Five Legs
Communion

Graeme Gibson was born in London, Ontario, in 1934 and attended various schools including Upper Canada College, University of Western Ontario and the University of Edinburgh. He has served as Chairman of the Writers' Union of Canada and of the Book and Periodical Development Council, and has taught at universities in Canada and abroad.

In addition to his fiction, Gibson is also the editor and photographer for a book of interviews, *Eleven Canadian Novelists* (House of Anansi, 1973). He lives on a farm near Alliston, Ontario.

Five Legs
Communion

two novels by
Graeme Gibson

Anansi   ●   Toronto

Author and publisher acknowledge with gratitude the
assistance of the Canada Council and the Ontario Arts
Council.

Cover design: Frank Newfeld
Cover photograph: Peter Christopher

Canadian Cataloguing in Publication Data

Gibson, Graeme, 1934-
   Five legs and Communion

ISBN 0-88784-073-6 pa.

I. Gibson, Graeme, 1934-   Communion.
II. Title. III. Title: Communion.

PS8563.125F5 1979 C813'.5'4 C094055-8
PR9199.3.G4815F5 1979

Contents

INTRODUCTION

by Leon Edel

Graeme Gibson's two novels, *Five Legs* and *Communion*, set in a familiar Canada but within unfamiliar "streams of consciousness," are of a kind we can still call experimental after half a century of fictional experiments. They are novels in which experience is not told in the usual way; it is refracted through the senses, emotions and intellect of the characters. The novelist has the difficult task of discovering the language in which to narrate evanescence. The traditional way of writing a novel had both directness and simplicity; the novelist took the reader by the hand and provided all the requisite information. The story-teller was always in the room. His presence held us—often gripped us—and we had a continuing awareness that Tolstoy or Dickens, Meredith or Henry James, were talking to us alone out of their abundant minds and quickened psyches. But even the old novelists had a wish to step outside the room and permit the readers, and the characters, to establish some kind of mutual relations, as in a play, in which the dramatist is usually off-stage. Tolstoy, in a few passages, foreshadowed modern experiments by using the discontinuous thoughts of his personages, or by allowing us to follow thought-impressions inspired by sensations—a smell of fresh paint or of bread freshly-baked. He also tried—as André Breton, the father of surrealism, would try much later—to capture the curious sinking moments when we seem to fall into outer space as we drop into sleep. One remembers how difficult Proust found it to capture the hypnagogic moment in the opening paragraphs of *Swann's Way*.

It may seem far-fetched to suggest that Graeme Gibson's experiments go back to George Meredith or Henry James. We have only to open *One of Our Conquerors*, however, to discover that Meredith (in 1896), without giving us the name of his principal character, puts us into his unsorted thoughts for some fifty pages. And in *The Ambassador* which many readers still find bewildering, Henry James busily manipulates us in a good-humored way, determined to reveal to us only what his hero discovers. This involves him in a series of genial but often fussy mystifications. One can of course resist this kind of story telling by clinging to the old forms. This was the burden of a remark Max Beerbohm made to Edmund Wilson in conversation. "Everybody has thoughts that go through their head, but it's absurd to try to make a novel of them."

Max said this in his old age, when one resists change or novelty. But as early as 1915, the absurdity of which he spoke was being committed by James Joyce in his *Portrait of the Artist as a Young Man;* by Dorothy Richardson in *Pointed Roofs*; by Virginia Woolf in *The Voyage Out* and by Andrey Bely in *Kotik Letayev*, published in Russia. The simplistic quality of Max's remark is dramatized when we remind ourselves that two years before the *annus mirabilis*, in which the English writers, and the Russian, launched their stream-of-thought novels, Proust had launched his *roman fleuve*, composed exclusively of "thoughts that go through the head." These novelists were not aware of one another until they appeared in print. Bely's novel courageously sought the impressions and images of childhood with the same sureness that Joyce's infant prodigy discovers sensation in the first page of his novel, that page in which the "moocow" is coming down the road. The ultimate use of this kind of experimentation occurred in Faulkner's *The Sound and the Fury*; undaunted by the linear-word, he sought to catch the disconnected world of a grown-up mute, a striking instance of the poet supplying words for the wordless. Out of such gropings was born what literary criticism now identifies as "the symbolist novel"—that is a novel in which language attempts to capture and represent the kaleidoscope of man's inwardness.

Mr. Gibson seems then to be on very old ground; but it is in some ways ground new to Canada; and ground so difficult and bewildering that the artist possessed of a certain kind of inwardness has a constant need to keep on trying. The bewilderment resides, for the reader, in his having to learn a new way of reading fiction along with the artist's discovering new ways of writing it. This is a tall order for most readers. Criticism, we might remark, has been delinquent in not providing some assistance. Critics talk of Thackeray and Dickens, James and Joyce, as if they all wrote the same kind of novel and used the same techniques of story-telling. The old story-tellers may be read with ease by anyone who has learned to follow words line by line, on a printed page. But the subjective novelists, attempting to create inwardness out of words, are novelists without plots, without continuity, and seemingly without selectivity. When Joyce was asked how he came to write "stream of consciousness" he referred his questioners to Édouard Dujardin's novel of the 1880s, *Les lauriers sont coupés*, an early work by a symbolist-musician, in which the author sought with difficulty to remain exclusively in the mind of his protagonist. When we read Dujardin we see how he was still trying to describe a room in its appearance, instead of capturing it in inward vision; for he had not yet learned to deal with sensory impulses and triggers, nor had he determined what differentiates inner from outer reality:

> La fenêtre est fermée... Et les rideaux? je les tire, voila... La nuit est supprimée. Dans la clarté amie, voici ma chambre.

This is charming, but we may ask whether the act of drawing curtains is not often involuntary; it is the "suppression of night" that conveys the subjective feeling. Dujardin was still trying to internalize the usual, as in an old-fashioned novel. Joyce very quickly changed this. He showed us how to dart in and out of thought. What we must ask ourselves is "What happens to the novel when this kind of experiment is attempted?" The answer is very simple. It becomes an "inside out" novel; the reader is looking outward from within. This was what, in its earlier stages, Henry James called "the point of view"—finding an angle of vision for the character and staying within that vision. In the post-Joycean experiments, there is much more: we arrive at many angles of perception, beyond the visual. The reader is invited to imagine the smelling, to receive sensory impressions, to experience the tactile through language as painters make us experience it on canvas. The result bewilders until the reader can take the jump: then it can become uncanny. It is a great exercise in synaesthesia. A.J.M. Smith has expressed it for us in his verse about McLuhan:

> McLuhan put his telescope to his ear;
>
> What a lovely smell, he said, we have here.

Nothing in our childhood reading is quite like this, for we ask words to touch the keyboard of our senses. The reader, as we have suggested, is placed in the eye of the character. He is inside Dedalus or Bloom, and he looks outward from within—he is on the inside, looking out. The vision becomes at once limited to the character's vision, and the character's capacity for vision, unless the author intervenes to supply external information. The novel becomes a lens, a camera. We are involved in much more than "thought"—we are asked to take notice of peripheral experience and inner response as it impinges on rational thought. Within this kind of vision, we are transposed into a changed system of time. We are *in* the moment of perception. In the old novels we were always in the past, in the "once upon a time" of history. We are now in immediate time, in human time, as distinct from clock, or calendar-time. Often we are in a split second of feeling. and we are lifting remembrace out of the past into a continuing present:

> RRRING! And aware suddenly of the day. Grey chills. blessed Jesus what a night, what a terrible night. Like a mouth full of

This is the first paragraph of *Five Legs*. The character slides from sleep into waking, into daylight with a mouth full of— and we break off in the middle of the sentence. We are asked to feel "grey" and chill and at the same moment remember the night. He or she (we don't yet know) has instant awareness of hangover (and what reader wants to identify with that? although many can and do). We are in time present; but also time recalled. We are in the given point of view and, by juxtaposition of words and perceptions, the novelist is trying to make us feel the simultaneity of waking and the discomfort of this particular immediacy, jarred we presume by the ringing of the telephone, or the doorbell. We must read on to find out which.

These are the new dimensions to be found within "inner fiction." We now must read actively, not be carried along by the simple narrative, more or less passively. We are asked to be attentive: and to recognize at least four principal and dramatic changes in story-telling. There is discontinuity, where there was continuity; we are in time present; we are in given angles of vision; and we are asked to react to linear narrative as if we were hearing the simultaneities in the world around us. The old novels flowed in a continuous narrative. Experience was sorted out and put to us in its most vivid terms by an omniscient author; he was always logical and chronological. Here, however, we are in Virginia Woolf's "shower of atoms." The novelist attempts to escape from the linear prison of his prose in the way that modern painting sought to escape from "representation." However, since the linear prison is unchangeable, a word-by-word-sentence-by-sentence-paragraph-by-paragraph world, the only escape is the one discovered by the symbolists and the splinter groups of surrealism. Virginia Woolf's verbal rearrangements are quite as complex as Joyce's. Someone says something. Then we have a page or more of thoughts, sensations, sights, smells; and only then do we arrive at the reply to what has been said. All this, moreover, has occurred in "the moment"—even if it has taken several pages to record that moment.

The total effect of this kind of experimentation is to give us a novel in which the author's data is scrambled, and with our old reading habits, we feel a need to unscramble it, to treat it as a puzzle, instead of accepting it in its scrambled state. Criticism must learn that scrambled prose can no more yield the old continuities of fiction than an omelette can yield the whole eggs out of which it has been made. The author, in this process, abandons omniscience. He becomes a stage director behind the scenes. One critic remarked that this kind of novel can't be read; it can only be reread. This is true if we read it in the old way. But if we make ourselves aware of what is happening in the here and now, we can discover a new way of reading.

The experimental writer asks the reader to remain within "the moment" and accept continuing surprise and mystery: recognize that he has been removed out of flowing order into a floating world of consciousness, with all the surprises of dream.

With time, I have come to consider these fictional experiments, with their limitations, and their tensions and strains of narration, as an heroic attempt to make language transcend "realism." The writer admittedly undertakes the impossible, and tries to create an illusion of possibility. At each moment a thousand things happen in the human computer (I hesitate to use the mechanical example and do so only to be illustrative)—a computer so delicate and fragile, orchestrated so privately, that no machine-computer can ever duplicate it. We have been, as humans, "programmed" since before the time of issue from the womb; and from the first flash of light, the first rush of the world into our ears and untrained nerves and untrained brain, our entire sensory apparatus has been mobilized to receive and deal with sound, smell, taste, touch, vision: and every child in its own way. How meagre the attempt of words to capture anything but a small part of this experience, an ongoing experience from birth to the day we die—and yet how noble and heroic. When William

James found the phrase "stream of consciousness," he recognized that he was using an awkward metaphor. A "stream" does not describe the chain-like moments of vision; and how trace the multi-levels of perceptual experience? Man's memories are lodged not only in our unfathomable brain, but in our nerve ends, in our eyes, our nose, in our mouths, in the taste-buds of wine-sippers, in the tips of our fingers. A glimpse of red or yellow, an odor, a few notes of a popular song, may bring back summer days of ten years before. Ascending a staircase into familiar rooms long unvisited, we are suddenly assailed by nostalgic memories of happiness or pain embodying the old experiences lived in these rooms. The machine-computer cannot begin to deal with phantasmagoria or orchestras of emotion. Computers are concrete; we live in evanescence. Trying to recapture a thought or a sensation—which is not usually linear—is like trying to catch a snowdrop in the hand to see what it looks like. In an instant it is metamorphosed into water. The image is William James's and he also compared our quest for consciousness to turning up the light in order to see what darkness looks like. This is exactly what the writers of our time have been trying to do, and we can observe it in the novels of Gibson immediately before us.

Gibson attempts to record a Canadian experience and since the ground has already been broken by Proust, Joyce, Virginia Woolf, Kafka, Robbe-Grillet, Nathalie Sarraute, Wright Morris, Conrad Aiken, H.D. and William Faulkner, a formidable list of experimenters, he absorbs their experience and uses poetic variants of their techniques. The imagination of our inner world can be rendered only through symbol and poem. We cannot pretend that we are inserting a movie-camera into the mind, because movie cameras can give us only instant visual images of a scene and the rarest kind of montage is needed to attain an effect of simultaneity. On this ground, we might observe, the moviemakers and the writers of subjective fiction have had to work side by side. The poetry of the visual, however, is quite different from the power of words: so much more of our inner sensory imagination is involved. And how is characterization to be achieved in a novel of flux? It can only emerge to the extent that given thoughts and impressions and emotions *express* the character. Small wonder that a whole school of novelists—men like C.P. Snow or Anthony Powell—have rebelled against the "mush" of stream of consciousness. Snow's novels exemplify the extreme opposite of subjectivity: they deal with diagrammed dilemmas, and there is scarcely a shred of landscape in which their personages move. We may wonder whether the diaphanous inner-world novel can ever achieve the substantiality of the old photographic fiction, but something else is given us: we are made aware of other kinds of reality, diaphanous-reality. The stream of consciousness novel has been called a *cul-de-sac* in modern fiction: but the little dead-end street is filled, in its brief length, with much wonder and much excitement.

It is no criticism of Canadian writers to say that the Canadian novel has tended to hew to the traditional. On occasion however we have seen acts of virtuosity, especially in recent times—the shift Margaret Atwood achieves from first person to third in her *Edible Woman*, the cadences by which Alice Munro conveys feeling. Graeme Gibson reaches from his reporting of the vernacular, the immediate city-environment, into the poetry of the perceptual world: and he is skilful in his use of the "indirect style" in which the author's voice intervenes to monitor impression and sensation:

> The river meanders as a river should. He can see sepia figures with parasols, gentle men with shiny boots, they drift silently beneath great black trees with rough bark, but the trees are dead now and the water is foul. In the guts of the bridge above him, a subway car rattles to Bloor Street. It's almost spring, the wind is cool: dirty water swells powerfully to the lake, eddies, whirlpools convulse to the surface and

vanish...Clearly pressed into the wet sand there are the
tracks of animals, exquisite icons, he doesn't know what they
are, he touches them with his finger.

Or the impressionism and "simultaneity" of

He must get up, the pressure of his bladder insists, he closes
his eyes, he opens them again. Children skating on a river,
their red toques brilliant in the sun. Their voices come to
him in the wind.

Canadian novelists, given time and place, given the sense
of the North, and the huge spread of land and the sparseness of population—which means sparseness of
communion—have had to struggle first with the immediacy of the material-real as distinct from the reflective-real;
have had to cope too with a far-extended society, compared
with the rich and intricate old-world societies of Trollope
or Thackeray, confined to a few cities in a small land. In his
subjective novels, Graeme Gibson explores the mental-real
against the material-real, the real becoming the
emotional-real. The reader, as I have suggested, must
develop a new relationship with the printed page. If this
seems to demand too much, we must remind ourselves that
Picasso and Matisse, Van Gogh and Rouault, and before
them, Cézanne, invited us to use our eyes in new ways, to
see beyond the photographic-pictorial. There are many
kinds of readers. Each must find his kind of writer. Some
will want to explore, with Graeme Gibson, the private
worlds into which he leads us.

Reared in Saskatchewan, educated in France, the
American-born Leon Edel was almost thirty when he left
Canada to become an internationally-known writer and
teacher. Author of the five-volume *Life of Henry James* and a
study of Bloomsbury (*A House of Lions*) Leon Edel is a

Fellow of the Royal Society of Literature, a member of the American Academy of Arts and Letters, and has been awarded the Pulitzer Prize, the National Book Award and the Academy's gold medal for biography. He was, in the 1920s, a member of the "Montreal group"—the discovery of "the modern" with A.J.M. Smith, F.R. Scott, A.M. Klein, Leo Kennedy and John Glassco, among others. He lives and writes in Hawaii.

Five Legs

For my wife and sons

Five Legs was first published in April 1969 by the House of Anansi Press.

"Unchained Melody" by Hy Zaret and Alex North © 1955 Frank Music Corporation. Used by permission.

LUCAN 1

RRRINGGG! And aware suddenly of the day. Grey chills. Blessed Jesus what a night, what a terrible night. Like a mouth full of.

Must not, can not sleep on this morning, of all last mornings. Awake. Cautious in established areas of warmth he lies and beside him the body of Rose. Stirring. Today maybe? Periodic flow.

Fructify dear God the mortal loins of us Thy...

Like I was, a student, and as I have become. So would he. Except. He's dead. I cannot let myself lie and dream.

Mild jactitation of the lashes. Awake, yes she is. Grey-green upper lids in cold light. "Morning dear."

A deliberate turn and she vanishes sighing under the coverlet. Waiting, we wait and Rose day by day.

Now after troubled sleep, a shift on naked arms.

"How are you feeling."

No response.

"Rose...has anything happened?"

"No. Nothing."

Morning and then the evening of the sixth day.

"But I feel awfully queasy or something."

That's good. Her eyes already wait another day. The sullen flow. Last night perhaps, the party. Could be, God knows. And smiling ruefully. "I don't feel any hell myself."

"Oh Lucan don't joke. Its serious. Feel just terrible and anyway you know I never drink too much."

Lucan Crackell takes his wife's dry hand. Explaining. Thought it might. Didn't mean, no certainly didn't. Everything in perspective that's all. He sits the better to comfort. Good Lord my eye! Take that! A baker's dozen red hot needles. Don't move.

Poised and bravely smiling at her side. Through the

pain of it. Rough winter winds impatient at the window; rattling southward over evergreens and through the wretched branches of a thousand naked towns. Great, just great. As if this stinking morning and funeral aren't enough.

Cold curtain-filtered light lies softly without shadow on the room. Day by day. Above all other things dear Rose, our sense of humour. Don't want to be losing that.

"Lucan. Would you get me a coffee?"

"Sure."

"I think I'd feel better if I had a coffee."

Softly now. Cup of coffee, couple of two-twenty-twos and I'm a new man. Easing out the old legs into…where in hell are my frigging slippers? Don't, good Lord don't look! Bare foot enquiringly down there in a draught. Important thing is not to move your head. Patience. Patience is the operative word.

"What are you doing?"

"Here they are. Couldn't find my slippers."

Rising, Lucan carefully from bed. Water's the answer. Five generous tumblers before retiring. Never does to forget the essentials. A good flushing out. Absorb and subsequently evacuate the poison. On woolly feet into the bathroom. Avert the eyes. Flick. Some terrible mornings Rose; in my youth. I remember one with my belly distended, hard as a bloody rock.

He pushes at the plastic cap with his thumb. Useful material, plastic. Raincoats to kitchenware. And three medium size, *format moyen*, white discs in the hand. Don't know where we'd be today without it.

Thought I should surely die. Probing, soft pads of his cool fingers. Probing. Doctor, I need a doctor because it has burst! Discharging unspeakable poisons. And thump-thumping on my poor body. Not appendicitis young man, but something you ate. Drank? Absolute alcohol! Dear-dear that was very foolish, very foolish indeed. Bespectacled professional stricture. And me so close to death.

With toothpaste stinging tongue refreshed and balding skull wet comb-disguised, he comes down the stairs. Shocking. Haven't been like that, not just like that since. Duty of course. Martin's supervisor so it is the least I can do. Carry him out in his own. Simply no way out, that's all.

Toast. A little honey might be. Just the thing to fill the void. Soothing. He crosses the hall in tartan dressing gown. Casually. Into the kitchen, January window light with crystals restless on the outer pane. Stinking winter. With gleaming kettle stainless in his hand Lucan slips in the toaster's plug easily, then smartly to the sink and a rush of water. A child would make the difference yes, a child...She must be! Sickness, that's hopeful. Nausea and everything. She's never been this long before. Six days at least so maybe she is, this time. God knows it isn't my fault if she's not.

Cups on saucers and the reassuring clink of cutlery. Domestic sounds. So important. Epitome of life's joy, the heritage and gift of children. And their fear of this hope was their failure, he's sure of that. He reaches for the giant jar. One cent on every shopping dollar. Distraught he was on Wood's bed next to mine. O Jesus Woody! I am undone, un-frigging-done. Fixed by the fickle finger and for.

What's the trouble?
She's up the pole.
Who for Chrissakes?
Beryl.
Not Beryl! Jesus Frank she even looks like a mother.

I'm telling you, when she filled me in last night I frigging near left town. Snuck in here and started packing the old books but was too upset. I mean really scared. Couldn't do a bloody thing.

Curtains bellied, sighing into the room. Poor bastard. Silly sexy bastard.

Can't Lucan. Just can't do the honourable thing. By her. Marriage! Mr. and Mrs. Walter Bronowski take great pleasure. And my mother! Lucan, my mother! Oh boy. She'll die. Disown me and die. I swear she will. Serve me bloody well right. Bloody fool! Jesus I feel terrible.

The bright tray neatly waits. Milk. Now get the milk Lucan. Nice girl like Susan, for example. Or Rose. Dark chill of the back stairs in cold light. Clean coat of white wash do the trick. Dispose of all this clutter; wash them down. Lying softly without shadow a mantle of light.

Unlikely. But hypothetically say. Most propitious of all conceivable circumstances...and anyone would. Terrible for her. Alone. Betrayed and alone. Man has responsibili-

ties, inescapable commitments far more extensive than
mere personal gratification.

You're right! Phoned Wells already and he said its
probably nothing. Probably nerves he said. It happens you
know. But just in case I'm supposed to see she gets lots of
exercise. Lifting things. Pushing them around. And baths,
hot baths are really good. For assurance he turned, surveyed and turned again. And then do you know what he
said? He said, I hope you're humble Frank, in the face of
one of God's greatest mysteries! Ha. The bastard. Still he's
a good head. Getting hold of some quinine...and ergot.
That's the stuff you know. Ergot.

Reaching into the milk box he feels intruding coldness
on his arm. The shadowy north and through the wretched.
A bar of light pierces the contained grey air. Squeezing
with one arm cold bottles to his belly, he shuts the little
door comes up the stairs. Smoothing on girls' bodies, their
slim girls' bodies, baby oil and iodine, in the sun: pale
shoulders and thighs easily in the sun. Nice looking pair of
girls no doubt: with their. Fine legs on them.

Curtains swelling into the room. Just hypothetically but
you'd have to. Complicity engenders mutual responsibility. Unthinkable not. There, push it right home. Nothing
like a bit of weather stripping to keep the draughts at bay.

From the smaller bottle he decants cream as the kettle
mumbles into life. The white with the white. Shadowed
from snowglare light, behind the desk he'd been with
turning pencil slowly in his hand. Oh God! You must see
Dr. Howell, that I can't you must know for you saw me all
lost and wild in those terrible days. Yet you. Chat on that
stinking phone. And you smile. Oh God. Tap-tapping to
the rhythm of his voice. Goodness yes, most unpleasant.
Certainly sir, of course. And by one of the Alumni. A
matter of decorum certainly. In the great hall. He's quite
right. Indeed. The shining receiver rested carelessly in his
long fingers and he raised his eyes to look at me. Obviously
a fat cat on the line. President perhaps. Solidly important
from behind his desk and he's sending me down through
this icy day! Very true sir. Respect for our university and its
staff. Without a shadow sir and if I might say so, a boost to
the university's collective morale. As well, a general
improvement in our internal self-confidence don't you

know. Yes I thought so. A smiling suppliant, nodding on the bloody phone. And slapping heavily at the window, a sluggish fly. Buzzing and slapping. Heavily. His life-blood dripping dark-staining the road of his youth. Seeping black about his head, a flower on the snow.

God how she struggled in storms of love. Wake all the dead! What ho! A pair of self-anointed worshippers, warm body sweat gathering gently on their brows, in the sun, their lips and stubble-shadowed under-arms. Moist and warm. Nice-looking girls.

By violence. Death. But its worse for her.

Her young man, lost. Struck down by a car, an unknown car last night. Had you heard? Soft features, condolence through his thin nose sighing. Shocking Lucan: absolutely shocking. The silver pencil, slow circles on circles inscribed. Such a pleasant young man.

How on earth did it happen?

Walking home, just after leaving that Susan girl, and a car...Fifteen feet she said.

Fifteen! Good Lord.

Fifteen. And then without stopping, it vanished. Never regained consciousness.

A hit-and-run!

That's it Lucan, that's it. Must have been under the influence don't you know, must have been drinking not to have seen. And as for not stopping...well, that speaks for itself.

Panic probably.

Irresponsibility. A case of irresponsibility carried to its logical.

Poor Susan. This will be distressing news for Rose.

Carried to its logical conclusion Lucan, and thereby becoming a social, a socially destructive force don't you know.

Really seemed to hit it off, the two of them. Since the summer.

Thought of that Lucan, thought of their friendship, of her living with you during Rose's course. Not simply a student-staff relationship.

No, not really. But.

And what with you being his thesis supervisor. Well, we

realize Lucan, you'll be wanting to represent the university at his funeral on Saturday over in Stratford.

Jesus! No. Way out. Not me, there must be someone, someone else. Haven't been back since. Since. The slimy bastard. Led me right in up to the neck. Six years, the son-of-a-bitch. Thinly sighing and smiling into the phone.

Lucan. Insistently. "Lucan, I'm calling." From the stair's top, insistently. Slow circles on circles.

"What?" Oh boy! For my head and mercy's sake don't, don't shout. To the hall, calmly, for chrissake.

"Bring up the paper. I've been calling and calling."

"Sure."

"The review will be in it."

"O.K. Be right up."

Calmly move, and think calmly Lucan. Deliberately he walks, step by step to the door, grasps the paper's edge poking in the letter slot. And pulls. Undue impetuosity is unwise. Most unwise on this morning of. Turning he surveys the entrance to their home. A pleasant hall. Successful combination of, of casual formality. Yes. Casual formality. The settee's effective. Believe I'll sit a moment to rest my limbs. Gather and conserve against the coming day, my strength. Aaah! Good quality. Pat-pat.

He unfolds the morning paper noisily. Hmmm. Missing Boy Found. Hmmm. Police call off mammoth hunt. Four bone-chilling hours. Police chief Simon Lunt told 750 searchers. Three year old Ralph Thirkettle. Found. Sleeping peacefully at his aunt's? Good Lord! And nobody checked? Good Lord. We used to live on Queen's Avenue, explained Mrs. Thirkettle, but who ever would have thought Ralphie would go back. Its all terribly embarrassing. Ha! I'll bet. Ha! In the drifting bloody snow.

Not nationalism but anti-Americanism, says industrialist. And so he better. Paranoia masquerading in the guise of chilly pride.

Continued Hunt for Mystery Car
Police Alert Body Shops

Provincial police, searching for the gray coupe believed to have struck down and killed Mr. Martin Baillie late Monday night, have warned garage operators to be on the lookout for a damaged right front fender.

The force of impact "Would most certainly have dented any normal fender" says Stratford Doctor Grant J. Small.

They saw and marked his irresistible wound. Fifteen and then. But for chrissakes why in Stratford? Lucan troubled with the sadness of this fact. Why indeed. A malevolent thrust. That's why. And sighing he gets to his feet. If one considers statistical probabilities it becomes immensely apparent he should have been born in Toronto. Or New York. One half our scattered peoples concentrated, cluttered there. From the hall, wind-fronted on the morning's chill, he walks: not lack of sympathy (who would not weep?) but preservation. You're right. Self-preservation. Or with his nails. Into the kitchen, where its warm. And the snow waxed now incarnadine. Jesus! He knows, thinly sighing in his bony nose, what it means and why I can't. After what happened? Unthinkable. Absolutely bloody well can't.

He puts the morning paper between her iron pills and sugar bowl. First with the best in Ontario. Then two moist slices into the waiting toaster. In his hand slowly. Save me dear God from the fickle finger.

Desperately there on the knees, mopping like crazy with their footsteps ringing closer and closer. Green beer, that's what it was. Saint Patrick's green bloody beer. Frantically mopping. Push it all under this bench. And the pickled eggs! Oh God its no use. If I could only disappear. Nimbly in behind one of these lockers, quickly, quickly for the sake of. Oh Jesus! Oh.

Don't look Julia. There's no use lurking in there Mr. Crackell. We've seen you. And in front of your students! Have you no pride? No dignity? You must be mad.

Fly! Oh fly poor miserable from the sullen.

A most distressing thing has been reported to me Mister Crackell. Could irreparably harm the cause of those, who have earnestly toiled amongst the young to instil respect for the man of education.

Terrible frigging scene that was! Good grief but I must.

Consumed with atrabile, Lucan collapses gently into the kitchen chair.

We can be very grateful. Miss Savage, a loyal member of our staff, has assured me she will be as silent as the grave. However. Discreetly his dry throat he cleared. Since, in your mind, our night classes do not aah, excite the same respect as your university work. Well obviously. We have no.

By images engulfed he sits long-staring at the clicking toaster. Alternative. But there must be! Someone. Oh for a snippet, a modicum of charity from this world; just a little Christian charity for my. Someone.

Clicking. And slapping. From his bookcase a shadow, halving his face as he sat. Appreciate your reluctance, certainly I appreciate your reluctance Lucan, but you're ignoring the significance of your emergence into brighter, better days. Out of the shadow as it were. You take that Lampman thing now, why you're proving yourself a man to reckon with. Very interesting I'd say. A pretty good indication don't you know, of just how far you've progressed with us since those troubled times. A source Lucan of great satisfaction. Very satisfying.

My God I can see it all! The excesses of youth dear Heaven, with self respect unthinkingly abashed. Lucan liberally smoothes, hastily spreads the melting butter. Scrape-scrape. And now from shadowless acceptance you must return O rash and overbold, return once more among the sorrows of the town. Scrape. Still, that cheerless bitch, she had no. Watch out! Than brittle unbuttered crusts Lucan, there's nothing worse. Watch out. Shameful.

Good Lord, the draughts in this old house that cut about the ankles and whistle up my legs. A gradual emasculation and for sure. Day by day we wait. A smaller modern place first thing; will please her and they're a hell of a lot more practical. Was a terrible frigging scene. Oh boy! They say it rises and it does. Right up the stairs and through the roof, leaving behind a dirty big vacuum for rough winter winds that come insistently, seeping in at the corners.

And more comfortable too. The toast waits in a damp pile as he spoons powder into the cups. And Howell intimated, yes he did. To ensure full coffee flavour. He as much as told me. That was President Scott on the telephone

Lucan: appears the Alumni Association is disturbed, disturbed by the trend in student dress. They feel it reflects somewhat unfavourably on the personality of our university, our public image don't you know. Fondly smiling his small smile. And its the clothes Lucan, that make the university. Heh.

Yes sir. Indeed. Ha.

Actually they're quite right I suppose. Heh-heh. Shadowed from snowglare light his face, completely shadowed now. Shocked of course. Hadn't heard you know, what happened to Baillie last night. A terrible thing, he said, who's going down from your department? Crackell, I said, Lucan Crackell. Just the man, his very words Lucan, just the man. He'll handle it well.

Dull red the skeleton frame rises from the earth. Very satisfying Lucan, just the man. And it will be. Virtually a new department.

To show the parents Lucan. It is in the response of friends that mourners find solace. Intimations of immortality don't you know. Furthermore, its through these, these difficult tasks that you grow with this university, eh? You understand my meaning Lucan. Be most unwise of you not to get along down there on Saturday. His small smile in shadow now. Completely.

God, just what I need. Once and for all today to drown these dull protests. Beguiled by true coffee aroma he checks the breakfast tray. Think I'd feel better if. Yes. And the serviettes. Don't want to be forgetting anything. Light glints darkly on circles turning in the cups. Turning in the loins, in. Rose.

Balancing the tray at a careful angle, through the door and up the stairs he moves surrounded by the instant coffee smell. Struck down by a car, a spreading rose beneath his head, a flower on the snow. Who would not weep indeed? An onerous duty. And yet the very least when all is said, the very least I can do. But whoever would have thought.

Tough worker ants intrude with spitting laughter in the sun, a wrenching of the earth, a scar and then bare girders with pale stones precisely clad. But from that echoing shell next fall will come a new department, of an equal size, and still there's no official word. Although. Be most unwise, he said. You're just the man.

Be going down myself Lucan but some people from C.B.C. have arranged to tape something of mine. Shrugging his shoulders. Oh it's not much you know, a little talk about a dog I had. In my youth. The Charm of Doctor Johnson, The Charm of Samuel Pepys and is at present working on The Charm of William Blake. His modest voice trailed thinly off as he squared the papers on his desk. Thank you Lucan, thank you. Nothing much, modest little books and yet...I flatter myself.

He pauses in the upper landing's warmth, inhales and quickly checks again the morning tray, inhales once more real instant coffee smells and then emboldened, marches into the room. She's a good looking woman alright. Her jawline hard across my face, her warm breath breathing in my ear. Dear God, Thy. Come on now Lucan! To be thinking. On this day of lurking traumas and in your condition... "Would you like a cup of coffee Mrs. Crackell?"

"Yes please. I would." Smoothing flat the covers on her thighs, her mortal loins. "I'm sorry I was so, so short just now Lucan, but. Oh that smells wonderful."

"It does, doesn't it."

"I know you were only joking, but I feel so awful and everything."

"Sure, I know." In her grey eyes the troubled sleep. "Its alright." Lucan takes the cup. "Were pretty late and..."

"No its not alright Lucan. Its not fair to you." Her teeth tearing delicately worry loose a piece of toast. "I mean, it upsets you too, I know, and still I act as if you didn't care at all."

"No you don't princess; and anyway you weren't..."

"Yes I was. And I feel just terrible darling." Her hand contritely reaches to hold, her dry hand squeezes. Jesus, I wish she. "I just don't know what's the matter Lucan."

"Look, there's nothing the matter love: its an uncertain time for us both, that's all." Poised and bravely. "What's the review like?"

"And being mean like that makes me feel even worse." Turning one by one the flimsy sheets. "But I can't seem to help myself."

"Last page of section one, I think." She turns the pages, searches expectantly and reads. Softly her small mouth pouts, tightens as she reads, she murmurs, smiles and then assumes a frown. "Not so good?"

"Oh its alright, I guess." Thoughtfully chewing on her toast. "But God, I don't know why they keep him on or anything. Listen." And shaking out the paper's folds she clears her throat. "Remember what he said about Godot? He really raved, and it was perfectly obvious he didn't understand a thing. But listen to this. I mean, its so stupid." And clearing her throat again she begins.

Listening, Lucan takes another piece of toast and gently chews. And nods. Could do as well myself and there was a time when. Interested in your work. And a book review here and there, but nothing more. A finer kind of prose if I do say so, and certainly more knowledgeable. Hmmph! Yet when my letter was published she fell upon me for a pedantic wretch. A stab in the back and what's more, an awfully selfish thing to do. And as Blair said, your academic interpretation was probably alright in the classroom, but for the theatre, the living theatre...and anyway it was a terribly successful production. Everybody said so. Hmmph. Oh well, its a dark and irrevocable world down there. Not up to the standard, her voice precisely reads, of their fabulously successful Paint Your Wagon. But certainly we are more than fortunate. Humorously moving her lips, scornfully. In getting one truly great show a year from an amateur company. "An amateur company Lucan! Blair's professional, so's Mervin and for that matter make-up's not amateur anymore, even if we're not being paid." She leans against the pillows, pouting in small anger. "And people will believe him too, no matter what they think."

"That's not strictly true Rose, and anyway he only means..."

"The actors, if you ask me, they're the only amateurs in this theatre. But that's all anyone cares about anyway. People talking on a stage."

"Now Rose."

"Its true. And anyway Wagon was the star show, with imported talent and everything." Frowning with exasperation, she shrugs her shoulders angrily.

In make-up since high-school with ample opportunity to act. Hart House. Her summer at Stratford. Not just jealous then. Lucan watches his wife's face, he watches and listens as she reads. Must be pretty hard to work with. Extroverts in an unreal world, fashioning pride out of ego; building ego on the sounds of acclamation. Beguiled by Okinawa charm and Okinawa brandy, goes on her voice, the industry of American civilization founders upon the island's simplicity. She's right good Lord, what crap he writes! The patient hours of experience, her understanding slowly won and then last summer's teaching. Very successful Lucan, a credit to you both. A credit to you both. A summer's school of drama. To you both Lucan, she knows her business and we were pleased to have her on staff. And Susan, the brightest of them all was obviously impressed. Doctor Crackell, offering her thin hand, I've so enjoyed this summer, I really have. Its been simply wonderful. Her hair whorled softly, sun-bleached about her face, her flesh-pink ears and golden throat. And I'm looking forward to coming back this winter and working on Teahouse with Mrs. Crackell. Really I am.

About his head dark-spreading seeps the flower of her youth. It hardens on the frozen earth.

Its all crap, it bloody well is! From the tilted cup he draws coffee into his mouth for strength and rolls it slowly outside his teeth before swallowing. Could I but...

They scar the earth, they wrench and tear with iron claws. And then they build.

A cigarette. Yes. Risk one, need one now the void is full and my poor old mouth's no longer foul. Selecting a cigarette from the pack beside their bed he holds it with dry lips. Out of the shadow as it were. And strikes a match.

Although slow in getting started, there is still plenty of humour. The author...Who cares for chrissakes! Who bloody well cares? Teahouse provides amusing fare. Jesus. Arrgh! He roughly coughs an arid cough. And coughs again. Whoops, my toast and coffee! Have you no. My poor and blessed suffering head! Oh God. Take care. And the morning's grey light breathes on the room.

On thinking back, he'd always known that youth's despair has nothing concrete to suggest, is negative alone. They were right. Every one of them. To its logical. And yet I...

Singing I have danced about a runty hydrant. Here we

go round. Drunk with useless joy I have danced night from the open streets, from eaves and branches, from between tomb homes at five o'clock in the morning. Here we go round and round.

And then that bitch Miss Savage, that...

But of course it wasn't her, it wasn't that shocking drunken scene but common sense, the maturation of perception that's made the change. A therapeutic shock perhaps, a. Nevertheless. Just the man. Hmmn. To reckon with.

Excellent Lucan. And smiling from his window, prospect of the still-new college (Crackell's castle I have heard them say), he will congratulate me on behalf of my staff on campus. It is a thrill Lucan, a real thrill and I'm not ashamed to admit it. Truly a remarkable job. This university is becoming international in stature, getting its name on the map...

Oh boy, that's all I want. Just a chance to get a crack at the administrative side. Boyoboy!

Gone at last is the unthought passion, a long time gone is the fool. And thank God for it. I'm no Peter Pan whatsoever and wouldn't walk again in the wind, no not for my life lived over.

Name on the map. And Lucan, the stimulus to enrolment! Old dynamo, you-can't-keep-a-good-man-down Lucan Crackell has made this college what it is today. Oh boy. At my desk in the clearness of evening I have sat, a lonely but impressive figure, and practised the hiring and firing in preparation. Oh I know what you think, but I don't want him and my voice was always strong and sure. No. No. And the curriculum. Aah! I've made such changes!

"Rose, I find this too depressing altogether. And anyway I have to get dressed." He puts the cup decisively beside the bed, he rises and slaps his thighs. Decisively. "A job to be done Rose, a miserable job, nevertheless a job to be done and there's a lot at stake." Pale eyes watch him above the paper. Can't calmly listen in this room's grey light, can't rest and listen. You understand. While at our backs the morning. "The man's a fool." Gently he smiles. He turns towards the cupboard and his suit. The waistcoat elegant, snug about his chest. Nothing like it. Immaculate indeed. I'll move with dignity, a fine dark figure through their lives. "I wonder what she'll do?"

"Who?"

"Susan."

"Gee, I don't know Lucan." The paper now across her thighs and she shakes her head. She's thinking of that time in the sun: two of them yes and their quiet talk; confederate laughter pale in the sun, their bodies white on the grass. My two sweet nymphs I used to think. And leaving for a moment my arid desk I would stand at the window and fondly gaze. Dirty old man. No I'm not. Innocence and experience: both sides of the coin in my house at once, both sides on the grass below.

Leaving his suit on the cupboard door he bends into the dryness for his shoes. My Blake and I ate it too. Hee-hee. Good Lord but they need a cleaning! Blunt fingers spreading and massaging, squeaking as the polish is absorbed. And the familiar pleasure rising on the scalp, as when the barber. Shave, shave and massage...ah the massage! Jesus but that's pleasure. The obedient hands on my head. Ah! An aristocrat born; a feline aristocrat bred. And after, yes after with my coat brushed clean and the warm air cool about my ears, I sauntered with my shadow on the glass. A cane, a cane and cloak are what I need. And a bottle-green dinner jacket for an evening's romp. Must get a cane. Click. Clack. And a drink, just one, on this sunny summer's day. Oh boy. A thirsty figure on shining feet past the upper half of a naked torso on her plaster back. Nippleless blunt breasts gazing through him on the glass. Gin was as. No painted tiny mouths shall suck on me. And tonic, just the thing.

"Nothing she can do, except go on." Dear Rose pushing herself, hands flat on the bed, from her smooth white back onto her buttocks again. Crossing her legs. "With her life I mean." Settling in. And reaching for her cup. "She's stronger than she looks."

"I know."

"Really a fine character. A very strong character." Sip and swallow. Clink. Deep-sighing with her gentle sleepy breasts. "But God Lucan, what a terrible time for her! She'll need her friends." Shaking her head mournfully she sighs again. "You'd certainly need your friends." And carefully smoothes the paper's page.

"Hmmn." I had just two, a couple of drinks that's all. For moderation is the watchword here. But I emerged reborn. The pavement hot against my feet, the bright street in my eyes. Self-control in all things and all things will be manageable. I always. Suavely twirling the cane-to-be he imposed himself delicately upon the streeet. Believe a glance at the paperbacks is in order. Tee-dum dum dum tee-dum. With a flourish in at the glass door and past the dear sweet damp-faced girls. With a flourish and whistling lightly. Ah you lovely pale gazelle. Yes nod, a quick nod to her almond eyes and then press on. To the books, the conjuring books. Delightful girl all flushed and warm, your hair a sweet disorder. Lovely. Because in my youth I used to pinch, I actually used to steal bright books like these. Graceful and knowing you brush the errant strands from off your brow and. Sly young fox. Blandly and clean-limbed in through the door (furtive in the eye's dark corner), blandly and clean-limbed up to the books. Careful now, wait till she...yes, behind the counter bending yes, and now a rapid glance about the room and. Inside the coat with it. Bang! Under the old arm against my beating heart. Ah ha! Pursed lips for a moment before some useful text, a studied look for the books as a whole and then to the door with wry disappointment; a nod of my head and the cheerful goodbye. Wow! Wouldn't have the nerve today and I'll simply browse. Besides. The Mirror of Art and his haunting face. That sort of foolishness is for the young.

There, by the window he'll stand with jealous admiration: the light angular upon his face, upon his smile while I sit graciously at my desk and his hands are like trembling vacant birds.

Contentedly he zips the zip and. Now where in hell. With braces hanging crisply at his side he rummages in the middle bureau drawer. My shirt, it must be. "Where's my shirt?"

"There. The drawer's full of them."

"No, I mean my white one. You know. With the collar." Jesus. Man has to have a shirt, a good shirt at a funeral. Can't. What sort of a public image is that? After all. "My good one."

"Isn't it there?"

"No."

"It must be Lucan."

"Well it isn't love, it isn't here at all."

"Which one do you...oh hell. Its in the laundry."

"Its what?"

"In the laundry." Oh Rose...its not! "I'm sorry Lucan but I couldn't find it when the man came. I looked everywhere and I couldn't keep him waiting all day."

"Rose, for heaven's sake I need it, I need it for the funeral." The world incompetent goes shuffling in the streets today: with freezing rain and fog it hunts me down. Jesus. Important. Can't get along down there in any old shirt, can't. Clothes make the. Rose!

"Well its not my fault Lucan. I can't keep track of where you throw everything for goodness' sake. I gave you a laundry bag." She's angry, she is angry for chrissakes! Turning on me at this desperate time, turning on me as if it were my fault. Goddamn it Rose. As if I should run the sordid details of this house. "Anyway you wouldn't have worn it, the collar's all wrong. Wear your blue one. With the tab collar." Smiling, she's actually smiling. "It looks good on you." As she wields the knife. "You look very handsome in the blue one." That won't mollify me you selfish bitch! You've never liked that shirt I know, but.

Snarling he gropes for silent words. And stands here as she smiles. So that's the way it is, eh? Holes in my undershirt and... To hell with it! To hell with it I say. There is no succour or compassion here. Obviously. Goddamn theatre and your matinee is more important than my... Rather transform into slipshod natives the plump-faced boys in stocks and bonds. For chrissakes. Your friend she is. And my favourite shirt. "I like that shirt Rose. I like it very much and I was intending to wear it." Bitter, that's what I: haughty and bitter. "However. Since it is in the laundry. I suppose I shall have to wear the blue one won't I."

"Lucan, don't be silly now." Below the smiling face her breasts lie gently white. A fine and slender. "Its just a shirt." He turns with dignity toward the drawer. With dignity he lifts out the cellophane-wrapped tab-collared bluest of shirts in the bureau drawer and holds it in his hand. With dangling braces. Nakedly crisp it is, starched clean behind its paper glass it stares with one breast pocket eye. Balefully. It is simply not the same thing at all. Can't tell me, from between warm sheets with this day out there you can't tell me. That it is. And that's all there is to it. From shadowless acceptance, wow, the softly sweating sunblown garden of our lives, I must return. He frees the shirt with claw-like hands, he crumples the wrappings and pushes them into the pretty little overflowing wastepaper basket.

Oh you just don't know! And the cellophane crackles with invisible fire, twists impatiently, expands into a disorganized mass and falls onto the floor. Jee-sus Christ!

Full bellying curtains and the back stair's chill. That's the stuff you know. Ergot. His young voice searching for assurance round the room as he turned, surveyed and turned again. Quickly quickly for the sake of.

Raw wounded earth and girders red in early sun; the bare and steel torn muddy hill that soon will have...

The flesh beneath her arm is soft and cool, her beckoning arm as she pats her thigh. And beckons. "Come on Lucan. I said I'm sorry." An uncertain time. Pat-pat. Never liked that, but. Moderation. Everything in perspective above all things. Waiting my kiss. She is. She knows I will relent at any moment. And so it goes. According to our rules. His wife's small smile as he forces his arm into the shirt's crisp sleeve. Oh Rose, dear Rose when green winds blow this arid time away... "Give me a kiss, give your poor dear wife a kiss." Very grey, her eyes already wait another day. Able to afford our own. Compact and modern. Buy a house and you're sure to have a baby. First thing. An exultant spreading of domestic wings. Or something. Everyone seems to. Hugo's little daughter and the Wilsons had one too. Feeling the cloth starched on his shoulders he fastens the buttons and crosses the room to Rose. A man to reckon with, I'll move with dignity despite the colour of my frigging shirt.

Ah this small gesture on my part (its a hard waiting time besides) is worth what it brings. Forgive me mother, for. He leans to the warmth of her, and kissing tastes the make-up from her face, feels the cool arm beneath his hand. And smiles. "Sorry princess."

"Oh Lucan, its so silly to be like this."

"I know love."

"We really must try to be more reasonable."

A tender thing when all is said and a baby'd do the trick. "Don't know how it starts my love. Its a hard time for us now. The waiting and all. But you're right we must try." Certainly should have confirmed the appointment earlier Lucan, but attendant difficulties don't you know, Senate acceptance et al, made it impossible. Past his shoulder through his polished window waits my new world on the hill. That's all right, quite all right sir, I rather felt. Knew you would Lucan, heh, knew you would (for frankly you had little opposition eh?) and that's the reason I was sure you wouldn't mind. And then we'll turn from the window; his bird-like hand will rest upon my arm. Certainly worth the hollowness of waiting and this unwilling trip to rout the past. The clear sun on his grey smiling face. Congratulations Lucan. Just the man. For the job. Yes now the waiting seems a proving time. Extends his hand in pale congratulations. "Once this awful uncertainty is over and we know, it will be better love."

"I just don't know anymore Lucan. I'm just not sure anymore." Her eyes moist as she holds her hand. My turning cotton-batten head. And her waiting eyes. "We should know by now."

"Don't say that Rose. You know its too soon and anyway I'm sure we're right."

"I hope so, oh I hope so. Its never gone so long before and I do feel sick at the tummy." What can you do? What can a man do with this unhappy woman. A kiss, a gentle reassuring kiss I guess. A loving take-heart squeeze for her hand and he kisses again her perfumed brow.

"Sure love, just you wait. And see." A smile of gentle certainty, a quick glance at her soft eyes and a pat for her shoulder. That's the way. "Now I'd better pop into the bathroom and shave princess. Time is running on." Again my quick and certain smile. Already some improvement for her eyes are bright. "You can relax there sweet, spend the morning in bed. Take care of yourself." Tenderly spoken with another pat and now into the hall. Quickly. Boy diplomacy in human relations is really something. Without a fine ear for the sounds of chaos in this world a man is lost. Unwilling though you may be, keep the old ears waving about: listen with care, I say, and pick your way. And just a chance to exercise this gift of mine in the responsible surroundings of upper academic circles. That's all. And watch my smoke. Wow!

> There was a boy
> A very strange enchanted boy
> They say he travelled very far, very far
> Over dum dee-dah
> Dah dee dah-dah

Glancing with his wry smile at the wryly-smiling self above the basin, Lucan carefully rolls his crisp blue sleeves. Not a bad shirt after all. Dee dumm dah-dah. But it isn't quite the same. Rubbing his fingers on his beard he stares more closely. Critically, I don't look too bad. Hah. Not an unhandsome face although I couldn't rely on it to see me through. A face of character. Yes, behind that face lies a man who is interesting to know. Ironic. Snorting briefly through his nose he wryly smiles again. A quizzical smile, objective irony. That's it. Hmmn. He takes the razor from its shelf, blows briskly to clear the hundreds of tiny cutting edges, bangs it on his hand and plugs it in. Jeez! This noise will waken my head again. So enjoyed this summer here with you. Certainly seemed appreciative with her golden thighs and sun-bleached hair. Sweet thing. And I'm really looking forward to working on Teahouse with. Would you mind awfully Doctor Crackell? I just can't reach right up the back. Would I mind sweet thing in this dark green summer's fancy heat, would I mind? The razor pushes folds of skin along his cheek. Baby oil and iodine heavy in the sun and I smoothed it in small circles on her back. Aah doctor Crackell! That's nice. Crescents of youthful flesh, her ears revealed by tangled hair. And my hands seemed strangely rough.

Pleasantly conscious of my stolen summer's drink and that beautiful pale doe of a girl at the cash desk casting her eyes at me, I browsed among the conjuring books. Tapping the side of my foot with the old invisible cane. Tap-tap. Good grief but there are lots of books. Who writes them all? And in all colours. Tap. Nothing like a haircut and a shoe-shine to liberate the social man. And whistling lightly. When I look up, casually, she'll be watching you bet; and the warm quick flush will reveal her. Hah! Can't keep her eyes off you, you sly young fox. Just easily raise the

old head and throw a wry and enigmatic smile in her
direction. Ready? Now! Well hello there. Its Susan. All
crisp and pretty in her starched sun-dress. How are you this
fine afternoon and why aren't you in the warmth of the
garden? Hmmn. I see. Well perhaps you'll join me for a
drink on this hot thirsty day. Dah dee dah-dah. The light
was shining on her face and her dress rustled sharply as we
marched out past those almond eyes. Ah-ha! A nod of my
head and the cheerful goodbye.

The terrible noise this razor makes outside my head
re-emphasizes the necessity of water. Lots of water before I
sleep. Oh boy. Dilute the poisons of a night like that. Jeez!
There was nothing for it but go down and meet her when
the play had ended. Closing his eyes he massages them with
a careful hand. And the razor snarls. Stinking parties with
her friends are like an entry to another world, across a
frigging ocean to an unreal world. Watching themselves in
the mirrored walls they moved in vague and frantic forms:
they twittered about me like bats in a desperate dream.
Shrill with laughter above it all, the actors removed their
make-up while we watched until tired and greasy their
faces appeared; they sat in undershirts or robes with flaccid
skin pale in fluorescent glare. Pushing the razor into the
top of his throat, he tries to catch the last remaining
whiskers. My name was called but the voice was carried
away in the crowd and my face too, was there on the wall.
Dark and nervously drawn. And because I once danced
with useless joy and absurdly flowed out and overlapped
my world. It is only drink that saves me.

Once again the summer street's hot afternoon with air
contained by stores on every side. Carefully on the hot
pavement we went to the light click-clack of her heels.
With dignity. A trim pony beside me on the window's
bright and jumbled face. Then in through the side door
with sudden darkness on the eyes. Click-clack. And coolness, blessed coolness as blinking you wait for Bert with
buttons tarnished by the air-conditioned air. The tray of
frosted glasses on his hand. Back again Mister Crackell,
you weren't gone long. Then with languorous and familiar
ease the drinks were ordered, cigarettes were lit and easily
we settled in to talk. Really nice and cool Doctor Crackell.
I don't come in here very often.

You don't? Well goodness gracious me my dear you really should. Yes indeed. You really should. A womb away from home as it were. Ha-ha.

Well Martin doesn't like it very much. He says he prefers the taverns to a bar. I don't know why. I think this is very nice, don't you? Its not so dark when you get used to it. I couldn't come in alone though. And anyway men are always waiting for girls in bars. I remember once in Detroit... You heard the lady. Coldly staring from my dangerous eyes; my pale hands resting on the table's top. You heard the lady, so bust off. Right away fella and play your games with someone else. Hah! Then lunging at me with strangled rage and I'd drop to my knee like a shot and out with the right arm, pow with straightened fingers driving under his breastbone! Arrgh! And the poor bastard's writhing on the floor. Make the others pause as well. Jesus mack, his voice astonished, you've killed him! He can't breathe. Then I'd loosen his belt and set him right. Oh Doctor Crackell. Thank you, thank you Doctor Crackell. Surprising speed for a man my age and size but its the thought-out move that triumphs everytime. Smooth pads of his fingers on the now-shaved face and his cool and calculating smile. Now I think you should stop this Doctor business, and call me Lucan. Think quickly, clearly and then the execution with finesse. Pow! Wonder if I could. Self-discipline and the rigorous control of movement should do the trick. Jeez! A worker's bony fist against my nose and mouth. Squash! The pain of it wow and I'm blinded by my ears and blood. At his mercy. Oh boy, its best to run like hell. If possible. But a man has responsibilities, inescapable commitments. Certainly wouldn't want to get hurt though. Winding the cord securely about the razor he returns it to the shelf, brings down Old Spice and liberally smoothes it stinging to his face. Nevertheless, self-control and. Could do the trick.

He's so unpredictable now Doctor Crackell that I wonder sometimes what will happen when we get married. But men change don't they? I mean, surely he'll see the necessity of settling down. Once we're married. He couldn't go on thinking the way he does. Oh I know young men are supposed to be dreamers and always want to travel and its probably a good thing too, but they get over it don't they? No, not another, not for me. I couldn't really. I've had enough already; I can tell, because I'm talking too much. Don't you think? And I feel all flushed. Lucan felt the ice against his lips, begged her to relent and waved again for Bert. A sad sardonic smile. Settling, poor bugger, down and he can't foresee it now.

Wouldn't fuss about him Susan, he'll find the compromise is inevitable and.

I get so worried sometimes. Like he wants to go to England or somewhere and he's going to teach there and write a book. Well. You know. It's a nice idea but its so impractical isn't it? We could go for a visit, I wouldn't mind going for a visit and staying in one of those old pubs and everything, but he doesn't see we can't live there. My Mother'd have a fit and anyway I have a girl-friend who went to England last summer and she knows all sorts of people over there and she says you wouldn't believe how expensive everything is.

Hmmn. I know. ah Bert, fine Bert with another frosted glass and the real world on the street seems far away. Just one more for I know her talk, I have lived it all. I was just like him and worse, oh shit... The surfacing past with Lucan's face reflected in the mirror. And that's why I can't go back! On that fucking road in winter twice a week I drove with drink and despair because she'd gone. But I mustn't think of that. Shaking his head he makes an effort to suppress familiar panic. they warned me but I couldn't, there was no way. We warn you Crackell...

Suddenly, violently. Horribly sick all over the floor and its splattered my goddamn shoes. Oh! Oh! Oh! Lucan stared numbly, through watery eyes, at the floor. My dinner there. Of pickled eggs and. Beer. Oh God! What a terrible mess. Pretend it isn't mine, clean the old shoes and hot-foot it out of here before. That's the ticket. Quickly he lurched away down the silent hall and. No. No. This will never do, for there's nobody else who. That's Crackell's vomit, they'll say. Who else would, it must be his, the drunken... Mop it up, that's better, mop it up and nobody will ever know. You crafty cunning beast. Long rows of lockers in the basement gloom and there isn't a mop. Or a cloth. Or even any paper to be seen. Just benches. And shadows from the mesh protected lights. Angular shadows.

What in this frigging world will I do? He stood despairing in its sour smell. Think. Think, for goodness' sake. My shirt! That's it, my shirt. He chuckled to himself as he struggled with his clothes. Hee-hee. Never let it be said that Lucan Crackell faltered. Good Lord but the suit coat's harsh on my skin! Hee. He chuckled again and began to mop and heard the women's feet and voices down the hall. Oh Jesus! Oh. Desperately there on the knees. Desperately. Oh God that time! A most distressing thing. Young and thoughtless I presumed to fight the winter world; yet lost from her longing arms, all lost with the terror of their memory on my flesh, I joined the hollow baying chase. Jeez!

The soap at first is slimy from the dish as Lucan slowly lathers up his hands. Back down that road to my misfortunes in the town. Two nights a week I went, to a stolid unresponsive class. English 102. Dear blessed Heaven, could I have seen! He carefully scrubs his knuckles and meticulously brushes the soap beneath his nails. Immaculate indeed, I'll have to be.

I guess you really wanted to do all these things too, when you were young Doctor Crackell, but you settled down didn't you? I mean look at you now with a nice home, a good wife and a solid job. But Martin says he doesn't want to settle down, he doesn't want to teach forever. I don't know how he expects us to live or anything and I can tell you I'm not going to raise a family on the terrible pay he'd get in England or wherever he wants to go over there. She sipped cautiously from her melting drink, she ran the tip of her tongue along her lips and reached for his cigarettes. He'll just have to settle down won't he. When we're married I mean. He'll have to accept his responsibilities as a man. Just like you did. Just like all men do. Reaching across the table he flicked the lighter's flame and it glowed upon her face. She dragged it alight. There you are Susan. Good God! My elbow's dragged good God! He jumped to his feet, he slapped and brushed. My drink on my lap. Ha. That was pretty careless, wasn't it. Ha-ha. And it's cold on my groin.

An old man (figuratively speaking) in a windy month he rinses the basin, conscious of the ache returning in his head. Clean it out Lucan. He dries his hands, careful to refold the towel, and rolls down his sleeves. Two more pills, a bit of water and a calm mind, above all else a calm mind to rid me of this weakness that seems to have returned.

Dismissed for drinking and I didn't because of the swoosh and empty fall inside my head, drive back immediately. I remember. Couldn't. So I walked in a driven snow-filled night and God how I walked. Solitary on long streets and wide in the numbing whiteness, the snow freezing in my hair and face, coating my chest and shoulders and I walked alone and away all dark and huddled. Pressed in my pockets, hard against my thighs, my hands were cold and twisted I recall, and the powdery snow was lifted in burning circles up my legs. Not a sound dear God as I passed among the street-light's pale illumination; not a sound but the wind's hush and the dry snow's rise and fall.

They know, the bastards, why I can't and what's in store when I drive down that road again to his uncle who is principal, his mother who smiled thinly at graduation and all the others in that dreadful town who know and maybe cherish the spectacle of my lost years. His fingers bumble out a cigarette, he holds it in dry lips and breathing in the lighter's flame he sighs and blows the smoke against itself upon the glass. What reason though? What possible reason except perhaps to exorcise the lingerings of youth; to overcome what vestiges remain. Your past is clarified Lucan, and conquered now: it gathers dust neatly on the shelf. Hmmph. And now, what was only a dream at my nightbound desk. Hah! Or else. A plot, a plot dear God, a filthy plot to keep me in my place! He groans and deeply dragging feels the sharp smoke in his chest. The buzzing fly that slapped between the window panes, buzzes and slapped with glass on either side while curtains bellied in the room and their persuasive voices were patterns in the air. White circles smooth and the jigshaw shape upon the snow. Goddamnit! The watch that he slips on his wrist says nineforty-three. I really must move, the past is coming on. So he brushes at the front of his pants, undoes the zipper and pulls his shirtfront tight, retrieves his cigarette from the basin's lip and leaves the room.

Leaning cosily on both pillows now she does not know the wind from the north and ancient land that searches and whispers about the town: she does not and she cannot know what the death of that boy might do.

"Did you see his picture?"

"Whose? Oh." He feels the sick impatience, a gentle pressure in his bowels. "No, no I didn't."

"Here." She turns the pages and Lucan stands by the bed. And there it is. Grey and impersonal, the undistinguished face of a young man in graduation robes. The image of a thing that once for a moment was. "Its not very good is it? But then he didn't have the kind of face that photographs well." Nor a face for memories. A wild and foolish thoughtless boy. There are english students, philosophy students, english and philosophy students— and then of course there's Baillie. And ha we laughed at my gentle knowing truth. "They haven't even caught the driver yet. Poor dear Susan." She turns at the melting windblown flakes. "Its a terrible, terrible thing. And his parents. The funeral should be an end, they should be allowed to forget and everything, but they won't be able to now." She sits for a moment in silence, and then: "It must have hit him awfully hard. Imagine. Crushing the fender of a car."

A brutal hollow sound and hurled by the rushing shadow, twisting in the air, his body struck and broken in the snow: the silence falls again in heavy flakes, settling on his jagged shape and the snows wax now incarnadine. "Jeez. C'mon Rose, its bad enough on a day like this." A curious dwelling on facts is just what I don't need now for my head. "I just wish I didn't have to go down to the bloody funeral, that's all. And the thought of all those people with a body in a church, I... oh boy." At rest in the Blackburn Funeral Home, from. A last deep drag on the cigarette, a deep and aching drag until the tip is suddenly hot against my hand. Take care. A kind invitation to view the remains. "And when you come right down to it, I hardly knew the boy and you certainly couldn't say we got along." Oh dear sweet Heaven, for its too late now and I've got to go: look after me and my aching head, look after my impatient bowels. "I wouldn't be going, if Howell wasn't so frigging adamant."

"You make me so cross sometimes Lucan." Her eyes unblinking in the room's grey light move past me as they glance about the room, they rest upon my face and then move on again. "What would happen if everybody, if nobody came to the funeral?" Above all else a mind that's calm, but she cannot see. She doesn't see at all. "I'd be going with you, you know that, I feel just terrible about it, but somebody has to make-up this matinee." She absently straightens the newspaper as it lies forgotten across her knees. And its warm enough in here, secure. "Certainly you have to go. And anyway Doctor Howell is sending you down because he wants you to represent the university. You said so yourself. You said it was a good sign remember? You said it meant you'll get the new department and that's what you want isn't it?" A weightless unexpressive silence wells within him as he sits. Oh boy. You just don't know. "I don't understand you Lucan, its just a funeral and you've got everything to gain, but you act as if." Hoo boy! You just don't know, that's all. This nausea pressing downward in my guts.

"Alright. I'm sorry. I'm sorry I said anything." He shrugs his shoulders ruefully. "I only thought perhaps you'd..." Oh boy if you only knew the fears and passions of a soul in flux, the anguish of a soul that's ventured past the easy life.

"Now don't be silly Lucan." Her voice, her knowing voice is eminently reasonable. "There's no need to feel like a martyr, there's simply no..."

"Look, let's just forget it. You don't understand and that's that." With thoughtless motherly unconcern you lounge about, presuming to understand the motives of my life. "The fact is, I don't want to drive down to Stratford to his goddamn funeral and you can't understand why. So let's just forget it. Okay? I feel lousy enough today without all this. Okay?" Jesus.

"Well I'm sorry if you don't feel well Lucan." She turns her hurt blank eyes to the window. Lost and distraught in the snow-wild night. Who would not weep? "But I must say if you had exercised a little control, if you hadn't..." Awwh well, that tears it! When it's only drink that saves me from that fearful crowd.

"Now don't go into that Rose. You know what those people do to me, you know and anyway that isn't what I meant."

"You had far too much Lucan and it was perfectly

obvious. Anyone could tell, the way you carried on. Showing off with that Whitefield woman..." Showing off? A Charleston, that's all and so what if I did get carried away. A bit. God there's nothing wrong in that. Showing off. Hah! And the thought of this day that was to come, that was the clincher, that was the wind-blown fear that drove me in circles through the room. Until. "They're my friends Lucan, oh I know you don't like them or anything, but they are my friends. And you made such a fool of yourself." The injustice of this woman! A fool? Not by a long bloody shot. A bunch of cruds. Jeez! And she turns on me who in human desperation...

"Don't come after me Rose, just don't come after me." I'm not up to that with this evil head; for the lack of understanding is one thing, but this positive assault upon my life is another. And its intolerable."

"Don't come after you, what do you mean don't come after you?" Rising sharply her voice with tears and woman's anger. He lights another cigarette as her damp eyes stare. "I was so, so—embarrassed and now you say. Oh Lucan! Sometimes I don't know what to think." He turns abruptly from the bed, he turns in the morning light to find his tie. This unhappy woman. Let's not make a scene Lucan, let us not give way to this depressing turn in the conversation but find your tie, put it on and escape downstairs for coffee. Before she cries and wins the day completely. "It wasn't just the dancing Lucan, you know that, it was the way you talked to Blair. They wanted to hear how they sounded, that's all, and its his tape recorder. So they could improve their parts. That's all. It can make such a difference." Her tears, her broken subdual tears are gathering and I'm in for it now. "Everyone heard you Lucan. Everyone. And it was their party, wasn't it?' Her pale accusing face, with damp eyes swelling, regards me as I fix my tie; she waits but there is nothing I can say. Alright, come along now Teahouse. Haw haw. This is your director speaking. With his goddamn bluff and tweedy face he stood and bawled for order and a reading of the second act. Pushing buttons, clunk, and winding tapes as people giggled how they simply couldn't stand to hear themselves. Right in the middle of a fascinating chat with Billie Whitefield, you fine lush thing, and he shouts. Silence please! So I belched. And went in temporary silence for another drink. With his foot on the radiator Lucan brushes at his shoe with an old undershirt. Something about the extravagant demands of the actor's ego. Or something. Hostile at any rate. Shouldn't have oh God I know it was a silly thing, but it wasn't the drink at all... it really wasn't. She just can't see or take on faith the extent to which this frozen day cuts out my liver and my lights. Haw-haw yourself you stinking catalytic crud. But I couldn't go back, no not where their voices began to rise, And fall. So I sat in the kitchen. Lucan stares mournfully at his shoes. That's all I can do and they're not much better for it, I'm afraid. With toes all wrinkled and full of dust. Jeez. And their sides all cracked. He's wrong, he's wrong because he doesn't know. Lucan he said, Martin's better off dead than marrying her. Because of the drink, he's wrong. You know how he wanted to travel and write and you bloody-well know that he couldn't with her. But Hugo he had to settle down: have you read the crap he wrote? Wasting his time with that useless crowd.

Lucan's wife sits and stares with her face full of tearful visions so he puts on his waistcoat, with its rolled lapels, and does up the buttons. There's nothing to be said dear Rose, you will not offer solace, therefore you have no place in this sad and, frankly dangerous return. He lays the watch-chain, with its fob at either end, across his belly and hears the telephone ring as he shrugs into his coat. Who would be and for what possible...

"The phone's ringing Lucan."

"Yes I know. I can hear it." Jeez. He stalks to the door, into the hall and then downstairs. Ringing, ringing, who in hell would phone at this unearthly time? But at least its got me out of that room in time. Stop that frigging noise for the sake of my head and my pitiful nerves! "Hello."

"Hi Luke. Its Hugo. How's the old bean?"

"Oh. Well. A bit ah, delicate you know."

"Don't I just! Jesus. That was some do. One thing about that theatre crowd eh? They sure. I haven't tied one on like that since well anyway, that's what I'm phoning about. You know I was planning to go down to the funeral today? Well, I just can't make it old son. I've got eyes like the behinds of two power driving eagles. Honestly don't think I can make it with this wretched weather and all."

"Oh? Well that's too bad Hugo."

"Yeah, well you know how it gets you sometimes."

"Sure do."

"I guess we're getting old eh? Heh." Impatient in my suit I wait with this goddamn thing in my hand as he goes on. Old! I wouldn't feel too bad myself if I weren't hung up between these worlds, suspended beyond the one sloughed off with the bright green time beyond my grasp. "Anyway, since I can't make it, would you mind taking Felix Oswald with you?" Good blessed bloody hell, that's all I need. "Promised to take him down and since he's, since he was such a good friend, I mean he was probably one of his best friends. I'd hate to think he missed the funeral because of me." Here on this morning that's bad enough, he saddles me with, with. Cold silence spreading in my bowels. "I know you don't like the guy, but hell, you know. What can he do?" And nausea's wings against the stomach's wall as his voice retreats, revolving in distant sounds above.

I can not go on justifying my life to them all. And my life's ploughed under in this world; the seeds are dead. The bastards! "Yeah, sure Hugo. No trouble at all." And my horizon's dark and sere. "Right, right. We'll see you. Bye." He hangs up the phone with an angry. Bang. Holy old bald-headed blue-eyed Jesus! I'm surrounded. Jeez. They retreat and disown this boy on every side. He climbs back up the stairs. The only one whose own poor life should be spared the ritual of his death, and to top if off I'm presented at this last inescapable moment with the living half of the dead one in that town. By all that's jesus holy! He slaps his thigh and glares at the shadows on the stair; he snarls and curls his sensitive lip. He'll sit cynically in my car and breathe all over us for chrissakes. His selfish idle breath.

The night wind softened the tracks of cars before their lights were gone: they passed through circling flakes and scarcely disturbed the night's white sound. Shocked from the sorrow of my youth I seemed to hear in that freezing world a yearning static call; a pale and yearning voice that called.

"Who was that?" And from that burrowing time this life was yours.

"Goddamn Hugo. Phoning to say he's not going down

because he's hung-over, because." This drive in the porous snow and the fog, this wet return on the Stratford road. Is to be avoided. "He's not up to driving in this bloody mess of a day. That's all." He can stretch on his bed and stare at the window while I with my own poor life must drive. Lucan runs his fingers through his hair. "And he wants me to give Felix Oswald a lift down." Oh the growing patterns of this day! "It makes me sick to... what do you think of that Rose? He knows my opinion of that guy, but he phones me at the last minute..."

"It's pretty typical of him isn't it Lucan? I mean he's a pretty selfish man, that's all. I don't know how Sarah puts up with it. Wasting his life and drinking the way he does." Her voice suggests. Is that a crack? Is she getting at me again in this... Jesus, if I thought, if I... "He'll be fired or killed on some drunk, you wait and see. If he's not. You don't know Lucan, what she has to put up with, you just don't know what he's like. He's always out drinking somewhere." What is she talking about for chrissakes? What do I care what he does, what earthly bloody interest is it to me? "How a man can have so little respect for." Lucan stares at his talking wife and he groans a wild and silent groan. She really doesn't understand! There is just no escaping the fact that my wife does not have the faintest idea of what is anguish in my life.

Driving alone from the empty flat, driving alone between black trees in the night snow fields. Alone. Lost from her life and compelled by the fear of the years to come I rushed down this silent ice-torn road.

Get a handkerchief or something. Or anything. To forestall this empty talk and to ease me from this room before I. Pointless to argue with or anger her in her sullen. And besides, with my head and this nervous stomach, I simply don't feel well enough. He rummages in the upper drawer. Not even a decent shirt dear heaven. But at least I have a good one for my pocket and an old one for the nose. Slip it into the old pocket and never confuse the two. Order, that's the thing. And as she talks and talks away I can turn my mind to other things; and it won't simply be an escape either. Because. After all. This dismal chore was designated in an attempt to. I mean there can be no other explanation can there? Because I am to be department

head he's sending me down officially. He closes the bureau
drawer and turns again to Rose. The next few weeks will
see it all settled, for whoever it is needs time to plan. All the
planning for a new life. Yes sir. He pats his pocket handkerchief into place and straightens his tie. Still, another pill or
so wouldn't be out of order. To calm the unofficial man.
Hum. Within her perfumed body grows my seed. Dear
Heaven I hope its true! Our lives conjoined and growing
into one. Our lives... "Should be on my way Rose. Can't
tell how long it will take on a day like this."

"Be sure to tell Susan how upset I am. Because I can't
get down I mean. She'll understand you know, that someone has to do this show." There is no distance in that
weather outside: its shape is encompassed by the swirling
snow. The park's black trees are indistinct, frozen in uncertain light. "I'll get a note off to her this weekend. Poor girl.
Its a terrible day for it." The room's warmth has gone and
I'm alone on that vacant road beneath the tree-torn sky:
one of the wretched figures who will walk and wait for the
earth's slow stain. "Lucan, for goodness' sake, you're not
going down with your fly undone? Hee hee."

"What? Oh." Good Lord. In the bathroom, after.
Couldn't have. Good Lord. He casually closes the zipper.
"Thank you Rose. Wouldn't do to." Jesus no! Crackell's
back you know whisper-whisper behind pink hands, and
how he has the nerve in a second-rate shirt with his fly
undone I really don't know. Oh boy, that's all I need!

"Be just like you Lucan, it would be just like you." All
sad-faced in your english suit and your fly undone as you
mourn. Dear Rose your taunts and your lightly mocking
voice are grossly out of order. Should be my help-meet,
should. And what are you, eh? And Lucan stands uncertain in his wife's eyes. "When the bird did its business on
you just before we were married and nobody noticed until
Harry...Oh Lucan you're always..." Ho-ho for chrissakes!
You weren't laughing then as I recall. "Came in with the
big wet patch on your coat and I thought I'd die, I honestly
thought I'd die with you standing there looking injured
and surly. Ha!" The bed she laughing lies enthroned upon
is burnished by the cotton-candy light and windows rattle
in the empty wind. Is it because I went too far or do I expect
too much? Oh God, I can't wander in myself today! Lucan

asserts himself; he straightens his shoulders and stiffens his back. Self-control in. I always say. On her white and slightly oily brow, a kiss. A final kiss. And then I'll leave. For time runs on. Once again he leans and. Kisses. "Now be sure to tell poor Susan how distressed I am that I'm all tied up."

"Right. O.K."

"And that I'll be writing her a note for sure." All levity gone, her voice is thin and earnest now as she screws the blanket in her hand. "Tell her that I'm thinking of her on this day and, and I have been ever since, well ever since her terrible. Loss."

"Sure Rose, I'll do that. You can count on me. Well, I'm off now." And he starts from the room. "Bye."

"And Lucan...pick me up a couple of copies of the Stratford paper will you. This morning's." Oh by God you, you. "I want to see what Mustard has to say about the production." Unfeeling bloody bitch! He turns incredulous towards his unsuspecting wife. With her brittle bloody co-ed's face. By God indeed! And you almost had me fooled with your. Frigging smarmy talk.

"Dear God Rose! Where do you think I'm going?" My voice is sliding embarrassingly up the scale to a squeal, can't control it; can't. "To a stinking, a stinking...picnic or something?" Keep it down for chrissakes, try to keep it down. And shaking his exasperated head. "I can't just, well what do you want me to do for goodness' sake, stop in the middle of the goddamn cortege?" There's a bit more control and the sound of my voice is better for it. Now calmly, logically explain to her how absurd it is to ask. "The point is Rose, you want me to think of buying a newspaper, a stinking newspaper right in the middle of a most disturbing day; a day so full of, as you should know, so full of possible, possible aah, trauma, that I just don't know, I just..." Christ. She doesn't understand. I can tell by the face that there isn't any use. Lucan begins to stalk the room with black dismay in the gut. And a roaring head. "I just don't know how you can ask me, that's all."

"Lucan I don't understand you. I really don't."

"That's obvious enough."

"No I mean it. You always make everything so dramatic, you're so unreasonable and everything. Just like your mother, your family's all like that. If you'd just take yourselves less seriously, that's all."

"Now look Rose, this is no time for a goddamn lecture, and I'm not going to..."

"But its just a funeral Lucan and you act as if..."

"It is not for chrissakes! Will you stop saying that! It is not just a funeral." Lucan shouting now, waving his arms and desperate. "If it were do you think I'd, I'd. Oh boy! How you can lie there and, and." Stalking and shaking the old head and I simply cannot find the words.

"I know its unpleasant Lucan, but people go to funerals every day and you hardly knew the boy. Its not as though..."

"You don't know what happened. I was drunk, drunk all the time after Vera left, and to top it off, well...well I was sick one night." Her eyes you terrible bloody fool, her eyes uncertain watch you as it comes. "I barfed at the feet, the very goddamn feet of an old faggot of a social science teacher. For chrissakes." God I must go to the john and relieve this tension in my bowels. "And they fired me." A certain Miss Savage and they fired me. "You didn't know that did you? You didn't know that your husband drank and puked right under the eyes of that miserable frigging town! Eh? Hah!"

"Don't be silly Lucan. That was years ago. You were a boy and everything; they're not going to remember...and anyway its different now isn't it?" Lucan distraught with a third of his adult life in her hands. "God Lucan, you talk about actors' egos! I've never known anyone who, who made such a fuss about their life."

"That's it! That's it!" Jumbled thoughts and why must I always speak like this? "Attack my life, that's the way! Feel free, go on. Boy! And you criticize my family when yours, good God when yours is a vicious outpost of..." Never a passionate longing, never: never the harsh wind of terror round the heart. Rushing gratuitously from deep inside, a dark and frantic freedom from them all. I'll kick over the goddamn wastebasket! No. Smash! That's the way and the twisted crap flies all over the floor. Bastards all!

"Lucan! Stop it. What's the matter with you?" Her small voice tearful from the petty life and its littered all over the place and I won't pick it up either. With the mark of my foot upon it. "Are you crazy or something?" No, no, an absurdly tragic figure, that's what I am, a pale and balding Hamlet from the comic stage. Tossed by the hopeless season's icy hand. He strides from the room and her breaking tears, he strides into the hall and down the stairs. Two at a time. Thump thump. A strong and angry unrelenting sound. Two at a time. We'll not be the same after this assault, not after your callous disregard for. His foot slips from the step. Good-bloody-grief but I'm. Hold on! Frantically he clutches at the bannisters; he cries a strangled cry, cracks his ribs on the newel-post and careens off headlong to the floor.

Lucan Crackell lies as he fell with a searching sob expectant in his chest. Too much, just too much. And the tears gather behind his eyes. "Lucan, Lucan, are you alright?" How can I be alright with this side of mine? Broken. All torn and wrenched. He lies unmoving and closes his eyes. Lucky, she's lucky I wasn't. Maimed. "Answer me Lucan!" I can't. My poor bloody head. Oh! And the sob rolls about, seeking release. I can't talk. He hears her bare feet hurrying to the top of the stair. Serves her right. He rises to his knees as she starts down. Arrgh. A frigging awful blow to my side and I feel so sick.

"Alright, its alright." He grunts and heaves himself to his feet. "Wheeowhw!" And clutching his right arm against his side he grimaces and shakes his head. He limps extravagantly with watery eyes and Rose stands uncertain on the landing. "Fell. My foot slipped and I fell. All the way down. Wow!" And he shakes his head again. Now. Maybe she'll.

"Oh dear. I, I...you are alright?"

"Yeah, yeah. Sure. I'll be alright." Christ, its become. But I might have been...she's lucky. This day is, this day is.... Oh God this day!

"Can I, can I do anything Lucan?"

"No. No thanks." He turns, holding his side and favouring his leg, to the kitchen door. "I'd better be going." Let go, let go of your side you stinking bloody sham! "Goodbye Rose." And he takes the sound of her voice through the kitchen and into the back stair's colder air.

LUCAN 2

Sighing he rubs his head, shifts. Sighing. He lights another cigarette and. His wife the queen; imperious in the basement, she oversees the ritual of masks. Bending she removes an eye-brow, peels black hair from a greying head, strips away the islander and finds the plump-faced boy in stocks and bonds; she moves in certainty while I wait, wandering as the evening begins. Reflected in the laugh, she's moving among them with cold cream and kleenex and I hate this world. The two young men who guard the door and watch themselves in each other's eyes; leaning on the wall some talk of methods, one nods to her drink and her hair falls down, but she does not avert her eyes. The convoluted sound of memories, of ego's plea and the laughter. Lucan longing for a drink from the bottle she poured, longing to rise from the room and walk in the gusting night. You who smile in this deadly room, you also have sweated in the green world's sun and I went over and asked you, I said c'mon Rose, for chrissakes let's go for a drink, let's go upstairs, I'm dying of thirst. Let's. I asked her but she wouldn't. She wouldn't. Later, she said, later for.

"...really a terrible thing. I still can't believe it, can you? Its so, so. Hard to believe." With a hint of a whine she's revealed by death, pinched almost, her face. She's Ann. No Nancy, I've taught Ann Sears and she's in the back seat. Nancy. Nancy, what? Lucan bemused by the mythical name of a girl, driving up Richmond past the Post Office, past the Cathedral, orange lit at night for drama, driving. Driving this drive in the sullen snow. Nancy. Thin-faced Nancy with glasses. Ugly Nancy. "Had his job for the fall and everything. A good school too." Her pause and the wipers' strain. Chunk. Chunk. Against the wet snow's weight. "The best in Stratford, by far."

"So funny at O.C.E. He really hated it." Beneath the uncertainty in her voice, there's admiration. Baillie had the way with girls. Got to give him that alright. Lucan's chilly fingers bumbling out a cigarette as Ann's voice goes on and. "Remember once in practice teaching." Reflex strangling of a little laugh and Lucan yearns for the summer sun, he longs for the certainty of grass. "He gave a model lesson, a really model lesson on death and rebirth. Or something funny. It was so good that the instructor analyzed it specially. You know? All about his question-

and-answer technique, his use of the silly chalk board and everything. You know how they are. Very serious. Recognition of individual differences. Evidence of thorough planning." Good Lord. She's got the same, his mocking voice! "And the point was, he hadn't prepared anything on it. And when the instructor had finished (this is what kills me), when the instructor had finished: Martin told him. You know that? Martin told him that he'd made the whole thing up. My God, you should have seen the poor guy's face! He damn near flipped." Her freer laughter and then this silence in my car. A pause. And then more softly. "He was always doing things like that." Chunk chunk and the heavy flakes are swept away. "Poor guy."

"He would have been head of the department for sure. In just a couple of years. You really make a lot of money then, and he would have been. Everybody says so." Careening from her mouth in whisper-plumes, her words fade in the warming air. "There's such a turn-over of teachers in Stratford. Everyone wants to go to Toronto. They were very pleased to get someone like Martin, I can tell you. Miss Schwartz is really ready to be retired." Department head in Stratford?—Hard to believe, Lucan, what you've done with Middlesborough in these two years. Its hard to believe. Light shines on his vulnerable face, it toys with the lines of admiration. You're really going great guns Lucan. Enrollment is staggering, already past capacity. We're really packing them in, eh? Rubbing his hands and his face (can I say it?) is awed. I'd better watch out for my president's job, eh? Ha.

Oh, I wouldn't worry about that, Scotty.

Ha ha. But seriously, I can tell you the Board is delighted Lucan, they're really delighted. Shaking his head. How you got that land for the golf-course, I'll never know. And the library, for that matter. Shaking and shaking, rubbing his greying hair and I don't want his job, not yet poor man, there's too much to do. And I'm freer here. A university of class, yes indeed, with that golf course we're attracting the better sort of student.

I know, I know Scotty. Do you realize that not a single student in Middlesborough was eligible for the student loan fund this year?

No Lucan! Is that right? Not a single one? Boyoboyoboy, what a coup! Wait till I tell that to the Board. Lucan, Lucan, you're a corker, a real corker. Laughing he takes me by the hand, laughing and clapping my shoulder as I rise. Ha-huh-huh-ha! The most beautiful campus in Canada, with the most beautiful people, eh Lucan? Right! Its too bad we haven't got the mountains like the University of British Columbia.

I'll see what I can do Scotty.

Oh God Lucan! You're a real corker, that's all I can say. I'll see what I can do! And shaking his head uncertainly he edges out my door. Could do it too. If only my. The ache behind his eyes, the pain of his battered ribs. Could have broken my neck, for chrissake, and died before her eyes, my strangle gurgling in her widowed ears. Shit! Staring at me wiping the spreading blood from my silent mouth. And somewhere the heavy thump of a futile fly, buzzing and thumping against the glass, buzzing as the cry grows in her throat, spreading its wings and growing and spreading until it bursts from between her teeth in a terrible flight of sound.

Rising in naked trees on either side, Richmond Street blends with the falling snow. A bus breathes grey exhaust, disgorging clumsy-footed figures at the hospital door: disfigured by wind and clothes they lurch and totter uncertainly, while all about our ears the sky is shredded on the branches' spines. Lucan trembling with, the echo of her cry. I don't want to go back. I don't want to go. I. Ahead, and beyond the city gates, it grows in substance on the hill. Must be the reason. Said so yourself. A good sign, almost certain. To get the Middlesborough. And she doesn't understand. My own wife, my Rose. She doesn't understand or know the. Swore I'd never go back, that I'd forget the whole, the fearful bloody mess that was my life. And since you didn't understand, get out of my. The fallible wings aflutter in my chest, for I can't be sure! My poor goddamn aching head, that's part of me; and this raw stomach is me too. Consciously, forcefully, he relaxes his hands on the steering wheel. And she will never know. It is all so perfectly clear.

"Poor Susan." And Nancy's voice is hiking still. "I don't know what she'll do. I really don't. She's never been interested in other boys, not for, for years anyway. He came home every weekend, at least almost every weekend; and when we were in high school, they went out all the time, as long as I can remember. Everybody knew they'd get married. We used to call them the Bobbsey twins. And now...."

"That's when he had the trouble with his skin, isn't it?"

"Oh yes. And it didn't make any difference to Susan at all." What's this? Bad. I don't have to listen, why in hell should I....

"Bad skin?"

"Yes Doctor Crackell, he had terrible skin. Terrible acne or something. You should of seen his face." Ugly Nancy, you relish this role, you really shine: the chorus, the thin but eager chorus for another's life. "And he was so shy, it was pitiful, so shy you hardly ever saw him after school!" Sorry he asked, and fascinated by the voice, Lucan glances politely, right into her, good Lord right into her sad sharp eyes! All I need, for chrissakes, picking at my sleeve, is an old man's bony hand. "But Susan brought him out of it because she loved him. Real love can do that you know, and she loved him for what he was. She didn't care a bit about the pimples and things, at least she didn't let on.... You know what I mean?"

An uncertain "Hmmm" for I'm no longer sure.

"And he started going to the school proms. Even to tea dances at the Pines. That's the club, you know, the Pines." She pauses and Lucan waits for the lights to change. "Of course, he really had to go to them." Knowing that I should ask why, that I should turn again with badly concealed fascination, that I.... But I won't. goddamnit, I won't! Not in my car, my own car, not today.

"What do you mean?" Thank you Miss Sears.

"Well Susan was president of the young people's club two years in a row."

"Oh."

"Yes." Staring. Good bloody grief but she's. Staring through the windshield at the road in desperation. What in hell is she talking about? Peering with his hands loose on the wheel. Probably isn't a kid, just another goddamn false alarm. Same as before. That vulnerable delicacy, that goddamn plaintive voice. "They were really very good friends of mine, you know. Martin and I lived right next door to each other, well nearly next door; just around the corner actually, and we grew up together and everything. We all went to the same schools." The wind that blows in this country, circling his shape in the melting snow. Martin! Her soft voice calling her man, her boy, her. What ho. She came from her bath with tangled hair; her face was flushed with heat and her eyes held mine: I almost put my arms around her, I almost drew her body against mine there in our hall, I could almost feel the breasts that swelled in her terry cloth robe and I did smell the dampness in her hair. But she looked away. She smiled her smile, and with eyes to the floor she tightened her robe across her breast and went on down the hall. Excitement in his throat as he watched her go, and it still warms me to think of it. There was a boy, a very strange enchanted....

"I've never known anyone who had so many friends. Everybody in Stratford's so upset."

"Oh I know Ann. I know. I can hardly believe he's really gone." Oh God there are tears on the edge of her voice, and there's nowhere to go. "Poor, poor Susan. I can remember so many evenings, so many...you know she really loved him?" Her voice is maundering clumsily in the scale, selfishly it reaches out and it pleads on my arm. Somewhere silently you possess a part of him, don't you? And with his death, your share of him grows. Or is that fair? "And he changed because of her, do you know that? He really changed. He used to be so silly. So silly, when he was young."

Struggling under a lowering sky, see me there, a heavy figure on uncertain ground: beneath my disgrace I bend and walk in the wind. But no more. Just a chance, dear God, just a chance and I'll prove what the well-considered move can do!

Silly. She's right, of course, its sad. His wasted youth. An assault of disapproving images, and Lucan shakes his head. For there he is, parading his silly wasted youth, and they say the only first he ever got was in public speaking! It had to make you. If he hadn't been so...for hours in the cafeteria, sprawled. Wrapped in that ridiculous cloak, cigar in his teeth and laughing too loud. Listening to his laugh. Polite enough, it wasn't that, he was polite enough on the surface. Wasn't that. Just. Underneath or something. He didn't care. You could tell from his eyes that he didn't care. Doctor Crackell, there's been something I wanted to ask you.

What? On the divan, in darkness with the girl.

Do you know what to do with an egg-bound hen?

Pardon, Baillie?

An egg-bound hen. You know, a chicken that can't lay. No. Ha-ha. I don't. Staring with horrid fascination. Why, do you have one? Ha. The girl's face and I shouldn't have said that, no I shouldn't. If you'll excuse me Baillie. And turning back to the undergraduates on the floor.

You make it do exercise, lots of exercise! In his shouting voice. And if that doesn't work you pour warm oil up its vent. Jesus ignore him for chrissakes, ignore him, and their embarrassed smiles. Oh boy! After his singing in the kitchen, after the drinks, dear heaven how many, the beer and wine in the students' house and his tilted throat? On the wooden table, perched, he sang to the bottles and the plaster hung in shreds.

> But now my memory it gives me pain
> For my long-lost Franklin I'd cross the main
> Ten thousand pounds I would freely give
> To say on earth, that my Franklin do live.

Very drunk now, on the divan, the girl across him talking about God. Motionless upon her back, his hands. And his eyes are closed. Above an astigmatic's liberated views, Lucan leans to hear her voice. As Baudelaire said, she woos. Surely, as Baudelaire said, even if God didn't exist, it would be necessary to believe in him? His hands respond with twitching motions down the spine, she shifts her weight. Isn't that true Martin? Hopefully her finger traces out his brows and ashen lips and Lucan stifles sympathetic shivers in his throat. If He didn't exist, we'd have to invent Him, wouldn't we? Through velvet curtains hanging on the door a jutting bull's head stares; turning jerkily it surveys the room, nods politely to Lucan, and then with warning finger and sepulchral voice: BAILLIE! He turns with staring eyes. BEWARE! BEWARE THE ARIS-TOTELIAN SCREW! And the bull is gone, but echoing loudly down the hall. ITS VICARIOUS, VICARIOUS,

VICAR.... And suddenly. Excuse me please, get out of my way! And tumbled, she's squawking on the floor. An instant of thighs, and Baillie's green face retching from the room, he knocked over my drink!

Got a thirst for water. To alleviate this head, to settle maybe, the uncertainty down below. Shifting from one buttock and easing his tender seat, Lucan blinks and lights another cigarette for clarity. Woefully talking of death in the fullness of life, sporadically sighing their unbelief and ugly Nancy simply can't have known him there! Oh no, you can't my girl, or you wouldn't be talking of change. The cigarette parches his tongue and assaults him from this bloody awful day. You cannot, huddled next to me, have seen the self indulgence at school, the angular obscenity that. Silly goddamn arrogance! He wore. Egg-bound, for chrissakes! And there were no, and this is the crux. By God! Clenching the wheel again, Lucan possessed by growing anger. The crux alright, for there were no signs, not a sign of change! He basically refused to care, that's it, whereas I...I. Driven as I was, driven down the lonely road of my disappearing youth, driven. By a terrible blow, my loss. By the unknown terror of my vagrant world; forced to follow, to walk in the burning snow. Lucan's growing panic and his body's protestations, and chunk the wipers' steady strain. For I always wanted, desperately needed even then, particularly then, with all my acid heart. To care.

Fumbling cold and the windows' eyes. The basement, the hall, the light, the lockers, the benches. Their menacing feet. Sweep it up, this rising stench, mop it all up, but there is no time, dear God, they're. Quickly, quickly for the sake of. Oh God! No use. No use hiding in there Mister Crackell. Have you no....

Hugh you're wrong, goddamnit, I know. Gulping another hefty gulp and I do drink well that's for sure. How many? Bottles singing as the refrigerator door is slammed and their voices dramatic in the other room. The unthinking life must end, you know it must. Milton anguished, not for the boy. He hardly knew him for chrissakes. Hugh's dark face, moustaches wet, is swaying before my eyes. Must concentrate, clenching his fists till the nails bite in, or I'm lost. Mourning because Lycidas had to die, the casual youth in all of us must die.

Don't see it, Lucan, don't see it at all. Lucan's cold glass in his hand; and clumsily kissing his mouth, the ice. Doesn't want to see, that's his trouble. Hanging around, invited to their parties. Too old, as the lines about his eyes attest, too old for the unconsidered life and Lucan impassively watching the yellowed teeth that chew his pipe. Not just talking about innocence, are you? Puffing and sucking as I shake my head. Thought not, thought not. And then through a cloud of smoke. But why then? Why does it have to die?

Its not appropriate. Carefully forming the words. Ap-pro-pri-ate. You know what I mean? Brushing with heavy hand the smoke between my eyes and his mouth. Teeth stained and soggy moustached. Shrill cries, laughter from the other room. Insulted them, I guess. Or something. The pompous bastard! And came with her accusing eyes in silence. Impulsively, desperately emptying my glass and with sudden insight. No. God no! Not innocence. Selfishness! Selfishness, that's it. Don't you see? Triumphant now and drinking deeply from the empty glass, rising to the bottle. Shakespeare's Venus! Selfish as hell, fearful from her lechery. Lurching, whoops, as he turns for a splash of water from the tap and this is important. Can't compromise or even share the poor young bastard's life because. Against the counter, a quick mouthful from the new glass, the, forgot the ice, it doesn't matter. And sitting down again. Because she's got no control over her desire. Totally selfish. See? No control. Searching through empty packages, have to light this butt. Longish, but crushed. And dragging in the smoke. Other forces Hugh, the world is full of other forces. The boar, yes, try the boar. Expect to impose your selfishness and. Boom! along comes some frigging great boar from the real world. Boom! Cracking with energy, the fist on my other palm. And he hasn't got an answer to that.

But hell. Lucan....

Wait a minute, let me finish. That's where they're wrong, you see? Desperately ordering, seizing into the buzzing silence. Revolving mind. Diagnosed it all. Wrong. Sip and swallow for some time to think. Star-crossed lovers, all that crap! Bigger than bothofus. Slurring my. Whereas, whereas the Capulets and Montagues are the real world

Hugh, the real world. The one that counts. My voice uncertain for she would have laughed, you laughed didn't you? Biting. Laughter and the sun. Hot on the shabby trunks. Made Adonis almost a fairy, Hugh! Cause he wouldn't stay. But he knew, Adonis knew. Okay? Poor bugger. That she'd destroy him with her carelessness. Arrogance. Pushing my glass away, I've drunk too much, have to. Can hear her lonely laughter even now. Think this out more clearly.

Christ Lucan, I think that's crap.

Waitaminutewaitaminutewait! Let me, Ah! Ferociously rubbing his skull but the trouble is far inside. Shit, what was I. Sweet Cytherea don't, don't for God's sake haunt me so. Too much insight! Rubbing, rubbing his head to exorcise, to efface, anything to escape that sound. Frantically rubbing.

Luke, hey Luke! What's the matter?

Nothing. Nothing except. Fuck off, please fuck off. Vera and leave me alone! You chose it. Your decision alone. And this is my reassuring-and-most-natural voice, except something happened to my eyes. Ha. Son-of-a-bitch, eh? But I'm okay now.

You sure? Jesus you look terrible.

Sure, sure I'm sure. Happens sometimes when I drink, you know. Ha. Pleasepleasepleaseveraplease....

Shifting tentatively for comfort and I should have. Would have too, slipped into the toilet before leaving, done something to ease. If it hadn't been. Her goddamn selfishness and that scene. A newspaper! Carefully, for under this slush its ice, sheer ice so handle with care. Hands light on the wheel, its the wind. The memories pain but its foolish to give in, God knows. Its probably. To exorcise my youth, this time of testing, and in days to come I'll recollect. A boy, a foolish boy had died, that's all. Happened to be a student in my care and I'll recollect from strength. A sun-lit office, my books, my stereo, and I might take up the pipe again. Yes. And smile at all this....

"Shouldn't you have turned? Doesn't Felix live up there, Doctor Crackell?" Felix? Oh God yes, Oswald, yes. The.

"Yes. Yes, I forgot." Turning slow motion, bumping diagonally on ridges of snow, sliding into this gas station.

"Silly, eh? I forgot where he. Lived." Its too much, its too much. Arrogant frigging kid. A symbol, a breathing symbol of the useless life! Jesus, we're always in the indifferent bloody hands of strangers! They search me out, with menacing cries they search me out; in glee they hunt me down. Rubbing the old head with chaos rising in the throat on this wretched day that leads him driving to the past. Crackell! Crackell! You're moving your ears. Stand still or we'll beat you. Have you ever been beaten, Crackell? Rigid, with watery eyes and perspiration bursting from his thighs, Lucan Crackell in a row of winter-bundled, awe-bedraggled boys. Does your daddy beat you? Plump-thighed and sweater-coated seniors smoking pipes and good at games. Their laughter with elan. At my ears, my poor large ears. And someone's skinny body in its heavy coat. Crackell. Does your daddy beat you, Crackell?

He used to Mister Brigham.

Hah! He used to beat you did he, your father used to beat you did he Crackell?

Yes Mister Brigham.

Did you hear that new-boys? Crackell's father used to beat him. Expectant now, his voice. Rising. Where did he beat you Crackell? Tell us where your daddy used to beat you. In winter clothes beneath the steam pipe's heat: bumbling voices under it all and from somewhere outside a young voice calls. Crackell! Crackell! Tell us, I said, where your daddy. A blurring column that narrows to a dark stain on the wall. Staring.

On the, the bottom Mister....

Speak up Crackell! Your voice, what's the matter with your voice?

On the bottom Mister Brigham.

Ha-ha! Ho-ho! So Crackell's father used to beat him on the bottom! Is that right Crackell?

Yes.

Yes! Yes what?

Yesmisterbrigham.

That's better Crackell, that's better. Been very interesting. Very interesting. Hasn't it boys. Hasn't it boys? And their voices in a hopeful chorus.

Yes-Mister-yes-Brigham-yes-Mister-Brigham-Brigham.

Languid applause and his voice is pleased. Now Crackell I

want some tuck. Anyone else for tuck? Savouring melted chocolate, he crooned rich words. Buns and crispies, coke and. Sweets they. Soft cream buns with chocolate thighs. Plump vanilla bellies for their adolescent nastiness. And Crackell.

Yes Mister Brigham?

On the way, stop into Mister Graham's room and tell him he's a tit.

Yes Mister Brigham.

Got that? A tit.

Yes Mister Brigham.

Right then, away you go. And make it snappy. We're hungry. Bastards rich, their arrogance. Flushing. Always hungry. Here somewhere, here below the dark hill's crest. And Lucan vainly searching where the wind is free, above the shadow of the hill. Me they have on days like this, Irretrievable parts torn off. Indignities. A certain sequence of indignities to which. Shrugging resignation of his shoulders. I've adapted. Had to, had to for chrissakes! And perpetrate upon myself? Now where in hell is this, why can't they? "Either of you know his house?"

"Yes, its just...just. There! That's it. The wooden one." Knows it well, but she's one of them with that echoing voice, the badge-like attitude they wear. Wonder if they've? Not innocence, certainly. As part of the general laxity, the essential absence of belief, there must be a certain amount. Of sleeping around. Hand on the horn as we wait. Huddled row on row, brick boxes, red: stuffed chairs in cluttered rooms and the kitchen smells. Plastic table cloths and the phony walnut mantle clock. Jeez! Part of the gang around him as he sat. Baillie and frigging Oswald. The horn again as he reaches for a cigarette. Smoke spiralling blue from the tip. And grey from the lungs. Taking his, for chrissakes, and we're short of time. Going on for eleven and he knows. This lousy day. From front lawns, swirling, the snow through scrawny branches lifts and blows. It tumbles in the wind. Wandering in late to class if he came at all. Hard blast. A long one and they stare from the passing car. "C'mon Oswald. C'mon, we're late." Behind him Ann moves suddenly.

"I'll get him, Doctor Crackell."

"Yes. Yes please." Turning as she struggles out. "And

tell him we've got a long way to go." Obediently and. Nice legs, small ankles in black stockings. Close the door, quick, quick its cold out there! Inside my shirt, the chill. Lucan pokes at his white silk scarf, arranges it between his overcoat's lapels. Rubs his hands. Blows. Leaning to look, her skinny face looking too, and their legs are good in winter. Vulnerable. Shapely, out of her swaying skirt, against the snow. Hah! I'll bet she does.

Laughter and her arms in that tree-top flat. Sloping walls, the red piano's music and her voice. Shouldn't, shouldn't, her image hesitantly comes its dangerous. Careful! But. Rubbing again, my hands, for warmth and Vera. Your crooning hands, the patient sensuality. I came and come: I, fastened and hopeful, ignorant at last of the real world's fear.... Embarrassment as always, paternal amusement at my young and learning time. Drinking eagerly draught beer in the King Cole Room. As clearly I recall. To fill the silence. Heavy swallowing, and your inviting eyes. An innocent, oh boy! And it was embarrassing. Small laughter at his youth's uncertainty. Shadowed leaves on the Museum windows as we turned alone, north up Avenue Road. Strong hand in mine and your husband, you said: I hardly ever see him now I have my own apartment. Big cars with red upholstery. Convertibles shouting by us as we walk, their music in the night. Turning where branches meet above the street, turning from cars we go, and up the hill. About the street lights, bright green leaves against the shadows and do I go in? With this Vera Demmett and her easy talk? Or am I? Kiss her married mouth. Oh God! Go in? But she gave no chance or opportunity, she led me by the hand through a darkened hall and up two flights of stairs. To turn on lights, bending. The incredible roundness of her breast and her blonde hair falling down.

Gently, with light from the other room, gently lying. From the window, shadows and. Her hair on the edge of my mouth. An awkward figure and how many times? How many beneath the sloping eaves, until I? Without offence, her mocking laugh: don't be silly Lucan. Don't be silly. This flesh and why can't I? What's the matter with me? For I like her very.

You think too much, that's all.

Excessive cerebration.

Whatever you want, my love.

But I've never been satisfied. Then more uncertainly. In fact, I've not been aroused. To any great degree. Lightly her hand and eyes.

Be patient. Patient. At least once, you've satisfied me. Physically. And it had been so long. So long. Rolling against him, her body lies across his chest. Hair in my eyes and her smiling face. Softly her brushing breasts and the weight of her thighs. And emotionally, every time I'm with you. Kissing gently my face and eyes. My ears her tongue explores.

Ha! It's ironic.

Mmmmm. Mmmmm. What is, love?

That right now, when I'm discovering this, I mean there is no longer any doubt that I'm. Insistent caresses and Lucan twists. To a degree, anyway. Impotent. And that at precisely the same time I should be reading Baudelaire. Because he might have been, too. Partially impo-....

Oh Lucan! Raising her head, and laughter. Lucan, you....

Its true you know. Martin Turnell says there are indications. In his work, that he suffered from excessive cerebration. Don't laugh Vera, its true.

Lucan you're such an idiot! How your mind goes on. Spilling and gurgling laughter. Baudelaire, for chrissakes! Have another drink Lucan, drink up for heaven's sake! Bounding soft and bobbing from the bed while Lucan rubs at his damp ears. But, its true, she might not see but its true. And shouting to her in the other room.

Its not uncommon among intellectuals! And its not necessarily a sign of impotence either! Naked and hanging, glass in either hand she pads and offers. Produces, sometimes it produces a temporary sexual incapacity.... Tapwater bubbles rising to the surface, she never uses ice; and drinking whiskey, rye in his throat what did Stendhal say? Drinking she's warm into the bed and Vera! Cut it out, hey! You'll make me spill my....

How many times her mouth, her hands? And then darkness. Back then I danced, danced with the best of them. Look at them. Oh yes. Exploding my discovered life, inevitably. Yes. Took his lousy time, alright! Skinny, hold-

ing her arm clumsily, and Lucan impatiently watching
their legs on the slippery walk. But not again. No. Because I
know that languorous world, I know it too well.

Cold air in at the door (hurry up for the sake of my):
scrape of clothes, and her body beneath, singasongofnyl-
ons, she shifts and lunges to make room for him on my
plastic-covered seat. And he has to slam the door. Watch
yourself, you young punk! Have no respect, the young. Its
true. Lucan has the car in gear and bumping sideways to
the curb, we slide precariously. Spinning the wheels. No
traction. Oh God, don't tell me! Serve him right, the
bastard. If he has to push. But then the jolting, the grabbing wheels and Lucan's away. Be good for him. There.
We go, down the middle of this lousy road: no use trying to
steer, other tracks, earlier cars. Command and lead. Teach
him that you have to pay your way in this world, you can't
always ride for free. Sense of responsibility. That's the
thing. Wipers clear away the crud and I can see more
clearly, although. Elegantly rubbing, they're expensive
gloves. This condensation is no help. And Ann, brushing
snow, brushing at her clothes. "Nancy, you don't know
Felix, do you? Felix Oswald."

"No. I don't. Hi there."

"And Felix, this is Nancy Haden." Bet it was him.
Refusing to acknowledge this girl, he doesn't even speak
and Haden, that's her name. Haden. No manners, none at
all. I'll bet he was involved!... He's just the kind alright.
Can't or won't probably, find, or even see, outside himself,
a single object worth his precious respect. Arrogant. Hah!
Just like. Whoooeee! A hell of a row and they never discovered. Questioned him too but there was no proof. A
terrible, and obscene and sacreligious thing to do! I'll bet it
was him. Lucan's sickness at the grotesque image and why
did I have to be the one to find it? The only frigging day in
the year I went early. Even if you didn't believe, even if you
don't believe. A shocking, stupid thing to do. Into the
science building. Somehow. Just to get the damned thing.
Shaking his head as in tracks leading back to Stratford, the
car is held. So premeditated! That's the real thing, so
carefully thought out. Some papers, that was all, went up
at five to finish the set. For a class that morning. Unreal
lights. Really bashing them off, because that's the only

way. Don't look up, don't above all things. You bet. The pile diminishing. Just six left, pausing in the desk lamp's light. Stretching sigh. Rising and stretching. Another cigarette as I stroll to the window in the gathering light, springtime, a job well done...what in hell's that? Lucan with horror to the panes. Peering. There on the muddy hillside hanging. A cross! Glistening white. Against the reviving earth. Running at first, but then, there may be. Somebody watching. He walks in the chilly air, for I left my coat. It is, dear Jesus Christ it is! A skeleton. Clutching to his feet like grotesque rubbers, the mud, wet seeping in his woollen socks. Cautiously he nears in silence, approaches and stands. The wind that cries through those bones. Above me suspended, I'll never forget, and hanging by its frigging feet those empty bones, and I had to reach up in wind and flatten the paper:

THERE IS NO EASTER

Behind me he sits and what am I doing with these strangers in my car? Felix. Fee lix. Funny name, a word. Feel-ix. Don't know them and what's more, don't. Want to. Them or him. Snow's cold on either side, untouched in the gardens as the town recedes: there the bus-worn road, the golf course sacrosanct and the dirty river's bed, in frozen. Western's penitentiary gothic, nestled. The naked trees. While I. Lucan Crackell, thrown so terribly into this frigging terrible mess of a situation. Jeez! And Lucan, in the mirror, sees a younger head that stares impassive at the passing road. Interference that we least suspect and from indifferent hands, for chrissakes! Lucan, its starting, don't, why in hell are you here among these clutching, bony hands! Reaching to prod the cloth of my suit, my Savile Row; to flick dismissal at my lousy shirt!

"Its sure a terrible day, isn't it." Argh! Good God, how can she say, assault us so? Appalled. Because that's what I mean, just exactly what I mean. The man whom sorrow named his friend, my forehead, I'm justified, you see? They do not care, not one of the whole shitty lot can even care! Deep in thought, for heaven's sake deep in thought as she stares at your face! The road or something. Insensitive Nancy, ugly Nancy Haden, stop poking at my mind. From her words expanding silence, spreading, oozing from the car: she tries again. "Much worse than yesterday. I mean the driving's worse and everything." Lucan's nod oh Jesus, Ann murmurs:

"Uh-huh." Whoops, in the mirror, his eyes are watching. Me. Back! Back quickly. Look! the road.

"Did any of you drive down to the funeral home? To pay your respects, I mean?" Lucan melting, pouring about inside, for she really expects an answer, she. Does. "How about you Ann? Did you...."

"No. No. I couldn't. I had a test in Phil. Wasn't prepared or anything, so I really couldn't. I had to work. Like crazy just to pass the damned thing." Not a chance boyoboy not a chance, you wouldn't catch me, of my own free choice! Not a chance. Back on a viewing trip, searching out youth's remains. My own. Horrified juggling. Surging and I'll regret it. I'll be sorry I didn't, for the sake of my bowels, this nasty pressure. Take the time. And how will I? What a horrible thought! Special room for the dead, for viewing: special chairs to sit on and stare. Eyes peacefully closed with abrasive cups (the old shell game), they hold the lids down; and a tube, under the arm there's supposed to be a tube. Hah! Every night a little man sneaks in, silently. Reaching under the dead arm, he pulls out the little cork and into a paper cup. Drains fluid. Dripdripdrip. Drip. Drip. White handkerchief delicate in his hands, he clears his throat. Straightens the lapels maybe, brushes the dust off the face "I don't think I could have gone away. Its such a gruesome thing."

"His poor mother and father sat there for two days, two days almost all the time. Mind you." Turning to me, looking at me, why? Why? "Susan was a big help, poor girl, she stayed, she insisted on staying so they could go out for a while. Go home and rest. Have a coffee or something." Susan watches and waits in the earth's slow stain: your garden's sparse and sere, the winter's. "And the flowers, you've never seen so many flowers."

"Particularly for this time of year." After silence, his startling voice.

"Pardon?"

"I said particularly for this time of year. You know. The winter and everything." Listless, already bored. Mocking her, I think he's. The bastard. Mocking. Glancing up, Lucan sees him turn again to the window's empty fields.

"Oh. Yes. There were gladiolas and lilies and everything."

"A veritable bank of flowers." Lower, more private.

"Aah yes," she sighs, "so beautiful, the flowers. Felix. You don't mind if I call you Felix?" Drifting open country in the wind and wooden fences snaking out of sight: dark evergreens march up the hill against the sky. And Oswald, muttering, shifts behind. "You went down then, did you?"

"No. No."

"Oh."

"But I've read about it." And Lucan wants to roar! Selfish. Arrogant bastard! He can't control, for he doesn't have the slightest. My stomach, oh! This day's combined assault, my stomach's weakness and my head! Sense of decency or manners.

"Where? I didn't know there were any." Confusion as she sees, and then quickly, stumbling in her fading voice. "Oh yes. You mean, in books and things." Silence drops again. Outside and above the party's noise, the laughter and embarrassed talk, his shouting voice. I WILL NOT ENTER A HOUSE WHERE THEY APPEASE THE PROLES! Drunkenly down our apartment's common hall, and Christ! If I'd known I'd never have. Spontaneity! It didn't please my wife, God knows, but how did I know they'd come too? Recalling tearful Rose, the uncertain glances of the guests, APPEASE THE! Tried to quiet him, say that for Baillie. He tried to shut him up but the voice went on and bloody on. My stomach tied in knots because I couldn't venture out and the police, dear God! Bluestanding creaking at my door and the neighbour's ruptured sleep. Oh boy! Aggressive selfishness, that's the thing. And apart from everything, everything else, it assaults the hard-earned calm in other people's lives. Now. Behind me. And he is baiting this silly girl, he. Oh boy! So goddamn arrogant, he's so! Shaking my head, and my hands again if only they'd. Stop.

Gargoyles capped with snow. Staring mournfully down the dull white land, they search for home. Shuffling Lucan in his winter boots. Trinity's panes like eyes in shadow; ivy thick as varicose veins. A careful knock. Shouts from the playing field, cold air lonely and down the hall a mouth organ begins. And again begins. Listening to his heart with his ear on the door. Yes, there it is, a clear invitation. Come in. Crackle sidling round the door, respectfully. Blinking in yellow light. Well. Crackle. What can I do for you? It bursts on the window sill, it chases the shadows from the room.

Mister Graham. You're a. You're a tit.

What? Oh. Who sent you Crackle?

Mister Brigham, Mister Graham.

Yeah? Well, you trot right back and tell him he's wasting your time.

I have to go to tuck first, they want me to go to tuck. Extending his opening hands with list and warm wet money. But I'll tell him after. Is that alright, Mister Graham?

Sure. Sure. And thanks Crackell.

Thank you Mister Graham. Almost regretfully turning, turning his back with the shining doorknob in his hand.

Crackell. Uncertainly Lucan returns to face the voice. Crackell, tell me. Pausing in mid-sentence and his question floats about the room, revolves indistinctly and then it blooms in the sun-drenched air. Are you happy here? Brown eyes before he looks away, and tightly curling hair. To papers disarrayed on his desk; senior math with compass and ruler. Trigonometry or something. Happy? The paper crackles from his hands. Far out his window, beneath a white-blue sky, lake ice is shifting, bruising with pressure, and dark birds drift and sway; briefly they hang in the window...Forget it Crackell. forget that I asked, eh? Birds in a pale sky above the breaking ice. And Lucan nods. Because I guess it doesn't matter, does it?

No. No Mister Graham. Lucan startled into movement; out into the hall he breaks as if pursued: under the gargoyle's longing eyes, a small dark figure on the snow, running clumsily, and they can not see from their eaves on Trinity House his tears. And they certainly wouldn't have cared, even if they'd turned down their faces and found my whimpering figure they wouldn't have cared. Those many days, dear God, day after day. "Anyone know where the church is?" His ragged voice.

"No" It doesn't matter.

"It doesn't matter because we're meeting Miss Morton at Wang Lung's on King Street."

"Don't you know where it is Nancy?" Doesn't even! Lucan's rising inner voice for you'd think! It almost seems a slight, a conscious rudeness! Hasn't even the courtesy, to acknowledge me. Tightened hands that clench, and he was docile descending; with one on either side and the neighbours' closing doors. Forcefully, one final time from the floor below, aggressive surly creep!

"Church of the Redeemer, I guess." WHEN IN DOUBT PUNT! Echoing with official laughter, c'mon now fella, c'mon now, in the stairwell smothered as arm in arm he went with them. "Its just behind Eaton's, you know. It'll probably be there." Ordinary voice and doesn't she. Mind? "That's where they were going to be married." If he was mine, by God. Grimly. I'd show him. Manners. I'd teach him. Married?

"Well why don't we go right to the Church, then."

"Because." Good Lord, but why? Why do I get involved? "Because she's arranged for everyone to meet at the restaurant first. That's why." My scathing voice, but reasonable for we don't want a scene, don't want to set him off. Or anything. "Have a coffee, so we can have a coffee. She's coming there." Listening silence: the plan, that's all. Not my fault, the thing. Arranged that way.

"Under her sorrowful eyes, the gathering mourners eh? Hah!" Open disgust, good grief, and he laughed out loud! "Get us all together, she'd like that. Lead us in properly wrung out by grief." By George he's, that's it. Emotionally unstable.

You shouldn't say that," and Nancy's ugly shrill, "you shouldn't say that at all!" Or else why would he? That explains it all; his drinking too, the way he is, that's it. And soothing Ann, she knows, she's used to him! Good Lord!

"C'mon Felix, don't be unreasonable." There is chaos and premonitions of chaos. I wonder if he's. Good Lord, I wonder if he's dangerous? Driving carefully with images of this boy amok. Blind doctor that I read about and a hysterical, oh boy! Hysterical patient scratching out your eyes. Wheewh! Pretend. That's it! Hah. Pretend to have a flat tire. Lucan chuckling now, for he deserves it. Even if he's not, he deserves it. Have to get up early, very early in the morning, for its the thought-out move, the well-considered man that. Ask him to get out and see, would you take a look Oswald, and then. Zoom! Off we go. Slush in his face! His tiny figure vanishing behind. Hah! Waving and running darkly in the snow. Furtively in the old rearview mirror, expecting, expecting...beady red-rimmed eyes, or? Looks alright, the bastard. Looks alright, tired perhaps but. Still he'd deserve it.

"I just don't see why we can't go right to the church, that's all." Cruddy fake! I'm the one, don't you see? I'm the one who shouldn't want to go! Standing, Lucan Crackell muddy footed on the springing hill. "I don't want to sit around a frigging restaurant, listening." To the past, god-damnit, listening to my crippled youth and she didn't see. A newspaper! That's the infuriating thing, they prattle on with their I don't wants and their stinking reviews; they're so bloody concerned! But I know Wang Lung's, I know every step in disgrace. "What will we talk about, that's what I want to know. What in hell can we talk about?" Scornful voice; insubordination. "A terrible thing, eh? Being killed by a hit-and-run driver." Fifteen and then. "People. Should be more careful, don't you think?" Smartass! That's what he. Insensitive, she's unaware of real agony; smartass doesn't know about death, and I'm tired, I am frankly tired of his nihilistic foolishness. I'll....

"Look Oswald." Be reasonable, remember your position. "The arrangements were made and they'll be expecting us, okay?" Officially my presence indicating. Concern on the part of Western for a student's death. Of course. But also, dear heaven I hope. Fruition! For I erased the past, rebuilt an image on the rubble of that loss. "Now if you want, if you'd prefer to go on to the church alone. Well. By all means go ahead. Its up to you once we reach the restaurant. You're a free agent Oswald, and its your own business." Keep it reasonable, the teacher's voice. Act like a child and the world responds. Petty complaints, they make me sick, and his lack of manners! "But the rest of us will meet them all as planned." Show him he can't. "If its alright with you." That's fixed him! Lucan with cautious expansion stretches, he yawns a little yawn and brushes ash from his lapels. Onto my gathering waist. Firmness, have to be firm. Assuredly speak from one's considered and.

"Oh keep the dog far hence that's friend to man, or with his nails he'll dig it up again." Who's that?

"What's that Oswald?" He's, the bloody nerve of this. Eliot.

"Keep the dog, you know. The dog. Woof-woof. Or he'll dig it up." Jesus fucking Christ! Cynical creep, we'll have a talk! Yes. After all this is over, for you can't have. Even a graduate student treating the staff like this. No sir! If you can't adjust, your sights Oswald. Shape up or ship out! God! Its all so. Flipflop Lucan's stomach, for there's no control. Despite me he's here; unwilling, already, as I was. For pity's sake! To drive this road. Why the hell did I have to bring him, why didn't I? Take who? Hugh don't be absurd. Ha-ha. Felix, the creepy and unstable Oswald-punk? Ha-ha Hugh you're kidding! And hang up quickly before he can reply! But I never think or act with efficiency and consequently here I am. Depressed and vaguely menaced by this day's array. And as the miles go by the structured past comes on, and it bubbles and boils as the pressure of distance is removed. Jesus! Why did I have to come back, what will I do? For I've got no control, I'm a broken moth that feebly, flutters. Day after day, they jigsaw into one: a Sunday night, meticulously clear in detail, but confused. Here he dances with a short fat boy, the perspiration glistens on his upper lip, and I can see the texture of rough winter cloth. In the lavatory, his figure with a cigarette; see how he leans toward the early morning window, his young cheeks blowing out the secret smoke. And with a gang of yelling boys he kills a skunk, or here, in the thawed stream, poised with a ski-pole, he waits for carp. More scenes. Lying in bed he hears the prefect's punishing stick; and later, chastised steps that pause on the stairs returning. Through it all, the narrowing lines that force the eye to young Lucan's hand, pale in the Sunday evening's darkened hall, ready to knock on the prefect's common room door. And I could not go in. Fading away to the bathroom, a futile attempt to void the snake of fear in my gut, then Lucan arrives at the door. Stylized figures, expressionless masks and indifferent eyes. They beckon. Frightened, and eager to please, I stand in this smoky room but why am I here? What have I done that these ceremonial figures stare, and what do they want? Well Crackell, you know why you're here? O God. For under their eyes he suddenly knows. Its not the. Shouting from the dark. And they think I did it. Lucan trembling as the head prefect rises and straightens his robe. You probably know; the Head has requested us to find the toughs who insulted his daughter Wednesday night. Some rowdy boys Crackell, some nasty rowdy boys running loose in the school. And we won't have it. A fine thing if a nice girl can't walk home in the dark, without having dirty things shouted from the shadows. Its a fine thing! He turns and the skirts of his robe are whipping about his calves. Isn't Montreal you know, Crackell. And it wasn't any of the toughs from town, for she saw their clothes. And we're going to find them! Because. Threatening, his voice rising as his anger grows. Because you know who they are! Lucan vibrates like a tuning fork.

It wasn't me Mister Scott, it wasn't me, honest! I was listening to the hockey game, Leafs and Rangers, anyone can tell you it wasn't me, it really wasn't, I can. Lucan stopped by the stare and imperious hand, his sneering voice.

It wasn't me Mister Scott it wasn't me, of course it wasn't you! We know that. But you know who they are, don't you! Shouting now, pressing close to my face and I can feel the spittle form his mouth. They're in your dorm, aren't they?

An automatic and withdrawing no. No. I don't know Mister Scott.

Crackell. Patience in his voice. It'll be easier on you, if you just. Tell us who they are. That's all. Almost smiling he walks away with confidential voice. If its the other boys you're worried about, well, well don't. In the casement corner, a stain; yellow on the whitewashed walls, a head with its nose on the cut stone sill. Its weak chin broods from the ceiling as his voice persuades. We'll let it get out that you didn't say a thing. Okay?

But I don't know. His voice a dying whisper, for I must not tell. Sad face on the wall stares back at this sad boy. Winter.

Now listen Crackell, we're being very patient with you; very patient. The paddles punctuation to his left. But don't be foolish. Listen. He stops walking and stares with his eyes into mine. We'll make it easier. Just nod your head when I say their names, okay? And you can go. Nothing simpler, nod your head and you can go. His uncertain eyes, unmoving. In mine. Simpson? Lucan's sickness weighs...floats; his serpent writhes. Desrocher? The names. Halter or Black? Lucan's perspiration is bursting from him; it gathers behind his eyes, the serpent's head investigates his throat. C'mon Crackell. we're waiting. Was it Black?

I don't. Desperately forcing he tries again: I don't know. Honest. Cannot, must not, I can not tell!

And away in that studied world, beside the frozen lake, the pantomine fulfilled itself. They got up. The steins hung lop-sided from the wall. Their hands reached out to punish me, to draw me down from the wind; and so, through spirals of silence the journey began.

The road with banks on either side, it drifts away and ahead in snowy wind and Lucan drives with his bowels. I should have gone. Before. This sullen pressure it keeps growing. Taking a moist hand from the steering wheel, he rubs it through his hair. A circular massage to the base of his skull. Relax the old tensions, stimulate the healthy circulation of the blood. Nothing like it. And I need it too. With the innocent sorrow of these girls and the tension of this goof, like cries in my car. Nothing like it. Job, I'm. When Rose. But I limped away and muttered in the back stair air. Between sheets, safe. She looks at. The review discarded beside her, she looks at the paper on the floor, uncomprehending. Or bending. Kneeling to tidy the mess from my foot. Oh God! Perhaps I'd feel better if I. A cautious shift to his left buttock and he relaxes his. Careful. Who knows what might happen, and what in hell could I say? Aaah. Aaah! There. Now I hope it isn't too noticeable. He opens the no-draft just a bit, smells the cold air. It could have been any one of us. And I do feel better. On this road to the past, with whiteness in the senseless bloody wind. She just doesn't know, that's all. That the past comes on. Stark fields roll up to skeletal trees, to stands of evergreens with sweating trunks unmoving in the snow. Showing off she said, and its just a funeral. Lucan runs his finger inside his collar and against his neck, trying to stretch the cloth. As if she can know. In that room. Diffused in the light she kneels and tidies, muttering selfishly. The bitch! While my very stomach recognizes that farmhouse. Its ornate stone and dirty orange brick, its windows and ramshackle barns. Christ but I know this road in winter! The power grid is just ahead. And these farms, with accusing eyes. But I shouldn't, after all she's my. And its hard for her too. Another rub at the base of his skull and he sticks a cigarette between his lips; he lights it and the smoke drifts grey and blue in the hanging air.

Lower my pyjamas and. The chair's back hard against my ribs. Lucan staring now and hurtling snowbanks fill the corners of his eyes. His knuckles are pale on the wheel. Clutching the best I could, my trousers and dressing-gown. Bundled above my hips. I waited. And I didn't tell! Again he asked me but I did not tell! Their voices behind me and I closed my eyes. Waiting for their expanding voices, their running feet, waiting for them to leap upon me, wrestle me unresisting to the ground, to club me with their fists and wooden paddles, to beat my kidneys, my spine, to batter with short sharp cries my exposed and quivering private parts.

Rising, the road, it curves to the crest of a hill and in silent fields, the valley falls away. Snow twists in the wind, obscuring trees and passive farms. It drifts on the burning land. With snow whipping about its legs, the flaking sign: mute in the wind's full force it warns.

REPENT or be DAMNED
for HE is an ANGRY GOD
and HELL AWAITS YOU!
!!!

Descending. Lucan drives with care on the hard-packed road that curves to the bridge. Rough gusts drive blindly about the car; they disappear, with melting crystals on his knees. He pushes the no-draft shut, the pressure increases inside his ears, he forces a yawn. Like roots, the naked trees reach up, the crouching cedars are like animals. Squat and threatening in the half light.

Even when they beat me, I didn't tell. My slippers back along the darkened hall with listening boys in every room and the air was full of their breathing. Silent whispers followed me into bed. Even when they beat me. Lying on my belly I heard them ask. Did you tell Lucan? Crackell, did you tell? I waited through that night for their praise. And in the morning Black and Halter were called before the Head. And caned.

The small bridge rises and falls over the river's drifted bed. Under a bridge. Or was it the night before? The earth was hard and sharp with nettles, the leaves were close against my face. I could see what pulsed in their white veins. At one point, between explosions, between the tortured clouds that mushroomed into the sky, I ran heavily on the road, heavily. And as the next explosion seared the place I threw myself back into the ditch, covering my face like the army taught, but I must have hit a stone, a protruding root for I cracked my ribs and the pain. The pain. I struggled because, because I thought there was safety by the sea. In the growing dark. Expanding with a terrible light. More clouds and their ashes fell like snow. The leaves were dead against my face, broken open, and their liquid had seeped away. Nauseous, their perfume sickened me and they rattled as I crawled. I had to get somewhere! Then I think I was crying and I know my side was agonizing and it went on and on. Voices too, from that no-man's land, there were voices screaming out in private noise. Jesus! Terrible. Terrible...That's all. Don't be silly, lots of people have them. Yet just as I woke. I realized. I knew with every little bit of me that there wasn't. Anywhere. There wasn't anywhere to go. It didn't matter.

A sloping narrow hall, badly lit with open doors on either side. No sound and the shadows moved like branches in a searching wind. Compelled step by step, avoiding the doors by clinging to the other wall, crossing and re-crossing as I went, for I knew they could not reach across and get me. Could feel them there, oh yes! Could feel them there, brushing together in the darkness as I passed each door. And then abruptly. And it always was the same. The wall against me opened darkly, and their arms came out to drag me in.

Lucan, wakened by rough hands, by the night's terror and these figures that press him back into his bed, smothering the cry that vomits from his throat. Twisting bedcovers and his body's protestations. Violent, their breath is eager in the dark. This is what we do to sucks, Crackell. Exploding fear, a futile struggle and he momentarily frees a leg

and kicking, kicking desperately, feeling the shock of contact in the knee. Hurry up for chrissakes, get him, get him,
hurry! The cubicle is full of moving forms and they force
him down. Immobile on his back. His rolling eyes and the
hand upon his flattened lips, his stifled cry. Another hand
comes down and he can not see, it stretches the forehead's
skin and presses cruelly on his nose. What do we do to
sucks. Quivering. His life is focused on the pen, on the
letters they trench above his eyes. No more body under
theirs. Only the digging on his skull that rolls the flesh
ahead in waves. Laboriously a curving stroke, a gouging
line and they whisper impatiently like bees. The pen and
its force, the head that is held by a terror of hands, all
joined by the word. Then they're gone. He's left. In silence.
He doesn't move. Quietly at first, one whisper; then others
in growing curiosity. Each cubicle sends an eager frightened voice, an awed. Lucan. Luke. Are you alright? Shall I
get Mister? Boys in pale nightclothes clustering at his door.
What did they. Do? Pushing through, unseeing Lucan,
running with hands on his head, running to the washroom
and leaning over the basin, staring at this shape in the
darkened room. Following behind someone flicks the
switch. In blinding light, from hairline to eyebrows, he sees
it:

SUCK

Bastards! From time to time he sees them in Toronto,
buying liquor at the Yonge Street store. On financial
streets, efficient wearing their pasts like uniforms. They
can! Lucan driving quickly in the blowing snow, behind
the tail lights of a diesel truck. A looming shape that
tunnels on ahead. For boys of promise and ability. Jeez!
And he hadn't told, that was the irony: he hadn't told! God
I've got to do something for it isn't simply wind. I've got to.
Get to the john, but how? I can't just stop at some gas
station, in front of these girls, and. Leaping, they're upon
you without warning! Humiliation. And instinctive carelessness, dear heaven! Cruelty, its their cruelty without
design. In this wind and these....
    Was the drink alright as my body protests, too much and
no doubt. But I knew. Even there in the theatre's rooms, I

could tell. Smiling, presiding. Hair immaculate and painted nails in those long mirrors. Rye. So I drank. Downed some quick ones before moving on to beer. Burning throat and eyes and she, Rose, drifting away in the darkening crowd....

The nerve, for chrissakes, to argue and make smart remarks! Staring and Lucan trying to, perhaps a belch. A careful release through the upper half, will. Ease this pressure, it grimly toys. Drifting selfish in the wind, and he's so lacking, so absolutely lacking. Arrogant eyes and body, behind me. There. And his hair's too long. Grubby, a rat's nest for heaven's sake you'd think he'd. Once a year, at least. So absolutely lacking, even in common courtesy! Not a bad suit, expensive looking, but you can. Tell a man by his feet, his fingernails. And hair all long and curling at the collar. Jeez! Small eruption in his throat. Watch it! Right of course, right all along. Nothing concrete to suggest, is negative alone. Instinctive carelessness.

Goddamitall! Should have. Oh sweet God, goddamn. Learned by now. That she won't be. Wasn't that drunk, for. Notatallnotatall! Coffee and bits of food, certainly wasn't that. Can't. Looks so good, dear God. In black. White thighs and flashing flesh she changed and watching, there I was. Rose undressing beneath the nightgown. What's happened, why? At this time above all else as you should know, so much. And it seems so long, so often now. Enveloping, I need your body's. Hardness. Softly I need. Yes. My hand, hopefully, but your body. Retreats. Following, I know its, I follow: no use, I know that silence and the shrug, it can't. Go on and on like this, its getting worse.... And impersonal! Outwards from the core, I'm going to be sick, she makes me sick. But then at least. Foolish as it was. Rampaging down this hill. But still, then; at least. Laughter exploding. We, I was a dancer; and every time a reoccuring freshness, Vera that truck is closer now, a transport and the hulking wheels drive snow on either side. Didn't complete my thesis, two frigging years and even my courses. A waste of bloody time that drove me to. Course work only adequate, Jesus. Lucan, halfway Doctor Crackell, lecturer; drunk on this, this very road, for chrissakes, and the selfsame.

Wind and these driving clouds, Susanna Moodie longed

for the formal world, for. London's parlour light as desperately, foreign in a forest land, they cleared for sun. From the north, where the wild fish blow, and it tempted Louis Riel, it whispered to D'Arcy McGee. Strong and free. Gusting now against my car as I drive through layers of time to Stratford. Trying to overtake that bloody truck. But it does no good. It does no good, for in Baffin's Bay

> ...where the wild fish blow,
> The fate of Franklin no man may know;
> The fate of Franklin no man can tell;
> Lord Franklin and all of his sailors do dwell.

Inappropriate that's all and where would I be? What kind of a life, if I'd gone, chucked everything up and gone with her? Lucan straining to see in the wake of the charging truck, pulling out for a view of the road that descends in a curve ahead. Lost in the wind. By God! Where the eskimo in his skin canoe, is the only one who. What kind of. "Will they Mister Crackell?"

"What. Pardon?" In hell is she, I wasn't.

"They won't leave it open, will they?" Blankly Lucan stares at this girl beside him, and then looks back at the road. "The coffin I mean. Felix says they'll leave it open in the church and everything." Christ. I hope not. Lying there with his hair freshly cut and his fingernails buffed clean, but. They might.

"Don't know, Miss Haden. I expect they might, although its hard to tell, isn't it. People do, of course. So friends and relatives. Of the deceased, can ah. Can pay their respects." Immortality. Lucan. Faces in shadow, setting grimly unaccustomed tasks, and the flood of light on that springing hill. Chilly in the air and it is by God, it is; glistening white in that day's half light. There is no. But. Just the man, you're just the man he said. The man that through these tasks, we want to grow. Develop with this university. Don't you see, Lucan? Don't you? A man to be. Reckoned. "It originated in the belief that, well. Long before coffins you know, when death was more immediate more natural." Lying calmly in an open bier, Lawrence's dead at Cerveteri, sleeping as if in life; like a phoenix, the sailor king, consumed with flames from the too real world. Seems. So hard to see but it does seem clear: accelerating up and into the diesel's burning wake with wipers' desperate strokes and the sound of great wheels pounding in the car. Lucan expectantly, staring in terrible noise; he peers to see the driving spume, he waits the darkness of another shape: sure it was clear, I'm sure. Straining against the jumping wheel, bracing his forearms' weight when suddenly, dark form another car and somewhere Nancy's shrillest voice: "A car, lookoutacar!" Car and.... Skidding acceleration as the windshields clear, and the back end slides: Lucan spinning to correct the skid; chunk, the implacable wipers. Chunk chunk. Wan faces stare in passing and we had...we had lots of time. False alarm, there was lots of time, nevertheless. Strong weakness in my knees and it bloodywell didn't do this stomach of mine any good. None at all. Breathing again. Could hardly see and we couldn't have. Lucan in accusing silence; wiping one after another, his hands. Say something, to fill this, say. Something. Couldn't poke along behind it all the way, couldn't. What can. "Well. That's a relief." Heartfelt and there was lots of time, I don't know why they. "Get behind one of those transports on a day like this and. Very difficult. To pass them. I remember once." Don't, don't for heaven's sake wander. Terrible there, frustration and the drink's remorse on this. Don't wander in your past, Lucan Crackell, don't! Selfsame funeral road.

"They're just the kind who would! They're just the kind of frigging people who'll make us file past him and."

"Oh I hope not. I think its terrible."

"And they'll want tears, pious words, they'll search in my goddamn eyes for, for. You know what Susan said when she phoned?" Petulant voice, a voice that cries for its own lost cause. He's almost a bloody beatnik with his grubby hair and beard. "There's something I think you should know. Get that! At six he dies, and at seven in the frigging morning she phones, there's something I think you should know she says, Martin's been killed. Ha! You know what I said? I said. You're kidding! Ha." Uncertain laughter as he pauses behind me. "What in hell else could I say? I was so." Don't want confessions in my car, don't want to hear. Arrogant vulnerability and his selfishness.

"Well, you know Oswald that death is a terrible thing.

For the loved ones. They can't be responsible for how they act, in the state of. Immediate shock. Death's hand is clutching cold, of shocking angularity. As the poet said. Susan, Miss Morton, probably had to do something. Probably had to feel there was something useful to do. So she phoned." Poor girl you searched, searched in the lonely land. Falling in the drifting wind and its leaves, the silence settles like an insect's death. "You can hardly blame her under the circumstances." But think of it! This nihilistic goon's assaults at a time! Nice girl like Susan. Man has a responsibility, can't just. "Think you're being too hard on her altogether Oswald." Sudden image of that violence in my hall. Hope he doesn't. No sense of responsibility, respect even. Don't want a scene, good grief, a nasty scene! Better soothe. "But its a difficult time, a shocking time for everyone who knew poor Baillie." Relaxing, that should do it. A bit of grease to oil the wheels, that's all it needs, and there is no doubt that I have the gift.

Dear girl, she's. Its. A frightful shock, an uncompromising burden that she has to bear. Even if she's. So young too and there's no doubt that her eyes held mine, she smiled that smile, a sad and knowing one as she went on down the hall. Even if she's. Better off. Rough hands and the oil on her back, the shoulderblades like beating hearts. Be alright, won't it, if I undo the top? I hate the line it leaves. Lucan aching in the garden's warmth, smoothing in circles the oil, his fingers timid on the flesh and I couldn't take my eyes away. Where she lay on the towel. Her softness bulged. Decent aren't I, I mean, it looks alright? Lucan's disobedient body; looks alright? Oh boy! Oil and perspiring in his hands! Gone now, and she's alone and searching, lost and this surly Oswald has the nerve, the utter nastiness to. "Sure. Sure. But she's more interested." Snide voice, bored, and there's no need, there's just no need for. "More than usually aware, you might say, of the, the opportunities, the dramatic opportunities of this...." Cruel, what a cruel and. Oh boy! Lucan amazed, simply amazed at the vitriol, the black dislike, but then. What can you expect from a life like his?

"What do you mean? Susan?" Nancy picks it up, the silly bitch! Playing his game. "Oh what do you mean, I've never seen anyone so, so." Expansive and scratching

beneath my coat, my knowing smile for I'm right, the point
is obvious; he proves it every time he speaks. "Why she's
simply wonderful." In the mirror glancing and he sees,
good Lord! The rushing truck, its chasing right behind, ten
yards or less with clouds of throwing snow and the sound of
its terrible wheels. Wouldn't you know! Soon as you pass
them every bloody time they speed up, they breathe right
down your neck. Lucan on the descending road increases
speed and its dangerous for chrissakes, we're going too fast!
Precipitous on either side, the porous snow and fences
rattling past with Lucan scurrying ahead of the brutal
shape. Staring and clutching the wheel for miles, it seems
like. Miles and we're too light on the road, we barely
touch. Skimming, skimming the icy surface and that stupid
boor stays right behind. My only hope, the only hope is
that he'll turn, perhaps. Perhaps he's going to Hamilton
or. Driving. Desperately driving. Rushing back too fast,
too dangerously: intently steering gauging the road for
miles and miles in the growing past and I've got no control,
good Lord this isn't the way, I must. Trees bare on the hill
and a wind that blows in those bones. Those cavernous
bones and I, walked in a rising, walked and saw. Dear God
there must be! I do. I do. There must. For I do repent, I
have and meaculpa have and do, I know. A wasted time
and when I moved into her bed I left my. Work and the real
world behind. Irresponsibility carried. God to its logical,
Lucan. I didn't, but should have seen. I didn't. Please
please forgive. Nightstreets we ran, pinwheel darkness in
my eyes and my thesis, hah! Not a line dear God, and the
course work only adequate. Never adjusted, that's the.
Doctoral work another life, and my years at Western far
away. Confession, he knows so well because I went down
there for my doctorate with a job promised for my return.
Forgive me. Neglect and responsibility and selfishness that
unaware. Overwhelms. Careless lives, day to day and.
Think I'm pregnant Lucan. Matter-of-fact, how can she!
Pregnant. Wow! Impose your selfishness and along comes
some. Pregnant. Ergot. Ergot and quinine's what they say.
Both hands clenched to stay on the road, swinging on this
curve, slow down, slow. Let him pass, for heaven's sake let
him. But then. Behind him, poking along in his filthy wake
and blinded. Sure you bet, the world combines, its the

whole bloody pattern. Why not a truck too? Not be pushed, no. Lucan Crackell's not your man to be pushed. Around. And grimly. Got to try Vera, we've got to keep on trying. Are you sure, for as much as I. Still I can't know, I've never seen her take them. Are you sure you're taking them. Right?

For chrissakes Lucan, that's not the trouble! (White-faced and bitter-voiced.) What's the matter, can't you see I'm sick! They make me, oh God they make me so sick. Bewildered Lucan, frightened. Patting her hand, pat-pat, an empty reassurance, jeez if I ever. Saw what can I? Lucan, cold serious, her voice, they're not. We've got to face the fact. Its almost three months now and they're. Not going to work. Turning away with strands of her blonde hair falling down.

What are we going to do, then? My rising, for I thought. Dear God I was sure they'd. A fly that buzzing, bumps, and. Inescapable commitments. What on earth are we going to do? Can't, she won't want. Oh what a terrible....

Not looking up as, faintly, her voice. What. Do you want to do Lucan? Oh God poor girl. Emotions soft, chaotic in this vulnerable time and Lucan feels the tears behind his eyes as reaching, he strokes. Honourable, must do. And pats. The thing, can't leave her betrayed. Betrayed and alone. Anyway she's said.

I think, I think, I think we should get married. You know that. I've said it all along.

No. I've explained Lucan, not like this. Wan smiling with her face. Wouldn't work, you know that. Pausing to consider the spring light on the air. I've had enough of. Strands of hair and her brushing hand, impatiently. Of marriage for convenience. Sighing, she stretches and her easy breasts. Huh! I'd rather.

Rather what, love? Terrible, a terrible thing but still. The only other way. The prospect of brutality, of sordid illegality. Dear God, I won't like that! And my melting heart at his woman's selflessness. You'd rather what?

I'd rather. I think I'd rather have the child and live alone. Good Christ, she can't. Couldn't do that, would would I. Into her eyes; she means it! People say, and what.

Good heavens Vera you can't be. Serious. You couldn't. Living alone, unmarried! Leaping to his feet and pacing in the room. With a, a. Baby! Just too much, too much that's all, she can't, couldn't possibly.

Why not, Lucan, why can't I be serious? Aggressive, in her voice her staring eyes. And what's wrong with keeping a ba-

Well. Quickly. Well, ah. There's. Money, money for example! You wouldn't be able to work or anything for, for months and I, I haven't got. Much. I mean, I'd help of course, you know that, but. Good Lord what can she be thinking of! Couldn't send her, not from. What would London. Good Lord! Certainly Vera, I'd help as much as I could, but. But how do you know, I mean. After all these pills and. How do you know it'll be. You know. Uncertain voice, careful, and her eyes keep watching me. That it will be. You know. Alright.

Don't say that, don't even suggest! Abruptly turning, rising to the window and her voice. You think I haven't thought for chrissakes, you think that isn't preying on me like, like poison? But Lucan, I. Hands, trembling hands in her shining hair, hands blue-veined that clutch at her robe's lapels. I just, I don't know what to do! That's all. Spring ice melting.

You know what I think Vera. Yes, yes! He overwhelms with hands and voice her futile protests. But you don't for whatever reasons, want it. Fine. I'm bound to respect, after all, your point of view. Cigarette, he lights a cigarette; reason's restraint, that's the thing, an ordered approach; and sitting, he straightens his trousers at the knee. Wouldn't, you know I wouldn't have it any other way. Deep in lungs and forcing, blowing grey smoke, clouding her face. Pensive, staring dully through the window's glass. Must say though, love, I think, really. That. Well I know how painful, lousy in fact, your marriage. Lucan puzzled, for surely she can't think that I. Not the same, surely she doesn't think it'd be the. I mean we've been living together, it's not as if. Just a casual, a promiscuous affair. Turning to me, she turns and:

Lucan, could I have a smoke? She's, she hasn't been. Good Lord, I don't think she's even been listening! She....

Sure, sure love. He offers and she takes. Abstractedly. The lighter's flame erasing shadows from her cheeks; falling, she sinks close-eyed and sighing back into the chair.

Unreasonable. Growing resentment and the lines about her eyes. The fact is I think she's unreasonable. Depression, that's it, lethargy, emanating; reaching out to numb me. But I won't be. No. Reason's restraint and action of some kind, and that's for sure. We have to. Act. You can't just muddle on. But how? She hasn't, not once, she. The smoke in whorls between us, slumping unhelpful, passive, hands blunt fingered against her brow, she stares. And smokes. What in hell am I? Three times at least, or four! Get married, I said and I mean it too; haven't just run off, haven't abandoned selfishly the way some men would do. But she rejects for chrissakes, surely she knows! I. You know Vera, there is, there is another way. I've said, good, I've said it and her face returns. It seems to me that, if you don't want to get. Married. Well. Staring, she's not, not helping me at all for God's sake, you'd think! Tremulous, her eyes and where's the hardness, certainty, she used to be so. Goddamnit she's! It seems there's only one alternative. That's all!

How, Lucan?

How! Good Lord, she's so. Leaving it all to me. she's forcing, making it look as though. Good God! C'mon Vera, you know perfectly well, don't. Don't make it any harder than it is. I've offered, you know I've offered, we could get. Married. Tomorrow! There, she has the choice and she can choose. And take our chances.

What do you mean, and her voice is sharp, chances? Too strong, don't want to. Overdo it.

Well. Too strong, I retract the word Vera. Chances is too strong a word. I only mean. You said yourself you don't want, that you'd prefer to marry again under. Under different circumstances. That's all. God what's the matter with her, where's the love and closeness? Closeness, where's the union that we've had? And, well as. Unpleasant as. You know. After all the pills and your sickness and everything. Twisting me, isolating every bloody word, she's trying to make me seem, the. It's just not fair, that's. All. Said so yourself, didn't you? That there's a danger, that.

Okay. Okay Lucan! What about the, this alternative then?

Aah! Well a friend. Decisive rising and once around the room. I have a friend who knows of a doctor, a perfectly respectable doctor, he's supposed to be. Very good. And it seems he. Turning away so I don't have to, blankly staring into the street, God don't. Don't look at me! Choice, you have the. Seems he will. Will. You know. Oh God Vera! And suddenly on his knees, Lucan Crackell, tears in his voice and kneading her hands. Vera Vera! He's a good doctor, I know he is and it's not as if. They do it all the time in, Sweden. Kneeling. Her hands are moist and cold. I wouldn't, wouldn't even suggest if. Resting his face on her passive thighs, and my voice subdued. But you, you don't want to get married, I know, and there is. There's always the danger. God Vera, you know I. Love you. You know I do and it only takes a couple of hours to drive out there and back and we'll. Her hand on his head and stroking, her breathing. What else can we do, desperate; what else can we do?

Nothing. Nothing I guess. Hands on my head and her lap. Thank God it's turned and I can. Hamilton obviously, wheewh! Easing the old foot and wiping perspiration, relaxing for that was far too. Dangerous. Oh boy! Piling ahead it disappears among the trees: Lucan driving still in its sound; rough churning wheels, inevitable out of the impersonality of night it comes, scarring the earth with violent intent. Brutal hollow sound, his body struck and broken in the snow. Sick from the open door, retching dryly, sobbing. Dead white, her face and clenching hands, again, I'm going to be. Stop the. Soothing, trying my best, four times or five on the journey out and I'm sure I've, couldn't have because there was no sign, but. Lost the way. Her body stiffening and Lucan's sad attempts to comfort her: sliding from behind the wheel, sliding to hold, awkwardly, to pat with selfsame anguish in the gut and vomit bitter in my throat. Clumsy. Perhaps I should have turned and my hands seem rough. Gas station there, back where the land falls away, but. There was no, there'll have to be a. Sign or something.

CRAPP, ONTARIO
HOME OF DOCTOR SOMEBODYOROTHER
ABORTIONIST
(Lions' Club Three Blocks East)

Can't have, it must be on ahead. Therethere Vera. What, jeez, can I say? Poor lost, my poor lost, my poor lost love on your brutal day. There Vera. There. Clumsy futile, what can I. Soon be. It will be all over soon. Before you know it. Filled with love and sickness, fear around my heart. The town, they know, they must. Lace-curtained watchers under shingled roofs, at strangers' cars that stop before this winterpeeled and battered door with broken gingerbread above, along the eaves. My foot at an ornate scraper for the mud that clings and glancing, a glance at Vera huddled in the car. Pale too, my face I'm sure and glistening whitely. Jeez, I feel so. Waving my hand back but she doesn't see, or perhaps. Perhaps she doesn't want to anymore and Lucan cautiously, dear God my heart transported by these muddy feet! Cautiously into this cluttered unprofessional room, with. Good Lord! Antimacassars for chrissakes and and tiptoeing, I'm tiptoeing over to this little bell. Ring and be seated. Eat me. So silent with the feet of mice in the walls. Careful finger, quietly, careful finger unwilling on the. RRRINGGG! Aaargh! Good grief its right. Wow! What a. Right above my frigging head. Lucan sitting dutifully, uncertain on this patchworked afghan and, tensing, leaping to his feet with cushions scattered to the floor as bursting through the door he comes. Good morning, ha! Good morning, my boy. Bending, Lucan bending to retrieve the yellow satin, purple and yellow cushion by his feet. Don't worry, don't worry about that and clutching my hand, shaking intimately. You phoned me last night? Anguished with the cushion in my arm; pale face and moist pale hand, he.

Yes. Yes, you see we. Garish and lumpy. Blurred reproduction, three colours, of Niagara Falls. You see, we need. Oh God!

I know and when people are in trouble. Glittering eyes, tiny, and rimless glasses; pudgy hand on his heart, a moment. They come to me. From all over they come to me. And do you know why? Do you know why they come from as far away as Detroit? Two and three times, some of them, do you know why, eh? Eyes wet staring into mine; tiny eyes that wait.

No I, I can't say that I.

Because I do a good job, that's why! You notice,

confidential lowering of his voice and jerking to the window, peering out, you notice that I haven't asked your name. Bent and turning from the curtain's lace he slowly winks, a long grotesque staring wink. Anonymity. He winks again with screwed up mouth and puffy cheeks. That's right, I try to use a little modern psychology to ease the burdens my patients bear. Oh I know, alright, how people feel when they come to me. I certainly do. Stepping forward in the room, I know how you feel! Yes I do, I do indeed, how much you need me now and I respect. Eager in the dark, mice beneath the floorboards scamper; lace-filtered parlour light, the shadows cornered in this room and pale, she's huddled, twisting there. Clearly. Tried, I've really, and it was yours. Eyes that standing stare, wet watching eyes and Lucan wilting, surrounded by accusations; terror and the rodent feet. Say, where you kids from?

Toronto.

Don't. Raised hands protectively, he turns to stare. Don't tell me about Toronto! Go down, I have to go down at least once a week. Sister-in-law's there, my oldest brother's widow, you know, and she. Gracious! I'm telling you, well. Intimate hand beside his voice, he leans. She doesn't drink to drown her sorrows; she drinks to forget. It's disgusting. Headshaking now, reproval and the twittering feet. And I have to drive down with her, with her supply I guess you'd call it. Ha-ha. Twice a week sometimes. She belts it back for a, why she must be, aah. Seventy-seven, yes. Seventy-seven if she's a day, my brother was. How can he, what's he? Swallowing, Lucan Crackell's focused on the civic pledge that framed and hanging, oozes laurel vined and smiling on the wall. Perhaps its, you might think its unkind of me to talk this way about family. But I'm fed up, fed right up to here. Do you know, indignant voice, she doesn't even put the exchange on her cheques! Pretty cheap, eh? And its not as if. She's got, why my brother left her very well set up, very well indeed I might say. He was insurance, you know, and a real go-getter, believe me! Shouting yet she doesn't even, I have to pay the exchange! That's what really takes the cake, you'd think after driving my poor brother, she drove him right into his grave, and make no mistake! Abruptly stopping. The shouting settles and his eyes are blank as pennies. Then, agitated in his corpulence, he zig-zags quickly in the room, he stops and staring at the wall. His wavering voice. You'd think she'd at least pay the exchange. Turning hopelessly and Lucan has to look away. Its only fifteen cents, after all. Fifteen lousy cents. That's not too much to expect is it?

I wave and she doesn't come: beckoning but she shakes her head, so muddy-footed once again I walk to the splattered dripping car. Changed your mind, but? But. Not going, I've decided I'm not going in. Good Lord! Overflowing ashes from the dashboard tray and they've fallen where I've thrown them on the floor: her certain, apologetic face; I'm sorry Lucan, I really am but I won't go in. Crossed her plump legs shining in the sun, its warm on my back. After all this and she. What are we going to do? But Vera, he's. He's not a bad guy and I'm sure, I know he. What on earth are we going to do? Lucan straining suddenly to see, for what's that, its a. Good God! Couldn't be. Wheels still turning and its on its back, a monstrous insect helpless on its back. Black and cream, its armour crumpled round the head and now their voices trumpet in. Babble in my ears. Skid marks and there's nobody, not a frigging soul! Oh how terrible. Braking automatically we slow. "No, couldn't be, it must be old, there's no one here."

"But the wheels. They're turning." Grim circles and she's right, dear God, she is. The wind! And they've all gone away, sure. That's it, they've left already. Frig the wheels and boy what a relief that was!

"There's somebody in the back seat." Trust him for chrissakes, trust him! A figure? Nononono, couldn't be, they've all. Accelerating, bastard Oswald, past the crippled hulk, brute black and turning in the snow, accelerating for we must get on; they'll all be waiting! Sickness, I'm; nausea burns the throat and my threatening bowels. Couldn't be dear God, bunch of blankets, yes cartons. Or something. My stomach! Sure that's what it is. "Aren't you going to stop?" Now don't my boy, don't get shrill with, what a! Couldn't possibly be. "I said aren't you." Rising accusation, insubordination that I won't forget if you keep it up. Chewing inside, but there would have been someone, someone else, there. Accusatory, don't you raise your; now his hands are pulling at the seat! "You can't just, just drive away for chrissakes, there was someone. There was somebody in the back seat." Police. Police and ambulance, we'll inform them and we're almost there. "I saw, Doctor Crackell I saw, just as clearly as, anything, a body? I'm sure there's somebody...."

"Now, now. Just a minute Oswald, don't, don't fly off the handle. Two things, there are two things. No three things." Receding in the mirror, dark in the gusts and there's a, he'll stop and see! There's another. Car. "Firstly. And I may be wrong here. I think you're mistaken, I don't." He'll stop and if. But Christ, there couldn't be! "I don't think there was anyone there."

"But, for heaven's...."

"Just a minute, just a. I know what you're going to say. What if there is, eh? What if there is. Well." Aha, he's stopped, and that makes it easier, oh boy! "Well if there is, and anything can be done, then." The coup de grace, here's the coup. "That car behind will do it." In astonishment they turn as I explain in my thought-out voice hah! Reasonable man is the one who overcomes, the well-considered, thoughtful man. "And the best thing we can do is, well, you know. Get straight into town and report everything to the proper authorities; alert the police, the ambulance."

"What if the guy's dying or something, what if he's really in bad shape?" Unpleasant. A thought. Good Lord. Private dying noises; crying, crying out from his no-man's land and we'd have to watch or wipe the blood from his broken mouth. Jesus arrgh! Terrible. "I dunno, I certainly think we should have." Backwards staring, tentative and; expansive Lucan, I think you've won, you well-considered man but then he, don't for, please my head! Slapping angrily the seats back, suddenly there's spittle, his lousy spittle for chrissakes spewing on my ears! "Goddamnit! You can't, you can't just drive by a thing like that without a look, without even looking at him for chrissakes! May be bleeding, may be bleeding to death and all he needs is a tourniquet, or something, maybe he." Jeez, what a sensationalist!

"C'mon Oswald. Take hold of yourself, for heaven's sake young man. Take hold. You're blowing this, why you're. Blowing this out of all proportion." Tried, exasperated Lucan for I've tried, God knows I've. "Explained it to you, very clearly I thought. And I'll say it. Again. Best thing we can do. For speed." Very patient, very clear and patient, that's the thing. "Is drive on into town and. Notify the authorities." Boy, doesn't he know. Anything? Amateurs can't just go dragging the gravely injured around, you know. Do great damage, irreparable internal damage, joggle and twist all sorts of things out of place you know, so even if there were someone. Which I seriously doubt. We couldn't have moved him anyway, could we?" That's perfectly clear, and. Crawling in there to pull him out, God knows what harm we might have done. "If its just a matter of. First Aid. Well, well the car behind will."

"I'm sorry. I'm sorry Doctor Crackell but that doesn't." Interrupting, he's continually interrupting and we'll have to have a. Talk. "It doesn't satisfy me. We should have...."

"Doesn't what? Doesn't satisfy? Look Oswald, I don't care if it satisfies you or not!" Jeez the nerve, the! We'll straighten this out once and for all, yes we. "I'm not one of your, your." Scathing. My best and biting scathing voice, arrogant punk, he has to learn. "Friends. You forget who you're talking to, I'm....'

"I know exactly who I'm talking to, and I'm sorry, but." Thunderstruck and God there's going to be. "But it bloody well makes me sick; driving away, away from." Don't want a. Scene. Good Lord! I'm just not up to that, my head and my poor sad nerves are not. I've got enough. Lucan's icy voice in the driving snow and Stratford now below that hill.

"We won't discuss this any more at the moment Oswald." Sternly, quickly, for I must strike fear, I must! Or. "When we return to the university, this whole matter will deserve, deserve a thorough examination." Ominously said, that's the thing, cow him into. Silence. "However. I don't wish to discuss it any further here. It's not appropriate."

"We didn't know there was another car, we had no way." Stop him! Raising hand, abruptly from the wheel.

"That's enough, I said! I refuse to listen or discuss." Girls' silence, awkwardness and Christ. This memory haunted landscape! And I didn't handle that well.

Rushing the crest of this last small hill and there, there! Burning wind, shrouded water tower, clumsy gate on the town's near edge. You're such a fraud Lucan, such a pompous fraud! Under the tree-top eaves, laughter and her body thick, fullskirted with my child; biting laughter and the sun. Hot on the shabby trunks. You talk about the book, but you're afraid! Come with me. Wooing. Come away, oh Lucan why don't you come with me! And I can't, I. Can't. Bewildered and frightened, his back to the room he stares on the street below. Why won't she? Marry me, even now, why won't she marry me and come to London, good job. I have a position waiting there. Folding behind me, stripping our rooms and folding. Packing, she's packing one by one the. Can't just! Oh God, she mustn't just go sailing off alone, pregnant and alone to have my baby in a strange town. She. Goddamnit Vera, turning desperately, you can't go off alone like this, you simply can't! In a strange town.

Then you'll have to come with me, won't you? Smiling, her voice and gentle. Or else I'll have to find someone else. What kind of? This, at a time like. Facetiousness is out of place and a tiny life is at stake. Helpless in her eyes, I must be. Firm. She's so frigging unrealistic! Wow! Can't go, go running off to England after her, so. Firmness, masculine prerogative. To assert the. But she went anyway, she just. Scattered redbrick boxes, ugly in the grimy snow and makeshift factories' concrete blocks, not a full grown tree, the builders root them all up and she went without phoning or anything. Just a letter and I. Terrible bloody position to be in. Christ! I did everything I. Could have, if she wanted to she could have married! Me. Moisture on these palms, handrubbing energetically; one and then the other. Wrote her too, I tried to help. Twice she. Blown mound, the service station there with shadowed pumps and lonely swinging washed-out lights; houses, of course the town has grown we all, weallhaveallhaveallhavealland I'm not anymore. Good Lord, that boy! Snow wild night, crisp underfoot with burning circles round my legs; young man a foolish, acid in my throat, I walked all night and self-afraid. Harsh weight upon me while dark birds drift and swayed; under eyes I've run, impatient voices crying in my ears like bees, suck, suck as the hands reached out and I.

HAVE WANTED SO MUCH! Are you happy here? Rampant snowy road, obscured the view and trembling Lucan staring cry-filled, plump and hopeless at that boy who, panicking, vanished under this bridge and down the never ending hill. Reaching hands to the cross; reaching to smoothe, on the hill, read the reluctant paper crackling on its chest. Cavernous lie! Unhealthy minds, for. Wilful obscenity, a vulgar prank and it's clear that. That each day breaks newly born or. At least. At least the possibility, there has to be that, the possibility! For once, singing I. Danced around. These streets! A dancer. Gloomy on fire these stores, the tannery they've all come home in reflected light and Lucan's falling, falling in the long hall, precipitously falling and he peels away like pages blowing in the wind. Lousy lie, its all a lousy lie! This trip and all, this fuckingawful drive and on and on I'll go forever hopeless down this filthy road. And as to, to what is anguished in me. Boy! She hasn't a, not a fucking clue as on and on. Have wanted so. But sickness, always wanting is the constant now and always, God! What am I to do, what hope for years or my life? What is there to do in fact (and the words in isolation clearly sound), what is there for me to do between this funeral and. The other? Not a prayer! Surrounding, the silence; and the answer's too well known, dear. Blessed. Heaven. Alone, sometimes and inescapable the answer that sickening, drags a question through my life. Nothing. Nothing. Can with the rest of. Happy? The hill and phoney. Nothing. To do and it doesn't. "There's the police station." Matter. What? Christ I hate that voice, I hate. Groping for, Lucan searching for the implication of. Yes, yes. The wreck and I mustn't, the wreck dear God and I mustn't let him see it slipped my. Mind.

"Ah yes, I know, I know but." Surely. There couldn't have been! Surely, surely they're. "Since we're behind schedule, I've decided to, to phone." Pretty lame, that's hardly good, but. What's that, a groan, did he? Bastard, the. Forcefully, take control for pity's sake, assert. "We'll phone from the restaurant!" What else can I? Can't let him see. Terrible fool if we went in there and the, the crash was old or something, feel a terrible. "No need is there, to get involved or. When a phone call's good. Enough." I'm flushing, again, I'm, angry for why am I? Here I am again.

"There'd be questions, signing papers maybe." Bloody inquisition and I swallow, every bloody time I. Useless argument and I'm so defensive with this miserable, this prick. Jeez!

"Let me out!" Startled Lucan turning, swerving startled on the road. "Stop the car and let me out." Staring, his eyes and angry into mine. Despising me. And reflexively back to see in this lousy town, breaking, to the roadside carefully. And icy wind through the door.

"Be a pleasure. If you feel." This way, oh God! So sick and overwhelmed, so helpless a bloody pawn, I am. Slamming cold behind me as he goes. For I'm defensive, bound about by. Forcing me, that's it, they're always. Putting me on the frigging spot and its all a hoax, a stinking fraud! Accelerating from the curb and I see it so clearly, so inescapably; how could I? On his side, they're loathing, despising me too. No, no! "Don't know why he's so upset." Ease their awkwardness and I must. "A phone call would have done the trick just as easily." Embarrassment at these grasping hopes, my poor life's futility, for all along they've simply. USED CARS. USED CARS. Above and reaching alone through the tearing sky an iron pole bedecked; torn plastic pennants gusting down to the lot's four corners there. SAVE! Huge clumsy lettered on this vastly wasted, broken carousel. DIFFERENT. DIFFERENT. DIFFERENT. In price...in trade-in.... How could I have. Believed, how could I? SAVE oh save me for I do. NOBODY EVER WALKS AWAY FROM HERE!!! Repent, I do dear God oh. SAVE! SAVE! Suddenly, violently. Horribly sick all over the floor oh. Terrible, the shameful scene, this growing stain of my youth and I did I sent her money, twice I sent. But she returned it. Everytime she. Have to get someone. Private, her life alone, gone with her own life somewhere and the child. Why did she, that's what I want to; why did she send it? Back. Why? Dirtworn above chrome and bright stores, this winter landscaped mainstreeet town: clumsy figures bundling lonely in the snow, burning the sound and sight of this past and underworld terrain. Almost nine, boy or girl of almost nine what kind of a life for a boy. Or girl. What kind of a life for her? Young, my figure walking still and driven the snow-filled streets: alone and away all walking dark and huddled here. Howling the night's white noise.

Delicate vertebrae, and her heart beating with ease in the stirring grass. Will you cry for me? Waiting aloof and gentle there for there's no one else, not a soul.... Please will?

Formal in the mind's blank eye she stoops through spirals of silence, she bends to tidy the room with tendons dark in her hands: pale her image, incredibly clear, as slowly she forces the paper back, stuffing and stuffing until I'm full. And mirrored their features; breathing their breath as she unmasks them.

Crying with their silence watching, pity clotting from their stifled breath. What can I do for chrissakes, what else. To be done? Searching eyes unhappy in the street's familiar hill: abandoned lives, uncertain stumbling in the snow-filtered underworld and somewhere, blindly, Lucan Crackell lost his life and love. Sad man, adapting to the world's disgrace. THERE IS NO EASTER.

Forget it, forget the bone's obscenity, their clutching hands, forget my past!

But I guess, beneath indifferent eyes. I guess it doesn't matter, comes the saddest voice and rodent feet of hope's despair. There's nothing to be done.

Susan!

LUCAN 3

"Gee. I don't know. But I'm sure you're right." Turning she watches me. "I can't imagine, I simply can't imagine that there could have been." Susan you look so nice and that's what I wanted to hear. A young woman, so much. The others just. Lucan Crackell sitting in his first warm face today and there's coffee, a cup of coffee being poured. Yes there is and even in grief you're a warm and a beautiful. Person. Hah! Drawn back, your hair's severe. Yes. Appropriate. And vulnerable there I can see as you turn to this group, I can see. "Can you Nancy? I mean, you'd certainly think that on a busy road, you know. As busy as that London road, well, you'd expect a crowd wouldn't you? You'd certainly have thought." Where you've combed it in tracks. And Lucan is pleased for its not so bad, certainly. Low ceiling beneath the gusting street, these booths I know and fear: certainly they remind but. Not a window, not a frigging window, nowhere can I see the day. But! Dismiss! Forget the memory of that slippered walk and the silence he brings. Coffee steaming circles upon circles and its just the thing. For hope. His shining eyes. Small and shining, he looks so old dear God, the lines and careful feet. Leaning to serve, is he the same? Cigarette blue-smoking on the counter's edge and other cups bitter in my throat. "Would you like anything else Doctor Crackell? Toast or anything?" Voice concerned out of friendship, and Lucan easing for its really not that bad.

"No. No Susan, thank you, I." Really isn't. Looking around; growing confidence expanding in the room. Another world actually. Oswald's gone (if only they'd lock him up. Or something) and Susan with watching eyes you're very nice. And helpful. Sympathetic, that's the thing for she knows. Lifting the coffee and my smile. "This will be fine." Intimate smile for I know your white shoulders, your. Breasts. "Thanks anyway."

"Anyone else want to eat?" Lovely girl, really a lovely girl and. Certainly an unpleasant thought but. She's better off without him. Really. "I mean. I think there's time before we, we have to go."

"Oh Susan, no! I couldn't think of." Reproval in her whine. "How could you think of eating on a day like this?" They phoned my mother, and asked why he didn't have a better coffin they said we'd have lent you the money if we'd thought you didn't have enough.

"Miss Haden I think that's beside the point." Firm voice to the rescue here. "Life goes on and that's the real thing." Lucan's strength and maturity, my growing certainty for she's better off without him.

"Well I didn't, I didn't mean. All I meant was that I don't want." Averted eyes, hah! She's left herself. "I'm not hungry, that's all." Wide open.

"So long as you." My knowing smile, Susan's eyes. "So long as you don't make a general principle from your own preoccupations, eh? Ha!" Feel better, honestly do and what a strange strange thing she said when we left the car. From her coffee, glancing: thin-faced with brutal glasses, winterwhite and sipping as she looks away. In the terrible frigging cold as we picked our way in the wind, dreading that sign and descending stairs and I should have worn my galoshes. Or rubbers or. But it spoils the silhouette. You know, Doctor Crackell, that I'm one of her very best friends. And Susan waiting gently here. Really one of her best. I can't think of anyone. Anyone who is as close, but you know. Conspiratorially, for the others have gone downstairs. She's a funny girl sometimes. I even have to admit it, her best friend. Go on, get in there for chrissakes! Get in, its too fucking cold out here! But she stands with the skirts of her coat blown apart by the wind. And she blinks stick-thighed in the swirling snow; staring as I hold the door, stupidly, and. What in hell am I supposed to? She made me promise not to see him.

What?

Martin, not see Martin in London. Enlarged eyes and pleading. She was jealous you see. Wool mitten on my arm, restraining hand as I try to push past her down the stairs. I didn't, wait a minute! I didn't even want him very much. Oh! He was a nice boy alright. A really nice boy even though. Moving inside her coat and her teeth are like claws. But I couldn't have, don't you see? Lucan ducks his head and shifts from foot to foot. You understand, don't you? This vestibule is too bloody cold. You do, I know you do because. Turning resigned, she removes her hand. Because you have sad eyes came her voice and Jesus! What a strange. Conversation. Drinking coffee and I feel better now, yes I. Sad eyes for chrissakes. the sadly eyes of Lucan Crackell. Shit! Now, blinking she waits, she sips her long lip deeply there and adjusting the glasses on her nose:

"Felix was his best friend, wasn't he?" Nakedly searching face. "His best boyfriend, I mean." Cafeteria sitting with their coffee, laughing, Jesus laughing with a stupid mocking racket! "Living together like that and everything, it must have been a terrible shock." Hmmn, a yesyes, they mutter yes while Susan's still, she stares at her cup.

"The trouble with people like Oswald." Careful, because his friends are. Sudden flush for Susan (can I say it?) eagerly, yes eagerly looks up, she's watching me. "People like Oswald, and mind you there are many of them in the world today, a great many. They don't have any honest emotions. Honest responses."

"Oh you're so right Doctor Crackell."

"They have to, to dramatize everything until its no longer real."

"And that's why he jumped out of your car, isn't it?" Breathing through her mouth: her pausing lips and perfect teeth. Without, even without her body in my hall, she's lovely. You'd have to say that there's a finely sculptured mouth. And perfect teeth. "So impulsive and it would have been just as good to phone." Yes.

"Certainly Susan. I think that's very apt. For example." Authority tapping on the table. "He's not here yet is he? And God knows when he'll get away with all the questions they'll probably want to ask."

"Maybe they'll even want to take him back out to the accident." Nasty, boy that's a nasty thought! Broken body or even worse, alive perhaps with agony and jeez I wouldn't like that very much. The dark blood seeping, clotting in the snow. No I wouldn't, for.

"Yes, and if that's the case, none of us would have gotten here in time and maybe we wouldn't even have made it to the. Church." Susan I'm. I'm sorry. Quickly change direction as she thinks of him. "But Oswald, people like him don't think of things like that, they dramatize, don't they, they act impulsively but not with thought." Careful! The Sears girl shifts and I guess the conversation. His rudeness was unforgivable, there's no doubt about that and we'll have to see what can be done; nevertheless. The conversation is. Unwise. Doctor Lucan Crackell turns, he turns and smiles at Miss Ann Sears; just like them, just like the both of them, she really is. "It's the nature of the young, I suppose, heh." Openly staring before she shrugs. She looks away. "Heh. And those of us entering middle age lose touch sometimes."

"Surely Doctor Crackell." Her returning head and here we go, for chrissakes, leaning professionally with fingers resting lightly on my cup; how many frigging times have I heard? "Surely that's why the impulsive young are a, a necessary component in any society ." Nodded sympathetically at arrogant faces because they've paid their fees? "Because without them you'd have no change, no progress." And she really thinks she's made a point, jeez! An original thought for chrissakes.

"Well that's certainly true to a point, Miss Sears, but...."

"I don't know much about philosophy or anything." Susan's effective voice. So Lucan leans back, that's the thing. "But I do know there's no excuse for being rude." Give her hell that's it, yes. "Every time I saw him he was rude." Enveloped Lucan small with need, climbing into that sculptured mouth and pink with her tongue. Expanding softly, her perfect teeth about him as she talks, and I'd like her to swallow me right up, yes I would, enveloped and warm and easy and....

On the day before my birthday Vera, you bought that bottle of champagne and hid it in the refrigerator and in the morning you woke me with an icy glass and we lay there drinking, hardly talking except to say how wonderful to drink champagne in bed early on the morning of your birthday, or any day, with a lover, with someone you love...Naked on my back, the body's need: passive. So slow, how good her hand, oh God her hand! Gently among the gathering hairs and strength: the sun is hot and her soft mouth follows her hand and you're so ugly Lucan, so lovelyugly, men are so threatening here and blondly shrouding my belly and thighs her hair.

Nine. Be almost nine, a boyorgirl and what are you doing now, do you think of me? "Nobody's fault really. I guess its just a matter of personalities, but I never. We never got along. That's all." Because of. Shit! My disgrace in this wretched town because of her and the job I'll probably never get and still her hand, blunt-fingered, and the leaves. "Never liked his influence on Martin: he was so different, you know, when they got together." You're like her Susan, a little thinner perhaps, yes not so plump. Somewhat bonier there at the opening of your blouse, nevertheless. Delicate. Yes. Cross-legged, after carefully adjusting the crease and God these shoes are a mess! Delicate. Happier Lucan with this girl, this mere slip of a. Its quite remarkable, it really is, she has the same. Perhaps. Drawn back her hair, not loose, but blonde like Vera's with melted snow. What if we. What if I leaned and. Stupid embarrassed Lucan Crackell for jeez, what kind of a stupid.... Wow! There is no. But the, yes, the chuckling, this day isn't so bad. Brushing these few ashes from my chest, brush-brush, and I mustn't forget the newspaper.

Rising, "excuse me for a minute," walking while I think of it, walking and good Lord! Stomping in all ruddy with snow. Four of them at least, no five and their laughter's confidence: jostling out of coats, their cries, hello, hi there, while starkly, one is standing dazed and bruised or dirty on the cheek: a brutal shadow under empty eyes. There's horror in the shadow of his hat; he's ready to cry! Looking but not seeing as they strip him of his dirty coat, then solicitously lead him past, they seat him. In my chair for chrissakes! With that stupid goddamn hat, what are they? Doing they can see my coffee there, they can. Boy! Some people, laughing and. Abruptly Lucan turns, demands the paper and I'm, I'm sure its the same one, but he doesn't see me here because his eyes are on that ragged man. Hands on the streaky glass and underneath the lichee nuts and fortune cookies in their trays. Yes, some cigarettes and slowly he bends, pulling the lever: wow! Swoosh the trapdoor opens and I hurtle through my floor, crash into the waiting rowboat; terrible struggle, oh God, my strangled cries unheard as they stroke in the maze of pilings and unspeakable filth into open water and the moon: pressed cruelly, my face in this bilgewater, and I can only just see one savage silhouette. "That's right, DuMaurier." From two quarters, my change and. "Thanks." Darkly to the waiting ship; and slowly to my coffee growing cold.

"And Doctor Crackell, maestro, teacher and veritable pillar of southwestern Ontario's academic community; do you remember me?" Cigarette holder as he talks and stands, presiding; silly old fool, heavy moustached.

"Certainly, yes, I have visited your. But." Show him, the arrogant. "But I'm sorry. I've forgotten your name." Enquiring Lucan leans smoothly, polite my smile. "Mister?" Superior, that's the. Laughter crackling from a blond, that meanfaced boy beside Susan.

"Mister? Mister? Haaaaaa-hah-haaa! Man that kills me." Glaring from face to face; avoiding me, his wolfish smile. "Hey Mister Max, do you have one, eh? Do you have a last name?"

"You'll excuse my young friend Doctor Crackell. He hasn't worked for eighteen months, have you Willy?" Subsiding, the blond boy back into himself inserting a finger into his nose, he digs vigorously. "Apparently they're not in the market for hairdressers with his background, but." Brightly back to me. "In his own offensive way, the boy is right Doctor Crackell, my name is Max. Max and no more." Slight bowing and turning up his palms; tight skull beneath his greying hair. "Eternal and humble student at life's banquet for the intellect at your service, sirrah!" Good God, what have I? What time is it and when can we escape this? Disengaging from his nose, the thumb and forefinger rolling together, they disappear beneath the table and in his hand, when it appears, a heavy-boled and leather covered pipe. Quickly Lucan at his watch, hot flushes and I better pop into the washroom. "Now let me introduce you to my companions: first, and perhaps you've met at one of my evenings, this is Pat." Lucan nodding to her incredibly white face, her midnight hair. "Pat you know is an *artista*: she paints and writes, don't you Pat. Hmmmn. A lovely girl. And here we have our court psychologist. Jerry Benfield." Round man rising, greasy, reflecting hair, his rings are hard in my hand.

"How do you do Doctor Crackell, I've heard a great deal about you and its a pleasure, a real pleasure I'm sure, to meet you at last." Holding, squeezing and staring. He sits plumply, takes out a handkerchief, rubs his brow, wipes his hand and from here I can see that its a bruise alright, a growing ugly green. Who is he, for chrissakes, this ragged man; he really looks drunk or something, he. Slouching down.

"You've recently met Willy, of course, he's a. He's an out of work hairdresser, but a man with...."

"C'mon eh Max, quit buggin me eh? Jeez!" Stuffing tobacco into the pipe: easy self-consciousness, poised. "Hey!" Alert suddenly with open eyes. "Hey man, where's Felix, wasn't. Wasn't that cat comin' down with you?" Hazel, or pale at least, and staring into mine. Well ah, unwilling Lucan about to speak, when Ann.

"He's over at the police station Willy, he's. No its not what you think, no: there was an accident, we passed a car. Why you, you must have passed it too?"

"Did we!" Darting eyes to the ragged man, and his wolfish laugh. "Man I'm telling you, it was really something."

"I was, I was quite certain we were the first car on the scene." Sticking a fresh cigarette into his holder and glancing, he's glancing at Lucan Crackell sitting absurdly frightened now. "Apparently he'd just gone off the road, one of his wheels was still spinning, so we naturally assumed we were the first, we." He, he for chrissakes? Who and what happened, was there any. Body hurt was there?

"We thought the car was empty, thought the wreck was old was there anybody. Hurt?"

"Well that's an interesting story doctor." Holder in under the ragged moustache, and considered flaring match go on, for heaven's sake go on! "We stopped, of course, pulled over to the side of the road and right away." Puff-puff for, what? "Right away, Willy here, saw the man in the back seat." Rising, Lucan's hair on the back of his neck, rising and.

"He was all scrunched up at the back of the car, right against the back window. At first I thought. I thought it was just a bundle of clothes or something, but then I saw his face." Without warning once again, Lucan rubbing the back of his neck and why didn't we stop, why didn't we?

"To continue. When Jerry saw the poor fellow there, we all jumped out, haste haste we cried, but none of us could match the alacrity of Sweet William: he was out of our car and swarming over the wreck with amazing speed. You would have been astounded Doctor Crackell, simply astounded at the conduct of this boy. There he was on his knees, cool as cool, wrenching open the door and before you could say, John Diefenbaker, he'd scuttled inside on his lifesaving mission. It was then." Bastard, shrewd eyes watching. Shrewd. Expansive hands and smoke about his head, he's milking it, milking for all its worth! "It was then I heard the ticking sound, like a bomb or something, ticking away. The ignition, I cried, or we'll all go up in a TERROR OF FLAMES! I'm telling, I'm telling you boys it was a suspenseful moment there on that winter road. It was the fuel pump I suspect, spewing fuel all over, indubitably, and as soon as Willy turned the key it stopped, but. But its a blessed thing that I heard it when I did!"

"Willy, for goodness sake, what happened?" Ann you're wasting, wasting yourself with frauds.

"Well. Like I was in there and I could see this guy; he wasn't moving at all and, man, I figured I'd crawled in there with a stiff and maybe Max was right and the whole goddamn thing would still blow up or something. Anyway. I was just deciding whether I oughta take his pulse, you know, see if he was getting cold or anything when I see his goddamn eyes are open! Man I damn near flipped and then he grabs my wrist and starts telling me about the lousy life of a travelling salesman."

"Dohnever travel." Mumbling voice as shifting suddenly, this dirty-bruised and stranger. "Don't any of you ever nice people travel." Good Lord, it? It is! "Eighteen years. Eighteen. And everyone of them god-for-say-ken." Rubbing his hand across his voice, his fading voice. "Goin' on nineteen." Must be the one and, and they've brought him here, they've come directly here. On a day of mourning! WOW, just who, who do they think they are for chrissakes! Susan's horrified and why not, shit when even Ann and Nancy stare? Bringing this, this. "Almost nineteen godforsaken years and then, last weekend...." Watery, eyes drift away: arms to the table top, his shaking head slumps down. "She had them put me in jail" comes his final voice.

"Willy, persuasive as ever, finally dragged and coaxed him out: and here he is, poor sod, a veritable broken, a broken reed! Aaah such are the...."

"What did he say, what did he say just then? About last weekend?"

"Oh man that's. He told me about it in the car." Wooden kitchen match to his bloody leather pipe. "This'll really slay you." Acrid smoke and his sucking mouth, the bright flame flares and wanes. "It seems," staring curiously into the coals, "It seems they had a party on Saturday night or something. Man, this is a, this is a terrible story. And sort of late on when everybody had been sloshing away at the old booze he goes into the kitchen, see, and there's his wife with this other cat. Climbing all over her. He said he thought she was fighting him off, and when she sees her husband she calls for help. Elmer! His name's Elmer or something. Help me! You know? So he tells the guy to get the hell out of his house, and he opens the door and everything, but the guy was pretty big and he refuses to go. Well. You know, what can you do? So he phones the cops. He had a couple of drinks while he was waiting for them and this big cat just sits there with his feet stretched out as if he owns the place. Elmer said it was really creepy: you know, all the people went home and his wife had gone upstairs to the bedroom, and the two of them just sat there, drinking and looking at each other." Puffing, bending his neck and blowing clouds upon clouds above his head, smiling suddenly: "Then when the cops did arrive. Jesus! Before the poor bastard could open his mouth, the wife comes tearing downstairs screaming that he's a drunk, get that, that Elmer here is a drunk and he's embarrassing her, and all her friends had left because of his violent temper, he was dangerous and was gonna beat her up again; he oughta be locked up, a decent woman like her shouldn't be left at the mercy of a poisoned mind. Boy! You know, on and on and she even cried a little, and the big cat just stands there nodding: he can't go home and leave her in the hands of such an unstable person. The cops didn't know what to do. They asked if she wanted to lay a charge and when the bitch said yes, they took the poor bugger away and locked him up in the tank on a drunk and disorderly charge."

"Oh no!"

"Yeah Ann. You can imagine eh?" Humorously shaking his head. "A whole night in the tank with the memory of his wife and her tall dark and handsome lover standing there in his own goddamn living room with big drinks in their hands. And grinning, grinning like crazy. Eh? Man, I mean that'd really drive you wild, wouldn't it?"

"That's really. Some people are so cruel."

"Mister Benfield is this man actually...do you mean to tell me." Bravo Susan, well done! Can't let them get away with this and Lucan leaning eagerly. "That this man was in that wreck?" I stare accusingly with her.

"That's right Miss. I'm afraid he was."

"But shouldn't you, he, go to the police, what will the police say?"

"I suspect they'll, they'll feel he should have gone directly to the station of course, but we. We rather felt he needed a cup of coffee first." Just who, by God! I'd like to know, just who these people think. Scorning the law, totally oblivious to grief.... "Furthermore we'll be taking him over as soon as he's had a chance to assimilate this extremely traumatic experience; one wouldn't want to, to rush him you know. It mightn't be. Wise." Turning his ring and leaning back. "I recall one...."

"Yeah, yeah. The poor guy needs a coffee, that's all. He can't go to the cops before he has a cup of coffee. Poor bastard!" Reaching his hand out he pats the resting arm: screwing him up, they're certainly. Be charged with leaving the scene, he will, they'll slap a charge on him so fast. "They'll probably put you in jail again, won't they?" Bloody selfishness, of this crew and jeez with a dead-beat life! "Man, he's lucky though, thrown right back against the back window and there's nothing broken, eh?"

"I recall a similar case, drunken driving and the authorities...."

"You should have seen the car, Doctor Crackell." Quickly brushing at his large moustache. "After Willy shut off the ignition and immediate danger was abjured, I had the leisure to, to examine the machine while they were inside talking."

"Incarcerated the driver, waiting for him to sober up, and. And this is the interesting thing. He never did." Collecting cripples for chrissakes! Encouraging all kinds of anti-social behaviour, they collect absurdities, they think.

And I've nothing but scorn, Lucan Crackell opening his cigarettes and coughing, Jesus Christ! This basement room, these booths; fan's greasy blades and faded lanterns meshed with streamers from the ceiling: bunched at the kitchen door, friends and waiters. Smooth skinned and drinking coffee in the juke-box noise. Another cup, I need one. Yes.

> Lonely rivers flow
> To the sea, to the sea,
> I'll be coming home;
> Wait for me...

"Front end horrifically destroyed so that a man would think, how can anyone be alive inside such a. Doctor Crackell, how can this fellow, I asked myself, possibly have survived the awesome collision between machine and growing life. That tree?" Waiter with more coffee and this is simply not the time. Or place. Even if and remote, the possibility, certainly extremely unlikely that I could ever enjoy. Sugar and pass it to Susan. "Yet there he was, amazing but true, lying in there chatting away to Willy. I stood awed, virtually awed at the resiliency, yes that's the word, resiliency; of this, the human body. There's a lesson, as in all things, there's a lesson here for those who see, for those who wish to use their. To see, and that is: man, if given half a chance man will prevail." Slurping at his coffee bent, this fool. "Isn't that so?" Moustache adjusted as he glares about the table at us all. "You're very quiet Pat, and you're the *artista* among us, the preceptive spirit. What do you think?"

"I think he's really an interesting talker." Leaning as if to touch, devour, this dusty man in his vacant trance. "And I think Elmer is a sad name. Terribly sad." Then to Susan: "He talks just like a French movie or something."

"Man she's right, that's true alright."

"Terrifically symbolic, you know."

"It was a real experience, I'm telling you, listening to him there in the car."

"I've been thinking of painting the climax of this one story he was telling us, its about...."

"Hey, yeah! Tell them about the time you went hunting!"

"Nono," he mumbles, "no."

"Yeah, c'mon. He went hunting once. C'mon, its really poetic." His delicate hand patting, pushing at the trembling arm. "Tell them, eh? Doctor Crackell is a teacher of poetry: he'd love, he'd really like to hear it. Wouldn't you? C'mon. Please!" Leave him alone, why don't they. Leave him alone, they're always bugging, clutching out and its jeez, terrible the way they keep him here. To entertain for chrissakes! Those shivering hands fascinating, his clumsy eyes that search. And search. Because of their selfishness, the police for heaven's sake, his charge compounded. Leaving the scene.

"Was burned over a couple or three years back." Tentative voice and sudden cough: rapidly licking his lips. "But the new growth climbed and was green all over the stumps. The birds had come back and everything." Pausing, and what are they trying to do to him? "That's good moose country. Very good moose country. Couldn't shoot one of them though, I could never." Dropping his mouth, sucking into the cup; slouching and drinking. "You're all young, you young people. You're very rich and I'm very poor, you're all young and innocent and." Christ this is embarrassing! Avoid, look away from their eyes; your shoes, look down or anything! "She had them put me in." Lucan, desperately say something, say:

"I think he should be taken to the police station." Briefly, but then they ignore and only Susan, for chrissakes, only Susan seems to know. Poor. Her funeral and what fantastic insensitivity to bring him here!

"Paddling, I remember I was paddling and the bush grew thick as hell to the rocks all piled and jumbled on the shore: birches, white birches and evergreens and as I came round, as I came round this point, I saw. I saw him suddenly. There, as close as that!" His arm thrown out and we turn: yes I'm sure its the same one watching us. "That counter, close as that counter!" Me. He watched me that way as drunken, descending I came in failure. Hour by hour. "A moose, a great bull moose, so strong and with a head of antlers like a man on fire. Oh! Oh! You're young with your lives ahead, so you don't know. I startled him, I. Yes, Elmer Workman frightened him because I am a man." Tears thicken his voice, the eyes; what kind of sentimental crap is this? "Powerful swimming, rising to the shore, water pouring from his back, God he was beautiful! He stumbled because of the rocks under his goddamn feet, he stumbled and then he was gone. God!"

"Antlers like a man on fire. Gee that's beautiful."

"What about the deer, tell us about the time you shot the deer."

"It really is, I think I'll try and paint that." Churning stomach for they're so, so goddamned pretentious! Selfish bastards can't see, they don't know. Lucan's second coffee finished; he shifts in his chair trying to get comfortable, trying to relax for this is stupid and I'll just pop into the john.

"Don't know why I did it, I don't know how, but I saw him, suddenly I saw him there in the new growth and before I knew it I'd shot him. And I killed him!" His head shaking; he stares at clenching hands, his cup. "With a sideways leap he fell into a thicket and all the birds were about my head: my friend cheered, he slapped my back and went running ahead, but I just stood there. Hearing the echo of my gun and the forest's breath." He savagely rubs his eyes, this foolish drunk and his pathetic fallacy, good Lord! How prophets were made for chrissakes. But its the, Lucan wiping the table's edge, the reasonable man, the thought-out move. Resting his elbow on the clean surface. That finally counts for something. Yes. "I'll always remember to my dying day. God! Terrified, you just can't know. Walking. Stumbling on charred remains beneath that surface growth. You can imagine eh?" Snuffling in through his nose, a wet nasty sound. "I knew just what I'd find in that bush, I knew, and the sun was so hot and I was sweating with the flies and, and." The tears again well up and Jesus one spills out and dribbles down his cheek! He wipes it from the corner of his mouth. "There were. And you know I'll never forget." His voice and staring eyes. "There were tears of blood in the palm of his hoof."

"You see, didn't I tell you? Isn't that a marvellous story!" She turns excitedly, her face a night flower and there are gaps between her teeth. Why do people encourage. Wide-fingered dirty nails, and he's rubbing at his head, I know that feeling well, Lucan Crackell years ago and; why this pleasure from chaos in the young?

Tremors growing from their silence round this man; breathing wetly, mumbling tears and God! I'm glad I didn't stop, boy! Lucan Crackell driving with Oswald, Oswald and this, this creature? Wheewwh! I've enough as it is, I've got horror enough without. Reads a bit, picks up a phrase or two and they think he's. Worthwhile for chrissake and poor Susan here, poor girl, I'll. Lucan smiling and shaking his head to show this lovely girl he knows. To show her that he. Cares, she's so. Vulnerable.

"Why is everyone so cruel, why can't they." Oh boy and cringing for we've come to this. "Why can't people love each other?" Breathing his tears, wetly in his voice; we've come to this maudlin, we've come. Naturally for chrissakes, one thing after. "You're young so you don't know. You young people can't know for love has gone from this world of today. The great lady. People can be good and true, they used to be, you know. They used to be. Good and true people." Stupid blear-eyed face and his cheeks are wet! I'll have to, I simply have to get out of here, I'll go to the, yes to the washroom and that will make me feel better. "The great lady in her furs and the poor woman from steerage, arms about each other and they sang. Why can't people always be like that? Loving each other and the ship went down." Breaking uncertainly, mucus, his voice and this is too much:

> Nearer my God to thee
> Nearer to thee
> Even though it be a cross
> That raiseth me
> Still...

Running tears beside that bulbous nose, terrible, jeez! But at least he's stopped. Singing. "Oh such a beautiful spirit there, such a beautifulbeautiful spirit." Scrambling, pushing back my chair, rising with a nod or something, anything, because this whole scene is fantastically embarrassing, crazy. With Oswald there in the door, clearly detailed; slowly he's taking off his coat.

> Though like the wanderer
> The sun gone down

High forehead and why, even from here I can see snow crystals melting in his beard, why does he move so slowly? Goddamn this singing and his drunkenness, goddamn their faces dumbly smiling, drinking as they smoke and listen! Jesus. Quickly nodding abruptly quickly away from this, from him and its that way I remember very well, down the hall. "Its all gone from the world, you know that? Gone, all gone all." Muddy feet to those glistening bones, walk straight for heaven's sake, with dignity! For I'm older, much older now and just the man. Free from the wind and its bare schoolyard with swings and bike racks propping the drifted snow. Repented yes, and I'm sorry Lucan that we've been so long in telling you. Those birds that are now his hands and I must be, its obvious that I'm just the man. Senate acceptance and all. Takes time, you understand. That's right, shoulders up and into the hall and out of their sight. And that's a relief. E'en though it be a cross. Whose feet are those behind me, in the shadows there?

"Just a minute please." The waiter and this shock as if the years return: uncertain standing, but he must. He must mean me, though I've done nothing, nothing at all. What have I done?

"Yes?" A yes in this hall with darkness in the eyes.

"Your friend. Its your friend." Blank my face must be for I don't. Am I afraid? I don't understand. "We can't allow it. There's a law." Directed somewhere else, his voice worried as another comes to blot the doorway's light. Silhouettes and their talk's strange past. Oh god this underlife comes on, this sickness: mice in loose whispering walls and the belly, the haunches of a rat, absurd with its tiny head. What are they jabbering about, who do they think they are?

"Which friend, and what about him? What do you want with me?" As many rats as people in a city and undoubtedly, they're dropping. Wetly from the stairs and boxes here beneath my feet.

"The singing gentleman. The crying one."

"That drunk? Good Lord! He's not, he's certainly no friend of mine, I've never seen him before." They can't, oh how can they think that creature's a friend of mine? Drawing myself up and patient injury in my voice. Yes, a man of substance. "Look, I'm here for a funeral and I didn't even want to come, you understand? Responsible business, you understand? I'm representing the University of Western Ontario. I don't even know these people, I don't know who that is. I've never seen him before." Relax a bit and exert the charm to ease me free. "The fact is gentlemen I'm, I'm working today." Perhaps they'll see this smile, my friendly teeth. "Just like yourselves. Now if you'll...."

"There are laws." What? The new one, taller, Bowing with the politeness they have. "Unfortunate laws, and the authorities don't like us."

"They don't like us anywhere. They think we sell opium, they think we keep our lettuce in the toilet."

"They say we put cat meat in the Won Ton, have you ever heard such an insulting thing? Its a lousy life. The health inspector is always gumshoeing his nose into something."

"We have trouble getting waiters. Its difficult, you understand, to get good Chinese waiters here in Stratford. Now our uncle is in Hong Kong, but do you think they'll let him come and help us?" Consumed, I'm. Consumed, Hong Kong and lettuce in the. What are they, why do they tell me this, for chrissakes? "Hoo! You have another think coming if you think our uncle can get into Canada." His voice strikes out and its airless here, that's the trouble, that's why the head and stomach. That's why I feel unwell. "And he is a most respected gentleman."

"So you ask your friend to stop singing, please?" And these men persist. "Tell him he's lucky to be anglo-saxon and he shouldn't take advantage of it."

"But he's not my, I'm telling you I don't even know him. And furthermore I have to." Nodding at their shadows, shrugging as I begin to move. "I'm just on my way to the." Waving my arm in this murky goddamn hall, turning again but Jesus! Gentle his hand restraining on my arm. Leave me alone! A sudden kick, that's the thing, smash into his jewels and an elbow for the other one, that would fix them. Quickly, a savage elbow blow across the jaw, like Cagney in that....

"Wait a minute, don't go." Heavy breath and it isn't doing me any good at all. "You don't know what its like. You are a university gentleman, a professor."

"Excuse me. Its been very interesting but I've driven all the way from London and I. I have to go. Excuse me." Breathing quickly, hurry! Stumbling on the uneven floor with his voice behind.

"It is our livelihood sir, its important to our business!" Not so loud for chrissakes, not so. They'll hear you in the other room. "So ask your friend to stop singing please?" Closing the door, locking it, pushing the bolt and this is absurd. I don't know. What to do and I must. Lucan's darting eyes in the mirror and am I alone? Carefully into the squatting position, fingers unwilling on the floor its pretty dirty and peek. Under these two cubicles for telltale feet and sagging trousers. There's nobody else! Good. Straightening arrgh! Bending has brought the evil rush of blood to my head, good Lord, or from it: Lucan awkward to the wall and leaning, breathing deeply because of the pressure and cascading light. A most unpleasant feeling, yes; very unpleasant and perhaps water, a splash of cool, this water will help. Gushing force and clear, but just as I'm about to, that tapping on the door. "Excuse me please." His tentative voice.

"Yes. What do you want. I'm just...."

"You are not angry sir?"

"What? Oh no, no I'm not angry, I just have to, to ah." Soak my face in water, that's all, for my dizziness and pain. I wish to hell you'd go away.

"We don't like to offend the customers but there are these laws, you understand?"

"Yes." Resigned and. Suck. Staring at my image in the glass for there's no escape.

"I'm sorry sir, I can't hear you. There seems to be water running, are you alright? I can't hear you very well." Good bloody grief but. Oh. Wrenching the tap shut and I mustn't in this silence be too.

"I said. Yes. Yes. I...." What, now what? I've forgotten what he. Said for chrissakes! "I said yes."

"Thank you sir. Do you think you could. We'd be desolate, very unhappy to think a customer was angry. Could you open the door please?"

"No. No I can't. Open the door I'm." Naked, horribly naked or something and I'm growing this hump, I'm. This very ugly hump. "I'm not angry, I assure you. I don't need to open the door, I understand you see, and I'll certainly speak to him. Yes I'll explain it all, yes I understand, I'll." Jesus Christ! Open the? "No I couldn't possibly." Away,

away fuck off you sneaky Chinese bastards! Hypodermics and innocent girls....

"Well if you're sure you're not angry."

"No. No I'm sure."

"We thought you'd understand. That's why we spoke to you. A university gentleman and you looked so. If I can say so. Understanding." Silence. That's the ticket, don't say a word and quickly the tap on full. These loud splashing sounds for a while but don't underestimate them; they're patient devils. Dousing coolness, delicate at the temples and around the ears so I can't possibly hear and that feels better. Taking some, rolling it around the mouth for freshness: Lucan chewing a mouthful of water, gargling a bit, but with care. Don't overdo it and gag, that wouldn't be very nice. Wet hands to the back of my neck and pause: I think they've gone away. A brisk rub with this towel to invigorate the whole head. Get the blood moving; brighten the eyes and skin. Listening carefully. They have, they've given up, there's not a sound. Good. Good. Now on to the business at hand; relieve this sickness in the bowels and I'll be a new man. Ready for anything. I only hope it isn't going to activate my piles. Bracing the door with my hip and bending to examine the seat, yes that's alright. Not too pitted or anything. Out of my coat and hang it up straightening the sleeves. You get a lot of cracks or pits in a toilet seat and God knows what filth's embedded, nasty diseases and. Everything. Pulling out a few sheets, carefully rubbing, polishing a little and it looks clean enough. What's that? Bending, there. Floating, aah! Paper and I didn't think. No! He must have meant the tank. Lifting the porcelain top; lettuce leaves, among the strings and levers? No. Rusty float. Be impractical here, there must be another closer to the kitchen. Back out to shut the water off. I'm sure they've gone: I'd try to see but the keyhole's full of dirt, and anyway, its dark out there. Embarrassing wow, to stare right into, into another eye. Jeez! Back to my cubicle, undo the old belt, jinglejingle, masculine bending the knees. Anyone, anyone with half a brain would know he couldn't be my friend. Worlds apart, we're. Yow its cold! But that's alright, they only live at body temperature. He's unobjective, sentimental, hopelessly. Whoops! Careful. I wonder if anyone's listening? Door's closed of course, but maybe. See if there's a peephole anywhere, a cold Sax Rohmer eye watching Lucan Crackell in this undignified position. Some kind of an air vent but it looks pretty safe. Twisting around, as best I can, but there's nothing else. Relaxing and the really unpleasant thing is they brought him here. Shaking head in disbelief. Trying to, relaxing but there doesn't seem to be. Just making me. It really makes you sick, the selfishness of these people. Feel worse, that's all; dropping pressure deeply in my gut.

Leaning forward, straining flat against the earth and sighting down the barrel at figures on the hardbaked path. Or hand grenades, lobbing them, their savage voice with dust and shrapnel bursting as I roll and move. Pow! Pow! Its Oswald, Good Lord! Returning my fire from that other hill. Clear-eyed Lucan Crackell, but with a certain fear, a sickness as he scrambles agile to these rocks and waiting. Peers in caution to the wood's green edge. You heard her Oswald. Cold-staring, dangerous eyes and at his first threatening move I drop to my knee and out with the right arm smash, like this, under the old breastbone. Driving hard!

Obviously a cruel presumption but what's more, its illegal, that's the thing. Illegal. Rubbing at the belly, perhaps that will help. Pushing downwards with stiff fingers. Quite apart from the impact, the chaos in her day, and that's bad enough God knows, there's the police. Jeez, what are they going to? Tense Lucan, easy. Relax. Serve him bloodywell right! Gratuitous pain and tension that he brings.

Mewling and stretching, a child in clothes grown small, sweet Rose. Walking in painted halls with cool stairs easy beneath the feet and nothing comes of it. Did you tell? Did you tell? Long night's wait for their praise, and then a mirror beyond this door in sudden light revealed. Oh God! Suck!

Or like Yves Montand in Wages of Fear, rock in my hand and there, crowbar threatening, cowardly. Put it down, drop it in the scorching sun. This clash of wills. I'm warning you and clattering among the boulders at his feet as he gives in completely and I throw the rock yes as hard as I fuckingwell can I burnitwithallmystrength and it smashes crushes his face and collapsing he falls in bursting blood and bone.

Just no use, gas that's all, I might as well go back out there. I might as well. Jeez! There's nothing here. Resigned, but Lucan Crackell doesn't know how I'm supposed to function, generate composure for chrissakes. With this frigging gut. No help, no help at all because she doesn't understand; its not the distance, no, not at all its her complete inability to understand. That's it. My own wife, a man's own wife. Its sad, isn't it? Boy its terribly sad.

Pushing out to the stained mirrors; distorted face. Lucan ducking his head, bobbing as a growth deforms, his eye and cheekbone swelling like a disease for chrissakes, and that's pretty disturbing. See if I can get the nose up. Turning on tiptoe and there! Look at it swell, grotesque and wow! a nose with yellow life, spreading, growing as I sway. Look sort of funny if. Grimacing Lucan Crackell, straining ugliness with fangs, popping eyes among the lines. Hah. A horror, a real horror, Hell's child. Eeek! it's me! Hah-hah. Well that's enough of that. Find a clear space, comb the hair and that little piece should swoop over here. Good. Wash my hands again. Another section of this hygenic towel, clunk clunk, and its certainly clean alright. A real blessing. Maybe if I could get my foot up here on this basin. Errgh my side! And the stomach's in the way. But there, that's alright. Now some of this muck off my shoes. Twenty-nine sixty-five or something shocking. And look what the salt does! Enough to make you weep. Lucan, awkwardly for the towel's too short, rubbing at the whitish stain. Careful! Don't want to slip, hah, this pinion leg go shooting out from under me or something. Don't want to, unceremoniously dumped again today. Safer to get them both back on the floor, solid. You've got to move from one firm base to another, solid motivation and you gain respect. Its true. Brushing hands at bits of lint and they should really have clothes brushes in lavatories. Yes. Thought-out moves and surely they've seen the change. Surely. Listening at the door and then into the hall, looking about, peering into the shadows. What in hell am I going to say? Just. Stop singing! Authority, that's the thing, fall back on the natural superiority of my position. Demand respect. Straightening the lapels before entering, check the old zipper and. Hey he's gone! Feeling of wellbeing, yes, of relief for its one less pressure. And Oswald, he's gone too. Good! Up to the table with my good smile as if I haven't just, unsuccessfully too, been to the bathroom. "Well." Briskly rubbing my hands. "Where's your white hunter gone?" Jocularity to ease the. They glance, no sense of humour, obviously. In the young and that Benfield person. Just goes on talking.

"Take the cow, I said, as a case in point. She wanders as provocatively as possible and its the actual sight of her, you understand? The image cast upon the mind that arouses the bull." Serious they sit and listen; what on earth? "The male only has to look at the female to get sexually aroused. Its biology. And then, do you know what he said?" Primly with shining fingernails and hair he smiling looks from face to face. "He said, are you by any chance calling my wife a cow?" And huh-huh, they chuckle, oh no! Too much, too much! Susan's glance to me, raising my eyebrows and her shrug resigned. "That's right, to help me. Huh! Just like a cop, eh? Huh-huh. So I said of course not, I'm talking about some basic facts of sex, about the biological source of our behaviour, your wife's and mine."

"Man that's pretty cool. Did he really have his gun?" His gun! Lucan staring and are they serious?

"He did, he did indeed and it was most upsetting, I can assure you." Your wife and mine, boy this sounds. Unpleasant. "I could see it glinting in the moonlight as he moved his arm. I was frightened, terrified actually for its always difficult to predict human behaviour under emotional stress. Even for psychologists. You need a whole series of in-depth interviews; I thought the best thing to do was keep on talking, appeal to his respect for education, and perhaps that way determine the nature of his syndrome."

"Ah Jerry, Jerry, you're a shrewd one and no doubt." Expansive waving his empty cigarette holder. "Mind like a steel trap. The kingdom is indeed fortunate to possess a...."

"Your wife's a beautiful woman, I said, an incredibly sensuous person and its not her fault, I said. I assured him of that. I pointed out that she was only functioning according to her biological nature. The female, and I really emphasized this, I really tried to make it as clear as possible. The female instinctively invites possession. Its a biological fact. Look at the roles of male and female in nature. I said." Reaching for the package, he nods and lighting a cigarette, exhales. "He looked pretty interested in all this, I must say, although it was evident he didn't understand everything. He's only a simple policeman, you understand." Smothering a smoker's cough. "Anyway. In the state of nature the strong male, aroused you remember, through his faculty of sight, goes about impregnating as many healthy women as possible. Whereas the male is aroused from a distance, the female is aroused through her tactile senses. That's why we have such strict laws about guys who feel up women on the street, but that's another thing. Well we have these males naturally attracted, and in their turn, the females instinctively, I stressed the instinctive basis for all this, the female naturally receives all desirable males until she's impregnated. And, I said, that's how evolution works. You know. Huh-huh! Its pretty funny when you look back on it. I had to explain impregnation; pregnant I said, you know, a bun in the oven. And then he thought I'd made her pregnant and he started shouting again and I kept saying I was speaking figuratively you know, symbolically but he was really angry and after all my persuasive talk the bastard." Pausing ruefully, rubbing his head and this is absurd. Lifting his face, turning again. "He pistol whipped me. That's right, just like in the movies, remember? When I had all those bandages? Well. That's how I got them." Shaking his head and I don't think I believe all this. "Stupid cop." Sudden chattering, their laughter's admiration one to another but she and I are different, we see, that's it we see. Destructiveness. Their gross faces and their noise. "No, no I couldn't report him. My mother. You know. If ever she found out she'd die of shame." As from above, Lucan and Susan, unmoving. Boy. It serves him right. "She said you are in some trouble Jerry, I can tell when my boy's in trouble. Bandages! Look at that face will you, you don't get a face like that for nothing. Do you want to tell your momma? You tell your momma. So its nothing, I said. He was only insulting the race. Ah she said, I knew it, I knew it. What is he an Arab or something that he dares?" Certainly disapproving, her small mouth: why not? Disrespect for he is dead, after all, their friend her lover's dead. And like him or not. There are demands, certain responsibilities. Who would not weep? You'd certainly think that for a friend, some pain, some. But faces gross and open, this appalling selfishness. Smirking friends for chrissakes. They don't realize, that's all. How important as joking here with brutal self-concern. Susan we're alone. Lucan wondering if there's anything I can do. As an older friend perhaps. Yes. Nice to take her somewhere, Toronto maybe. A complete change of scene, that's the thing, a chance to talk it out for hurt those eyes, her face and my unhappiness. Time like this you certainly need your friends, oh don't I know it! Lucan Crackell knows difficulties and pain, yes the real thing. Boy. A companion, for I knew you'd. You have such, well not really sad but I do understand. Reassurance, that's what she needs, a little comfort from me. Hmmmn. In rattling talk Lucan trying to catch her eye, staring hard and perhaps if I concentrate. Intense eyes, that's it. Susan. Sooo-saahn! Can you hear me? Dully she sits and what's that a birthmark or something, a wen where her temple beats?

Warm bodies, deep inside us hear the easing limbs. Receptive. Sweat's invitation for there was a time when the earth was full and bones didn't sing between us and the heart.

No certainly not make love to her! Good Lord. ha! Lucan's protestations for she's not Vera after all and a good girl. She's recently bereaved, anyway I'm married, Jesus Christ I'm. The Plaza's roof with drinks and talk: that big city and lights define the world below us. A little therapeutic talk between two old friends, that's the ticket; and maybe see a good movie or something. Eat a smorgasbord.

Susan. My child's in England or somewhere, isn't that curious? We've never seen the child, my wife and I, because it went away before we met. Rose doesn't know anything about it, I've never told anyone you see. You're the first person I've mentioned it to. But its there. Somewhere. And the thing is, I don't believe I'll have another, I don't believe she wants one. Isn't that sad?

No words left: crass and spoken. Boxes piled in early morning light. Can't go, I can't desert this life and order, patterns that I am. Oh Vera! in that heavy silence, but you'll never know. What could I do there for chrissakes, what would my frigging mother say? Wanted so much, I wanted to but young, I didn't know what to do, that's the thing: I didn't know what to do. And anyway, I didn't think. You'd really go.

Hairdresser's up to the john so I'll just slide over and take his chair. Smiling at me, nodding yes to my glance and I will. Lucan rising and what can I, in sudden silence, say first? Controlled walk, that's right; the shoes are better and I wish to hell they'd keep on talking. Here we are, sitting, adjusting my trousers. My small smile and quietly. That's the thing. "Where did, ah. Felix go this time?" They're listening, jeez. But at least she looks relieved to see me here.

"I beg your pardon?" A little louder I guess, and Lucan raising his voice, leaning.

"I was just wondering where Oswald had got to. This time. Hah. I mean, he always seems to be."

"Oh. Oh. He's taken that drunken person to, to the police." Eyes rolling and is that? Yes good Lord its sweat, light there in the hairs of her upper lip. "And not a moment too soon, I might say." Poor girl, oh you poor. I didn't realize, I couldn't see from over there. Terrible ordeal, just. Just frightful and what can I do, what on earth can I possibly do except. Smiling with compassion, and perhaps I can. Reaching out to touch. Pat-pat. For reassurance. Oh she's a fine looking young woman, hmmn, and sensitive. Pat-pat. Sad. It wrenches the heart to hear how sad, vulnerable her voice. Under her breath almost, softly and her eyes. Doctor Crackell. I just don't know what to do. Therethere child and did she say it? Oblivious, chattering, they're really selfish devils! Selfish bastards. Therethere and smiling. Young sorrow, dark in this room. Pat. Strokestroke and a little squeeze because I understand. We're different aren't we? This day is painful God knows and all I ask. I only hope that I'm as good for you, as helpful as she is for me. Yes. How could I have come without her? Jesus! Tears behind my eyes, that's right, I'm grateful, so strengthened by this girl. Really an emotional experience to discover how much she means to me, how much easier she makes it. Different, yes its different, I've position. Representative of the university, just the man. But years ago, driven by loss I drank, I drank too much; that youthful shame. Oh boy. Couldn't live without them. How can a man let his woman and child just go away? And drunk in this restaurant, slippered feet, time after time with despair as if I'd let them die, as if I'd killed them and then. Oh shit! That terrible frigging incident, that. She knows, certainly she knows in a town like this, but even if she doesn't. She understands. That's it. We're the same kind of people. Not like these others, no sir. Two, six, nine of us here and that, another table. A real gathering. A writer, what's that they're saying? Susan, her fingers briefly on my hand and that's nice. But where's she. DON'T GO! "Excuse me." Softly eyes to mine and then, for the others, louder. "Excuse me. I must talk to." Nodding at that group. Brushing her wrinkled dress at the thighs, her tummy. Who's a writer? Stay, please, after I've moved like this. Makes me look sort of, silly.... Stockings together, thighs as she walks.

"I'm shattered."

"Who?"

"Me."

"Why?"

"Well Max, I never knew, that's why." Turning at his wolfish return; standing, sneering at me in his chair. "Did you Willy?"

"What, did I what?" Eyes from me to her. Running his fingers through his lank hair and I, I don't think he'll say anything or, I hope he won't.

"Did you know he wanted to be a writer?"

"Felix or who, what are you talking about, c'mon eh?"

"Felix, for heaven's sake. Felix." Black-sweatered, an *artista* for Christ's sake! Nothing but scorn and imperceptibly, curling my lip. Certainly she's got a fine body though. But Susan's more. Animated with them there, she's more, more. Refined. "Did you know he wants to write, I didn't ever know that."

"So what's to know? Everybody wants to write." Rolling forward, he leans on the table and what does he put in his hair?

"Ah Jerry, Jerry you're virtually that famous old Greek philosophizer." Blowing through the cigarette holder, and a look inside. "What's his name, Erueka with a lantern searching for the honest man." Staccato old man's laugh; snapping his wrist, shaking saliva tobacco juice from that dirty thing. "You persist in seeing the real person." Grandiloquent wavings, thin his stupid arm. "The bald truth, the testament within this envelope of flesh."

"Well its true isn't it?" Purring voice and this old fraud eats by feeding them. "Everyone wants to write, but we'll all teach. That's the way things are." Fatfaced smiling and piggy, his eyes are too close together; watching me, plump-fingered he twists the elaborate. Vulgar ring. Perspires, I'll bet he sweats all the time and eats peanut-butter sandwiches. I certainly won't rise, don't, for he's waiting, don't rise to this innuendo! For there's nothing to say. Bloodystupid, that's all. Jesus! They're well past, too old for foolishness. Its no longer. Appropriate. Just look away, you sly young fox, pretend you didn't hear. Unwilling sadness? Easier, she looks much happier, natural there. Light still her finger's touch. With pain the things I'm here to feel? death's youth, my own, and breaking words on faded bones.

"Ah Mister Jerry Eureka, or whoever you are." What's the word? Bizarre, really a bizarre and embarrassing. "You're too cynical." Not me, no wonder she left, not Lucan Crackell but this foolish bloody old twit. Explosive nasty, laughter rising in the scale. "You decount the individual."

"But man, he knows it! Cause he's a shrink and you better believe it." Aggressive selfish all, bursting with anarchy, their talk; and arrogance, jeez! This goddamn undergraduate mentality, their literacy misused. Maybe I could just get up and join her in that waiting chair; wash my hands of this lot. "Anyway, if Felix was writing, we'd know about it."

"Why?"

"Like Logan."

"Yeah, that's right. Logan's really involved, you know, he really believes. And Oz, well he's too...."

"He's never been up to my studio or anything, he never asks about my painting."

"Sure. Like why isn't he writing, its crazy, if he wants to write. Man you can't just...."

"How do you, Willy, how do you know he isn't?"

"What? Pardon Ann?" Good legs, black stockings and the curious wind: to my car easy, they came on the frozen walk.

"You're all talking away as if everybody's got to be a, well a fink because he is, Logan's a real fink. And just because Felix...." C'mon jeez Ann! Laughter as impatiently they shift. Good for her, hmmmn. Leaps to his defence against us all and I'll bet they do. "But he is, you can't deny." Lucan sees her leaning, sees them nuzzling on her arms cool-nosed like puppies and hah for heaven's sake he knows them well I'll bet his eyes his hungry mouth.

"For chrissake!" Bastard's voice, cheap condescension and I'll just slip my hand into the old pocket, poke at this wayward. Get down, get down! "We're not talking about personalities you know."

"That's right, who cares what a person's like so long as he's an artist, who...."

"Cause personalities aren't important, Pat's right. Its passion. Passion! There's your answer." Cross my legs with elegance, stuff it, get in there! Aaah. "Commitment to a world." Lucan passive, leaning back with sensitive, my mocking smile. Although. Its still a bit.

"After all, who really cares? Look at Genet, look at, at. Why I've had artists up to my studio...."

"Shit Pat, you've never had a, a real artist within a. Mile of...."

"I have Willy, I have too." Defiant voice and selfconscious, really selfconscious twits. "From Toronto, and Montreal, from everywhere." They are. Lucan shifting because its still awkward, but. There. That should do the trick. "And just because they're Canadians you know, it doesn't mean they aren't any good." It seems. Shifting, look unconcerned! it is so long and it isn't fair. My body unruly oh Rose, I. I wasn't drunk you know, I'm not. After the coffee, the bits of food, then your coldness, my clumsiness and frozen shapes, dark birds unmoving on the sky. Retreating, my following hand and I don't know, I just don't know what's happened, what to do. Go on like this, it. Breasts, translucent gowned and bluntly hanging, bending she bends (straightens dear god, she tidies) her buttocks' shadow under blue night cloth. White. It can't go on, this angularity how can I? Stronger, rudely overcoming, smothering her cries, yes that's the way: ignore the protests, desperation yes, a little firmness I should have screwed her down into the bed overwhelming for underneath she must enjoy it need it like I do oh Christ at this time particularly now? "Some of them draw like Picassos, if only people would recognize it. Like I know one guy from Montreal...." It would be much better, you know Lucan, if you could wait, why don't you wait until you see that I feel like it?

"Ah! Picassos, Picassos. That's the man, that's the man for." Energetically rubbing his face and there doesn't seem to be a bone or anything left in his nose. "Yes sir, that's your man alright, a virtuable prince. Say." Leaning forward with Lucan Crackell desperate, how. Can I get away, get out for a. "Say Pat, you're the one. I've never asked you. What do you think of Picassos?" Earnestly exhaling, tapping his holder on the crowded ashtray. Clink-clink.

"Picasso, what do I think of Picasso Max?"

"Yes. What do you really think?"

"Well." Arranging the cup and saucer, this studied pause and her thoughtful eyes. "Well. Prolific." And suddenly she pushes the cup away. "But not very profound." Nodding confidence, her turning smile and Jesus! Turning to look, the swinging door with waiters smoking, laughing and she's serious for God's sake, she's. Quickly I'll go and have a couple of. Have a beer or something.

"Yesyes, I thought you'd say. Something like that, but still and all you must admit, a prince. A virtuable prince of a man among painters." Lime green or something walls, the varnished wood: stale air with tables cluttered and aluminum chairs, the snow and stumbling past. Looking to see if she's rising, ready to go; and at my watch. Blue-grey pickled eggs like testicles in jars or babies stillborn, hopeful with the wind and I'm sure there's time, if only I could just to my feet and. You can make time.

Lucan's not your man to be fazed by an inescapable little thing like this; what is life, after all? Nevertheless. A couple of drinks or two would help. Because. Looking for a window, but hah there isn't one. The sun must be over the yard-arm or wherever and things are really an unholy mess. Beer to freshen me up, that's the thing, brace the mind and spirit. Good ale does more ha-ha, than Milton can. For my trembling soul. Clean-tasting and a food. Beer's a food, after all I didn't have much, as preparation, by way of breakfast and beer is, everyone knows what a particularly nutritious beverage beer is. Yes. Oil, as it were, to ease me through this day.

"He must be forty."

"Oh no Ann, no! In his early thirties I guess, about Doctor Crackell's age or something."

"But he's never published anything Pat."

"He's not quite ready, lots of people are after him you know. But he doesn't feel he's ready yet."

"He still gives those readings in Toronto doesn't he? And there's the guy from the C.B.C. who's always wanting him to read on radio."

"Sure Willy, that's right. But he refuses, not yet he says." A modest little. Sad because they're not, he knew, very good. About a dog for chrissakes; I could do as well, if it weren't. "He works all the time, as soon as he gets home from the office he pours himself a glass of sherry wine and, and after writing copy all day too, that's a terrible job you know, he starts working right away, on some poem or other. More likely he's rewriting, reworking an old one." Admiringly she shakes her head, her pale face with Lucan sitting here and once I thought I'd write. She leans severely. "He must have hundreds. But he's just not satisfied with them yet." White, her private smile. For heaven's sake why can't you wait until I'm in the mood until the time is right we'll never have a baby if you force me climb all over me you're "I'm telling you Ann, I've got to, well you know I've learned a lot about him this last year and I've got to. Like him. Yes. He's a very devoted poet. Why...." Looking from one to another of us, sliding her eyes past Lucan's, pausing. Rubbing his forehead quickly, yes, for my damp hand and put it back under the table. What is she, his lover or something? She certainly has black hair. "He won't stay late at work, you know. Even if its something pretty important he, politely but firmly refuses. "You know. Tells them to screw off...he has this obligation."

"An obligation worthy of the noble few!" Rising his

voice and mock dramatic, silly old. "It is, to my mind, his insatiable thirst that ogres well, an insatiable, one might even say endless, thirst to digest the theory of his Muse. Aaah, but the conversations we've had!" Hardly the best (Lucan with chaos just beyond the eyes) of testimonials, talking as they are. "Plato's castle and the moderns, yes indeed, we've discussed the bard." Poets battling in a coffee house and publication isn't everything you know. "Argued over a bottle of screech or something more...." Raising his fingers. "More salubrious. Oh yes, many's the night...." Gnarled, they're stained and.

"He's even lost some jobs because he wouldn't compromise." Waiting, they try to hold on with thick and yellow nails, uneven at the edge: indifferent to the table down. Waiting. Hands and their talk of writing, they go on and bloody on with Lucan Crackell relishing, for the moment, his. Disdain's the only word, for these people and their. Ordinary hands that rustle and crablike reach, nobody ever notices hands. A pair for each, a brace of scuttling, suddenly hands that feed, they pander to the body's needs. Abstracted and obedient. The Hands of Orlac, or the terrible story of the severed hand, revenge-bound servant clutching up the drive and with trembling heart he heard it at the doors, it searched about his house, it grasped a stone, it hurled itself against the glass, bursting in with dumb intent, it lay a moment silent on his floor, waiting: terror-bound, he. Frozen. Heard again the fingers scratching, felt it pulling at his covers as it climbed toward his throat. Boy, that's a. Pretty good story. Ha! Lucan loosening his tie just for now, relaxing, show them my ease. Before I. Cruel hands of strangers, prying fingers....

So soft, trembling as if its heart would break. *Un buho. Si. Is you. Regalo, es un regalo.*

He says its an owl and its yours. Heavy returning to his drink: sipping mescal, blowing through his teeth. Then staring blue eyes from his shaggy head. A gift. *Un regalo, verdad?* Glancing, but he hardly sees them nodding. Seems you've made a hit. Sardonic bastard and aloof as Lucan's three-week admiration grows. Quite a hit with the natives. Sweat commingles around the tiny body, wings and thighs imprisoned: nothing, almost nothing but its warmth and fear.

Muy bonito. Un buho, pero. Free laughter spreading among small men; dark bodies' odour and their strength. *Cuidado!* Snapping, pecking with sharp fingers as it lunges, twisting suddenly with open mouth, its eyes. *Pica.* Such a beautiful and trapped, whoever would have. Boy, these are moments alright! Red tiled roofs, white walls and cool bars with Lucan's welling soul, yes sir. Search out and isolate the magic drunkenness: remember! Ephemeral mood, your owl; the hands, rough nails that pick harsh music Vera, and the sea. Somehow suspended, yes that's it, three weeks suspended, unfolding here in the sun like the flowers at my window. You'd have loved this Vera, where are? *Pica.* Jostling humour they crowd with fingers reaching out to tease the frantic head, the beak, the body's terror in my hands. Culpa, mea culpa. Blindly Lucan, through them, pushing to the bar. Did I let you, why did you send the money back? Perhaps. To my drink and they'll leave it, leave it alone!

Gracias, muchas gracias. Thank you, its. Bowing uncertainly dark face tipping again beneath the hat, and spittle-white is dropping foam between his feet. Feet and benches' legs, benches and lockers with their footsteps, the stench and shadows don't. Lucan Crackell's turning, don't for chrissakes, turning as the barman laughing leans to probe, taunting the ice pick handle: stiff hair and blue in neon light. No, don't No. But *gracias, gracias,* how do you say? Helpless bowing again, twisting my arm so it, careful! Smiling gratefully, but don't let it get at my wrist.

Absently smiling, tired. Blind man's guitar again, random thoughts and the barman's sagging face. Its three at least and maybe. Lucan's glass is, my glass is empty and the owlman, my benefactor drifts away past the fat policeman, rumpled and sleeping. Have another, how do you say? He'd left his third, this fourth or fifth cantina of the night, I didn't see him go. I didn't realize until. Incredibly generous people and I feel. Mechanically pouring, the barman fills my glass and Jim's. Quite moved, touched by; passive the bird lies now. Its the gesture and their warmth. Strangely in the laughter, blurringsound, he'd stood. A bundle of feathers in his proffering hand and what, what is it? *Un buho.* For the *gringo sympatico.* For me? So pale they're brown, the bulbs suspended naked at each corner as we walk; Jim and Lucan in Mexico and this free night. The warmth I feel, but. What can I? Walking. The sound of our feet, Lucan's searching warmth and admiration for he does so much, he is so. Free. Yet how can I? They're lucky these people, they can and do. Declare. Men's arms enfolding men, embracing they declare. The ease, their life's emotions; no shame. Reaching from the sea, encroaching sand on the cobbles underfoot, our muffled steps: across the street, sidling the broken shadows of pariah dogs, and the owl stirs futile in my hand. Wow! To think I've met, found already in my new life, I've found a friend. Like this. We must be like them, declare to live and that's the. Truth. Lucan Crackell walking out of London and away. Jim. Bubbling in my chest and throat, exhilaration and my friend. Jim.

Yeah?

Jim, I've been thinking, I don't want to go back to my goddamn thesis. Listen, How can I, how shall I say it anglo saxon to him? Simply. Why, so why don't we get a place together here? Eager, hopes tremble. You know I, I've really. Well we get along, don't you think? Mottled and tenuous, a ragged cloud is bright before the moon, while shadows scurry in the street. We walk and I'm up from foolishness, my fear. Boy! Why I could, I know I'd be able to finish this novel for sure, you know. And Jim....

Don't, I really don't know how long. Bearded, his face turns away. I want to stay. With narrowed eyes.

Well, ha, that doesn't. Where are you going? I mean. Faster, he's walking much faster and Lucan jumps to keep abreast. It doesn't have to be here. Does it? We could rent a house or something, couldn't we? Somewhere. And while you're painting I. I could work on the book, it would be really good eh, and. Rushing the words to hold, persuade, they tumble out because. You're it would be fine for me, be fun don't you think? You're good for me, because. Drawing inside himself, staring and resolute ahead, I shouldn't. You know Jim, you know because you've done something. From the beach, beyond his house on the corner, ocean's cool and early morning air. You're an artist, confident, but. I need assurance, I do, not just anyone's assurance, you know, it has to be. Someone I admire. Faster and faster my voice and his walking, the moon. And I like you, that's what I'm trying, I've gotten to like you here, we've. Hands deep-thrust, why he's. Brittle uncertain Lucan Crackell, for he's. We've had a lot of fun haven't we? Suddenly, incredibly tired and the drink, I'm tired out of my mind: my legs and drifting this sand. Because he's, and I should have, must have known. He's offended.

Shame that comes mnemonic even now, sporadic through years as leaning foreign in that music, drink expanding with my heart, I'd told him Vera, once again I tell him of your flight, my guilt and watching. His watching eyes: self-betrayal as I wooed him; ego hopeful of his condescension and I think, host as I am to parasites, these scars, I think. In retrospect he must have, how could he not have despised me?

After evasive, the awkward pause and goodnight (will be, tomorrow it will be, oh boy, embarrassing and what will we say?) alone with this hopeless staring body. Shame, the shame of my life for this land has prevailed. Crescent beach and the mocking sea with head-bending Lucan Crackell cooing reassurance to the heart that's beating, promising. Freedom and underarm swinging upwards, releasing the tensions and the unravelling feathers a hectic shadow bumping, bouncing one scrabbling bounce on the sand, the clawing climbing flight that's lost against the dark forest.

Rub the hand, harsh-rubbing on your trouser's leg. Its gone. Hold this shell, press it to your ear as somewhere in that darkness, unremembering, it twists to separate the feathers from your sweat, escape the imprint of your hand. Listen to the sea and hear your life; the echo of your blood, its scornful pressures.... Doctor Crackell, he's the one. He should. Assaulting bodies and their hands, the passive terror of a child that running jagged figure weepweep who would not "You must have seen some of it Doctor Crackell." Shocked by this sudden attention, what. What do they want?

"Somebody had to." Rushing words and sure of herself, expansively she stretches white and black. The nerve, the frigging.... "That is, if he really is doing anything at all."

"That's right."

"Tell us, help us prove." Insistent, eagerly they ring me, waiting with their eyes. They draw me in. "What kind of stuff is he writing?"

"Is it any good, I mean...."

"You must have seen it, somebody must." Prove to us, help us prove they rudely press and Lucan Crackell cannot find his voice, it squeaks. He stammers:

"No. No, no." I stammer, "no...I've heard of course. I've heard, but." Hugh what crap he writes. "But I don't know. I've never seen, actually seen any of it." What am I, are we doing here? I haven't felt my owl, not just like that, or heard the sea...Oh Lucan-Lucan, on this focusing day, these images, my past, and hopeless chances Vera, down I went a-hunting, down to leave you and my love....

"Well even Martin, according to Martin himself that is, even, he, his best friend, you know, and roommate. Never saw...." Poor Martin, poor, they sighing eat and drink.

"Obviously then, he's." Expanding, thinly expanding as she's sure, her easing worry. "Not produced any too vast an amount, eh? Hee." Eyes regard me, mocking with certainty: I cannot meet them. "Not if nobody's seen." Brushing black her straight hair, brushing hands, large, with strong and silver nails.

"It won't be the same." No it won't, agreement nodding, smoking. Sipping at their coffee. "Without him." Reminiscent hope, a wish and. Not for him, good Lord no, ha! Certainly not for him but to show, to spite her. Strong hands and staring eyes, that's all. Yes. Pretty funny, ha! Lucan amused, shaking head with this smile at the possibility of Felix and. A talent, a real talent and why this hope on my, why should I, what possible reason? He's such a, an irresponsible and undisciplined person that its most unlikely, I'd say. Nice. I'd like to see her face if, if one day he. And Hugh thinks so, that's the. I've always wondered if perhaps.... But not Christ, not the way he's screwing around there now, he'll have to quit, get out. That's it, away. Not me. I, jeez, too long, was. Afraid, I.... Young yes. Got the time alright, if he believes, if he's. Desperate enough....

But that's absurd! Even with the drinks, the sickness walking from them, even yes I was persuasive. Yes. Hugh's too much like them, his mistake as I should know. And its not. Appropriate. But what if he, Christ! What if he made it?

I heard cruel laughter from that other room, I heard your freedom there. Pride. Fear at hopeful faces, transformed by her caressing hands: her image possessing and I said come up with me Rose, come out and have a drink but no. Not now, later later, for she does not know the wind. In the mirrors, other worlds, and flesh familiar all but mine.

Standing uncertain behind me: her voice in the back stairs as coldly limping, I've limped ashamed into this funeral day. Up and embraced by the land I've come, as she stoops to tidy, to stuff all that paper back.

One o'clock. Phony mournfulness, selfish bastards, with Susan patient there. Gentle and apparent ease, for they seem like a better, a reasonable group. Not like.... One o'clock and Lucan seeing her hair, wisps at the neck and ears yet severe in keeping with. An hour, still an hour so there's time. Felix suddenly, wet hair and chilled, come in, I didn't see him and I'll bet he's had a drink, the. Just seems to appear, he comes, goes as he pleases while here I sit, I. There was lots of time and its a good thing. Lucan smiling wisely, its certainly fortunate I waited, caution, didn't rush in there for a drink. Oh! Oswald, yes. Was looking for you, wanted. Wanted to know, Ah. Boyoboy, you have to think and act with speed, finesse. What the ah, authorities expect of us and didn't know. Wasn't sure I'd see you, there'd be time in church. Hoo! Lucan you're a sly, a fox. "Reasonable about it, trying to find a lawyer. Phoning Windsor or somewhere for a lawyer." Lucan leaning, what do they?

"Jeez, poor bugger, eh?"

"Has he got money, couldn't we maybe help...." Expectant, what must we do and what do they want.

"Well." Fingers flexing, rubbing his hands for warmth. "They want you people to go in after the funeral, he's really. Quite decent. After the funeral, to answer a few question." Oh God a watershed, despairing Lucan; I can't go in, not after. Driving by and everything, they'll. "He said they'll just hold on to him until he's sober." Stylized with piercing eyes, this ritual of masks and did your father beat you Lucan, did your daddy beat you Crackell listen everyone you newboys listen.

"Well ha I don't see why they, what we can." Dignifor heaven's sake! Your dignity, position control your. Lucan, control your voice! My reasonable voice, considered and my smile. "Surely they don't need us, you must have explained? We didn't see ha. Don't know why but we didn't see anything. Helpful." From one to the other, watching this group, I turn and surely they don't want to. "Did we? There's nothing we can add. Is there?" And Susan listening there, her face, she understands, she....

"We talked about that." Ignore, avoid the eyes! His moment and standing pause: I'm so calm, icy almost, while. "He insisted, he argued that we'd seen the wreck and we were here in the restaurant too." Didn't object too strenuously I'm sure, doubtless you welcomed, sonofabitch, the opportunity to shaft, to screw me oh! "But ah, I. Prevailed so...." What what, what's this? "Persuaded him our car could add nothing to their investigations." Amazing, this boy, I certainly didn't expect? "How, I asked, since we didn't stop, since we didn't feel there was anything to even interrupt our drive, how can any of us. Be helpful? Eh?" Accusing for me, talking and I do believe he's trembling slightly, lips and fingers. Soothing through me, settling my stomach and I do feel better, yes. He's young, young but. Lucan impressed, impressive yes. Not so, well he's better than, oh God yes, all these others yes, my warmth. Or something. Lucan touched for the boy's not bad, and anyway I'm not so small a man as to be worried by arrogance, selfishness, not when I. Perceive, see the good ah, the. Well. The hope that's mired in his youth. Entertainment for them, but Lucan Crackell's reasonable, an eminently ah, considered man. Yes. For if I'd been forced to. Jeez uncertain, needing to please, explain from guilt, why didn't we stop? Oh boy. Ha this relief and revolt, in the young is understandable; he did take the drunk, kindly, so much kinder to him as he took him back. Than these.

Freedom Lucan, yes. Beer from his moustache, licking foam. Anyway freer than most of them. He's really not part of the Queen Street clique, nor the old man's, Max. He's not. Sucking pipe, his swarthy face is indistinct as Lucan stares. Awful death and wound I concentrate, I....

But. But that's. Hugh, youth's freedom is ephemeral and that's why they all die young. My heart with voices: Lycidas and tragic, Romeo.

God Lucan, what're you? You're saying there's freedom

in youth and on the other hand, only a, bondage when its gone!

Yup. A respectable bondage is the best that we can hope.

Christ that's.... Don't, for you've got him, don't give an inch. Quickly!

Pain's the average man's alternative and chaos. Hammer it home, and remember to use them again some time. Ha!

I don't believe it for a minute, Jesus Lucan! But he can't, Lucan Crackell drinking strongly, for incredulity's no answer here, he can't, assail. Brushing ice to my mouth, the shape of her thigh when I left, skirt-tucked and her belly's tension. Chaos, shame and chaos. Why does she, God oh my, throat's so dry! Impulsive swallowing. Come wet, wetly from them to retreat, refuse me hopeless, hoping Rose.

Down walking away; the snow and wind, I walked and walk. USED CARS USED CARS Merry-go-round, this shabby pole bedecked and SAVE SAVE. My figure, young and lost, with icy circles on my flesh: from the streetlights, my shadow dark on the snow: exhaust and distant tail-lights, cold my hands deep-thrust, and clenched. Drink's fool. REPENT. This thirst, the ease, oh God what ease I crave! Escape, if I could only. NOBODY EVER WALKS AWAY FROM HERE. Standing, somehow with chair pushed back, impulsive going for a. Smiling Lucan Crackell as they stare, curious at this clumsiness and I'll say. "Excuse me I must." Must what, will I. Say? "Ah." Sudden coughing in my hand "I've just remembered something, have to buy." Shut up, they. No need to explain, no need at all! But swirling head as I turn, begin to turn, "Some stockings, my wife asked me to buy." Oh God don't. "Some stockings for her, she." Bastard, silly fucking bastard smiling, bowing, their eyes, their. To Susan's face. They'll know, they know where I'm going; stockings for chrissakes, stockings shit! and he grabs his coat. My fumbling hands. Terrible frigging cruds every goddamn one of them, they're. Irresponsible Jesus and their nerve, stupid goddamn arrogance! Accusing for Christ's sake. Me! Rough shrugging at my coat, my scarf, don't forget as to the door, I hear:

"Doctor Crackell, Doctor." Her soft voice calling, reaching me in this heavy coat. "Just a. May I, before you go?" Turning with her words, her voice; and other figures fade. "You are coming. I mean." So vulnerable, she's: lovely girl. Warmly Lucan pauses, for its touching, really, how much she. So uncertain, she's uncertain. "You'll be at the church?"

"Yes, why yes. Of course." How could she think, does she suspect, do all of them behind her know? "I just have. I only have to do some shopping, that's all. Rose wants." Blurting my bad excuse, they. "She's very sorry, Rose asked me to say this. Because she couldn't come. The show, she said you'd understand. It only opened last night and apparently. There's nobody else to do make up, she has to. You know how that place is, she has to work." Her hand on my lapel her voice.

"I'm so glad you came." Is close to tears, she's, oh! An old friend to rely on, just to get away from. Perhaps she'd, would you. Join me on this thirsty day as you have done ha. Before? "We've always talked so much about Martin." Hmmn. Unblinking, my eyes while in my hand, her forearm trembling rests. "And that's why I'm so glad you're here." Then I spilled my drink, our awkwardness, the closeness of two friends. Real friends. "Do you know something?" Urgent her hand at my breast is tugging now.

"No, what?"

"Wednesday night." Vulnerable, she's mine, my best friend. Here. "Before he left, before he was. He'd come to insist, he'd come all the way from London in the middle of the week and he was. I could tell he was upset, that he'd." Reaching for you Susan, reaching in spite of their curiosity, I reach with all my heart. "He'd decided to see Miss Schwartz, to take a job here. Isn't that wonderful?" Surprises me so don't let on, surprises me for I'd have thought. More and more that it wouldn't work. Out, I was. "Of his own free will and on his own, he just arrived and. Told me. He promised he'd see her in the morning. Thursday and that we'd be married in the summer and everything, but then. While walking home, you know...." Parted lips, her tears, my helplessness and how could I have misjudged him so? "Isn't that a terrible, he was killed just as he was taking control of his life." But never mind, therethore, he's gone and Lucan's need, he takes her shoulders, gently as she, looking up. And brave, so brave she smiles. "Do you remember Lucan." Pausing cautious, blinking and her smile. "Can I, you once said to, can I call you Lucan. Now?" Subdual tears abrupt, harsh sorrow and the need in my throat. Oh!

"Yes, oh my dear. Yes. Yes, of course." Shaking my head, my welling eyes averted for.... Relax, tense hands, groping affection clumsy at her arms.

"Do you remember that night when we drove and drove? We'd been swimming, a bunch of us, at the quarry and Rose, poor Rose had one of her headaches, from the sun or something, do you remember?" One of her, sighing Lucan for even she's seen, you've noticed. Driving at night from the town, in the radio's noise, how many times? The glowing dashboard's light; driving with trees, flashing fenceposts and the road, your legs. Singasong of nylons, tucking as you stir. "And you said, you were joking I know. But you said you could imagine Martin living somewhere in the bush, in the woods all alone and then. Once a year maybe, coming out for a terrific, a real bender." Her talking face, and did I say, I actually say that, she remembers? Sad and are they mocking eyes? Her moist pink mouth, no. Pale. "Well you were wrong, don't you see: You were terribly wrong." Squeezing my arm, smiling with Lucan feeling something, there's something curious; she likes me alright, there's no doubt about that, but. "And I knew it all the time, I've known. That people, he could change." Suddenly clear, clearly she knows about me, sure, for everyone, they all must. How could they not? She sees that I've changed yes, and. That's it! Ha. Lucan flattered, yes I certainly am, I'm. Whirling for she understands. Ha!

Greengrass the somewhere, above us branches clutching brightleaved the wind: bruised green beneath our bodies and the heat, with branches searching, watch...and this time Vera I'm the one, my knowledge caresses, eases forbidden doors. I'm sure you're not, no not with him! Light air, your innocence, my tenderness explores: hand, your thighs, my hands in circles on the calling flesh. My sweet return....

Finding himself bundled and walking, chilled in

unpleasant slush and the gusting street. Clinging brown, soaking the shoes and eeeh! Oh, that's...Lucan frozen, precariously balancing on one leg and I should have, quick to this lamp-post. There's a nasty patch of wet in my sock. Again balancing, its safer, and running my finger inside there and scooping, finger-hooked and lifting out what's left. Curling exhaust from the cars: I'm the only, there's only one other form, its sheltering there in the doorway and. Waiting for a bus, waiting for a friend? More carefully, pick your way with greater care, and thrusting hand inside his coat, drying the finger in his armpit's warmth. Pulling on my glove; walking away, alone in a mainstreet town, and....

Done this before, a déjà-.... Behind me Susan, among them, me yearning and guilty, shoes between the ridges, walls and towers of that dark world at my feet. Uncanny, Lucan's feeling—I've done it all before. Walking in shadows on the other side but were you Vera then? Or Rose. The door with yellow opaque glass. Will I or won't I, I'm not, its not as though I couldn't stay out. Ha! If I wanted to, if there was a reason. No. Man of decision, Lucan Crackell's not your man to be driven by whims. After all, I've. Settled Lucan, you've changed and youth has died. Hmmmn. Behind as he saunters and she certainly couldn't, over there in her doorway know that I was going in, a bit of refreshment. No sir! Perhaps I'll still, of course there's that. Possibility, yes. I mean, I'm out here now aren't I? Jerking straight his arm, baring his wrist and its cold; another, another forty minutes or so...WARNING TO MINORS. Rippled panes to his left this time and she must wonder what I'm up to. The law, it is an offense. Dark figure retracing steps; slowly the cars and their noise. Oblivious. Caught newspaper, awkward moth, it beats as I pass, the futile wings. Suspicious, she leans, she watches. Really a clumsy silhouette I guess, against the light: staring, if the truth be known, unseeing with water on his shoulders, in his hair. Reluctant feet in mud, muddy imbedded, the bones for me, there is no. For I'm, that image on the glass before me's just the same and he's an angry.... Relaxing back, quickly to the door and is that a smile, does she smile knowingly and who's she waiting for? Voice calling my name: crouching cars like animals behind me in the glass and my face was there on the wall. Nervously dark, and drawn.

Christ don't be ridiculous! Warm air in this familiar room: what's the matter with a beer or two, we used to. Not long ago beer was a morning drink. Food for the day, yes. In this harsh land, a bit of strength. There. There by the wall's a table. For two. Lucan in their eyes, on tiptoe between these chairs and loosening his coat; as I have done. He sits and I don't think a single head has turned. I pass. Rheumy eyes and underworld: unmoving figures alone, impassive. Shaded life: world without sun, a man. With swollen hands, unemployed, the drunk condemned. I did not know death. Had undone. He sits. Green, pale walls with chocolate trim and, I'd forgotten:

NO SINGING, DANCING

OR

SPITTING

Gambling is Forbidden

Here then is Lucan Crackell once again, careful. Careful not to drag your sleeves in the table-top beer, these puddles. Jeez! Do I ever know this place and there's not much. Change. Wow! Desolate figures, the heavy smell. And we sit, so curiously bleak, we sit as far from each other as they can. Turning to look, for I'm not. Turning easily, with confidence: whoops! Sudden man, the waiter and his tray. "What, what's on tap?" Politely, for you never know. He's a different one, I don't seem to remember and you never know with these fellows.

"I don't know." Clunk the glass before me.

"Ah. Is that." Smiling to question this stolid rudeness. "Is that ale?" To point out clearly, that I know, that. I'm not like. Not one of them.

"Its all the same buddy." Jaw firm and waiting. Rough accusing voice. Bored. "You wanna drink or not?"

"Ycsyes. Hmmn." Lucan gulping, pausing. "Yes and I'll." Swallowswallow, burning in the chest. "I'll take another, better leave another while you're here." Foam that slithers in the glass, his exchange, I'm alone. With this new. And boy, his. Lack of manners, this. You'd think, certainly they'd get a nicer, better class of. Waiter. Or something, it makes me feel quite sick. It does. The squalid, but anyway. Another mouthful, clean and it does much to.

Alleviate, freshen the mind and stir the blood. Yeah, and stretching, Lucan back into the seat, for there's lots of.... Shit! Oh goddman I've forgotten her goddamn. Newspaper, she'll.... To hell with her! Wait she says, waitwait for fuck's sake Jesus wow! Empty glass. Until. You see I'm in. The mood. Jees-us Christ what does, how can she? That's it. Fuck her! Boy I wouldn't be surprised, if tweedy Blair, that. Bastard. Not in the least. Waving at the waiter for there's not much, weakfingered snapping, its important hurry please for what if he does, they do? Oh Jesus!

White flesh lazy, his arrogant hands that clutch, his pornographic body fat it makes me feel beneath my heart a swelling sickness slim, so slim she. Pale. oh pale spreadeagled, Rose possessed and willing, where?

Gagging at the new glass, no, coughing. Rubbing hand across my mouth that's stupid, that's. And a, perhaps a cigarette. Left quickly and into my car, quickly back, what? Nothing, no! In at the door to hear their voices? Small sips rapidly, Lucan's drinking: cold and clean, it eases. Just a mumbling at first as lightly up the stairs and shallow breathing, her laughter leads him on. Head's so light, my head: behind that door, yes, that door and in my bed. Drinking to still, explain this rare excitement, quivering; straining to hear each slightest sound. My head. Until it hurts, inhaling and hold it, why do I. Prolong? Smoking and injured Lucan Crackell, lust's imagination in slow motion, bodies wrestle, bedsheet entwined they're flowing into one.

Tied up or something, in their power, jeez there's too many. Cruel ropes that sear my wrists, my eyes averted longingly. You make a sound and we'll, yes we'll kill him sweetie, little lady if you don't. Cooperate. At her blouse rapacious hands, tearing buttons and her skirt, her eyes with tears, her stifled cry oh no no and the vicious swipe across my face we'll kill him baby and its nothing new for us...moist mouths her nakedness and eager eyes as one by one they screw her on our bed and stirring yes spasmodically she wanton twists, she turns beneath them, eager now, eager her arms around them desperate hold, she "You wannanother?" Shaken Lucan struggling for change, nodding dumbly and that's. Clunk. You simply must. Shifting carefully to ease the pressure, ha, that's a shameful, really. I mean, to think of your wife. I simply mustn't allow myself. More slowly, just a taste, not too much. Rolling bitterly on my tongue.

God imagine the feeling! Felix is right, oh boy back there, her body's gift: dark in the jail and alone; their laughter, his hands, her...twisted, oh! Dark at the water's edge, this landscape, roots between us and the sun....

Softbody bursting from my hand to rise: rising from me at the edge, lost in that forest, lost. Crouching past and their chattering arms reached out like bees and there's the terror, for I knew. It doesn't matter. Dark birds accuse about my head, they cry: it doesn't, for I've always known.

But I've danced in shadows and my songs, me laughing....

Rude, most certainly, but here he is again. Keeps his eyes open. Efficiency's a virtue I admire. Cold glass, and I've really been quite harsh, too harsh with Oswald. After all. Lucan sipping, savouring, for after last night, oh boy! It tastes surprisingly good, it does. Hmmmn. He's young after all, serious and.... God! Sad yes. worse for me in a way. Jeez. But if he did, if someone. Perhaps I didn't, he might. Get away, yes FUCK THEM ALL! Be the one that. Be good to see...the one. Inhaling so it hurts and tight lips blow the smoke. Large hands, what? Reaching they toy, arrange the, what on earth is it? Longer engine life and no internal knocks, I'll bet! Mechanical images, electric blue, and there's no sound: sincerity, teeth glittering as Lucan stares. Mouthings, animated eyebrows; empty face for me. Impersonal down from the wall.

Heavy shadow, brutal impact hurls his body, sharp and awkward for a moment in the air; red blood a rose beneath his head, and eyes, the youthful eyes.... An animal pause, uncertain drifting in that night and wind.

The force of impact would have crumpled any normal fender. Shit a most unpleasant, terrible, I can almost feel the. Blow, the jagged wound, its sad. Cut off, as it were, just as he'd. Abrupt I must. Its almost time. The watch, there's only time for a. Quickie, yes. Raising my head, and he is really on the ball. Yes. "Thanks," nodding, "thank you," and this better, this'll be the last. For sure. Turning glass in its ring of foam, Lucan sees her smiling. And she's holding my arm, she's. Oh!

Lucan Crackell drinks and stretches, rapidly blinking, staring. Got to assert the mind's control! It's a most, sip and swallow as he lights a cigarette, a most curious and a vulnerable situation. Yes indeed, oh yes. Ha! Calmly smoke in wreaths about his head. A superficial, but essential order. Yes, that's the thing. I know she. Likes me, yes she does! Perhaps she'd....

Once, dear God, there was a ship! Vegetation from the sand as growing from her. Pirates, they seemed like pirates, ragged for my youth they came all foam bedecked and sweating to Mexique Bay. Come with us, they said, we need another. Tanned and bearded, eyes stripped by distance and their strength, their laughter's....

Work with us, why don't you. Come along?

Six weeks in San Francisco to refit, they said, and then. At night, their laughter easy, oh so easy...The Hyacinth. Something over a hundred and ten feet long, was built in Scotland and freely there, she's riding, rising from the sea. And then to the islands. We go, to the islands. (How shall we set sail for happiness?) So come with us. Come.... *Un buho*, the prisoner owl, the feathers, sweat commingled, his and mine. And was that just two weeks, two weeks ago? Crescent night and swooping arm, alone; lifting clumsy at first, the unexpected flight, clawing. The climbing hope to this forest and the sun. Then springing, magic they came for my dreams; but here I am, still in an empty bay I'm standing Vera, for I couldn't go, I couldn't simply throw everything, my thesis up and all my life, to follow that ship. No, no I couldn't, you must. See! No not after his rebuff not with! Embraced by fear, my shame against their strength! Oh God, if I could only....

But in my hands, life! I too have held, staring suddenly at these, my opening hands with dark hair curling to the wrist. Life in these hands! Goddamnit, I. Have! Dry-folding lines as fingers close to the palm; they're puffy, too much blood, or something? Strangely rough, because. I let it go? Fresh glass, swallowing: to salvage this day, I must. Clearly think, and concentrate. Clearly act, must choose and I did.... Silent gathering despair, I turn, oh slowly bending, staring between these legs, they're such a mess, a christly mess....

Bumping terror from me and away: I took her, I

insisted, you won't get married, there's no other. Way. Muddy feet obscene as rats at dawn beneath the cross. THERE IS NO EASTER Just have to. Lucan, think about that, and. Maintain, dear God control! Exploding terrible chaos and my.... None of them, a man's own wife, she doesn't. Emptying glass, handrubbing hands because. REPENT, there must be possibility, a chance to, repent or. See. Yes, a choice, a. Lucan Crackell's not your man, he's not the kind who falters. So there is no? GODDAMNIT THERE MUST BE! Decide, that's all, just. Nobody, they're all. Alone you must assert, be. Strength for. CHRISSAKES! Clenching now this glass, they're bastards every fucking one of them are bastards! Yes, defy them all, the yes, I'll. Throwing, hurling that's the thing, its empty glass. Shattering horrifically and silence, Hah! The fuckingbastards, shit! Pukefart, pisspisspiss, boy I'll. "Hey buddy, hey!" Here he bastard, here he comes. "You can't do, who?" Quicksilver sickness, shame....

"I'm, I'm...."

"Who the bloodyhell do you, what'd you go and do that for?" Suspicious, aggressive there. "You want we should call the cops?"

"No, no I'm sorry, really I'm." Fumbling quick, get out, get out of here. "How much, I mean. Here, this is for. The glass, I'm." Rising the chair, oh Christ I've hit the chair, its falling! Stumbling Lucan's lunge to save, caught it, I. Pretty good, at least that's. Pretty good reflexes, for a man my. Thrusting bill, avoiding don't catch his, eye don't hear his. But muster, God muster dignity! Sternly walk among and past them, dirty old men: faces lost and hopeless grey. Uggh! Shutting his coat, the searching cold, turning he pushes the door. Their laughter and violent warmth. Thank God I'm not like. Boy! Inverted and raw on the hill.

My arm in confidence, a man can change. Her smiling faith, a curious elation. Decision, its decided. Yes. With hands he walks in the slush unconcerned: heavy cars and a bus, forging by and the streetlights weakly shine. Maybe I should just keep going ha! California, I could work in. Or.

Laughter's unaccustomed in my throat, my chest expands and. More quickly, light and strong. Running and to hell with the crap that's soaking my shoes, he even

skips. There was a boy. Dying figures huddling past for I
was wrong, perverse. And wrong. Romeo died, (I want to
shout) and Juliette, because they. Cared!

> There was a boy,
> A very strange enchanted boy.
> They say he travelled very far, very far
> Over land and sea.
> And then one day,
> One magic day he comes her way...

Smiling eyes responsive: in my hall she smiles, she
takes my arm. Leaning blond hair falling down, leaning
to whisper: so glad, so very happy and warm, her
breath infects my blood. Oh Lucan. Lucan help me!
Calmly, Lucan reaching gently, in gently subduing
light we lie with shadows in the other room. I can taste,
on the edge of my mouth, her hair: oh Lucan help me
for I don't know what to do!

You sly young fox.

FELIX 1

You. Studiously bouncing your ass against the rad. Bouncing forward to your toes and shifting, back to the scalding metal with another patch of flesh and trousers, bouncing again to the toes with this imperceptible arch of the back, shifting because more than once on the same spot's painful. But hold on, forget the pain because other people, soldiers and saints have smiled in pain while you, you're just playing here in the vestibule, watching the mourners. Waiting for his body. In how many classrooms have you closed your eyes to swallow the panic? Rattling papers, pages turning all around you, and how many times and in how many rooms have you borne down on darkness? Bouncing now and rocking, you're cringing from their draught as they push in at the door and the iron ring crashes behind them. Loudly from the street, with voices falling in self-conscious echoes as they come to bunch and crane at the inner door. Pausing before you they reverently stamp and sniff in droplets glistening from the nose: they nod abstractly, one by one, and meet, you have to, their eyes! "You're from London, are you? I mean." Plump voice that interferes with his breathing. "You must be from the university." Gasping and standing too close, wheezing his smoker's breath in my nose and then he turns away, quickly over his shoulder. "I could tell, you know, just by looking at you, that you're one of his friends from university." Waving a silent wave and smile, and then again his breath while his eyes are moistly. "Well. Heh-hum!" Patience thrusting its hand. "I'm his uncle you know. Uncle Martin, his namesake." Trying to withdraw, I try to get my hand back, give me my goddamn hand! I mustn't be, really mustn't make a scene but he clutches, clutches and kneads, he pats my arm! "Its hard to believe, he's really gone." Sadly shaking his round head. If you don't give me back my hand, I'll! Struggling and pulling, grunting audibly. Give me back my hand, give me my hand, but he'd only laugh, the bastard, clutching even tighter. No, no its mine now, mine all mine. I've got you! Those people coming in stop to stare as I wrench, I twist and extravagantly jump. He won't give me back my hand! Leaping like a fish I topple chairs in furious noise and shshsh, they whisper, shshsh, inside the congregation stirs and some crowd back: the word is spreading, feet are running in the aisles. What, whatwhat, what's going on? He won't, pleading as I wrestle him weeping to the floor. Its mine, all mine now, mineminemine.... Straining, but its no use, pulling with all my heart to rescue, pushing my boot into his armpit for the extra force. Please, please give it back, please give me GIVE ME BACK MY GODDAMN HAND! Shrieking down into that face, jerking and shrieking, close to tears myself from the mourners pressing in! Christ the mother's coming, here she. What? Stumbling on the preacher's arm. Whatwhat, would Martin? Think, his favourite uncle. Ferocious into tears, oh Christ I've done it now! Accusing faces ring about me, shame on you and. "Young man, I'm sorry. I don't, know your name?"

"Oswald sir. Felix Oswald."

"Ah yes, you. You shared his apartment didn't you?" Nod to his saddening smile, nodding. "Yes, yes of course." And slowly, his head. "Yes, I knew didn't I? That you were from the university, I could tell. I have an instinct." Breathing asthmatic punctuation, his eyes are vulnerable. "For these things. I have an instinct, have to in my business. In your case," a smile of satisfaction stirring at his lips. "In your case it was the beard, I could tell by the beard. And a handsome one too, I might say."

"Thank you."

"There aren't any beards in Stratford any more. There used to be, oh yes I remember. Many years ago." Stiffly smiling to contain the. Oh Christ why? Why do I have to, shift here awkwardly, he wouldn't want me to, to.... Have to! Why did he come back, why to this solemn world of uncles and they're all so, all of them, they're old! All this respectability that's pushing in, he's dead. "My grandfather had a beard, very big it was I remember. And bushy.

Right down to here." Pink hands at his throat, he smiles imperceptibly and I can hear his breath inside. "Covered his necktie, it was such a big one. Came right down to here, he didn't have to wear a necktie." Smiling politely, stiff because there's nothing to say about his grandfather. What can I say to this face? Over his shoulder, bumping from the street with bursts of wind and snow they stamp and nodding, push calm-eyed and staring from.

"Mine's too small for that, I'm afraid."

"Oh yes! Hah. Ha-ha! Still and all, you've got one and that's something."

"Yes, but not like...."

"Not like my grandfather's, is that what you were going to say?"

"Yes, I was going to...."

"I knew it, you see? I could.... But its similar, isn't it? I mean its the same kind of thing." Turning. "Ah!" He expands, grows before my eyes, holding my arm again. "Mister Oswald this is my wife, my better half." Sad-eyed beneath her tortured hat his aunt a shining face with powder in the wrinkles around her parted mouth; a shining face. "And her sister, this is her sister. Miss Smith." Take her large, extending! Taking her dry firm hand, I nod and....

"Pleased to meet you."

"How do you do."

"Miss Smith's from London. Perhaps you've seen her." Shaking, I begin to shake my head. "Walking her dog, she has a three-legged dog."

"Oh Queenie, yes!" Squeezing my hand in the dryness of hers, she smiles and slips her tongue wetly along her lips. "Yes, my Queenie, she's a lovely dog. We walk every day in the park, Queenie and I. Perhaps you've seen us?"

"No, no I don't believe...."

"That's curious. We go very slowly." Her look is disbelieving but I, haven't, no, I swear I've never. "We have to, walk slowly, as you can imagine. She only has three legs and naturally, handicapped as she is, well. It takes some time for us to get through the park." Slightly frowning and pinkly again, the tip of her tongue rests on her teeth. "Are you sure you haven't seen us?"

"No I." Look desperately thoughtful, try! Pause, concentrate for her eyes and think with your wrinkled brow. "No. I'm sure," and then escape, explain more quickly: "but I don't often, go into the park you know."

"I always wear a red coat, a bright red coat." Her fluttering eyes, she bows her head to watch me curiously.

"Trees make me nervous." Hah.

"I shouldn't, it really isn't, my colour, I know it isn't my colour, but, it's a good coat a very good coat. Warm as anything. So I can't bear to give it up."

"Why Frieda, why should you then, why should you give it up?" Her eyes are darting now and the tongue leaves moisture at the corners of her lips.

"Well, its.... Red's a colour, its the colour of passion you know."

"Oh. Now Frieda, come on now. Let's not...." Uncertain flutterings at her mouth; she takes her eyes away and turns.

"Didn't you know that, Martin, didn't you realize that red is symbolic? Of passion I mean, the colour of passion?"

"No. I." Blowing suddenly, exasperation as his wife applies her hand to his arm. "Wheee-ooo!" Then in silence his uneven wheezing breath, it reminds me. Of something it. Suggests from somewhere back I can't recall, at the moment I....

Out there somewhere; pulling the pillow from under his head; unceremoniously pushing (is it hard to do, is he stiff yet?), closing the lid and what sort of laughter from what kind of men can they be, doing dead conventions? Or in the hearse already, bringing him here. Grey billowing exhaust about them: sleet soiled, the deep expensive shine, while they adjusting cuffs and smiles, they flick the ash from laps, they swear at the dampness of their shoes. "It is though, it really is." Insisting, strange dry woman, why do you. "Surely you've seen us, me in my coat?" Turn threateningly on me like this, when I've. "Every day, every single day, as regular as clockwork, we set out." Jesus, no I've! Shaking my head, this my most emphatic, yet my understanding smile. "You couldn't mistake her, poor thing. Her left hind leg is shrivelled, handicapped from birth she was and its no use to her at all." Sighing she's jostled as more crowd in, they come unendingly, they bottleneck at the inner door: growing with impatience they're shoving back in silence, rudely resisting pressure from outside. "She hops along as best she can and that's." Forced in against me now, they're spreading to the walls with sudden hissing sounds and angry faces staring back. Look away from her wet mouth, but still I smell the lines about her eyes. "She does very well considering, she really has adjusted very well. Clickety-click with her front feet like this." Pawing her large white hands at my chest, leftright, leftright, like a slowmotion horse. "Clickety-click, clickety-click and her little back leg has to support all the rest of her weight, can you imagine? Click. Click. Click. I hold the leash quite tight so she won't fall off balance, but still, her poor little paw's deformed from the extra work." Crowding faces grow with anger, thinly reach while fat ones fall in surly wrinkles to the throat. What, what's going on, so many. There's so many, why? Why don't they go in, what's happening? Surging about us, faces blending in one voice, their eyes pressing her to me, beating me back against the radiator's heat, her large breasts flattened upon my arm and I can't escape this sad, her faintest smile. "I'm sure, I really am quite certain that you've seen us." Gentle dizziness behind my eyes, I think in this noise, her taunting voice, I think. Radiator at my back as dizzy, we push and sway: he takes his eyes from me to her and never. I swear I've never, seen her, please, so many there's so many, why? Why does she grin like this, insist and....

"Leave him Frieda, there's no need."

"But Martin, there is. I know alright, if he's seen me." Stripping me somehow, smiling her eyes stare me bare and cold. "I've seen him you know, oh yes. I've seen you lots of times."

"Stop that! And leave him alone." His face while voices all around begin to snarl, cry out and his wife's swept away. "Just a...." Rising to see her, find his wife. "Just a, minute, I'll be, right back. I'll...." Wedging into the crowd then pausing, he leans to us here and warns: "You leave him, cut it out and leave him be. You hear?"

"Oh Martin, you're so, silly!" Choked laughter to a cough behind her hands and he's, good Lord he's gone.... "Isn't he, isn't he silly?" Gentle coughing but steady gaze. "We get along fine, we understand each other." Even stare, shallow-eyed. "Oh I think so, yes I think so. Do you know why I asked for a dog like Queenie? I did you know, I especially asked for a poor little handicapped animal that nobody wanted, I asked everyone. The Humane Society. Everyone and do you know why?" Dear God, what, how can I? Weird unanimity of her face that's waiting and her sad, that smile, I...don't know anybody,I...Jesus fucking never! saw.

"No."

"Well, in Mexico, we were at the zoo in Mexico, they don't call it Mexico City down there, just Mexico. Its rather confusing, they say I'm going to Mexico and if you don't know, well you wonder. If you didn't know, you'd wonder, wouldn't you?" Swirling for I'm all alone, I could almost burst, I could just cry I feel so. Straining alone to see, look through and past these ugly faces, why? What ever possessed him to leave her there, come back down to this world of old animals and Susan? Sorrowfully away, sorrowfully, for if he hadn't left us to return, he wouldn't be dead, I wouldn't be: mourners' faces, heavy like there by the door, soft-jowled another arrogantly rises. Annoyance pushing, grimacing flesh. He's gone Val, didn't you know?

What do you mean? Breathing our breaths together, me fiddling with the dial.

To Stratford, he left an hour ago. What happened, he was....

What, what was he Felix, tell me what?

God I, you know, he was. Unhappy. Angry. What happened? Her silence, palpable regret: her pause, I cannot tell her, he's gone down to hunt for a job and....

We had a terrible. Misunderstanding, no it wasn't, not a misunderstanding: falling away, a terrible fight. And he's gone? Yes and to marry Susan but I cannot. I. No....

Yeah, but he'll be back, you can be....

No! Sharply, crying abrupt in my ear. He won't, not to me he won't. I know. Silence again and then. I know. Her voice retreating from the phone and to herself: I think I'll get drunk.

C'mon, c'mon Val, I'm sure. But that scene, his anger there: righteous in the kitchen drinking, stamping violent and you know, she hasn't got a serious goddamn bone in her body, you know that? I mean, gimme a cigarette, let me pinch another cigarette. She's got such stupid ideas, I mean, shit! Later with convincing anger, crumbled patterns of his talk, he said, I'm going down to marry Susan. Find a job to live how I know I am. Val, can I do anything Val?

Ha-ha. No. Ha-ha, this is too much, there's nothing I can do, nothing: burning behind, this pressing heat and shifting, agreeable, always polite as my mother. But blank, my smile couldn't be emptier, yet still. "Wide paths and beautifully spacious." She goes on and bloody. "Areas on either side. The animals, they look so happy. All of them with. Mexico has such a wonderful climate, don't you think, have you ever been to Mexico?" Intently focussing, searching my eyes. "Well really you should go down there some time. The poverty's dreadful of course, but its a wonderful experience and anyway, I do think, I've always thought how happy the poor are there, you know what I mean? How much they love their animals and that makes it easier to bear, doesn't it? You'd certainly never guess from the zoo that there are poor people, its got." Insidiously shaking her head as we're rubbed together, she rests her hand on my arm. "An artificial mountain for goats and for the birds, why there's the biggest cage you've ever seen its really huge, so they can fly and believe. I've always thought maybe they believe they're still free. That would be nice wouldn't it. In the middle of all this, right in the middle, and this is what I wanted to tell you, this is why I specially looked for a little deformed dog like Queenie. Bless her heart. Because right in the centre of all this, the fountains and the peacocks running loose, we came on a crowd, a really kind of ghastly, scruffy crowd of peasants and beggars you know. The kind that stare at you like animals and ask for money: they were gathered at a smaller compound, so many they blocked our path and there were peanut shells all over the sidewalk. They were all laughing and pointing at whatever it was; some children, little children of the street you know, were throwing stones. We didn't want to get too close, seeing how it is down there, you have to be careful, but they noticed us and started calling, Lady Lady, looksee look and when they parted I saw it was a water buffalo or something and it had five legs." What is she saying Christ what is she going to say? Horrible laughter gargling in my throat so I can stare, for a moment staring in her eyes. "That's right, five legs. Hanging useless from its right shoulder, the extra one was terribly ugly, it was so sad. All the bones were elongated, unusually long you know, so the toes, or whatever they are looked like bony fingers." Raising her hand from my arm again, abstractly she gazes and clutches at the air. "It was just awful, the poor poor thing and I was so embarassed because they'd all turned to watch except one filthy little boy who was trying to throw a stone that was too big. I knew, I just knew that I was going to cry or something, so we pushed through and all the rest of the day I could see that poor animal's suffering face and its. Leg. I realized then and there there must be hundreds of just such unfortunate animals born that never find a loving home and I vowed, I promised myself that I'd try in my own small way to do something about it." Smiling, bravely smiling, searching in her purse to wipe the corner of her eye. "That's why I got Queenie. I'm looking now, now I hope to find a deformed cat, but do you know." Firm disapproval rising in her voice as she taps my chest. "They destroy most of the pitiful things at birth. So I'm having a terrible time." Transfixed and yes I think, that's a great. Idea, reasonable and humane idea. Destroy, yes at once, des.... Oh Jesus, this is becoming, she's too moist, her mouth. Destroy them, that's what I. Touching my arm again, so insistent at my sleeve, she turns to. Returning anxious, they thread and balance, pushing to her side. "There you are Martin, there you are." Is that pressure on my arm, on purpose? "We've been having a nice little, a talk and I think, I do believe." It is, dear God and what's she, sudden tremor from my gut, she saying, going to say? "He's beginning to remember me. Aren't you." How can she, can I answer, staring what! "Isn't that nice?"

"Oh Frieda, no! You've not been, surely you haven't." Wildly at them staring, could I? Maybe I could, just; excuse me, excuse, you see, I'm overwhelmed yes, under this, inexcusable this tension and my life.... He's on my side, is so unhappy and people, you see, they always: my uncertainty, sucking it into their hearts for fun, the bastards every....

"He is, he really is! You are, you're beginning to remember, aren't you?" Tugging from her hand to shrug, but glittering, God how cold those eyes and. How manymany Jesus times, the faces coaxing and this fluttering, my heart?

Elongated bones with toes dragging in the dust and peanut shells.

"Yes I. Actually." Shit, she's seen, like all the others, yes she has and I "Do believe Miss Smith is. Right, I've..." Brusquely as I try, he takes her arm; his glance for me, disdainful as they turn away.

"Come along, come, Frieda. We'll lose our seats." Her face calm as they, she open smiling at him from my rising voice.

"I have, she's right you see! Uhhm. My.... I generally, generally I'm. Preoccupied, when I walk. I don't usually, notice." Lofty, they move away with knowing eyes again, the secret smiles, again, a.... "The people around me, that's why. But I do, I recall this time I'm sure, quite sure that once and maybe. Twice, I've seen, I recog...." Jesus Christ the pushing strangers and these fucking tears as I pull out, lower my hand beseeching, God how does she know? What is it in my face, what invitation is there in my eyes?

And his eyes, you're kind young sir, kind as we picked our way, him unsteady on my arm: deeper green and spreading bruise in the shadow of his enviable, I'd really like a hat like that, to wear at university. A kindness that is all too lacking in the youth of today, a real concern like soldiers have when the chips are down. Whoops! Slipping badly, clutching once as the wind, the snow, but holding him, muttering careful whoa! Hold on there Elmer, that's the way as we pause in the marquee's lights, we're almost there. Weakly flashing, shadowless bulbs and all around us freezing rain. His eyes. Used to be and this'll surprise you, I was a major in the war. Self-conscious steadying, firmly planting his feet in greybrown slush as figures bundle by. You wouldn't know, looking at me now you'd hardly think. Sniffing in moisture, tearfully at veined nostrils and tentatively, thick fingers play, apologize. That I hold the Queen's commission, that I.... Shaping fingers clumsy on, jeez that's a nasty bruise! Wait, don't.... waitaminute please! I want to, tell you. Listen! The dampness in my shoes. A young officer sailing from Montreal. Can you imagine? Full of courage and a sense, we really had a sense in those days. Queen and Country, I was. Handsome, a fine young.... Snow blows about his shoulders, water from his broadbrimmed hat. Purposeful for this instant, the flesh of his jowls seems strong, but now before, I've never seen before my very eyes, his crumbling face, a thing like this; he turns with tears, uncertain columns down his nose and look at that, his fucking cheek! As if some spastic thing was trapped beneath the skin: it stares through his eyes. Face declined I take his arm. I can not meet, look anywhere except, to this hand unwilling at his elbow guiding, for we must. I can not stand too much of this!

C'mon, c'mon Elmer. Let's go. Major Workman, but he resists as his voice cascades, shattering out.... But but these people scornful figures come.

I was. I was a good soldier you believe, you believe me don't you? A good man, I didn't used to always. Headshaking dumbly, searching my face, I didn't used to always be like this you should have seen, oh young man I was young!

Yesyes with familiar panic, trying to, how can I get him moving for.... Please we must, I believe you, really I do. I can see but they're waiting in the restaurant and I must, I have to. Yes that's. Good. Thank God he's, beginning to shuffle, here we go out from under the marquee, yes that's. How keep on. One of his laces has come undone, poor bastard. Drunk driving at least. Poor bastard....

That's right, every summer and some winters too. Not to one of your cottages no, no sir I'd take, I had a canoe then, really a. Beautifully balanced and painted, red and green: I'd carry it, so easily then, from the baggage car to some.... We went together, at first we went a couple of times. My wife. But that was. Turning suddenly with frantic hands again, it didn't. You heard what she's like, it didn't work out! Terrible springing chaos what, does he mean what shall I do? Oppressive cold about us; falling before me, all his face drops away. It was, harsh awkward voice the war, it was the war you know, that's what did it....

Look why don't you just, that's the. Eagerly pressing his hand, why don't you get on a bus or something, I won't. You could be gone and nobody. Nobody was hurt, after all there was no one hurt you only rolled it over and I wouldn't tell, I. Can't, dragging him there, hating myself: the cells and a tattoo showing beneath that uniform's sleeve; perhaps its. Do you need? I have some, struggling at my coat, some money, I could give you....

But I'll always remember, do you know that? I'll remember what I was and that's a comfort. Don't you think? That's a real comfort in times like these. Puzzled at me for a moment, then turning, stepping out to lead me, struggling to keep up with his drifting voice. Maybe things will be good again. Some day.

Maybe, maybe! Submissive bastard, didn't have to: I wouldn't have, said I'd let him go and yet, his dreadful bruise again, he. Stared accusingly, yes for me as they prodded, eased him to the cells. Drunk driving. In stillness the bastard, the dirty bastard! Inflating panic, for I'm just. Like him no, yes! There's no avoiding, there's no. Him dreaming of the past, his memory's comfort as they. Bullshit! It is, I'm.... Stop chewing your thumb, bouncing here and chewing like.... His crutch, and on he drifts. I've got to settle down, settle or get out, I must assert become for I can't be simply, I can't go failing on like this he flunked me and the Anglo-Saxon jeez its almost lost completely lost I've....

Stragglers quickly through, relieved to be on time and look away, these nodding strangers. Driving with curtains drawn and the coffin, Christ I hope they don't. Open it when they get here, I hope they. See them shifting, impatient turning and from here, even from here their whisperings, sibilants rise.

How can Jesus, I act or. Be when ineffectual, I'm so soft; too often now this, drifting away until my body's left alone. Glaring so they'll notice, glancing only see, surely. The passionate staring mask! I try so hard, this phony, to find a way: a predictable self, any, a person for my. Always this same, the hopelessness!

Crumbling footprints: they fall with spreading brown, the dirty slush to water from the door: blunt nosed and seeping flood towards, I'll have to, my feet. Blurring susurration from the waiting room and as I, sudden! Man's hand along the pew: with spiderflexing fingers, seizing at her shoulder. Who are they there in the door, no sound? That hand caressing flesh beneath her coat.... Perhaps, the puddle at my feet, perhaps it'll pass right by, searching down the easiest way; perhaps I'm safe for the moment if I don't move.

To marry her, for chrissakes leave a woman like Val, such a woman. Sensuous, I just don't. Fatherly figure (a pall-bearer too?) surreptitiously, stealthy hand behind his back and down, digging at his ass? The cuff lifts above his shoe. Digging at his, ahah, I caught you! His whole leg trembles, scratch-scratch as glazed eyes flit, his vacant stare. Look away.

Makes me goddamn annoyed, that talk, what's the matter with your generation? Knife and fork clattering to his plate, resting on the table's edge for a moment his hands are clenched. The trouble, young man, with you is. Do you know what your trouble is? Pointing finger at my chest. You and your generation? Expanding tension as she bends her head, the thick black hair drawn tightly at her neck and rising our voices, accusing. You don't believe in anything, you hide behind our skirts because. You blame us for everything and won't accept any. That's your trouble and well. Well I'm sick of it....

Through shrouded streets among the trees, naked, dirty with this day the hearse is bringing: from every room the lives come breathing out, those faces at the glass and pigeons in the eaves.

Mechanical voices and the carousel, drifting in the summer and fading from the wind against my face until running, I remember the ferris wheel: against the sky it turned spasmodically and the cars swayed. Running closer to the town and closer, my past excitement awkward in the chest and vibrating then, alone in the cacophonous air, beneath the jerking wheel and conscious of harshregular, that rasping that I know from dreams. And then the silver trailer and, oh God, oh Christ, its....

SEE! SEE! SEE!
FOR THE FIRST TIME ANYWHERE
the
GIRL!
in the
IRON LUNG
INSTRUCTIONAL FASCINATING
Hear her breathe!

ONLY   Don't miss it!   Kiddies
50¢   25¢
ONLY

Patiently jostling figures, in the loudspeaker's terrible breath of the girl inside, lining to the door. She lives but she

cannot BREATHE, come-along-come-along, A MIRA-
CLE OF MODERN SCIENCE STEPUP, STEPUP! She
SMILES, see her smile and she WAVES AT YOU! You sir
and how about you come-along, we have to do everything
AND I mean EV—ER—EEE THING for her! Come-
along-step-up, come-along. Staring fastened (everything,
he has to....) fearful at their eager pushing, turning laughter; savage jaws, they're eating, wetly drinking and as
pressing, more with clutching money crowd about I.... All
this for half-a-dollar, lookit that, four bits to help the little
lady, come-along, and move right in. SHE WILL NEVER
GET OUT! They're here, through the town, the urgent
word and movement, "the hearse is here, they're here!!"

"Here it is, are you ready, is everyone...." Had to do
everything, was it real? Carefully, and what am I, pallbearers supposed to do carefully, through slush and water
spreading behind me now. Or did she, did they let her out,
stretching and bitter, how old? Politely nodding, each
other usher to the door. Into cold that's searching to the
skin, behind plump legs and delicate shoes: efficient double
doors are opened, snow already glistens on the gathered
curtains.

He would have wanted. Shit! That cheapness: would
have wanted you to, would have wanted you there beside
him Felix! Stupid goddamn blackmail on her terms, a
mother's. I'm his mother Felix so I know he would: you'll
come won't you, you'll help us? Curious faces in a passing
car; with ski-rack another, loaded like those rocket
launchers, shushing cars wetly as we wait and watch.
Gleaming metal rollers and while he's gliding it out, he
beckons solemnly, encouragingly he nods. "Alright fellahs.
He's waiting for you." Savagely, struck emotionally dumb
he's. What, in this day did I? Incredibly polished, what
kind of wood (bottom's cheaper, pine or something for the
profit) expensive looking wood and hardware, waiting for
chrissakes, waiting? Obedient crowding ahead, their
hands on the bars to pull, pulling and I must get in there at
the other end, it slides and now, the weight, you brace
against the door but. Nothing, they must have, its light. All
the weight. Unrhythmic joggle, awkward shuffling to the
steps and if I crouch a bit, just bend my legs, I'll miss the
weight. Up they go! Arrgh, its not so easy going up and it

wouldn't, you'd hate. To drop him or, shit! And what would it do to this organizing prick at our heels? Be almost worth it.... Slowly don't jar him, easy, whisperwhisper that's the way, now straight ahead, that's it. Mind the door, don't.... Step by step, the coffin swaying in the afternoon. Careful, as staggering slightly, hah! Feel our sudden concentration to correct, control the faltering, that's the. People do some times, they've been known to....

EEEK we're falling, have done it, look out for your? Quick so it won't break my goddamn legs or anything, dashing out from beneath with a crash at my heels, it. Look it. Jesus Christ its burst open! Tumbling down the stairs like a Laurel and Hardy piano, these passing cars in the street, they're full of open mouths, over, I'm overwhelmed, they explode in hysterical silence, they brake while. Sliding awkwardly, running. I'm away, that's the best thing, keep on going, yes sir! Wildly down the sidewalk with my stride and round the corner like a shot, gathering speed on this uncertain ground with the wind in my hair, for he tumbled most horribly out: he was lying beneath that fucking thing. He was. And he had no pants on!

Hissing. "Just a moment," and his handful of kleenex, rubbing at the glistening droplets, polishing. Renewing the shine. "There, that's better, not." Smiling from the back of their heads to me. "Not that the finish stains easily you understand, its ah, a first-rate box." Intimately, one to another and over his shoulder, red-lettered on the wall. Please do not throw confetti in the vestibule of the church. Thank you. "Its for the. You're not family are you? No, no I thought not. You've got to do things right for the immediate family." Leaning to tap my arm, shaking his head. "We don't want to carry him up that aisle among his friends, all these good people, with any imperfections, that wouldn't be very friendly would it?" Then rustling black and white the preacher past my arm; starched and he shaves the back of his neck, he pauses: surveying them waiting there and turning, his face is young, so young. "By the, I admire your beard, I really do. I hope you don't mind me saying, I'd really like to work on a beard like that." Jeez does he, really did he mean? Now clear as a bell, rising from him as we move.

"I am the resurrection and the life, saith the Lord."

Scrabbling, rising unevenly ahead on either side and turning faces pale and small beneath the ceiling's height. "He that believeth in me, though he were dead, yet shall he live: and whosoever liveth and." Changing to catch step, to stop our clumsy swaying gait. Left. And. Right. Lengthening this sad slow march of mine, left. With him inside and dead. Right. He's really inside, its hard to believe, he's. "Shall never die." Grotesquely past watching faces, furtive eyes because I've got his feet, they must be here beside my hand. Left, that's it; better, much better and right, we've got the cadence, got this rhythmic crawl, and we're only. Careful now, don't lose it, that's the way, lehp! Rye-yeh, lehp and sweating on the parade square's sun, they'd foam at this, oh brother. What's that? "Let not your heart be troubled? ye believe in God, believe also in me. In my Father's." Somewhere ahead, her cry: echoing hoarsely with young, his voice so, mingling in the air above our heads. Some faces dumb while others shift to see as, her voice rising, his words.... "I would have told you. I go to prepare a place for you." Uncertain flight, the curious wheeling of his words among her cries, she dominates; this sobbing, Jesus! I wish she'd, why I wish she'd, why does she indulge? Gripping, manfully, forcing shut my ears because the tears, once more this goddamn swelling, weakness, behind the eyes my goddamn....

Darling I'm so happy that you. On the window sill, her rings above the sink as she pauses with soap on her hands. You don't know how much it hurts me to see how far you've been from God. I pray, every night of my life I pray to Him, hoping He will guide you. Jewelled frames her glasses and the eyes, blue eyes magnified and watching as I. Quickly, finish this fucking plate and behind the cupboard's open door to put it in the rack. She can't see me here. And every day I ask Him to help you, you know that. You know I do?

Yes mother, I. That isn't, shit that isn't. The point, she doesn't, they never understand, so why do I bring it up? What makes me confess like this, argue and? They're all, they're good Catholics and intelligent, they're concerned Mom. They, well they don't just accept....

But that's the point Felix, Catholics have to. Shush, don't let your father! Busily turning, blandly washing with his footsteps from the pantry and I can't, they've learned to live together, but I.

What are you two gossiping about? Wanting to talk. He perches on the kitchen table but I can't look, disguise myself like this.

Oh just, Felix was telling me about his friends on the staff of the university. Rubbing the cloth, washing them clean. Have you told your father that some of your best friends are graduate students this year? And even young professors, turning briefly to him, some of them are professors. Aren't they dear? stiffly nodding, I have no life, I....

That's nice.

They sound very interesting to me. He was telling me how interesting they are. Resentment burning for the fake the avoidance and my: just not real, I'm not. Don't let your father, mother hear you talk like. Vigorously rubbing, drying.

I was telling Mom that I'm pretty interested in their. Pausing her stiff hands in the soap, her tightening mouth. In their Catholicism, its the first time. You know for the first time. Calmly, with calculation and I know, I think I know, I'm sure what. Brazen I'm doing.

"Know that my Redeemer liveth, and that he shall stand...." sobbing, will we never pass this snuffling, slowly step by step? Mounting fluidly before us now, beneath the colours and between the empty choir stalls and there's the. Juggling, but more smoothly up, the carpet really helps, it makes a difference and steady there, that's.

Only her not standing as we passed her body, crouched on the smothered sobbing and from above, his father's hand, pat-pat her shoulder, bewildered fingers playing with her hair. Shut up!

There's the stand and, lifting slightly, that's the way. Pausing on either side and cautiously, don't for heaven's! Uncertainly turning inwards, shifting with his nod, I guess. We are dismissed. We can, carefully to the steps and down in a bunch among, these waiting faces. Here, with grace and individual control, to where he motions Jesus! I wish she'd stop! Dear God I.... Empty pew and in. "To this world, and it is certain we can carry nothing out." Pushing along and should I, will they kneel and pray? To the end and turning formal with his voice. "The Lord gave, and the Lord hath taken away; blessed." They are, at his lead, folding to their elbows on the polished wood and shifting, for room. "Be the name of the Lord." I'll just sit, bend to demonstrate, acquiesce. Please dear God look after everybody and make her stop crying because he'd dead, that's all for chrissake, all this doesn't change and what's he got to say to her?

I did, I really was. Disguised with protests, yes but I wanted, I clutched their moral condescension, cried out loud, yes grasped and welcomed their paternal, I was afraid. Focused always to that night. Strung out like we were, and physically with drink, the music when suddenly, so hushed and reverentially, his voice: Beauty, such as this, without the strength and security of the sacraments, is too terrible for man to behold. Jesus Christ their mute agreement, their bond! Except for me. And the Mahler (last movement of the third?), silence but for Mahler and their yes, yes! Repeating and acknowledging, so true, it was terrible and set apart, my back against the wall, an emptiness that melancholy slowly filled....

But don't you, can't you see? Professors, they're professors and. I've had considerable contact you know, and I think, I'm not a fool. I've seen a lot of them. And they're intelligent. Sincere and serious Catholic thought and. Smoothly scathing as I dare. That's more than I'm accustomed to, but he's oblivious.

Look son, your mother's right, I agree with your mother. Slipping abruptly from the table to the counter, mixing a drink and why, how did I get involved? Last of the dinner plates dutifully into the cupboard and I'd like, but I won't ask, I'd like another. Drink. You just don't realize what you're getting into Felix, you don't.... The Catholic organization is, surely you know what that's like? Tasting, sucking at his glass and slyly: a highly organized business. Quickly slipping then, triumphantly. And where would your freedom be with them, eh? Snatching with venom, silver to be dried for how can I explain? That's the trouble with your generation....

For heaven's sake now Father! Turning, Jesus, moving to pour a bit of this whiskey and turning my back. My generation always, never me....

Darling don't think us....

Its true, certainly its true! You want everything your own way, you. Glittering behind me, her rings on the sill while its splashing amber into my glass. The Pope will be telling you what to do and all of the priests! And where would your precious freedom be then? Sharpness in my mouth and swallowing: I think I'll go out, I'll. Sipping again for the futility of this and what's it got to do with....

Don't think us unreasonable dear, I've. Always liked the high Church, the Anglicans, you know that; the ritual, but Felix.... Rome?

Now don't, don't go off half-cocked, your mother and I, we're naturally. Very pleased you, that you've begun to. Think about God. And all that, but....

The Catholics Felix! Then with intensity, predictable emotion so she dries her hands: Oh darling you mustn't! It's so wrong. Promise me you won't just accept what they say, that you'll think seriously!

That's right, be critical and don't do anything rash that you'll regret. Comforting voice for her and always, I have to prove, to mock them with. Probably just a stage, young men go through stages, I remember how many times.... And your professors seem impressive, they seem. That's the reason, it must be why I do it, for I know they'll fail. Well you know how teachers influence the young.

They shouldn't be allowed to do it, that's all. They shouldn't. Oh God Mother, neither of you, no they don't understand!

We're not saying you shouldn't see them, of course we're not. We're just asking you to be sensible about it. Not do anything rash. Always we're on the brink, the very edge and I've forced them, picked at their weakness with my bastardly....

They're everywhere, they've even taken over the Immigration; if you're not a Catholic you can hardly get in anymore. Why Rose Anderson, she's your Uncle Simon's sister's daughter. She married one of the Andersons from Winnipeg and she was at Immigration in Toronto and she said, she was trying to get an Irish girl you know, a maid because they're cheaper, and she said the office was full of Italians and Catholics of every kind.

Now mother, that's, oh brother, that's....

Doesn't it bother you? I was reading just the other day

that every computer is run by a Catholic! It's true Felix, doesn't it, but. "I held my tongue and spake nothing: I kept silence, yea, even from good words." Good grief the others have all: straightening, I'm the last, I am, in this row! Shifting, to avoid, yes, attention from their eyes; straightening ever so slowly, with confidence and maybe I'll even. Bending my head again as if to search, looking for something. Dropped, you see, hah! Wasn't, no I wasn't praying all that time, good god no, hah! Dreaming, just remembering vaguely. "My heart hot within me, and while I was thus musing." Random memories, that's all. Oh yes, in churches, like this, remember others, brief misleading times? Huh. Silence made only more desperate and ashamed, until....

Actually, since I haven't been able to differentiate between a feeling of social (them nodding there with me against this wall) and spiritual envy, I've not placed too much importance on the event

Indifference now, or even stronger yes, for once we, one time we laughed at my suggestion, wild and forcing, Martin hey, let's laugh at God! HA-HA!

At God, let's laugh! Ho-ho-ho?

Yes, let's you know. Laugh. Laughter, you know, ha-ha. HA-HA-HA! Hoo-hoo, hee!

Hoh-hoh, hoh-hee-hee, HA-HA-HA-HA! GAWD! OH HAWHAWHAW! HA—HEE—HAW!

Hee-hee-hee-hee-heeee-haaaaw! Harsh self-conscious barricade: an overlapping sound, accusing and my eyes, are they bright, do they stare like his? AT GAWD! HA, ho-ho. Guilt twinging and more difficult, ha. They, faces from shadow, watch silent and in the kitchen door is Max. Ho, at God. HOH.... His squinting face, the troubled stance and grimacing from a cigarette. Vast silence, their faces and was he right: Even if He doesn't exist, do we still have to believe?

By expense, they try to make it less ugly but still it sits, unnaturally squat and cumbersome; pretentious hardware and a deep-down shine that lasts and. Immutably horizontal, heavy where all else architecturally strives, rising around him symbolic where faded, the air is full of regimental colours and the glorious dead. Dead he's dead. That's all! What more can we know, what have I ever seen but words?

He's dead. Gone, that's all and no more.

> Martin Baillie's dead and gone
> Boom tiddyboomboom, boomboom
> But his memoree lingers on
> Boom tiddyboom....
> BOOM—BOOM

Trying to imagine what he looks like. Eyes closed, for sure, the artificial flesh prepared packaged for worms. Blind worms for empty eyes. Folded probably, across his, breast they call it on the dead, and tallow white the puffy fingered; is it still a it doesn't work like a hand? Flexing, long fingered closing on my knee with, these dirty nails again, I can't seem to. That's a hand and so is this other one reaching into my pocket, because they work, they wrinkle amazingly in the palm and stretch as I wish. With this split match between my knees, digging under the nails, cleaning and smearing the dirt between thumb and finger.

Oh Felix, Felix she's superb! God I could die, she's so superb, I'm telling you, I lay with my face on her thigh and stared up over her belly, and she has a magnificent belly, oh God she has this long lean belly and her breasts, they're like pigeons Felix, pigeons.... No! Not.... Beautiful birds, that's it! Jesusjesusjesus. Screwing up his eyes and rubbing at his scalp, teeth clenched and grinning ecstatically, while a stranger beside him, vicarious I watch his cupping hands towards remembered breasts. I could write songs he bellowed for each of these ggrraaowwhll! And an epic, a whole screaming epic for that stuff between her legs. Awwrrowgghoboyoboy! Throwing himself, rolling back and twitching on his bed, kicking his feet and jumping. Superb, absofuckinglutely superb! Struggling to sit crosslegged and this, pause. And you know something Felix, you know I like her? I really do. Staring back in wonder, his open face.

C'mon Martin, for God's sake, how many....

No this time its different! So help me. Convinced, dreamlike, but how many times, how many promises? I'd die, if I lost her now I really think I'd die. How many, yes, with only Stratford. Susan for his guilt.

Why? Into innocent, his unseeing eyes. Why then, for

chrissake Martin, I don't understand; why do you go on? Tension, sudden in his body. Seeing Susan. Abruptly springing from the bed and to his feet, angrily: the familiar agitation as he strides, to the bureau and his cigarettes, but push on, I'll.... Every weekend, almost every, eh? Deep eyes retreating as he drags, gasping he inhales and blows grey smoke, now breathing out the match. I mean you don't even, you don't like going back to Stratford, you know: How can you....

Don't talk about it, don't. His voice down, angry introspection for a moment. She's inescapable. Shrugging turn to the window where the shaking leaves, green, they stroke the sill and whisper. You think I want to go back there? You know I don't, I want to get the hell out, I want! His face again. God Felix, you know.... I want! I want and want his desperation and and the whimpering leaves. She won't though, she'd never take a chance. Vague hand rubbing in his hair, abstracted hand alone. And that's why Val, she's so lovely; she'd go to Europe, we've talked about it and she says a writer's got to live, he's just. Got to, you know. Experience things, to sing. To laugh. To fucking dream, look! Let me show you. Hands thrusting under the mattress, reappearing with his journal: opening as he sits, spreading it upon his knees. He reads: *To write one line, a man ought to see many cities, people and things; he must learn to know animals and the way of birds in the air, and how little....* a rendering for chrissake! He speaks as though he doesn't read: upon the page, his fingertips and really he does, I never knew! He wants to write, everybody for Christ's sake, we've talked but I never...*to think back the way to unknown places...and to partings long foreseen, to days of childhood...and to parents...to days on the sea....*

"For I am a stranger...." Indeed and, we're strangers with these partings long foreseen: and failure. "O spare me a little, that I may recover my strength: before I go hence, and be no more seen." For once and finally in the dark I saw, so many volumes in her empty flat behind Victoria Station, and the cold. (I never knew she liked it so, I never....) "Glory be to the Father, and to the Son: and to the Holy...." Incantation, my automatic lips, remembering, remembering shame because I'd assumed, presumed and all the while she must have read so privately from me.

Uncertain amens scatter about me, fading behind: awakened, I was, by an old man's singing voice. Dancing from outside the pub in the street below, rising against the rain, a lonely voice to this window and her empty room. Those recent antiseptic halls and the sound of starch in her walk, her creaking shoes. You must stop coming down to see me, we're wasting our time! Past official doctors and rigidity, we stalked, we two to the street. Felix. You can use the flat this last time, but you'll have to be gone by Sunday at five. That's when Ellen gets off duty and you know what she'd say....

Won't I see you at all?

No, I'm. Peter's picking me up right after work and we're. Oh Felix! We can't go on and on. Fine rain and occasional hissing tires to the bridge. Lying here, sixteen hours and eighteen rides from Edinburgh and she's really gone! Harsh shrouded by dusk and the clinging sky, it chants to the wine, the accordion sound. Nan, oh Nan this time's the end and rolling to my side, struggling beneath her blankets here for warmth, I see again the bookcase and my egocentric bastard, how many, in how many ways, God have I known her at all?

Refuge and mountains: all for the body this geography of words, while really, the curious fact of his reversal, why. Did he come back to her, do I know? "Thou turnest man to destruction: again thou sayest...." in a manner of speaking, why? Pressure in the throat, don't.... Goddamn his voice, this ritual, oh shit! Be pretty silly, you don't want to go snuffling past, pushing to the aisle and out through their, no sir! "For a thousand years in thy sight are but as yesterday: seeing that is past as a watch in the night." His voice, his role, predictable along the path of self-effacing words and I don't. Raising my passive eyes along carved benches, screens and rising, now from his shoulders, searching assured in the quizzical air, it mingles with his words. I don't believe it anymore. No, did I ever? Even for a minute (last year, was it as long ago as that?) with Mahler and my willingness, surely.... Around me, the fair. Above me swaying cars and squeals: harsh-regular beneath the noise with jostling figures (she smiles, see her smile??) patiently, to the door's black shadow and her creaking breath. SHE WILL NEVER GET OUT. A miracle of modern...cut down, dried up, and withered. SHE WILL NEVER....

"For we consume away in thy displeasure: and are afraid at thy wrathful indignation."

...*and one must have memories of many nights of love* (his face upon her thigh, he said, about her belly God!) *no two alike.* Her magnificent, its enough to make me start again, her breasts like beautiful birds...*and the screams of women in childbed....*

"Thou hast set our misdeeds before thee: and our secret sins in the light of thy countenance."

...*one must have sat by the dying, one must have sat by the dead in a room with open windows....*

"For when thou art angry, all our days are gone: we bring our years to an end, as it were a tale that is told."

Do you know, bright-eyed to me from his journal, do you know who that is Felix, who?

Weak words, from fear, create these gods and explain our death: with his clear voice they reach in hope, in self-degrading. Bastards, fat who unctuously accept their death; it doesn't matter to their lives! "...and though men be so strong, that they come to fourscore years: yet is their strength then but labour and sorrow...." Surely you can't accept? You can't, it, life is....

Rilke, that's who! Rilke and he's right by Gawd, he's. Tenderly almost, closing the black book and turning, he pushed it back under the mattress. That's the wonderful, Felix Val's wonderful that way, she.... Stretching uncertainly back along his bed, his drifting voice. She wants me to move in with her, what do you think of that? She says. Reaching hands beneath his head, arms bent-elbowed into stubby wings. And I mean she's right, what the hell, why shouldn't I? Briefly, eyes to me shifting, blinking as he looks away. You tell me, eh! From the open window, night, the leaves by his head: clumsy wings and gentle voice of the trees upon the sill. You tell me what's the difference, I spend most of my time there anyway. And. Who's going to care anyway? No one, I mean. Nobody has to know, do they.... Curling suddenly to his side, with hands between his legs and knees bent to the chest. I'd like to. I really would. We get on so well. Together, we're very compatible. You know? Rising for one of his cigarettes, I....

Struggling slim and alone with her black hair falling down and I'd better, I'll have another. In my own kitchen for Christ's sake! At my own party.... Desperate gulping, stop that stop that, trapped I'm. Energetically huge, her shadow on the wall as she pulls with single purpose past the door. Muttering help me, for help; will someone help me with this christly thing! Oh dear oh dear, what can I? Trapped. Maybe I could.... Grunting, she's. Shame as she drags it, my mattress for chrissakes! Dragging it in the hall with helpers now, laughing they're into the living room and I'm so depressed, I feel. Do things just wear away: FELIX and I shrivel, too late, too late, I keep on dying. Felix and I will sleep in here tonight. Oh, awwhh goes my soul, oh in their formal cheers, their encomium. HOORAY FOR PAT! CLAPCLAP! HOORAY! He'll never get out.

Lighting it from his and puffing, deeply dragging; caught in the window's air, grey smoke between us gliding and his voice. We're going to Paris, did you know? Well. We are and I'm going to, teach or something. Eagerly towards me, bouncing, pointing with his hand. There are schools you know, high-schools and English teachers, teachers of English are.... Oh! Oh! Felix I want, I want. Rising to sit and reaching, stretching his arms with fingers splayed and strong; grinning, yellow teeth and grinning to the ceiling; funny bugger for I can't believe he'll do it, really go. We're going to do so much, Felix, we're going to break out, free ourselves and. Go, yes! Cracking his hands together, crack! Yes we are. Boy....

Down there at the end of the hall, yes she is. Through the sounds of them and their silence in the bedrooms and into the living room where she's stretched out on my mattress, lying there on the floor all ready I guess, and open for me while. Drinking away at this, clinking ice alone because.... Shouting out, she certainly shouted bloodywell out, Felix and I will sleep! Amber acid to my stomach now, my throat from drinking, how does she expect? A man's got some pride, you know, I. Jesus Christ what am I gonna do? Bottles, some half-empty, all around me on the table; bursting, air about the window frame behind me and they've all, either they've gone home or. Laughter rustling in the bedroom darkness (what are they doing are they doing it?) Zippo lighters snicking into flame and shut. On her back maybe, she's lying in there, how's she waiting? With slightly parted, her legs and smoking too I'll bet, her breasts. She has nice breasts.... I am not, afraid, that is not the . Pouring another, this drink and sipping. A bit, strong yes for this time of night and it'll be better for a splash of water, that's. Sitting again, and there's definitely at my back, a draught, a definite draught. Scared for fuck's sake? Crap. Absolute crap. But ha, I can't, how can I go in there to be swallowed, that terrible assurance? I can't, that's all. Felix. There is to it. Felix, she's calling, shsh, Fee-lix I hear her whisper, hoarsely down the hall, are you coming Fee-lix, shsh-shsh for goodness sakes! Bedroom door, awh the hall, you've done it now! Gulping at my drink and bored, look. Martin, I'll bet its. How do I appear? Above it all, that's it, as padding he comes, ruffled and I'm simply not interested that's all.

Felix oh. I thought. Squinting from the light at Felix, me among the bottles, cartons and my elbow suddenly in this creeping puddle, shit! His head inclined towards the front of the house, I thought. Impatiently brushing, angry at my sleeve for its uncomfortable, bloody. Secure now comes his ordinary voice. Pat's calling you, she's....

I know, I know for chrissakes. From my hands, kaleido-scopic lights: hands pressing briefly on my burning eyes. How must I look, dejected. So back leaning now, I'll bravely? Uggh, I wish she'd (and I mean it too, he cannot know how much), I wish she'd go away or....I'm not....

What's the matter, are you sick or something?

I don't. And this sounds pretty silly. I don't like her very much.

Christ Felix, boy oh. You mean you're not. Boy! What are you going to, tell her? Jee-sus, hissing through his yellow teeth, he turns for the bottle by the sink with eyes. You ah, better have another, eh? Returning to take my glass, his face as he pours, watching. Staring to the door. And you'd better think of something pretty good, because....

Felix, yoo-hoo, where are you? Fee-lix.

Listen to her, wow listen!

Ready or not, here I.... Louder and louder she's coming, her voice in the hall and where. Here I come! Desperate face, my searching about, where to hide? Under the, Christ no she'd. See for heaven's sake, grotesquely underneath the table while the window behind, I can hear, its far too cold. To rush outside and where would I go, at this hour? Footsteps, hers at the door and God! They're, yes they're. Bare, that's it, alright, that's enough! She has! She's taken off her shoes, her stocking and her.... There you are! Felix, I thought you were hiding on me.

Embarrassment and flushing, even now because she's, I guess she's become. Back there and grieving but I won't, won't look no sir because. Since that night, some kind of symbol for us, you and I; pervasive sickness as my voice returns from then, and I do not like to think about it, I cannot....

Nan's perfume on my mouth, my limbs caressed, caressing limbs and by my face her sleep-filled hair with growing tension, gentler still; all tremulous (the accordion much later) Nan, uncertainly muttering Nan, oh Felix and drawn to her, waking, warm, even with the sound of my blood from the hitchhiking cold, I welcomed her secret protests because....

Act, I can not, never get out. Of myself, I am. Afraid! No, I know this argument and shifting uncomfortably, for its automatic, still I'm sure. It isn't simply fear, it isn't for I can't presume, that's all, to let them force me, prove she has to, Nan, I know you are, believe you, yes.

And I wish I wasn't, I shouldn't be. Is that wrong, is it wrong of me Felix?

No, oh no Nan, no!

I want it to be you, so much I want you to, sometimes. This hand, our hands belong, it fits so well in. Sometimes I can hardly stand it, wanting you to....

I know, soothing into her luminous eyes and myself so close to tears. I know. Subdued voices, body strong along the body's length and her breath in my ear.

But I can't, I have to think, I. Pressed now into my throat, her face so soft the mouth. I don't know what to do!

Alright, its. Calm dulls at the edges of desire; after all-night waiting in the lights that passed beside the road, after the cold, after the damp outside, this image of rest on the mind. Repeating, its alright; I pat her shoulder, residual aching as I turn away and drowsy, so. Tired, who wouldn't after thirteen hours on the road, so. Sleepy, yes although her body's warmth, so, her thighs because there's nothing I can, really to say, there's. So. Can't find it in myself to force the change, that's all. But desire, how many many times, how many times?

Bare, absolutely and utterly naked but with, dirt, is that in the folds, the creases in between her toes for. Who paints their toenails anymore? White her reaching legs beneath the pleated skirt and busying, Martin's back at the sink; soft around her hips and clinging as she poses, muscles stretching in her calves. You're not hiding on me, are you Felix?

What me? Hiding ha. In the kitchen?

Grotesquely pouting, come along then: her voice and leer, she turns, I. What can I, don't want a scene with Martin motionless now, his fingers waiting on the counter by that drink. C'mon. With me and dutifully, following but what, Jeez what can I say? Flatly her walking feet away, and from bedrooms here and there on every side, they're listening; hey I could fire out the door! Down the stairs like a shot and out to the street, but. But. Its not that I. You understand, don't like you Pat, you. Its just that tonight I don't. Want you physically. You know, I. Won't do, it, no, no won't do. She wouldn't like that. I'm drunk, that's it! Impotent, look I'm staggering that's the thing and I have this terrible social disease, can hardly stand to touch it myself let alone....

Life's electronic breath as bumping, I ran with her growing sound in my chest, she'll never get...their faces after me, their eyes as I ran from that wheel and I must. If I'm ever going to write or. Anything, I must get out, I....

You've made me look like such a....

Strong feet, pale on the bottom as stretched she lies, dark sliced by this angle of light from the hall and expectant, she beckons for my drink and pats; intimate, hand imperious she draws me down. Come; lie here. You're such a funny boy, oh! Grimace tasting; dark mouth at my glass and reaching her body out to the table, forbidding she....

What are you doing with my drink?

Felix, its too strong darling, you've had enough. Black rope her hanging hair as she shifts, her folded legs so white, soft-eyed above me with the gash of her mouth. Silly boy, hiding out there in the kitchen.

I wasn't, honest I.... So lightly. Cross my heart I wasn't, honest. Drink's confusion. Resignation. Briefly her hair across my eyes, she lifts my face to the crook of her arm.

Silly baby drinking, hiding when Pat's got something better, so much better for you. Electric softness of her breast beside my mouth, so easyeasy, oh so aaawh! Gah-gah, gurgling pleasure, blinking, filling the world with her body's must, her. Nipple, where's the, aaawh in my busy mouth and hardly aware of there, her crooning voice, that's the babybaby, so much better for you. Aaaawh! Confident reaching through my body, hers, a moistening suction cup as moaning, back, she throws her head with tendons stretching white along the throat; strained and gasping and her loosening thighs, moaning Felix baby oh my.... Felix! Pushing, scrabbling in panic to my knees and crawling towards the door, scuttling, this maw and now her shrewish voice: Felix where are you, what's the matter baby, are you? Felix! Stumbling up from the dark and onto my feet, run run, that's the no! Walk, elaborate casual walk, tucking my shirt and away from her voice. Felix, where are you going baby, don't leave me Feeeeelicks! Feeeee-licks! Reversing, back down the hall, and into her cavernous eyes.

Shush-shshsh for. I'm sorry Pat I've changed. I mean I. Can't. I'm most terribly sorry but. Well.... Bright kitchen's light again, alone thank God he's gone. Pouring with these remarkably steady hands, gurgling, whoops! That's a pretty big. Water's cloudy bubbles in the glass as drinking, swallowswallow for she's making, that's a godawful noise she's making. SHUT UP! Oh dear oh dear, running as best I can with this drink (ice, should have some. Make it smoother some ice), running and back here before her angular, her figure in the sofa and she's rising, she's reaching, so quickly—quickly, I'll say! Do you have to be so goddamn unreasonable? Towering, my height impressive, do you? And Jesus, Jesus God she's, shuddering she subsides and cries.

You've made me look like, wet-injured her voice as she slumps. You've made me look like such a fool.

Pat shshsh, I...no I haven't, not so loud they'll.

Yes you have, youhaveyouhave!

Don't be silly Pat, I. Jesus what an unpredict! Shshsh, for heaven's....

What did I do. Rising and common, that's the. Boy this common voice of hers and I think I've. What did I ever do to you eh, what?

Nothing aah, nothing why, I mean. Drunk too much, I think I'd better leave her, go. I mean, that isn't. Surely that doesn't, it isn't the point!

It is, it is! You've got no respect for a girl at all. Figure accusing, bent shouldered she turns away to cry some more while I with the sound of Jesus! Her bawling, clutching shadows from the corners, I. With liquor acrid in the throat and to my stomach burning what. Can I ever....

Crunching, sound of my feet in the tire's ruts, leaping the wind, it glistens in the air with snow from the banks on either side, the light from street lamps; settling, it falls in circles to the frozen ground, while from here (how strange) I see his empty stumbling, arms deep thrust in pockets and that body, night alone and the crystal wind. Lost, my mind is from its poor machine, Pat wanted: I drift back farther, to empty winds on his face.

Gas lamps on the glistening stone as carefully in the rain and turning right to wander, slowly with music stirring in the air; past and lost in the empty street and right again to Picardy Square. Fingers in the steaming grease, a sixpence worth and rolling, this melancholy in my throat; twisted in doorways, figures passive after closing time. A legless veteran's eyes, his medals tinkling as he clatters by on little wheels; a peg in each hand, among the legs he pushes to the ankles of a blowsy leaning solitary woman at the wall. The rain. Crouching there below her bulk. Shouting a name to her head, he calls her crumpling, folding helpless to her knees and toppling with her hair, yellow in strands of water to the street. Rapidly now, awkward to her side with swivelling glances, bony as he thrusts inside her coat and bending. Opening his thin lips, bending with eager, hungrily he attacks, kisses attacking the flesh of her mouth, her throat, and as the encircling legs obscure, she stirs: I see the automatic arms reach up and fold about him, drawing down....

"And why stand we in jeopardy every hour?" Tried so

hard, I. "Protest by your...." Phoned the Red Cross, offering myself, I. "Die daily. And after the manner of men I have fought with beasts." Will go right now to Budapest, immediately to help. I must you see, surely please there's something more than folding faces to my voice, impatient with teacups on their desks. As a stretcher-bearer, anything. "If the dead are not raised, let us eat and drink for tomorrow we die." Eat, drink and be. "Not deceived, evil communications corrupt...." My hope, to Glasgow even, hitch-hiking I went but politely. Always no, thank you I'm sure, we have so many. But I have to! Don't you see, I. Closing faces thank you, I'm sure; returning stares from beside gas fires, its doctors we need and nurses. Qualified people, you understand. "I speak this to your shame," as back to the street from their damp cardigan smell, with you don't have. You haven't the qualifications to do anything over there. Cups on saucers firmly as they turn away. Do you, what can you do?

Descending police and struggling through their laughter, leave 'em alone, poor bugger he's never.... Taunting retreat from their clearing space. Leave 'em, c'mon for chrissakes! Coppers, aawh coppers. Leave him be! United now, faces turning to wait in the rain as more converging uniforms in pairs; they join their boots to shifting, one to the other foot ring and, a-hem! A-hem! Clearing his official voice, you two. Come along now can't, you can't be doing that down there. In a public place, come along now. Haven't you got a home?

Around the corner once I sat and watched one violent enter the room and shouting. SO YOU'RE AT YOUR MOTHER'S ARE YOU! Breaking sound of his fist, crushing the face with her lover staring up, at that brutal. Obedient, she gathers on her feet with streaming red blood to her dress and silent, we watch them to the street.

Hands at his back, her white hair clinging to the pavement as reaching now and bending the figures pull, trying to lift him, suddenly—clattering on rollerskate wheels, his little wagon skitters out to the gutter and from his struggling, half-a-body in their hands, this terrible howl. About my ears, from back around the corner in the rain muffled as off I walk, my hands deep-thrust and heavy, rising Arthur's Seat above me; heavy light, the rain about my eyes as I walk. "All flesh is not the same flesh; but there is one kind of flesh of men, another flesh of beasts, another of fishes, and another of birds. There are also celestial bodies, and bodies terrestrial...."

NO LADIES ALLOWED

Preoccupied from my tea and bun, to the blowing street. I'm sleepy. Tired and can hardly hear his howl as I pause, drop my face to this hand-protected flame and. Want a short time for a quid johnny?

What? Oh. No! To this weedy, wow this creature, thin-lipped smile and desperate to my eyes. No. Thank you, I'm....

Awh c'mon Yank.

No, nono, I'm. Anyway I'm a Canadian.

Well you'll give the lass a fag, anyway? So thin inside her belted trenchcoat. And she's cold, poor. Sharply belted to her hips and knowing eyes.... Fumbling, offering take one, take them. Bony hand, pathetic reaching hand and in the lamplight, knuckles chafed and red she knows, her body oh! Take them all take, but feet away, she's going; walking and her tiny waist. Couldn't, no I couldn't ugly thing disease I might. A terrible.... Disorderly turning, my back where she pauses there and I've never had, that's the sad. Vicious inhaling deeply to my lungs I've never had. A woman. This way johnny, here to my room, you have such beautiful eyes and I'm sorry I called you a Yank. There are so many. Here, that's right, I'm really a princess in disguise, I'm not. Shshsh, there that's the. Such beautiful eyes. Gently to me, her breasts, the room's so warm; together to her bed with shallow her breath, expectant while my hands in sureness grow about her thighs, her belly and I rise. I grow in strength in passion fuck I fuck I.... Don't, don't look for chrissakes, look or turn! Jeez, a terrible.... I'm, look I'm a fucking twenty fucking-one-year-old, a virgin! Write or anything, how can I? Can't, go on like this and on and....

"...sown in corruption; it is raised in incorruption: it is sown in dishonour, it is raised in glory it is sown in weakness; it is raised in power: it is sown a natural body; it is raised a spiritual body. There is a natural body, and there is a spiritual body. And so it is written, the first man Adam was made a living...." Beautifully balanced and painted, red and green, I had a canoe then, yes I. Carrying it, his body younger every summer, to some desolate pier. "...but that which is natural; and afterward that which is spiritual." Oh the looking back young sir, the looking back!

Bright air across the Saint John as I climbed among great girders pocked with rivets, up I'd leave the pebbled beach and rattling waters down below and further, twisting weedgrass, rolling in eddies there behind me by the shore as up, with up the bank beneath and steel to the crest I climb to see dark forests ragged into fields on the other side. Dizzying outward on the ties suspended, high in the wind above the water's distant sound until I can hear the sky thud down with echoes from the past and country. Running suddenly with warning rails in terror by my feet, running for the first time and scrambling beneath the shaking tracks, over the water swinging a moment by my arms and crouching here as screaming, tremendous the engine and it moves above my head with steam in clouds, vibration and the steam.... Below me, waters move against the prow and cold perhaps, a skimming motorboat with someone who waves to that small figure tightly pressed in the V of two red girders high above.

Young and solemn, very solemn public voice, reading the sound of words carefully, not to raise his face and see the coffin with stuck eyes tight, hooks and the chemistry of decay: but solemn emphasis repeats, thin hand balancing his voice from one. To the other. Corruption, putting on. Incorruption, mortal. Jesus, ritual this talk and hollow teetering! Tongue ahead as she turns her face, wet tongue along her lips and she searched into my eyes, yes for the sadly lurking animal there, she squeezed my arm and coaxed....

First her hand and assured between my legs; blown rain at the windows, glistening film on the street below to Holland Park with her hand to my heavy cock, her mouth in silence at my ear. Growing from passive, I'm going to shout. YEEOW! Hot in my, awkward hand inside her clothes, hot blood behind my eyes, although. We couldn't, could only. There's nowhere else, God help us all, there's nowhere else to go! Oh boy, I should have stayed in London that's the. Thing, I should have....

Back instead for the goddamn degree, back and now

correctly, oh! The jeezly M.A., oh, Jesus, I.... Anglo-Saxon almost gone and Crackell, bugger's failed me. Shit! Extension yes, he gave me, grudging an extension on the frigging thing and then. Without warning. Hello respectfully, hello, cautiously. Hugo? And turning from the rows of soup, his face from a shopping list.

Hi there Oswald. Staring for a moment from battered eyes. What's this about your moderns course?

What do you mean?

Well Crackell, Doctor Crackell's failed you on your essay. Gentle scrutiny and then, his sadness. Didn't, oh. Didn't you know, he hadn't told you? And I stood, boy I must have stood with my face hanging out.... "...Jesus Christ his only Son our Lord, Who was conceived by the Holy...." Know, used to anyway, most of the words but I don't, with them shuffling dumbly around, I can't say it anymore. I won't. "Was crucified, dead, and buried: He descended...." Ascended into heaven settled on the right hand of god the father almighty from whence he shall judge, I do, you know, I still know. His following voice and why, so young and how can they choose that kind of life? Skinny, beneath his skirts like scissors, pellucid shanks and limply hands at rest: thin-lipped devotion to another world, don't. Move your lips, don't even pretend! To reconcile, how could he, Val and Susan? Catholick, I remember. The spelling, how curious, CK.... Monday's desperation, every time he'd. Belly, oh God Felix her belly, her breasts like. Rising, his voice and leaves unfolding at the sill; each week consumed with memories, how many nights of love before the, guilt, his journey back each time to Susan, ancient mourning world. Kneeling at his nod, the prick, again the bodies down and bending as I sit, just. Drop my head a bit, respectfully. The words. Boom-tiddy-boom-boom: and pause. Boom. Boom.

FELIX 2

Turning their faces as we lurch back down the aisle and pass, feet shifting among the pews behind: shave neck leads us balancing, swaying above the floor among blooms, pellucid faces in row. Empty voices as we pass and bodies leaning for their coats and still he sways and leads, he draws us to the doors through uncles, Frieda leave him Frieda be and smile, but look! Away. From her ropelike hair, don't look. Past blindly despite, to the vestibule and pausing as he leans to see the shine, his bending knees. My beard, did he actually say? Forward crouching now he breathes a film and elbows work. Hovering there attentively, work on a beard like mine? Breathing again and rubbing where the shiny grain's like a mass of worms, then gathering back with folded arms to smile and sadly smile and smile. Please do not throw confetti. Plump hand pushing to hold the door as, into the swirling cold, the air we lurch to the steps and inch and stagger, slipping ahead as....

Tripping and lost him! We've dropped him again for chrissakes, shit in this swarm of. Dumped him again but its not my fault, this time its not. And rolling him bastards, clumsy out to sprawl downstairs and lie grotesque, quick with their single groan, quickly.... Bending and stuff, quick as they pressure in horror, around, these limbs and the terrible gaping mouth....

Funny how cold my feet get, damp. Dragging, clenching my toes to activate the blood; exhaling, with voices in the enclosed air. Grey hanging smoke and voices, pressure of driving snow about the car. With pennants shaking, one behind the other, cars and ahead the hearse: winding, a mechanical line beneath these staring houses winding and the trees, past figures in the snow.

Standing useless while they rolled him in, clamped the door; standing chilled, then turning and there. Crackell. Looking at me and his. What's he doi.ig, winking and. Why does he signal, he's grinning and nod, he's winking, at me? Peering about, he must mean. Staring back at his eyes, he must mean me! There's nobody else. Nodding again, slow teetering head as he turns and threads to, emerging Susan to her side.

"It is. I'm sure it is."

"Well, you never know, do you?"

"As soon as I saw him I...."

"Some people!"

"Said to myself, that's him alright."

"You'd think he'd be embarrassed."

"After all these years."

"Some people...."

"Coming back here as if he owned...."

"Just the kind of thing he'd do."

"What?"

"Hasn't changed, you can tell just by looking...."

"What'd he do?"

"Hasn't changed a bit."

"What...."

"Give people like that an education...."

"That's what I...."

"And they vomit all over the floor."

"No!"

"So I asked that nice Reverend Stackhouse."

"Yes?"

"And he said, that's him alright, that's him."

"Well. Vomiting! Ugh."

"Of course I knew it was. You don't forget a thing like that."

"I should say not."

Smooth grey and the other one brown, two mean voices from behind. Lean to the window, drifting back cold from the glass, and stare: winter mirrored lawns, the voices brown and grey while hissing, this heavy car, we pause. Matted coat with crouched above that steaming pile, its ugly body, stupid searching head; it turns, sniffs. Shit on the sidewalk behind. Forehead briefly, sharp on the glass and focussing cold while. He is so, pompous son of a bitch!

Only this morning, it. Funny. It seems like weeks ago, that car and the wheel. Why the hell didn't he stop?

"They say he even used to...." Heard so much about. You'll like. Crackell, my God yes he's marvellous, you know? He'd ah, have his graduate seminars. In the tavern for chrissakes,! Before he went away. They sit around and. Wow, he's terrific, really a. Really a civilized guy, I. Must. Bored hired face as he drives and beyond, deserted swings in the park and the mist: abstracted, chewing mouth and eyes, beneath the plastic visor, straight ahead. I must, settle down, I've got. To work and. Three hours minimum a night, from five to eight or. Maybe even four to eight every day except Saturday. That's the thing. Maybe he'll let me write a test, exam to make up, maybe another chance he'll.... Red and yellow frames beyond his face; gusting mist around slides and the climbing bars, funny. Thing, really. Parents. Absurdly crowding to the elevated ring, that pack of scrambling boys for faces, parents laughing below: hands adrift in the heavy gloves, thin-armed like monkeys and my smile uncertain for her, there she is. Her tilted face and talking for a minute, falling the slope away behind her to the lake, to white waves brushed with air. Here, gruff voice and Oswald, here; big hands, the cloth on my face, can you see? Oswald, stand still! Can you see?

I see nothing. And nothing inside, withdrawn inside these gloves.

Can you see?

No sir.

Well here, stand over here. My shoulders in his hands, directed. Thumbs in my shoulderblades. Now parents, all you mothers and fathers: this as you know is the camp's annual Blind Boxing Frolic haw. When I blow this whistle the kiddies will start swinging haw. Heavy belly nudging me, his big voice ragged in the clearing. Keep your eyes haw peeled for any young brown bombers haw! Now. Adult laughter in the leaves. Are you ready boys? Bumping words against me with his stomach, can any of you see? No. Are you sure? Lifting his hands. We wouldn't want to spoil it, would we. Drifting, as he talks. Well then. Ready. Steady. Whistle and the sudden whack on my head, another and wildly trying, stiff arm swinging out to thump and elbows, blindly skinny arms tangled. I with chest in

heaving bodies, thump and.... That's the haawh-haaawh
way, hit out hit out, smash oh! Heugh, choking laughter
heugh-heugh! dumbly, blows in sobs and heaving, desperate breath, the laughter, laughter and more contact as I
rush through arms and sobbing, push to...Oswald what,
what are you doing? His hand across his runny mouth as
stooping, he's into the ring. Put that on again, you can't!
Around me sightless figures paused and I stood in those
faces, crying I. Crying I don't want. To play.

Why did he signal to me? He did, extravagantly nod,
winking some secret between us; there was nobody else I'm
sure and yet. Vague distance, always his reserve for me
especially and his critical eyes, we don't get along, why did
he signal? My temple cool on the glass. He went and took
her arm, he stood beside. And I didn't look back. Funny.
Maybe if I. Settle down and work, must. Finish what you
start Felix, first things first and when you've got a. Tightening smile and calculating eyes. Look son you must accept
responsibility, you can't. You never finish anything, you
just drift along. And frankly that's what worries us, your
mother and me; we. You can't go on and on in life just
quitting what you're tired of.

But I'm looking, I....

Looking! My God Felix, you're.

There's nothing, what's.

Do you realize, my God you're almost a man!

I don't like it, that's all, oh. You don't understand.

I understand that you've already failed a year. I understand that. And I know you're not going to. You make me
so bloody angry!

Well I'm. Sorry, but that's. The way it is.

Don't you, don't take that tone with me young man.

What am I supposed to do?

Its those friends of yours.

Look father I don't want....

No good for you, no good at all.

They're my friends.

Bums, that's what they are bums....

They're my friends and just because they're different.

Different, different! Oh. Hah! Voices harshly and into
the kitchen, she'll be leaning there and is that the thanks I
get? Spend every afternoon cooking a lovely dinner and

what thanks do I get? Bickering; every night, every single dinner spoiled by your. Oh Felix it makes me so sad.

Martin Baillie's dead and gone. Boom-tiddy. And outside, mist along the earth. Straightening abruptly, takes control of searching this, crawly things inside my chest, if only. Hot in pressure, hand to my forehead rubbing, pressing against the bone and I straighten, easily cross my legs. There's only a couple of months, if I could only work! Boom-boom, the engine's strength and my random thoughts. Boom. Boom for chrissakes settle down the voices, boom, and watching eyes and.... "Surely the point."

Boom.

What?

Did you say something?

Young man did you?

Did you say doom?

Boom-boom

Oh. I see. Boom.

Boom, they wait condemning. Boom. I told you so, another. Boom. Irresponsibility, up there at Western what, God knows, goes on? Free love, I guess, just. Oh I've read the books and heard. A thing or two. Revolting!

"Small wonder Martin came down every weekend."

"So eager, he was so."

"If they're all like that."

"He was a good boy, Martin." Boom-boom.

"God rest his...."

"Always so respectful."

"A prize in Susan too."

"That girl is...."

"A princess."

Princess shit, a bloodsucker that's what. Coaxing him with guilt (and Crackell, why, her arm). There! Behind that wall? Amazing thing, that's the. Because he decided. Going down to marry Susan.

You're kidding!

No. I've decided.

But Jesus Martin, what about Val, I thought....

Its all decided. Refrigerator door as he comes back to sit. There's no future in it.

But what about. Europe and. Boy, I was sure, I was positive you'd....

Felix! Staring. What would I do over there?

Write, well weren't you.... Write or something, don't you want to....

God Felix I've never done anything, not a fucking thing! Harsh hands press his scalp and rub, then smack the table's top and bottles rattling as I rise, retreat for another beer. Its all crap! Crap! Slumping body down. And you know he's right!

Who? Avoiding his gaze as I pour. Who's right?

The Whip. Pausing. My father. He says if I'm going to write, he says I can do it here. Harsh rubbing hands again. And Felix, I know I can teach, I do know that! That's something I'm sure of.

But Martin, for chrissakes, that isn't....

She's a nice girl Susan, really a nice girl. You don't know her like I do, she's. Look I've known her, she was really good to me when I had that.... Turning away, increasing the sound. I had a skin thing, a. She really was! Drinking purposefully. She is, she's a fine girl yes, the Whip likes her. Hah! Slipping, whoops, skidding sideways down as we turn, between grey stone, cemetery gates in muffled snow; turning down into mist and trees, their icy prongs. Vague in hollows as we glide, evergreens sagging white and black above the tombstone mounds. He left, just half an hour later he was gone on the evening bus and boom-boom here. I am.

Where?

Hung up. Between.

Closing one by one, the line to a halt; carefully out, watch the jeezly! Snow in my shoes, Christ. Along the fender here, picking my way and just enough, there's room between this chrome as slipping through and stamping feet. Lousy winter, lousy fucking soaker for chrissakes! Stamping and jumping. Shit. Don't want to but, I must. Already gathered there by oh, more steps, the double opening doors so forward, don't want to yes, but forward. Has to be, can't. Quick, turn and dashing, watch these new cars at the gate, staggering briefly, then off like a rabbit and breaking new ground. Off their road and away through the snow, not a track ahead and up this hill, the voices down below. Hah! A moose, thigh-deep and lurching, proud, that's it a moose! Piss on soakers, their cries behind. Hey (what's his name?), hey you! Grunting up to these trees at the top, up up and away! I'm almost there. Hey Oswald. Come back back, hey! We can't carry him all by ourselves, come back! Nimbly now on the crest and among the pines, turning strong my proud figure, above; and bunching down there by the road, the grasping hands, I pause. For breath, deep breath and shaking my head, turn away. Now trotting easily upon the frozen crust, between the stones I skim and hear their trailing voices out behind and to hell. With them, I'll show. Through branches pursued by branches, released from heavy snow, sighing they rise behind me as I run, falter, tire. Do I tire? And where's a path for, is there, must be one for the goddman snow impedes me now and I've done it yes, can't stop running for.... Gasping for air just ahead of their dog-like cries with snow about my legs like lead, my chest for breath and cries, they've got me, staring back to see dark shapes that reach oh Christ they've....

Show 'em, I could.

So? Wide-eyed and staring echoes; so? Anything's better than. His coffin. Bracing, shifting to sway with its weight, their steps more confident and surely to the steps. Anything's better than this, he might have. Maybe he'd....

Shit as they nip at the heels, just as their laughter reaches to haul me down, just then the surface, it holds! I'm on top of I dart on ahead, my stride and lean this disappearing figure in the white. Waist-deep behind in snow, first time, the voice turns back upon itself confused.

Concentrate that's, careful to the door. What's this, another chapel, what? Sadly smiling man, he's brushing, at my feet for Christ sake! Do we have to do it again? A broom, bristles about the ankles, "That's it. Don't want to be traipsing in there with mucky feet, do we?" Please don't throw. Undertaker's understrapper while flapping black, another leans intently, polished in streaks, the drops; a third, its cold with briskly hands is staring at my beard. His opening mouth is pink. Why can't we just bury him?

"O.K. fellahs, just put her down over there." One hand gestures to the corner, darts back to the other twitching on his vest. "On the machine." Rubrub the dry skin rustling as we lurch again in their voices. "Care-ful!" Quickly all around. "Careful fellahs."

"Oh"

"Careful."

Bells and flowrets against the purple cloth; lilies and things, all white and pink and tight along the wall, their cloying stench about us (straps and chrome below me) and someone's grunting, we bend and release, what's that? Out from the others, a fucking great leafy wreath. HE WAS A GOOD BOY. Good Jesus. No! And bent-winged and beady-eyed, a bird, its *stuffed*, a great stuffed goddamn bird stuck on there grimly Jesus, winking right at me, he's. Frieda, it must. A GOOD BOY, why. At me, I'm sure his crazy wink and he's nodding, he did.... Is this day ever going to stop? Back with the others into the crowd that's spreading, feet scraping, coughing, I'd better. Desperate on the green, the jagged artificial leaves, you bird, your glinting eye at me: much better than joining the fucking hunt, you're right! It is much better to be hunted than to join in the chase. Amen, it is much. But I'd better. Sidle in here from public view, no use. Undue to myself (what's his name?) and still they're cramming themselves, more and more as the dirty slush to pools on the floor. Bunching forward, teetering from foot to foot and there, threading in a tear stained line among hands that reach to pat, to touch with dumb gloves as they go. "Poor Susan, poor thing."

"Who's that with her?"

"I don't know, poor soul."

"He's not from...."

"Oh that!"

"Yes...."

"He's from the university. Or something."

Right in there alright, he's certainly moved right in there as they shuffle; families, Susan and Crackell, what the hell's he up to? Straightening his tie as he rocks and vaguely stares at the flowers along the wall. "Its silly to say this I know, but. He looks, Martin would have looked like that, don't you think: If he...."

"God rest him."

Turning, the smiling bastard to her face; responding flicker, she leans as more come between. I can't see them any longer, so many now along the other walls and, bulging. Wet clothes, damp smell and heavy of the cloth. With dying flowers in the air. Shifting, "excuse me," now some whining kid, pushing "excuse me" to see him there and shit! That tongue, her. Eyes and darting tongue.

"Hullo again." And leering eyes, what hiding me? In the kitchen, yes oh. God her pushy hands, mouth all wet and opening, fingers on my arm; I must excuse me, get but her hand restrains. "Aren't you tired from carrying that heavy thing?" Eyes and mouth enfolding, breath and eyes, my arm. "We girls don't know so tell me. Tell me, what's it like?"

"Oh. Oh. Not so bad you know, not bad there were lots of us see and...." Faces all around, my idiot words and sailing, Jesus preacher to the coffin's side I'm saved. "Excuse me," finger to my lips I nod ahead and quickly disengage. "We'll have to...." Again, the breaking wail of that bastardly child, will someone. Take the thing outside! Will someone. Why? Poor kid, now darting face ahead to see, the preacher, what. So calm will he, can he do? Swivelling desperation and my flopping stomach, flipflop its her eyes, her crippled animals for chrissakes I am not! I simply turn away; calmly survey the shoulders, heads in front, I can hardly see flipflop, her shape beside me, leaning? To that lifted face, focus on his nose with open nostrils, placid jowls and. Doesn't he shave? She leans and shifts, I move. Shuffling behind us, stragglers from the door and. What am I going to do with this leaning, she's almost rubbing woman! Get out I, awkward, excuse and pushing desperate from her, what, oh dear to the front and running....

Movement so I stop, we stare. I'd sure like to work on a beard like that. Plump face with narrowing eyes, I surely would. Sudden odour, sickly of the flowers at his feet. And I look away! This weakness, this. Preacher again, his eyes, those fragile hands with fingers shining on the page, then carefully. Back to the undertaker, he bends, white-cuffed he's bending, fat hands tug at the nylon grass; hissing, it slides and bunching to the chrome, it.... "Man that is born of woman." Rising embarrassed with his voice, backing to the wall and nodding, agreement yes and. Here we go again. "Is full of misery. He cometh up, and is cut down, like a flower; he fleeth as it were a shadow, and never...." Composed and solemn, this bored, my beard for chrissakes! In the midst of life. "We are in death: of whom may we seek for succour...." In the midst of life we are in death how true, oh right in the middle, now for instance. Voice pleading O Lord O: rising chilled air from, our boots and bodies twisting in their clothes. In the midst. Thrill of familiar words, the cliches' strength. For the. Value of ritual's in the order, yes. Remember that, the value of the ritual is in the order it brings. Another epigram, hah. God is order, and our fear personified. "O Lord God most holy, O Lord most mighty, O holy and most merciful Saviour, deliver us not into the bitter pains of etenal death."

"Thou knowest, Lord, the secrets of our hearts; shut not thy merciful ears...." Propitiation's whine. Not me, no sir, I.... Don't need, no! these pleadings, need his petty life! Or words. "...spare us, Lord most holy, O" Jesus moaning, a terrible! His mother's face collapsing and crumpled to her knees again, she. "God most mighty, O holy and merciful...." Shudders, horrible shudders and her animal tears. "...Saviour, thou most worthy Judge eternal..." studied voice word by word as the father, son of a bitch, poor. "...suffer...us...not, at our last...." Leaning sideways to her, white knuckled on her shoulder; staring slack-mouthed, turning and shaking his head as his face peers away in layers....

Eyes protective, thank you back to the mourners, crowded; unwilling audience at her, they stir embarrassed while my ears, despite me, goddamn ears have isolated, stop! They register every fucking note will she stop and Max. His profile, hurt by her grief he whispers to her and instinctive reaches. Gentle Max. I'm growing from you, I...Pat! Beside him, right hand absent through her hair, my flushing sudden. Large pale hand, the sickness rising for. You've made me look like such a.... No, no! Just a symbol, some kind of.... Painful back to her voice on the floor, then Max again, I'm.

"Forasmuch as it hath pleased Almighty God of his great mercy to take...." Hulking forward with upside-down a begging bowl his undertaker's hat at his back "...the soul of our dear brother here departed: we therefore commit...." His body to the boomalay deep, what? Angle of the hat, its changing, his hand edging out. "...earth to earth, ashes to ashes...." Earth, falling in lumps with sweat, Jesus! you can't bury a man indoors, from a living hand it slides and pointed there, his shoe at the switch. Poking

impatient, poking and then with a jerk and a gentle hum.
"...dust to dust; in sure and certain hope of the Resurrection...." Huummmmm, the coffin descending into that
hole in the floor, creaking with straps and groaning noise.
His mother's voice and the patent leather's spidery cracks,
tiny in his shoes on that stupid goddamn grass. Christ. If an
ant stumbled out of there, lost he'd squash it flat, he really
would. Get out of my grass. Squish! Rubbing fingers his
hand retreats, clutching to the hat; smoothly he presses
again at the switch, but. Huummm. Machine obvious; he
steps again and kicks with dignity his polished toe and
faster kicks, he kicks and kicks, now teetering on his other
leg and waving, furiously smashes and jumps, the sweat is
bursting from his dome! Huuummm, insistent hum while
straps alive! What's going on down there? Bending self-
conscious, belly unwilling as flustered he yanks the lever,
pushes. And it stops. Hooray! Sickly smiling, vaguely panting to himself and grunting, he straightens and backs to the
wall, mopping his forehead as he goes: pugnacious eyes
search the floor for ants as he subsides. I'd sure like to
work.... "Lord have mercy upon us."

"Christ, have." Unwilling voices, have mercy, "Mercy
upon us. Mercy," mumbling all around.

"Lord, have mercy upon us." Clearly spoken, then
enquiring, pause for us. "Our Father." Who art in. Growing stronger, background to his, this whispering about my
ears. Thy Kingdom but I will not say, I. Stifled sound,
because I don't. Anymore, this use of our fear. Felix
Oswald, head bent, awkward in this crowd, a hypocrite
among, lifting his head clear-eyed above them to. Crackell's eyes, oh hold it! I glare, he twists away, instinctively
lowering his head. A-ha, ho-ho! I've won! Alright, who else
now, try to stare me, looking around who else? These
bodies in prayer around me: bowed, yes properly with lips
beneath their faces, stirring lips and mumbled. Strange,
such foreign lives, their tacit. Breathing together, words
and sighs about me here and I don't. Belong, but he turned
away, he really.... Upwards, above this awful mumble,
many times and in how many. Does it always come to....
How are you fixed for blades? Hands that spreading,
drunken laughter in the corners; nasal and how are you
fixed they taunting pressed around me for a. Fight. Again

rising, again uncertain, how many times? Even in the sound of his reading, anger and trembling even now, among these lousy people.

Selfish extravaganza, that's all, my mattress for chrissakes! Dragging it, laughing for everyone to see, and me? Just prey, could of been anyone, a convenient object. Rituals of fear. Black hair, blue with moisture there at ease on her shoulders and confident scorn. Max, she. Dominates, I mean a symbol now, for me and even Martin's gone. From his passion Felix oh, her body is my, Felix! Back convulsive on his bed with glee, my own life too then. On and on, the words go on and on.

But Jesus how, Christ Martin, look can you go back to....? Puckered flesh, dry skin in wrinkles: rasping goddamn shapes that bunch and automatic, whisper prayers.

What are you talking about?

How could he? Dull and listless, habit goes on but I couldn't go back no sir. I can't....

I don't understand you Felix

Hung up, that's what I am, between the two; but I'm different yes.

I've never heard such nonsense! Trouble with your, you won't accept responsibility.

Words. "...with whom the souls of the faithful, after they are delivered from the burden of the flesh, are in joy and felicity: we praise and magnify...." Public mouths, bartering, praise and majesty; want me to live like you, I....

No I don't! Pride in the night, that's not. Don't hit the curb! His clenching voice, her breathing's shallow in the seat behind; my instinctive, still this urge, goddamn, I....

Why are you always so critical of me?

I'm not, I.... Appeasing, his tone with hands relaxing on the wheel. Look, son, I'm only saying....

You are you know, you insult my friends.

Oh, now! Exasperated sighing and well now. If you're going to talk like. Hah, his voice uncertain because he cannot answer. Bash on, pursue it and knowing, why do I?

They're my friends. And you're critical of everything I do.

Darling that's not true, we're very proud of you, but....

You give me, young man, give me one good reason why I shouldn't be?

You seem so. So aimless darling.

Mother, I'm just not interested....

I'm sick of your selfishness, just a. Minute you hear! Your father, I'm. Flashing cars as he jerks the wheel, with glaring lights, his face. You and your generation....

My generation, why can't you talk about me?

Because you're all alike, that's why!

We're I am. Not, I'm...oh God he doesn't, I....

Some childish fad and right away, you all jump on the bandwagon.

I don't want what they want!

Always critical, sure sure, its easy to be critical....

That's not fair.

You give me, you hear? Some real suggestions how to improve the world!

O Jesus, gasping oh!

Darling don't, you mustn't use the Lord's name in vain.

Well, well! What do you say?

It makes me so sad to hear you....

What am I supposed to....

Oh yes, its fashionable to be disrespectful, but what do you do? Nothing, not a God damned thing! Silence awkward in this moment and we're hardly moving, coasting by the curb. Ungrateful, the whole....

Ungrateful? What do you....

Ungrateful, that's right. The whole lot of you.

What do you expect?

What, what do you mean by that?

Well. Careful, oh God here it. Goes. What have you given us?

Given! shuddering car to a stop, what do you mean by that?

What kind of a life. Or world, that's what I.

Aawh! Turning his face with. The bomb again is it, the end of the world? Hah! Arrogant hands from the wheel. My boy. He doesn't. Bastard, he doesn't understand, I've known. So long, its futile, he doesn't. You think you're different, well let me tell you something. My generation had prophets of doom too.

But now its different, don't you....

Its always been the same. When they brought in the airplane, everyone said. And I remember. Everybody said its the end of the world, they. The war to end all.... Even the, even the tank. Think of that now! The tank!

Its not the, that's the point. My shrill voice rising. They're not the same!

And gunpowder: the end of the world. Hands secure on the wheel again as we move, he is so sure! And I've lost. Control because the worming tears because.

That isn't what I meant anyway.

You don't know what you mean.

You're pretty sure of that, aren't you?

Don't talk to me like that.

Well its true. More softly, but I won't give in. I won't.

What do you mean then, tell me that? Face waiting; white road slowly, he waits for my voice.

You wouldn't understand.

I understand you're mucking up your life, I understand that! You've never finished anything, never been able to say; well! There's a job well done.

I don't want to talk. Fading, so louder and. Don't want to talk about it anymore.

You don't want? Felix, I don't like to say this, but we've got to straighten you out....

I'm not a child.

Your mother and I are concerned.

But I'm not a child anymore!

Look young man, so long as you live in our house. Something snapping, breaking away as he speaks. We're paying for you still, you remember that, we're.... Its starting again, they're blurring, I....

Don't want to, don't say anymore!

Listen to me, young....

I'm not going to, I won't!

Felix! Felix! Startled and me bursting out the door, his sudden, braking to the curb as I stumble, Christ my knee, then up and racing with lights wild lights and Felix! fading, Felix! "...come, ye blessed children of my Father, receive the kingdom prepared for you from the beginning of the world...."

Self-conscious striding from them, purposeful now on the balls of my feet and relax, that's the, thud thud thud, but pat is better, lightly pat, patpat on easy feet with arms relaxed, that's it; my hands carried high among cheers and breathing's the thing, your breathing like swimmers', yes, controlled and even, blowing out, patpatpat and. In, patpatpat and. Out, you graceful and patpat-thud you mustn't. Never look back, someone may be gaining on you, gasping now and there! Cut across the lawn, the house and windows gawking at the lean and freely running figure of the night; perhaps some silent aghast, a watcher in nightclothes will reach for my tears, perhaps. I think, what's this? Christ a hedge, a darkly squatting but no sweat, I. Lithely striding Longboat, poise and settling in for the hurdle, reaching legs and straining ease as up we.... Shit! I've caught my. Terrible awkward, I think I'm headlong sprawling crash but rolling quickly, back to your feet in the watcher's scornful eyes! A clever acrobatic stunt but no, some drunk he'll say, turning indifferent to his woman, some university student by the look of him. Do I pay taxes for that? But was he really crying, she'll ask; how funny, what's he doing now? I'm bravely. God my shoulder! Bravely loping with blood, I'm sure its, streaming down my shin as lamely I lope in other eyes and shadows to the park. Jarred something loose I'll bet and then they'll. Me in the morning under a bush and he's bled to death from his shin! Oh shocking! Why was he alone, where were his family, friends at a time like? Oh shame! Jerking to a walk. He was all alone.

Sloping ahead to the railway tracks, what am I? Against the wind, black trees on the sky and if I don't turn my head, don't look, there aren't any houses, no lights. I'm alone with the stubbled grass, this ancient stillness, northern land.

Leave the tears on my cheeks, in case somebody: I saw the most interesting fellow, tragic, alone in the park last night, a human individual and oh so sad, he was sad, alone there beneath the cold and screaming stars (bleeding he, yes a nasty wound), he wandered aimless past the swings, down to the poplars by the tracks with blood (I'm sure of that) in the prints from his feet as he went and I saw where the tears had dried on his cheek. Trees shiver with the leaf-loud wind as I walk and hear far-off engines: faint anonymous feet to the tree where I once saw, sudden raccoon away, I almost stepped on it, then heard the claws escape among those branches from me down below. But he's not here now. Squatting against the bole, ready for anything. A man of sorrow, yes, with all my faculties intact and vanishing, post to post, the fence in shadows from my. Bit of strain on the legs out here by myself at this time of the goddamn night, I must've been walking for hours can't they, why can't they see I'm, goddamn it old enough! Electric cricket and still no light: boxcars hunched like animals beyond the fence, I'm not a child. Boy, if they only knew! My cricket, with leaves between me and the sky; I'll bet they're worried, but. Piss on them, shuddering, sigh as I rise. Piss on them that's what I say. Ssh, like a commando, quietly through this hole in the fence with humming wire to darkness as I push, stumbling to the tracks and houses, piled shapes there against the sky; alert and balanced now, Felix Oswald on patrol. Sharp ears for shadows, softly he glides on the balls of my feet and they'd be sorry, they'd boy, if. POW! Rifle's explosion (my shin!) as he hurls himself down and rolls in the vicious RATTA—TA—TATTA of automatic weapons. POW! pow RATTA-ta right on my goddamn shin, I've. Vigorously rubbing, oh! Descending silence jeez, I hope nobody. Pretty grotesque, I'll just lie here and that really hurt. Quietly rubbing. The night between me and the town. Better, that feels. Better and I wonder where my raccoon went? My good suit off the tracks and great, into the ditch for a. Great! Peering up over the edge; unlikely at this time of night, I'd be surprised, I. Still. Wriggling up to see and if it weren't for the shivering trees between us, crickets there on the fading town of noise, I'd probably cry again. Or something. Jesus! What a yes, a fraud you are, belting off like a fucking movie and he'll use it against me, for sure, some time he'll scoff and Felix. You'll certainly have to demonstrate a little more responsibility before I'll, Jesus whatever it is, whatever I'll want or need! You can't expect and its for your own good that I. Jesus Christ what's that? Horror to the earth and straining to hear: a breathing sighing breath in the darkness there it is again! A cough, oh Jesus straining fingers what? Heaving a sudden animal, breaking cough from there in a shadow I can hear it in clustering sighs with bodies shifting in cattle-cars shadowed oh…. Closer, what a terrible, inching cautious towards and dragging God, this wounded leg so bravely with boxcars and listening. Alone.

Blood swelling I rise, pulling myself on this iron rung and silently forward; hard-eyed and glinting to where they groan and helpless wait for me. Sharp cough but now I know; here I come!

GOT YOU RED BASTARD! Quailing from, this roar I shrivel in monstrous shock and quivering, Felix Oswald dies, his heart with agony explodes HAH! Crunching blow to my shoulder, lifted now and hurtled (done for, that's it! they'll be sorry) my husk is pinned against the cage. I despise, YEAH! Rolling eyes and roar, his spit on my face. I DETEST all PINKO PRICKS and BOLSHEVIKS. Teeth grinding, threatening grind with his meaty hand at my throat (goodbye) and COMMIES and so-called liberals or RED by ANY OTHER NAME YOU!

Butbut, gargling words he's choking but.... Pale hand I'm brushing, I can barely see, at his gnarled arm butbut....

You shaddap you!

Stranglegloop, I'm flailing hand and mother will cry, inconsolable and where. When your son was: Strangle-strangle beneath bright stars....

RED COMMIE FINK YOU! Teeth grinding to the gums then leaning HEY! And loosening, air! Thank Christ, with closer face. Hey, I seen you somewheres eh?

Arrgh I, don't....

Where eh? HAH I know. Rough laugh and trailing giggle as he slaps his thigh. At the Legion, you drink at the Legion?

Unngh swallowing nod for air and still my eyes for flight; this goddamn, this crazy man he almost....

Well okay then, I'm sorry eh? Chuckle; you're alright. I thought you was. Fading conspiratorial voice, this looming nut to me. I thought you, maybe was a red, you know. Here. Friendly crushing hand round my arm, while sensitive, my own to my tender throat. I useta work in the packing house, you know? In Torawna. Stopping to listen, he's neckless, stupid bastard's got no neck at all! That's where these ones are going, I useta. Flicking his red-rimmed eyes, his teeth in a sudden grin. I useta bash 'em onna skull thunk, with a club you know, or give'm a fucken big shock with a prod ZAAP! Really laid 'em out, the other guys.... Accusing pressure on my arm. Was a really good job, it was, until the fucken goddamn RED

BASTARDS! Smashing his thigh and white electric, his eyes and smashing his hand, smashing and.... You know what they did? Sudden fearful fucking crash on the wood beside my head and how can I, what can I say to a? Tell you what, they let the goddamn cows, YOU KNOW THAT? Smash CRASH thump that's what they! Gangs of commie finks, creeping around an lettin all the cows go before they'd get to Torawna and then there weren't any goddamn cows anymore or anything so they hadda fire me. Jeez I wish I could get my hands on one of them. Grinding teeth and half this way and lurching away, a shadow and maybe I could, my legs. Are stronger now and maybe I'll dash off home like a shot down the tracks and over the fence before he. Love to strangle, kill somebody grind them with jaws as stumbling, crazy bastard further, here's my chance, I'll whoops! Back abrupt and his voice: it was a fucken good job. Close, that time. A good healthy job, here. Feel.

Ha, I think I, backing off, I....

No, feel!

I'll. Believe you ha, I really I....

LISTEN! A healthy job! Have to jeez, in this terrible staring face and reaching, biceps clenched and how can I. Christ he is; strong, as harsh, clubswinging he shouts at the dumb and waiting, grins and clubs and clubs and that's, my God not very I'd better.

Yeah hah, I'm sorry, about. About your job. Its. Smiling, annoying, I. Handrubbing, waving on down the tracks. But I better get home, its been, they're waiting, expecting me, Mother's. I better.

Into a staggering lope and his voice has stopped. Milling about me, people to the door. So long ago the killer's hand at my throat and underneath my feet, in the dark, as I ran, the creosote ties....

Moving aimless past me from that idiot grass, bumping as they go, voices rising at the door. How curious, still; by straps suspended still, unmoving still beneath the floor with laughter in the mist outside. Where do we take him now? Turning to avoid, avoiding possible nods and her head bent by his shoulder Max. He's gone, descended from your need and this strangeness I feel, so strange. This strangeness as you go, I go and you'll remain. I have to, can't go on like this for I don't believe and I am. So desperately said and straightening for their eyes: I am not like him oh! Why did he come back for chrissakes, marriage? Jesus to her and he loathed it at O.C.E.! All withdrawing, all: space about me, cold air from them bunching at the door, while formal. Crackell installed, family the waiting group for. What? Shall I do now and. "Surely you...." Shit I forgot! "I'm sure you'll explain, Martin said. You were his room mate? So you'll know." Her goddamn hand and panic, startled away from her eyes and voice can I run, can I.... Squeezing fingers as she leans, she. "Did he really propose the way she says, do you really think he did?" Flustered how, how should I and this is no time! Hand and moist her lips, softly along the teeth; insisting she presses my arm. "Do you think he did?"

"I really couldn't." This woman is unbelievable, what does she? "Miss Smith, I'm not sure." This woman I won't be drawn, she cannot. "Really."

"Oh but you must." Knowing smile the gentle, smoothest flesh in folds: "You must be." Her bloating pause, she knows with steady eyes; she waits I flinch. And turn. "What." From knowingly, so calmly said, "what about his girl in London?" Darting my eyes away, and frightened Jesus by her touch. With the family there and. Bursting, Christ resentment for what right, she's. Goddamn animals, she's forcing me. She's waiting. So assert, that's it, you. How does she know and what. For chrissakes else? "I know, oh I know all about her. Yes." So empty me inside, the stillness for I won't most assuredly. Don't have to answer you. "Know I used to see them in the park, when...." Bitch, she's a bitch insisting. "Always the same girl, that's how I know, it was always the same girl." What, what is she saying so loud, can they hear. "A real girl too, she was...." Felix shrinking, disassociate myself and edging. "Prettier than Susan don't you." What, oh is she? Edging from her, desperate for someone, an excuse. "And more exciting looking, you know what I mean?" Nodding, I shouldn't nodding and bobbing here; the family's shape in the corner of my eye, engulfed by her breathing and her steady eyes. "What's her name?"

"Oh!" shit....

"She used to speak to Queenie." Eyes, she reaches....

"Oh," squeezing and.

"What's her name, I'd like to know." She's caught her breath expectant tongue in the corner of her mouth.

"She likes animals. I guess."

"Oh I could tell, an interesting girl."

"Ha," and swallowing. "Hum."

"I remember...." Standing so close, her body and they're nearly all gone her breath, she's. Standing too close, these fingers. Tell me, clutching now more forceful, hardening into tears. Tell me her name but I won't; I try to turn, break to the door and outside, to the calm and the air but her hand's on my arm, I strain in this terrible cry: TELL ME HER NAME! Clustering mutter like bees.

Is he botherinya lady, you just....

Step right up, rightup.

You'd think he'd be ashamed.

After all these years.

Tell me and I'll....

Look, look!

HER NAME HER NAME

I? For one I admire his beard and I'd certainly.

You shaddup you!

OH HAWHAWHAW! HA—HEE—HAW!

Maybe things will be good like that again some day. Hee-hee-hee-hee-hee heeeeee you've made me look like such a fool, such a fool. "Val."

"What?"

"Her name's Valerie." Dead he's. "Valerie."

"Oh. Valerie. But why did he come back?" Because, was he. Afraid, was he afraid. "That's what I'd like to know." Was he afraid. Swallowing fear because I'm not the same and I will break free from this. Hung up between the two and he chose, he. What can I do I can teach, he chickened out, he.... "I mean I always felt." Intently, "I still feel" and knowing hand at my arm. "She's a very, well you know, a more. Interesting yes, that's the." And with pressure. "Wouldn't you say?" Nodding, blankly nodding into her I fiddle with my tie, I nod and see me nodding, nod-nod, nod. "A more interesting type, wouldn't you say?" He was afraid and turned his back in the kitchen. "So why do you think he did it then?"

"He was afraid."

"Oh now!"

"And turned his back."

You'd think he'd be ashamed.

"Oh," Felix and I will sleep! He was afraid that's all. Afraida. Fraid, we'll sleep in here. I was afraid. They had a fight a terrible. And drawing myself up, a fight and final separation. Come to somewhere she said, or Europe but he couldn't. She wouldn't settle down, she said, so there you are, and I agree. I. Words and earnestly agree, I hate my....

"What of, for heaven's sake" with her smile. "What do you mean, afraid?" They've all, this emptiness around, with Crackell. Turn abruptly, turn, why did he. Did I'm sure he signalled. Here he comes and I have to. Settle down the bastard, flunked me will he let me write perhaps an exam or something surely, oh my gut there isn't time.

"There's beena-hem, a change in plans." To turn, to trample out the door like a hungry elephant MAKE WAY MAKE WAY and watch me diminish along the road. "Oswald." Yes oh. "Yes?"

"Yes?"

"I said there's been a change."

"A change?"

"Felix aren't you going to introduce him Felix to me Felix?"

"Yes we've decided" Pursing his lips. "We've decided to...."

"I'm Frieda...."

"Go out to the graveside, the plot. Oh." Swelling with cheeks (dear Jesus the grave, there's more...), bloating before her eyes he drifts, a balloon on his toes, drifting he bounces and Christ inflated, he's soaring and blimping. "How do you do? I'm Doctor Crackell."

"Oh doctor!" Oh for chrissakes doctor.

"Yes," expectant? "Yes?" Get out, that's the thing, I must. Get out and away, poor Val he was afraid.... Such a prick, such a prick but I'll change I can change and go for the voice; you must live it, says and escape, you must. Have memories of many nights. Of love no two alike to write one line, you must. Change and you can, this despair. Felix too, why did I tell her? Hearing Martin's voice: hung up between hope and the world. I've seen too much and too deep and I can't go down to Stratford leaving Val because I'll never be, because.... Oh Val he did, settle down settle down. What will I do over there I know I can teach.... I'm not the same but why, do I talk like that? Flushing, I revealed, her control so I told her. Why do I do it? Her mouth, complacent, death.

Sudden the voice, hah-hah, with biting knot behind my ear: I see nothing I see a frightened boy with skinny arms (the gloves, so big the gloves) and a scarf across his eyes and the whack, the sudden whack and laughter, inciting pressure upon the thuds and panting shrieks I don't want to play I don't like this game I waiting in animal breath, a cough. Cavernous tearing sound from the boxcars as I rise, damp from the search to see; they wait to pay, vacant with animal jaws, their mouths attack and grinding chew at meat and candy floss while laughter, the air is full of spittle and damp wads of bread. Impatient they shift (with mustard glistening on the chin) they jostle never get out she will NEVER GET OUT! Spitting laughter, busy-mouthed around me there, they mount and stagger three steps to push inside....

"Yes. His mother wants it that way and so we thought...." Conspiratorial leaning hand to my arm and naked. If you play their game, I have to get. "Actually I think she wants to." Turning for I've missed and drawing back, I don't know. What's he saying? "To get it over with, you know. Poor thing." Muttermutter. "So we're, just the family you understand and. Pallbearers, you. Of course. Final ceremony. Into the ground, its frozen. But just the immediate, we're. Leaving in a few minutes" Get out, oh boy screw off for Jesus Christ, what's he talking about for! Yes this panic, mood. I have to. He thought he could stay. "...very pleasant, it was and I'm sorry about your dog."
"Don't be, oh doctor. don't be!"

Never you will never, never get out; a fucking underworld and you're dead if you play their rules so why do I? Swaying about the mother there, to the door; teetertottering step by step and he does not see: smiling he smiles and bowing, smiles with Susan's anxious face, she's stopping but its not for me; turning curiously as still he's swelling, bouncing lightly on the floor, blimping his. Mother ahead with Susan, vulnerable and dark the queen's procession. To drifting snow. She beckons and her silent mouth; Lucan, mouthing Lucan. "...alive with it, absolutely alive so they sewed her back up."

"Doctor Crackell."

"There was simply nothing they could do."

"Poor soul. Oh dear, the...."

"Doctor Crackell, Susan wants...."

"What's that," condescension. "What's that you say?"

"Susan wants, she's...." God his soft face, why do I bother? "They're going." Vaguely waving, my hand with startled his....

"Goodness, yes, thank." Sudden shaking. "Thank you its been very nice." Grabbing her hand and flustered, rolling eyes, he's shaking saying: "You'll be out, Miss Smith, at the grave then, very nice. To meet you." Turning muttering as he goes: "Oswald, yes. We'll see you. There." Trottting off on absurdly small, his pointed feet and back to her; they're leaving me with this. Helpless but. I'll, this time. I'll if she, one word from her I'll. Felix firm-jawed, cool and killer's eyes, her prying bloody. Five-legged whatever-the-hell for chrissakes! HE WAS A GOOD BOY towards this light-reflected eye and winking bird HE WAS. Afraid, he was and peeking from his...Jesus! Without a nod and bustling after them, her too. They've all....

Now climbing alone among the steel (so rough, those girders under my hands and feet) and high in the wind with over there the country, forest: too far for listening and so dark as, tightly pressing, higher from the water's edge and snaking grass I climb from the noise and higher to the rails, the ties are sweating oil and tar in the sun. I lay in blustering air beyond the trees, in the wind. Screaming primeval wind with chunks of stinging rain and clouds; through crevices, howling the channelled rock as we're driven back, scrambling back to the leeside calm, with laughter in my lungs and sheltered now. Exhilarated smoking, violence of air while the steep slope falls to the palace calm in the park below. Felix Oswald, rushing slow-motion to the edge in driving rain; so awkward. Stumbling earthbound and clawing to this plateau in the open sky, crawling. Beyond and fierce (oh Martin that's once!) Felix alone on Arthur's Seat with shadowy blue, Edinburgh around him and grey below, he's stretching awkward, imprisoned in mist and thrown by the wind GOT YOU.... And weaker, he's weaker and blown and the warning voice and mindburst as wilder he higher in each explosion GOT YOU sudden the hand out of silence! GOT YOU RED my heart oh FUCKEN BASTARD dying, I. Lifted and crashed, pinned my husk against that terrible cough dear God I'm afraid....

Tentatively Oswald and gently again, "Oswald?" Jarring soft voice and the smell of snow on his coat: wet wool's voices, subdued laughter, what. Have you got, its war you know. "Are you coming?" What qualifications we want doctors, his tentative face and. Waiting Crackell's eyes, for an answer watching....

"Oh."

"They're waiting." Oh, patpat his solemn voice, his hands. Christ he thinks, that sad. "Its hard, I know," his fucking voice and: pause, he thinks....

"No I!" It isn't him. "Not that, I...."

"Lost a friend, she. Left...." Unfamiliar, squeezing fingers, then bravely: "I know how you feel."

"No!"

"What?"

"I'm not," to his eyes, more. Naturally and possessed. "I was just thinking I shouldn't have been surprised."

"Surprised?" He starts away, then standing. "At what, what are you trying to say?" Hardening stance and shifting eyes, watch out....

"That he came back to marry her. You know." Shrugging, his body. "He left. Edinburgh at Christmas, he came back then you see!" Stop babbling stop! Reaching to him with this private, that life.... "We climbed Arthur's Seat in the wind, really a terrific wind." Demeaning, my voice is strange, reverberating but he doesn't turn, he keeps on going. "Eighty miles an hour easy," as trotting after him please don't, another word.... Leaping cat-footed upon him, they do not know and grabbing, iron fingers to his throat, you son of a bitch you listen, to me! Steely glare into collapsing his face. You listen to me or I'll kill you, twisting hands till he gags. I don't give a good goddamn about you or your lousy course, don't get me wrong! You can stuff it up your rosy red ass; but you'll listen to me now!

Stranglegloop; his folding knees and opaque eyes. Somebody's got to listen!

He had a choice you see, just like I've, maybe even you

had once. Quickly quickly for they're waiting and you're in for it now, boy you're sure. He might have made it, but he couldn't he went back down before the top. Chicken.... Frantic signs from his face and Felix snarling, really a dangerous man. He came back, that's what happened. Loose weight on my arms and falling, he's. Better off dead than here. Pausing, but I'm right; and they'll put me in jail, I know. Sweat and panic, the tears of death down his nose but I don't care I'm. Different I don't care if you fail me, I'm not like him so SCREW YOU FINK BUDDY boy, I'm....

Shshshsh, with finger warning to his lips and eyes to the door.

What?

They'll hear you, shshsh. Straightening his collar, throat red from my fingers as he smiles conspiratorially. I'm interested to hear you say that. Dumbfounded, I'm.... For I've always thought, well, You seem the type that will live in the bush and in years to come you'll. Burst down on the city, all ragged and torn and get plastered, really drunk for weeks and then you'll vanish again. Smiling primly finger tips to the pulse of life where his collar's white. Don't you think? Felix descending in curious faces, knowing groups that lean together, darting eyes to him and his scrunching feet on the drive: settling snow, past Crackell's nodding to the side, a door, they've brought it, him. They watch, then flicking cigarettes among the flakes and hitching, bodies' preparation once again, the. Welcoming touch, snow's touch above the collar; shirt-sleeves cold inside his coat as he moves aloof. Finger flexing. Lean and aloof so, piss on them all! Clenching fist, sure, bracing feet I'd. Take him alone, pulling, it slides and coasting on that other end instead of, staggering. Awkward beast. And stretching, lifting arm to the rolling wheels and the weight has gone. "There we are."

"Lift her. Up!"

"That's...."

"Herrg, ha! Shit...."

"A bit more."

"He's a heavy one...."

"Push, that's...."

"There." They're gasping back, stamping feet, puffing

for now he's almost one of them. The closing; polished
fingernails on the closing door. "The same cars, eh men?"
Muttering assent, they turn from the door's expensive
sound. The sky in delicate pieces, broken and falling, the
fallen sky exhausted among them: ragged shapes groping
across the treacherous ground. The sky in his face and
melting like blood in his hair. Sure-footed Felix, lithe
(what an interesting fellow, so lithe!) and easy anonymous
strength. Felix Oswald, and he can't go back. Not after,
tightening smile. Attacking Professor Lucan, oh boy
Crackell M.A. Ph. D., no sir! Body drained and dry beside
the door, unmoving, what do they do with the liver? Into
the car with his body ahead: maroon curtains (not after
that savage assault), polished wood for a shell. This whole
day. That's a troublesome, thought; its a pretty big organ,
they say or over. Three pounds of brain for chrissakes, dead
inside the skull! Tentative legs in the car. Those chickens,
Jesus. Carefully wrapped and returned to Dominion.
Cough. Cough. Here! Angry and sure....

Yes sir. Efficient pause. Can I help you? Then spotting
the bag, bending to peer inside its mouth. Chickens?

Rotten chickens.

Oh sir!

I mean really rotten.

Did you, flickering. Did you, swallowing, buy them
here?

Um.... DO YOU THINK I'D HAVE BROUGHT
THEM BACK IF I DIDN'T? that's what. YOU PRICK I
should have said but uh, yes. Um...at least I didn't, at least
I'm not smiling....

I said. Staring suspiciously at my beard: I said, did you
purchase them here.

Yes...I did.

Well.... Taking a breath for another plunge, whipping
open the bag and vanishing, his face his whole face OH NO
inside! Felix appalled Oswald away with rising gorge,
cringing from stronger. The muffled voice. Well.... Well-
well, rustlerustle and poking around, but he did he
ruined! Our dinner, Jesus, what's he doing, eating IS HE
EATING THEM? Churning stomach, these stabbing as
he reappears and Felix looks for grease on his chin. Well....

Yes?

No wonder.

What?

You left them in their wrappings.

Professorial assurance, his condescending look as shrinking, Felix is sure I'm sure that's. Shiny smear at the edge of his mouth, its grease.... Counter chickens. Hands on his chest and rocking with stains on his belly and groin. Counter chickens must always be taken out of their wrappings. Blunt finger into his ear and digging. Innards, scooped from the body cavity and put in a separate container. Otherwise. Smiling to the gathering crowd, projecting his voice for those at the rear: some people try to do it with a wooden spoon, a spatula ha, but. Light reflecting from his chin. That's not a very good idea, no sir. Encouraging now, he looks from face to face. Anyone know why, can anybody suggest why its not a good idea to force out the innards of a counter chicken with a spatula? Customers shifting. Puzzled faces, eager to please; they scratch at their heads and shift from foot to foot. Well. Well then I'll tell you. Because, leaning to hear, expectant. They wriggle to see and hear, because you'll damage, the sharp edge of a kitchen utensil will bruise. Or even pierce the succulent liver, the heart.... Deathly hush at his words and wisely nodding head: he begins, I ask you! Short steps pacing from the steaks. What would happen if I, slapping his chest, me, your friendly neighbourhood butcher. Smiling acknowledgement for snorts and titters from the crowd, he passes veal and pork. What if I dug around inside these poor animals with a spoon or a, a...breaking fatfaced, a shovel? Eh? Pausing, mock horror back past hamburger, he turns at the spare-ribs and returns to interested mutters.

Good point.

Sure is....

You wouldn't catch me....

I'd never thought.

Eating any of that stuff anyway.

Its funny what you pick up.

Oh!

Tastes of urine, it does! I can always taste it.

Staring triumphant into mine with hands still at his chest, he whirls: you've got to be considerate, its not just MEAT you know, not simply CHUNKS OF MEAT!

You've got to have respect, you can't just....

That's why I never eat lamb.

Why?

You can taste the wool.

Even in stew?

RESPECT! Because its FLESH, its FOOD. His body's earnest sweat as grabbing he raises the bag and waves it. You take these birds, these poor birds: THEY'VE ROTTED FROM THE INSIDE OUT!

But they, feeble my voice oh jeez, from the inside out! I try. Whole chickens, they. Weren't....

I beg your pardon. Young man? Scruffy young man? I said....

They were fresh Saturday morning. ALL our chickens are fresh.

They were cut in halves. For the barbecue....

YOU BEARDED PRICK

I had them specially....

YOU WANT TO LOOK IN THIS BAG?

Good lord no! Heaving at the thought, I.... Glaring he grabs a butcher knife and taunting:

Go on now, LOOK IN THE BAG!

NO!

Shame on him.

Some people.

Probably didn't even....

Beatniks.

Don't let him....

Give 'em an inch....

Some people, and they'll take.

Such a prick.

Don't let him get out!

Backing away, but still he comes on with his piggy eyes and the swinging bag as I turn, remorseless still through their midst after me. Stay dignified oh! Jumping oh, as he lunges, careening through their voices, scattering faces to the door. YOU EVER COME BACK HERE AND I'LL GIVE YOU A PIECE OF MEAT YOU'LL NEVER FORGET!

Shaken, boy even at the thought I'm. Stomach and nerves, and nausea. Cool, glass to my forehead; dancing snow and the crawling road to his empty grave, its all. So closc and mist-enclosed like water, underwater's drifting claws. The silent seas, head bouncing gently on the glass, with indistinct elusive shadows crouching all around and. An appropriate, poor Martin day he's gone, that's all. Here for a while and then he's not. And I guess that's the only change. "Certainly changed." At any rate, there's.

"Oh I should say," there's nothing else to know.

"A different man." Confusing words, their smoke exhaled through the car.

"As you say, he's."

"Yes."

"And everything's moving."

"Lickety-split." Crackell they're....

"Along." Talking about. Crackell, that's it! Startling recognition, *we've*. He said, *we* have decided; the sly old bugger, they're. Right! Felix shaking, ha-hee-hee, begrudging admiration as he shakes his head. Right in there, he's. Part of the fucking family, that's it he. Boyoboy like a dirty shirt, I wonder what he's up to?

"Must have been very close."

"Um."

"For him to be."

"So concerned."

"Solicitous."

"Yes." Groaning Felix Oswald to himself, oh. Signalled, why did he signal? Nod? Whatever it is I'm here to tell you, don't. Not a word, oh please.... That its not for him, not Martin's sake, Christ! No. Siree, impulsive. I'll explain, how wrong oh. Don't.... "They say he was his supervisor."

"His what?"

"Or something."

"Yes."

"His ah...."

"Supervisor." Fuck it....

"Yes. How can I.... He ah. Supervised Martin's ah. Well. Whatever he was doing." Bit your tongue not a word....

"His M.A."

"Yes. That's right."

"Well no wonder." Calm about my lips, laughter breaking in my chest; to the tombstones, glaring concentration as we lurch. For heaven's sake to control my glee. That was it! All the time that was! Patting her hand and ponderous, leaning for chrissakes. He's on the make! Ha. So many times! In from that sweltering summer, the sun to the cool and there they'd be. And I kept wondering. Two of them yes, his wife and Susan, she's kind of angular God knows but jeez, she's. At least she's better than. Dry, so always humourless; royal blue suits or something tailored, always thin, that predatory mouth. Slowly descending curve among the dead with shattered trees by the day and silent-leaning, those shapes beyond my eyes. People find each other and I really did, the time they spent. Even in the cafeteria, talking every morning after class but what can you say? Martin, is there anything, I mean you know, going on between. Your girl (your girl?) and your thesis supervisor, there they go again! Rhapsodies, look at their opening, their mouths, too serious. Too serious and that's lechery, not much control there, look. Breathing in and out, talking all over each other; twisting bodies in their chairs and talking, arranging their limbs and that's a pretty sexy performance if you ask me, they behave like that in public, what do they do oh Christ! What an absurd. Crackell? Pompous bugger'd die and Martin. Kills me after a weekend with her and I think maybe, maybe this time so I rub her breasts like crazy, they're nice, they really are so I kiss 'em and nibble and suck and rub like they were magic lamps. Glaring at his hands. But nothing ever happens, never. She dies on me every time. Watching, uncertain glances as he drinks, then. Curiously tentative voice. Sometimes she lets me, you know. Go even further, sometimes. Abruptly to the window, pausing with branches scratching at the pane; returning embarrassed he drinks, slumps back in the chair. She lets me, you know. Put my HAND UP INSIDE HER SKIRT! Groaning; I wait, he sways with all the pain I know and hoarsely says: and you know? With awe. Its like a prune, like a withered up old prune.

Jesus!

What are you gonna do, what's a guy gonna do?

You're kidding!

Just like a big old prune, no life at all. Aghast, I'm. What can I, what on earth do I say?

I. Jesus Martin, that's. Watching, recessed eyes above his glass. I know, exactly what you mean I. Escaping to the fridge for another beer and my mind's bending.

I don't think it even has a hole in it.

That's terrible. Bottle cold in my hand as I turn for the opener. Terrible. I can see now....

Yes! Yes that's why. Val's alive, she's. God Felix she's wonderful! She's got a cunt like a horse collar. Jarred, I. Intent on the opener, I don't think. That's nice I.

That's interesting. But he doesn't see me shrink, and that's. Not very nice about a girl you like, Val's a fine girl and. Jesus, a horse collar! Heavier, snow unmoving now, we've stopped; their bodies to opening doors. He's left me alone, copped out and Val, any Val's worth more than that, he certainly. Snow in my socks, who cares I'll, screw the path and Christ! Up to my knees! Screw it, get to the hearse with dainty picking feet above me on the road. Serves him, it serves him right in a way. Left Edinburgh Felix I must, the Whip. Calls me home and you know the Whip, guardian of my inheritance, I must go back....

Walking.

Streets, gaslight, shadows, silver rain: circling anonymous, slowly with music in the air and walking, oh. I see. Hope and silence bursting inside. And outside, I see I see....

Hands on bodies tense in doorways: ravenous moths with caught breath as I pass to crouching there. Calling her down and insatiable, mouth and stunted body to her throat she opens, even for him, she....

Time's attenuation, sounds from the isolated world: in rain and rising chill that old man's begging-song from the street below; NO LADIES ALLOWED oh Nan! I cried, back down the hill oh Nan! Will I see you at all?

Running.

Footsteps in the empty street: running I loved you Nan. Alone in the lights that barrel down the road alone, in the cold the damp. Cardigan steaming to my ears, you're not. Qualified. Come along what can you do?

"Come along there," harshly whispered. "Grab your end," who's that. Officious o-kay bastard hold your. Glaring at him, startled I'll. Eyes diverted, they're all. O-kay o-kay, I'm. Staggering, we're....

"Hold it!"

"Pull him out."

"Careful...." Steadying, the best I can on the path; bracing against the hearse with melting snow on my back the bastards. Here he comes, sliding. Floundering around, they're. Knee-deep for heaven's...Felix Oswald's crooked grin down the shimmering coffin to, disconcerted. Strangers stuck and muttering in the snow why; don't they. Watch where they're going, backing off the path and right into what can you expect? Ha. Pulling, I'll heave and pull them free ha. Errgh!

"That's...." Snow in circles as I. Heave and save the day. Beneath him they pant and, he hauls them ahead! Or could have. Absurd skit, struggling without movement, kneeling precarious on the snow and trying to stand; gingerly, one foot testing yes, and now. The other, that's. Briefly the surface holds for one as another goes down. "That's the way!"

"Get...."

"Oh!"

Erggh

"I...."

"God."

"The way."

"I can't get."

"Up, that's...." Pitching through crust and grunting: Felix above, silently sinking. Chaotic in our wake, the spoor of a dying animal, some wounded and wolf-harried moose. Eyes rolling, desperate heaving lungs among the tombstones, crouching evergreens under their snow; I don't want to play this, thin legs through the crust, it stumbles and ice shards pierce to the succulent bone and my body's awash! Down, in this tremendous silence. Nobody moves in the rattling wind. Pause, with bolder shadows closer; darting just outside the vision, loping in the closing day, faster. Faster they're closing in, throw out a serf to slow the bastards, scavengers on my tail as, scattering bodies from the sleigh, frantic we surge against the drift. More, oh more who's next I'm forcing, the coffin bruising, teeth at his, body out to the teeth and following eyes it goes, I'll travel lighter; now light and away from the last, the failing cries behind but the bastards, they barely pause and they're back and what. WHAT'S THIS?

Among the closer forms who's that, its. Leading the pack empty-eyed, its Martin there, the faces! Nan I know them, closing on me, I know them all you smile so, reaching out.

Just gasping breath, that's all; awkward the coffin, resting on chunks of broken sky. Again then, struggling: desperate for purchase, trying to rise and knowing now he's alone. Slow-motion bodies, they wait. Embarrassed. Aware of each finger, nails to the palm with muscles up my arm and the weight's there too, in my shoulder, down my back to the side and pulling hard. So slow. The din of my legs, and loud, the snow I crush, each breath that I breathe. On and the same clumsy on, as heavier flakes we slow. And slower to them clustered but its trampled down, its easier here by the. Grave. New grave while turning, we shift and guiding it, careful, on either side and "No!" Frozen by the voice. Horrified with frantic, it comes again. "Feet first! Feet first!" and staring faces. "Not that way, the other." Windshifting, we dumbly stir; the family there and Crackell. "He's got to go...." Martin, what are we...? "Turn around!"

"The other way." Huddled group by that stone, a rising group are they gnomes?

"Come along there Oswald!" And Crackell's reaching voice from the other side. "Turn it around," I'm.... Surrounded, jeez and I'm laughing, I'm Jesus gasp, this shuddering gut oh. God I mustn't. Pushing they're dutiful, back against my clumsy hee, my legs and ho! Straight-faced manoeuvering, shit I mustn't, not with Martin here but Martin stranglehee, feet-first-feet-gnomes for.... Careful! Foot by foot to the. God to the edge and there's. Water, the fucking thing's full of water, that's a. Chuck him down in there, sobering thought. Plop. Carefully plop, along the edge, dislodging frozen chunks that plop, hollow and falling, splash. Another fuckingawful, skinned with snow another machine with sodden straps and bending, relief as we release, retreat from the edge in a bunch and Felix withdraws. Not with them, I won't. Sidle away ten feet. To the gnomes, they really are. Graveyard trolls behind that sweating stone and peering out again to, good Lord, to shout! "Not yet." Waving, what's he...? "They gotta saya prayer first!" A flurry away from the grave and everyone's staring through me subsiding, my gnome disappears in the

earth. Disturbing alright, and what.... Striving his voice
for order, muffled words as unobtrusively, picking my way.
Grotesquely torn, our path back there and my feet are
soaking; in my pockets, hands against my thighs and raw
from falling plop. Numb feet carefully for chrissakes, what
are they doing down there? Intrigued, yes anxious. But I
can't go any farther, no. I can't. For people. Turning
dutiful, Felix me. Receding shapes with easy the snow like
piss on it! And that's final. Blindness to the eyes, I'll.
Cautiously at first, very cautious sneaking away because.
He's dead and what do I owe? I'm not moving. Them after
all, I've. Carried him shit! Goddamn expensive coffin and
he wouldn't, no couldn't have expected more. Tiptoeing
anyway. He would have loved this day. Seen the gnomes
and I guess that's something. Briefly turning, there's the
family, that's. Curious, his arm and hers entwined. What's
going on? The voice is gone; settling slowly into the snow,
they're sinking, churning now but soundlessly up to their
throats. Solemn descent, with faces terribly calm; Felix has
won. Not moving. Slowly their farewell hands, but he does
not see. How curious. Liberated steps. Crouched and
smoking, three dark men emerge from the ground with
arms and hands protruding here and there: six eyes watch
me come. "You'll want a smoke after that." Nodding.
Relief as I crouch to the flame, deeply inhaling and
breathing:

"That's what I needed."

"They've all gone then."

"Yeah." Smiling, crouching I smoke. "They've all
gone."

FELIX 3

like I was crazy or something. Not caring, this headache but not caring; strange with them and I thought, these small dark men, I thought they were gravediggers....

Uncertain; wind with turning Felix as grunting to their feet and hey, I said. "Hey, aren't you." Leaning to that yellow muck, aren't they.

"What?"

"Aren't you going to, I mean. Isn't anybody going to, you know, cover him up. Or anything?" I thought, I really did, I was positive.... Confused, my face to the grave, its indistinct for the snow is rising and their eyes. I really am, I'm sorry, unsure I'm....

"Not ours anymore."

"Oh." We turn, he gestures to figures from the mist in single file. Oh....

"He belongs to them now." Others that crouch, peer from the edge, their voices in the snow.... Belongs to them?

Then into this tunnel, walls as we go and its dry underfoot, dark up ahead and where are we going, what passage is this? It feels so dry and growing warm, I must be, thoughtless I follow just like I was drunk or something. What happened to Martin? An open door, they nodded and stepped into the earth, the earth for chrissakes! Right into the goddamn earth.... A tunnel with cautious feet and unaccustomed eyes from light behind, this breath in my head, I'll. "Don't look back."

God, "What?" This sudden admonition. "Why?" Pausing and is that light ahead?

"The eyes." Yes it looks like, the eyes. "Won't get used to the dark if you stare back at the light."

"What is this anyway, where are we going?" His standing shape is clearer. "What is this?" But he shrugs and the others continue ahead; strong against, it must be light. Turning he shrugs and there are, that's why its warm, yes pipes along the ceiling. Unzipping coat, a dry warmth and faster walking because he's right: after the snow and blowing light, the eyes begin to see

easy in single file without him. Tombstones, grave still open plop. Feet. Worn path to the road, the car: and its done. Buried. Felix Oswald to the car. Door opens. Closes. Opens for them; closes. Waiting. Family passing, Crackell briefly. Disappear. Doors and voices, boom; cigarettes from the back seat. What did I leave back there? Moving plop, its done. Driving. The earth with trees on either side, the trees, the earth, the gates, the road, the heavy sky. Its done. Seeing, not hearing: trees and houses, cars, the house somewhere, the road and cars, their house, Martin's, a drink...it doesn't matter. Give me a drink I left something....

Felix and Lucan Crackell in Martin's house. He waits for me to speak. Sipping punch. Anything. About the funeral. Why didn't you stop? Flunked me too. Felix straightens his shoulders, shrugs. Familiar faces grown strange: do I know them? No noise but movement on the steps, his; he doesn't know me, offering pack, is he trying to know me? "Smoke?"

"Um." His hand is trembling, why? Pinching to free c'mon, c'mon. "Thanks." Hands, two hands. "Thank you." Hand to my pocket, scratching, flame, his face with shadows, the eyes. Lifting smile, why does he smile? Curling paper with flame, blue as I inhale; the smoke in my lungs. Martin's picture on the sideboard. His empty stare.

"Oswald, the um. How's the, ah, that fellow. You know...." Felix inhaling. Accusing from the walls, laughter from empty eyes with Felix, can I laugh, why don't I laugh, don't I dare like that? Boy its pretty sad if, how? Can't even laugh. How, I mean. "How is he?"

"Well" Jesus, he's hah! Pause then words: "He's got that bloody awful bruise you know and stunned, he's lucky, Christ...."

"No I mean. What's going, you know. To happen to him, what'll they do?"

"I don't" Gently he went. How? His stupid hat. "How should I know?" CAN'T MEET HIS GODDAMN

EYES? Even the question: distant around the room, these people, that stare, his voice. What happened at the grave?

"Well thanks anyway."

Beg your. "What...whatwhat" for what is he saying, why? I don't understand.

"You know, for arranging." Sudden again to his side. "You must have been at your persuasive best ha, I mean. Since we don't have to go in. To see them." Cigarette stub and trembling. "Just a" turning to the ashtray. Me thanking, Christ! driving past a face, so white, staring, I was sure. The bastard! Pumping grotesque, writhing, his blood, the snow. Watching, yes watching he'd hardly see and driving, he'd drive right past! Leaning to his toes, rising, teetering there, rocking back on his heels. Sipping and rocking. Professional level gaze; studied pause and swallow, what's he, for Christ's sake? Wine glistening, pulpy lip protrudes, invites some terrible, yes some confidence I'm sure, my life: eyes hooded, smiling eyes for me I will not speak, I don' wanna play for chrissakes maybe, oh maybe he'd let me write an exam! Blurring room, voices barely reaching; settle down I must and work...if he'd only let me....

Walking, again I do not feel, cannot, what am I going. Empty body, walking rooms, walking sillybugger! Youth, indulgence yes, with rain to my eyes this hah, oh Christ! You silly bugger, if I'd only, boy if I'd got to Hungary I'd have had something...to write about or....

What'll I do if I fail? Another fucking, this stone, the words drop through me I can't write, another failure. Depressed with closing lights, windows, I have nothing to say.... I don't know anything, I don't feel.... Anything! Muscles, air, lungs, throat I WANT smog-yellow, sky absurd, his hands and touch: guilty looking, and close to tears I don't do anything at all. Guilty he pauses, peering sillybugger through the night but nothing, silence and rain on my face. There's nothing here for me, no sign or no hope: what am I? Night, windows and rain. Sort of an anguish yes, I qualify; because, who is this Felix, frightened (a virgin for chrissakes) what'll I ever...underground. "You're doing some writing." Sudden pain and glaring, I.... Nodding, and. Its crap, all crap he.

"Yeah." Ducking my head, thinking, I've been thinking. Uncertain and smiling.

"How's it going?" Who told him, shifting; how does he know?

"Well, uhm," its....

"Difficult, yes." Rocking he bends, he smiles with laughter in the room. "Particularly in Canada it seems," what? "Have you read, do you know Brown's essay?" He doesn't wait. "A sound analysis, it seems. Rather helpful. Yes. Its difficult alright and he suggests, well. The problems of a real Canadian literature." Sudden silence. "Do you know the piece?"

"No I'm afraid, I...."

"Never mind, but you might. Its well worth." Hand to his eyes, shaking head, fingers massage. "His point is, one of his points, that." Beer is it? Alert for jeez, the bugger has he.... "Goddamn Puritan mentality doesn't simply you know, inhibit the development of naturalism or anything no! No sir." Swallowing, glaring he swells, he grows. "It fears, that's the thing, it demeans the very role of art itself!" Muttering "bastards" and that'd explain, if he has, the smile, his nod because he did, I'm sure..."andandand the, its the same with, with what he calls the frontier mentality, yes. YOU'VE GOT TO PAY YOUR WAY!" Afraid because he shouts, and they stare with Felix, I'm aloof, not involved no sir not me, notme in faces, empty eyes. That's why. Earnest leaning. "That's why," confidentially, "I'm making a change." Embarrassing voice is hoarse. "That's right, I'm going to make...." Abruptly scanning, searching for, nodding to Susan and her smile. What?

"What sort of...."

"I can't just tell you the details yet, but...." Winking for chrissakes, what? "But you'll see soon enough, I'm going.... Well." He must be; emptying glass, he's drunk or.... Clutching my arm. Urgent voice. "You see the time's already come, you understand? Put it off and I'm lost, I've got to. Climb, that's it, back out because there's nothing...." Why does he tell me this and hold my, he's got my arm alright. Why, what does he mean? "Do you know why I'm telling you this?"

"No, I'm.... I'm not completely sure. I...."

"You don't?" Staring and waiting. "C'mon Oswald, try...at least you could try!"

"But I," my voice. "Really I don't, I haven't...."

"Well you should, by God you should!" Gentle touch, almost gentle hand. Christ! this is silly for chrissakes, stupid: shaking awkward for I don't know, why should I, bastard he's drunk or something flipped.... "You've got to learn to live in the wind." Live in the what? Be stronger, shit; I don't know!

"I don't know what you're talking about."

"You will." Relieved to look with him, its Uncle Martin: respectful nod, my parents' child. The wind for...hot air and why? Abruptly, slight bow with a glance at me, he excuses "excuse me" waving his glass and mocking, he leaves me with this uncle, me defensive yes, uncertain; it can't be, its, no its not fear! Of what? Whatwashe, talking about for chrissakes? What, what....

"I have, I thought you'd like." faint wheezing: "There's a bottle of something stronger, you know. For the pallbearers. That is, if you'd like." Soft difficult breath and this remarkably fine gesture, I'm. Grinning to him, happy yes.

"That would be very nice sir."

"For the cold and snow." Relieved and all I can do is smile.

"Thank you."

"You just ah, come with me then." His round head away; very decent, a decent sort of.... A pleasant calm. Don't seem so bad, not to easier Felix; like a cat, lithe as a cat and ready, expectant I pad, see me pad, I'm strong, a famous (or dangerous; good?), a figure look at him, who, who is that? tall, thin, look at him, bearded

behind them, pausing in mild surprise, but more like curiosity on the threshold of a huge goddamn room, a cathedral ceiling: its huge and this is where the light comes from. Flickering light and the smell of kerosene; two small lamps at either end. As he approaches on the uneven floor, he sees that the lamp is on a triangular table, and chairs are clustered about two sides of it: against the wall there are rectangular frames of some sort. Two of them arrange the chairs, then sit, the hunchback (was one of them deformed?) goes to the frames and reaches under a pillow: then returning with a bottle, he gestures Felix to his chair. Waiting and watching until they drink and lifting the glass, sweet yet musky, fruit wine and nodding appreciatively, that's good gentlemen, "thank you" and sipping again, rolling it on the tongue and savouring, rinsing the teeth a bit, that's good alright; drinking and hearing movement in the dark. Shading his eyes and leaning to peer beyond this circled light, straining to see and rising, these few steps with my shadow from the table, both hands up like blinkers, bending from the waist and there! figures, walking and standing, small and stocky figures; they cluster two or three at a time and whisper, that's the rustling noise, like the wind. Felix surprised, he's still walking, careful from his drink and coat for there's something interesting, a stall or bench and yes, a sign ahead. Growing accustomed and they're not frightened as I come although, its true, they drift away whenever I remove my eyes; not when I'm looking, not when I see, for they've all stopped moving, they're silent and posed like mannequins; yet when I look again they're further off. But they're smiling I can tell, I can feel that as I move among them to the sign and what does it say? Two words and squinting hos, lips clumsy forming dolhosp

DOLL HOSPITAL

Pausing with gentle sounds and movement again but he doesn't turn: funny to see this shop, because it is a shop (doll hospital?); how funny there's no glass. Closer he can see there are no walls behind this storefront, false front, stage set propped before the cluttered tables and shining, what's shining? Hurrying around the side and excited, there's a, sitting on a stool, his rough voice sudden: "You might've come in the door, its usual isn't it? to use the goddamn door!"

"Oh I'm...." Startled and jumping back for I've offended, quickly around to the front, but what can I say? Maybe I'd better, reaching, maybe I can buy something; digging for change, pushing in at the door with cowbell jangling at my head, horrific it springs "excuse me" oh! but he's reading, now he doesn't look up! While it does, thank God and there are two tables, one a workbench with the lamp beside him surly bugger and the other's for display. Leaning to see, fascinated to pink and broken bodies, plaster- chipped this jumble of limbs, these silent shapes: a shattered head, skull and sockets. Felix staring back at faces, some eyes closed, half closed and one with no lids at all: compelled to try and isolate the heads among these bodies, limbs and tangled hair, I try but can't, I have to turn away....

Tittering is that laughter from the dark and do they know my thoughts? Revulsion in their searching breath, a cough, but how can they know my thoughts?

Past the bodies, faces, farther into the shop, I was right: a work bench and by his elbow another pile of hair and marbles, for chrissakes they're eyes! Accusing as Felix turns to bars and wheels, what's this? but he ignores me as I pass, what are they, weights? Good Jesus Christ they're, that's a.... Felix awed, there must be hundreds of the goddamn things! A slanting bench with straps for the feet, and on each side there are weights for the hands: ropes piled by springs, they look like springs and carefully putting my feet between these bloody iron discs; they've simply been thrown, they look as if they've just been tossed into this corner and that's it! They're all brand new for chrissakes.... Pausing to stare, bending to see: they look like boots, iron boots. On impulse, just to see but its too small for my shoe, so slipping it off and then cold metal, the stiff strap on his foot. That's, that feels funny and balancing, other shoe off and stocking foot, careful into the left one hee, its cold hee-hee and Jesus Christ they're heavy. Dragging his torture boots like Frankenstein and lurching, waving his arms for balance and clomping a step as they hold their breath: then another towards the huge weight on its frame, straining a third and thrashing for strength with his shadow broken on the wall. He is intent, slowmotion as he raises and reaches his arm and he cries, does he suddenly cry out now, for he staggers, he falls in rattling laughter: it reflects from the ceiling to where he waits, their scorn at Felix Oswald down and ready to cry. He waits, he should jump grinning to his feet but it hurts and I must get up so struggling, I must, get back for they're closing in, I can hear the feet. Rolling desperate to my belly, grunting on all fours. Prepared. For the change. Then wildly erect with his face at me and I'm scared, I stare as he nods and tries to smile, then I'm away: I'm off, skinning out of his boots and light as light in my socks out the door I run, that's the way! like the wind to my drink and coat, I've got to climb are they chasing I can't look back but I can hear yes, Christ! and I hardly touch the ground, I fly with my body's sound, the rush of my blood. The worst is over I'm sure, for they smile as I come and one of them is. He generously welcomes me and rises: welcoming eyes, and cradling his drink who's that other? A figure mnemonic, who's that leaving, vanishing along the wall? I know him, Felix shocked and knows too well but: who is it for chrissakes, calling "hey! hey where are you going, I know you. Who are you?" Brief turning face in the doorway "STOP" and reaching with my voice turned shrill? "Why are you leaving?" But he's gone and I'm scared

plumply gasping, wheezing. "His skills, the hunter's I mean. His daring you might say, initiative. Above all his. Initiative, why...." Nasty living-room and his mother. Susan. Christ! "Do you realize, a good hunter. You know. Very good hunters provided for the whole community. That's right." Cigarette. "They were the natural leaders; they were. And do you know why?" Sharper voice but I won't. "I'll tell you why. They knew," fist cracking to his palm, "how to get things done!" Smiling. "That's all."

"Gee."

"That's right, that's...."

"He's right alright."

"...Martin for you."

"Look at the boy scouts."

"Exactly. Get a boy out there in the woods you know, oh I've. Many's the time I've...." Private laughter, what's he? A bore, Uncle Martin you're.... "Early in the morning."

"That's right, none of your lollygagging about till noon."

"Breathing in God's air as He meant it to be you know. You've got a man. Patient," convulsing face, grimacing smile. "And resourceful, dependable. For I've said it before: a good shot, and I'll say it again. He's a dependable man."

"He is, and that's the truth." Nodding, agreement, muttering into drinks.

"It takes a steady hand for hunting."

"And the eye, don't you forget the eye."

"Oh I wasn't, no sir."

"The eye's important."

"It is."

"You've never seen a blind hunter now have you?" Ho, chuckling hah, politely; cigarettes from the pack.

"Its got to be a quick one too, the eye I mean. If its ducks you're after."

"Oh God yes, but...." Gulping wetmouthed, glistening. "I like the running game myself, the bounding game."

"Well Martin I don't know, birds...."

"Gives you" Fat-smiling confident. "You know, every man basically knows what I mean; it really gives you something to shoot at, a good-sized pow, good-sized kill." Thumb-cocked triumph, thumb-cocked and sighting along his finger POW! Dismissing. "I can't understand, really I can't, and I've...." Sharp laughter. "I've shot birds, oh God! Thousands of them." Face and calm humour. "I can't understand what satisfaction a man, you know, a man gets from blasting some stupid bird out of the sky. Hah, you give me the bounding game!"

"A really satisfying kill."

"Yes oh, when they fall. You know? They really fall...."

"Martin I know what you mean." Breathless: "You hit a bird, even when you hit birds they're so small." Hands clutch the air. "Sometimes you can't even find the goddamn things."

"That's right, now you take the moose for instance." Focussing voice. "You ever hunted moose?"

"Have I? Well," dropping face away. "No, but...."

"Well there you are. Now when you've hit a moose and you know you've really hit 'em, when you squeeze the trigger and...you know...." Gaze past us, awe: the sullen birdman shifts. "By George that's a, a satisfying feeling!"

"God damn!"

"Yes...."

"You just don' know."

"Deer of course, they're good too, and bear; bear's got its own reward you know, but moose...oh yes." His face. "Moose", grinning. "Moose is something special."

"Goddamnright!"

"Rather like the deer myself"

"Oh deer are good, I'm not saying, make no mistake...."

"They're faster I think, and nervous."

"I'm not saying you understand." Gathering Max,

"there's no reward in deer, good Lord no hah. You know I'm." And Frieda as he swells he pats his chest. "You know me I'll, hunt anything that moves because I love...." Rising voice. "THE OUTDOORS, the great OUTDOORS! I really do, I love it...." Arms wide, his arms embrace us all: "I'm only saying that moose is a superior quarry, that's all: don't get me wrong, a more rewarding...you understand...."

"I'd never" Max what, Christ! "Shoot a moose." And Felix scared....

"And anyway, don't you agree? Its the hunt that counts, I don't know why...."

"Or any other of the round earth's living creatures."

"What?" Turning silence to stare.

"Let me illustrate ha!" Finger to thumb, conducting his words. "Gentlemen, for you are I can see." Dentures as he smiles. "To illustrate, let me...aaah! A parable yes. What's more, salubrious, more? Effictitious than a parable from my own, how shall I say? My own poor life, poor hah! but rich, rich in that greatest of all boons that poor, we...." Folding mouth, moustache, drinking. "Salubrious, what a...wine punch is, very. Salubrious, I remember." Swallowing again, eyes above the glass; cringing, shifting and this time Max I won't betray...stirring, their strength and mockery.

"Well ah...." Smiling to his friends. "I believe you've, hum, missed the point of our little discussion."

"Not at all, notatall." Smacking lips and laughing suddenly, dentures in his mouth: "Paddling my canoe, I was." Abruptly for silence. "One summer. In the northland, very far north, away...." Splashing to the rug as he waves his arm. "Away from all this on one of my." Rubbing it in, pressing his foot to the dark patch there. "Ventures you might say. I was working, one of my jobs. Ha-ha-HA! Oh you don't know, I may look, but...." Tapping his head, "I've done a lot." Offensive, goddamn leering at them. "Anyway! There I was, paddling (I've done a lot of it, believe me gentlemen in my day) when suddenly, right there!" Again, spilling hand, they start. "As close as that, oh my you could've breathed me down, I was amazed, absolutely: why I never, in all my experience and so close, as close as...." Enthusiastic body performs; he points, they turn unwilling: "Rising you might say, up and out of the water, emerging like a." Searching laugh, aggressive "Hooo-eewh! Heugh-hugh! A myriad, yes. Just like a prehistoric myriad of old."

"Did you get him?"

"God damn!"

"Stumbling on the shore and rushing to the bush like a man in flames."

"Christ I can see it now."

"Bet he didn't have a gun."

"Blam! Blam!"

"Antlers I tell you, like a man in flames!"

Got you red bastard

"...silly old fool didn't even...."

"How big would you say...."

"Like a man in flames."

"That's lovely, absolutely...."

"IN FLAMES!"

"Isn't that always the way?"

"...lovely." Sly Frieda with these men, shoving.

"And he paused, here's the wondrous thing, he paused to turn and look at me, he did!" Words, his voice. "Looked right into my eyes, stared deep in here." Sharp fingers at his eyes. "Do you know boys?" Sudden stare. "There were tears of blood in the eyes' dark corners."

"Awh c'mon!" they shrug but he doesn't, does he see?

"Isn't that, wouldn't you say that's an interesting experience?"

"It ah, certainly is." Flesh-white chin. "But you see old man, we're having. You understand, a private conversation don't you know, so why don't you...." Stronger, harsh face. "About hunting and since, you're not a hunter."

"Indominably not!"

"You don't like hunting." Accusing breath.

"I will not hunt." Silence. Hardening smiles. "Oh I'm telling you gentlemen I've, yes I've had the opportunity. When I was in. Its not that I...." Twisting fingers, his moustache, his eyes and laugh. "Oh no no-siree, no-no I've had the.... HAH! In Africa Afreek, the great white rhino, fearsome! Of the dark continent, I know. What I'm talking...."

"We haven't even been introduced."

"...about, I surely do."

"I mean I mean," bursting voice: "who the devil are you anyway?"

"...is this?"

"Absolutely frightful."

"Bursting in on our conversation."

"India, Ceylon, Kenya." Sipping he doesn't, Jesus he doesn't see! "And Burma yes, I remember once in the monsoons it was." Reaching neck, laughter with bobbing tendons. "We were on the track of a particular tiger who'd been, well you know. Rampaging off the land. Little children and things." Shrugging, "you know. Very nasty business, the tiger."

"Eating little children!"

"Oh yes. They do it all the time in Burma."

"That's," staring eyes. "A lot of bull!"

"Well, just a." Asthmatic I told you. "That's hunting isn't it? Hum, you...surely you have to admit that hunters, in this case. Why...the society. Needs them, depends upon...."

"Just a...."

"Their courage, their...."

"Just a moment sir!"

"What?"

"Then, even then I say, with the cunning beast in my sights, that. Rampaging carnivore...."

"Cats are like that."

"In my mercy, so to speak and I couldn't...."

"You can't trust cats."

"Oh." Wailing she turns and "how can you say such a thing?"

"Its true, they're a selfish lot. Cats."

"I couldn't shoot him, even then."

"And a good thing too if you ask me." Sniffing moisture in her nose. "Cats are lovely creatures," then suddenly. "You know" and his arm, "Perhaps you can...."

"You couldn't...you COULDN'T???" Outraged, "that's outrageous, that's. The kind of SENTIMENTAL THINKING that undermines...."

"...help me. I'm looking for you know, for a crippled cat, if you ever see a crippled cat...."

"Undermines." Wheezing. "The basis, the very BASIS

of our social fabric, our...."

Extravagant "Madam" from the waist: "There's no shortage, no sir. Some of my best friends."

"WHOLE COMMUNITY!" To them with fury "I'd have to say thats a, why GAWDDAMMIT that's...."

"Yes. Oh. Yes!"

"Tell me, whoever you are...."

"SUBVERSIVE."

"Whatever your name is."

"What about the children?"

"The women and children?"

"The DEFENCELESS LITTLE KIDDIES!"

"You selfish old...."

"Bastard, that's what he is, a...."

"Just give me one." Icy voiced. "Just one practical reason for your...why are you so disrespectful?"

"Well. You want, I see."

"That's right. C'mon!"

"Tell us if you're so...."

"Subversive, I mean."

"I see, you...." His trembling hand for calm, I....

"Don't even know who he is."

"Want a defence, an eloquent...." Hand to his eyes. "I meditate a lot." This numb caress. "I do, I really do. A lot of hard thinking and its come to me, you understand...."

"Now just a minute." Straightening inside his shirt, shooting his cuffs! "You listen to me old man." Sure smile for all? "We're-ah, fairly hah, a successful group."

"Yeah, what do you...."

"Goddamnright!"

"Yes."

"For a living, look at that...."

STOP!

"...suit. Old man...."

YOU BASTARDS

"Like a bee, thin bee."

"And do you know why? I'll tell you why?" In chorus because, *"WE know HOW to GET THINGS DONE!"* Hip-hip the bastards, clapping hands and I haven't. Not a word, I passive, so fucking I'll never, afraid, be anything, I've got to! So vulnerable, old, do something, what? Clothes about their bodies, screaming words with me

standing: the smell of a voice in the wool of my suit. Max I
can't. I don't know what happened.

"I know a man in the ranks// And he'll stay in the
ranks!"

"Immortal poesy."

"Do you know why?" In unison, hands. "I'll," fistsmack
in sudden palms: "I'll tell you why! Because..." Allsmack,
handsmack, smart clap in time: "He doesn't know how to,
get-things-done!"

HOO—RAH! HOORAH! Clapclap. Hoo-rah. "We're
hunters. Hunters, that's right." Smile for me, so coldly
sure: "The community needs people like us."

"The country."

"...whole free world!"

"Depends, the social fabric as we know it depends upon
the hunter's, you understand." Got you. "His ingenuity."
Red bastard pig!

"Its easy, you understand, to be critical. Oh yes. Its an
easy thing to be negative, while the others, the practical
men, the hunters." They threatening sway, "as it were
provide, providing through the ages for the community."

"The community as a whole."

"For people like you!" Hand-prodding they circle
closer, they're overwhelming his grey face...running in
breath; ran yes, dizzy, in girders above, alone.
Sky-hurtling wind. Air-beating faces, mouths, words lost, I
turn carefully in this ugly room for another drink. And its
not, for sure not as good. I didn't care, I crouched to the
light with car after car behind the hill: smoke to my lungs
and breathing confused, slow motion.... Terrible echo,
heaving cough: running, I've run wet-wool, failed so often
what can I do, am I the same? I should have Christ, have
Jesus, they're hunting him but not a word, not a fucking!
Bastard Felix I ease away: that's emptiness. Cold hand
with voices somewhere. Dead tongue in my mouth, this
glass and no hope. Like when; what night? In Edinburgh,
silly bugger breaking away from me, tears (that window's
face, reflection on my empty room) and running voice: is it
wearing, my life is it simply a wearing away?

"Like all of them, he had...." Scornful, sharp pointing
Christ, where can I, they're turning I: "You can see, no
sense of responsibility." Disdainful flowers, am I blushing?

And Max to me; hand on my arm: they snort and laugh. "Silly old fool," they fade and I did not, will not. What happened?

"Goliaths sirrah, variable Goliaths. Pay them no heed my boy." To me, he's come to my eyes, his voice and Felix, "Oh Felix" with hand and sudden "Felix."

"Yes."

"What can I do, what can an...."

"C'mon Max, don't...." An old man do?

"Did I embarrass you, I don't want...."

"Shit no!"

"You know I never want...."

"You didn't, no hah," awkward: "you didn't. No!"

"Yes I did, they were offended. Were they offended?"

"Christ Max I don't...."

"I offended them."

"I don't care, they're not...."

"I can tell."

"Jeez," smirk and stronger they stare with this sudden: "I'll get them hee, old Max," filling glass from the bowl: "has a few tricks up this sleeve of his." What are they thinking? Discomfort, this friend you are, he is but cannot any longer; I've got to go, get out goodbye, so often. Failed, not changing like I must what must.... So drinking, wine and citrus, run I'm going to.... What think, what do they think? Aloof their eyes, he leans, whispers: "I'll get them, I have. A little something." Bony finger beside his nose, "a little appropriate something, you just wait."

"I just had to." Voice for him. "To tell you just how really kind I think you are."

"Dear lady oh." So courtly, Max this would-be lechery. "And you are. A dear lady." She blooms, reaches as he calls, waving his arm: he calls her down. "An inspiration, yes with your poor little dog, a model...."

"Cruelty's so...." Fluttering lashes, tongue, "so cruel, I think," her darting tongue

to the arch and through; they enter (he went this way, my stranger, I'm sure) so follow, I must and straining to see the three of them slowly ahead on their descending road. Who was he, pale and briefly staring face; he paused, then why did he leave, was he frightened and why did he rush off like that? Musing and walking (this is a pretty funny place!), easier walking, there's light ahead; some light or other and I can see better, that's the thing! eyes for the dark. Able to see passages that lead away and some of them are bright with noise: Felix more cautious, for others are terribly dark and shit! Shapes, who are they in doorways as we pass? strangers watch and shift; threatening bodies and the sound of my feet.

Faster walking, they're almost trotting, swinging their arms for speed without a word, not a word and faces, straight ahead. Don't look back, straight ahead in shuffle, the shuffleshuffle sound of our feet, pursuing sound of our feet, pursuing echoes as we descend....

What if, wow quickly and don't look back, what if they're all chasing, they've all joined in for chrissakes bunching behind me and reaching, reaching to grab THEY'RE SNAPPING AT MY GODDAMN HEELS! Startled Felix into a desperate scrabbling run with their feet and breath about his ears, they've got rifles....

Christ I'd like to, can I sneak in and see what the hell's going on, can I? Dragging behind for its safe, there's nobody following, that was, shit that was silly. And there, that's a likely. Have I got the nerve? On impulse, more like impulse because its empty and only pale light, blue light and they haven't noticed, there's time, so Felix quickly in from the main tunnel, this light and peeking around: another short passage. Its brighter without a sound, I'd better hurry. Quickly, light of foot (so quiet) with fingers to rough, the concrete walls, peeking WOW, this grabbing chill. Holy Christ! A giant TV? Keep your head back! Edging carefully to see some man or other running in panic who is he? Fingers trembling on the wall as uncontrolled he runs deserted streets, a slum and straight through an intersection; winter light and the terror, its all reflected in smaller screens a hundred times: electric blue and soundless, Felix sees standard sets; some on tables and others in shelves or something, hanging on the walls. From blue to changing grey or black identical images and he's tiring yes, with coat-tails flapping he stumbles but desperation drives him on and on, he lunges flailing now and all these cold good Christ, these watching eyes!

Against the concrete, Felix aghast....

They sit, how many? An audience as he runs and there's

hundreds, there must be...staring with flipflop panic...he's running from them and its all too much too much too much I press my cheek to the stone...the charging blood the futile heart....

It can't be, can it be true?

Close-up now of his gasping body, terrible heaving and beaten he leans on gigantic, a what? a roadbuilding, a machine with iron wheels: his changing shadows, their heads deformed by earphones everyone, they listen, what do they hear? Slowmotion, almost gentle, he crumples, the camera on his hand, it strains to hold him from his knees, on his knees to the earth, to the earth his face and, hands deep into the earth....

"Hey you!" oh, my. "Listen", my shuddering, the hunchback in shadow: "You can't do that...you can't just, wander away. We've been looking for you."

"I'm sorry." He's angry and turning, he's...so trotting behind him. "I'm sorry."

"That has nothing to do with it." And out to the others, accusing for empty Felix among them. "He was in there after all."

"Aaaah!"

"I'm sorry, really I'm...."

"We've lost." Abruptly staring at his watch. "We're half an hour behind time now."

"You don't know, you didn't stop to think, did you?" Injured and petty-voiced: "How hard it is to find some- body in all these rooms."

"We'll have to rush."

"Its not as if we didn't...."

"I said I'm sorry, I didn't realize." Obedient now and surly as off we go but I thought. How was I supposed to know for chrissakes, its not my fault, no sir...they should have. Right, if there are rules then, obviously: keeping up easily with them, short-legged bastards, they should have told me. "How was I supposed to know?" but they don't even answer so piss on it. "I just wanted to see." Shit. "That's all." Purposeful walking, thin-lipped about me and watching cautious, I know they don't trust me, they're...fucking keepers that's what they are! Boy. Hurry- ing with shadows about us to the walls, hurrying sounds of breathing, our feet and I'm, what am I a fucking prisoner?

Empty doorways: silence as monotonously step after step, confused and always descending....

Captive Felix, yes I am and confused. What would happen if I disobeyed? Three small men and twisted, rodent bodies: we're underground. Where, "where are we going?" Polite, I'm friendly, properly respectful "where" to rustling clothes; pitpat quick feet to the earth and no reply. His shoulder's silence. Pumping arms and faster, shapes around me in the hall and somewhere voices whisper, a man is running, look look how he falls into the earth!

Possessed and expectant with them and I follow, I see and follow, ignore those other passages, their life and noise: sadly observe my body, fumbling with them, threading their way...how many times have I lost my life?

"PISS PARADE"

Voice command and bumping together, turning left "LEFT TURN" in a rank and pausing. "QUICK MARCH." Shoulder on shoulder, forward to the edge of this tumbling hill. "HALT" as he should with them, pause again; then clumsy pulling it out be ready! to ready, aim, "FIRE!" All pressure released uneven, four glistening arcs. What is this ditch, crevice, ravine where he stands? Two feet balancing, pissing heartsick, knowing the ground's eroded, feeling the fall about to come yet hopeless, obedient...polite I am, instinctive to please

what can she want? Hesitant because I can't, she knows I've Jesus seen her and I can't escape! Arrange, Felix arranging for mothers, quizzical, intelligent and somehow yearning. My body gallant yes, I mutter: "Mrs. Baillie m'am" and stare. Our eyes. Now speak, say: "A sad day" or something.

"Oh Felix!"

"I'm sorry, Mrs...."

"Felix, oh!"

"I really am."

"Felix I don't know what." Choking, searching my face. "I don't know what I'm going to do."

"Yes." I know.

"So sudden, its all so sudden."

"I know."

"In the midst of life."

"Yes."

"Felix!"

"Yes?"

"He was a good boy Felix."

"He was, yes...."

"A good Christian boy."

"He was."

"Oh Felix."

"Um...." Straining I think, staring at her vacant staring face. I've drunk a lot....

"Such a loving son." Fingernails absently trace her forehead. Clumsy fingers and the sweat under her white arm. "Felix." Pointed, threatening....

"Um...."

"Are you a, tell me...." Swallowing, then in a rush. "Do you love your God?" Argh-oh a, dirty, what?

"What?" and sick, she's.... Reeling, a foul, glaring she pursues my eyes.

"Are you a loving son?" She did, Christ my heart! ARE YOU A LOVING.... Sickness and listen that's it! I'm not a child anymore, not a child. Seizing breath, their sighing breath, there it is again! Bursting from the door and desperate to the park and nightalone....

"Um," a loving, "what do you mean?" Deep breath. Another. Don't speak. Fat bitch. WHAT DO YOU MEAN? Guilty. My eyes to the room and away: see him come, glass in either hand, earnest from; white eyes, he's coming, he rescues. I nod, he smiles, she takes the glass; we nod and smile. We smile.

"Reverend, do you know...." That's his throat, that's his collar, those are ashes. Plop. "This is Felix, Martin's room-mate Felix Oswald." Bobbing. Hands extended. Those are his hands.

"Hi."

"How do you do."

Undemanding hand. "I'm pleased." Ashes.

"Its a pleasure...."

"Felix only...." Warning in her, "Felix only looks like Jesus. Don't be taken in Reverend; he doesn't go to church, he doesn't love his God like Martin." Jesus fucking Christ!

"Why aren't you like Martin?" Bastard bastard he's better off, he's better dead. "Every weekend he came home to go to church with us...."

Martin!

"Well you can't be sure Mrs. Baillie...."

There's time.

To die, wear away....

Smoke and spaces. Bodies, funeral blooms: he was a good boy. You can't be sure of I'll get out that's the thing.... See him clumsy suckhole smile; this is my smile.... Knowing Felix desperate voice, the sudden want: of many nights no two the same of love GET OUT I felix or I'll never Felix out I "Felix" what, returning what, her voice? "Felix, you have...." Where am I? "There are still some things of Martin's in the apartment. His gramophone I think and a clock, his electric. Clock." She wants, she's going to take Christ everything away from me! Sour throat, I wanted, he was my friend.... I really do...eyes swimming can she, can they see? And I nod, yes. "Do you have them?" Nodding yes but....

"The record player's broken. It doesn't work."

"That's, oh Felix, that's all alright!"

"A long time, there's something...."

"I'm not, Felix I'm not going to use it. Its just you see...."

"There's something wrong with it. Its broken."

"I'm collecting everything," insisting Jesus, "for well. Upstairs." Head rolling to the stairs. "His room upstairs." Hands. Her spotted. Together. "I'm you see, I'm making kind of a memorial up there."

I'M MAKING KIND OF A MEMORIAL UP THERE

"You don't mind if I have them Felix, do you? You don't mind,...." Voices accuse, what've you ever. Laughter. Nod. The clock, yes his clock, the clock in the museum. "I knew you wouldn't...." Squeeze LET ME! "Thank you Felix, thank...." Sniffing, so sad darling, it makes me...she's squeezing my hand, that hand, my body in this room. That body. Mine? Who are they there? What are they doing? "Um. Professor Crackell seems a fine sort of man." Felix. "Dear Martin always spoke so highly and I told him, yes I did, I said Martin what sudden figure, figures bursting in noise? Enchanted Felix because they're real, they talk and laugh (I can hear their noise), not like those doorway ghosts or other judges judging that dying run, his face into the earth.

Boy this is fantastic!

It really is, exhilarating: smiling to faces, Felix grinning as they come, well-dressed from passages ahead and excited more and more, they fill the corridor, a mob. From the theatre. Good-natured to the street like this, joined by some exciting, some show, something.... Expensive, low-cut at the breasts all tanned and heavy, elegant summer dresses, white and glistening lips, their bright mouth's laughter, and arms, their round arms, shoulders that pass by me. Felix, eager, silent Felix at the edge of a crowd, madras jackets, bermuda shorts and brown knees; cigarettes are lit, the flame from mouth to mouth and shadows on soft throats, breasts tanned and heavy...they look so nice...oh boy!

Pressed back to the wall and delighted and there's more and the first ones move too slowly, they're pausing to talk: there must be dozens for pity's sake, hundreds more, they push and chatter to one another; they wave from their toes and smile, they haven't seen me yet....

Everybody certainly seems to know everybody and boy, I wish they'd.... Felix resisting, forearms up and elbows out as again he's jostled, Christ. Straining to see and that's curious? really creepy...they're talking alright...yes they are...a muttering noise but there's not a word, I can't recognize a fucking word! Jesus Christ, leaning worried to a voice, it sounds like a voice but THERE ARE NO WORDS boyoboyoboy I'd better.... Searching excited, frightened eyes and above them, there! is that? Yes. For Christ's sake they're, they're...look at them clutching up there at the ceiling, bastards among the pipes: desperate and holding afraid, I'll signal; I'll wave so they'll see, like this and stretching higher, this. Felix waving, arms in giant motions left to right and crossing, right to left but they don't look, they crouch as Felix "Hey" is jarred by this vacuous prick, "c'mon, watch out eh!" Shoulder pushing back to show him, angry Christ they shove as if I wasn't there at all. Be firm then. I'm going to leave, get out of this and join them. On the other side, YES: so if I push along the wall, just edge against them to the end (there must be an end)...inconspicuous along the argh, the wall like this "excuse me," then I'll cross over and that should do it. Stronger and a little louder: "Excuse me" but they still don't move. Pressing harder for chrissakes, hand to a shoulder. "EXCUSE me, PLEASE!" and stumbling, shoving, grunting into another. This is hopeless.... Felix desperate prying them apart, lunging into an instant's gap and even when I trample on their goddamn feet they don't respond. Urgent on he goes and on with breaking sweat inside his shirt: keep to the right! don't leave the wall or I'm lost, swallowed up in this sludge. Levering at them, knees and elbows out and slipping by in their wordless noise.

Rising to judge direction, yes stretching up to see how far.... WHAT'S THAT! Who's that for chrissakes, there he is familiar again I know him God, I do but who? he's seen me, can he be, he hangs by his arms then falls away.... Letting go. Down into the crowd with driving need to follow, discover who it is and where he leads, he's leading me somewhere, he...and he's getting away!

Body harder as more press in and stand; lashing out he snarls "'get away, get away!" but they jostle him sharp against the wall. "Watch out will you, Jesus will you watch out where you're going...." Eyes blurring, what are you going to do? Eyes clouding and panting afraid: "I have to find him oh please, excuse me I've got to get through."

Prepare that's it and body intent, Oswald-at-last will show them, sneering bastards, savage he'll lash out... attack....

Another blow and they don't care, nobody cares how I feel, my body in the dark or what I want I want from clawing shadows these houses and the night

blonde and pleasure of Ann: my dark, my face for her. The haunting smile. "Hi there."

"Felix you look." Hair to her grey eyes. "You really look surly." Laughter in her throat. "And you've been ignoring me all...yes you have, don't try! You have." Mocking pressure, she is she must be on my arm. "Flint-hearted boy!" Not true, I'm not.... "But I forgive you."

"What do you mean?"

"Its true, oh yes it is. But I'm accustomed to your cruelty Felix Oswald. I am resigned." Fingers down my sleeve to my hand, they rest. "You know that. Don't you?" Gentle. Fingers....

Funny. We hold. I fall away....

Her eyes are grey.

My flesh is soft, she says and full; my marrow burning...if only you'd bring yourself, and give yourself, and lose yourself.... Grey eyes, hand. Forgive.

I'm afraid.

Rain on streets, rain at windows, breath in my ear, her mouth, I could with you, with her if I yes if I could....

White, hair black on my mattress, white-armed, my baby baby reaching arms encircle, draw me down I'm sorry, Pat I've. Got you! crying I don't like her. No! Five legs, three legs. I've never liked, don't you....

"She said I only look like Jesus."

"What?" Startled. Hand, its touch.

"Isn't that wild?"

"Who?"

"Mrs Baillie." Worlds! There are worlds in me....

"Oh." Hand gone. Eyes. "Here comes Susan." I'm sorry, you've made me look like...who Susan? "She wants you Felix." Ann I'm reaching, see it, my hand, I need you. "I'm leaving Felix."

"Ann," whose voice? "Ann don't go." They're all....

"Felix." Voice, I turn. "Felix, how are you darling." Leaning. Cheek. Struggling, breath....

"Susan," please!

"Oh Felix." I do not move. I mutter.

"Susan," mutter, then PUSH HER! Push her away! Skirts.... He was right. Shrivelled-up prune between her legs....

"We were engaged to be married Felix, did you know that, did you hear?" Voice, songs, an epic...he won't, I know! "So glad you all came down, that's why...." not to me.... "So many nice people...." Back there. What happened, why am I? "They've come from all over you know, from Toronto...." Into the snow, from the snow. So many nights. "Ottawa, and his uncle Bill is down from Montreal." Going back, so many....

Forgive me.

Ann! Where is....

Back my head. "Particularly Lucan, he's so...well...so

human, so understanding. I simply don't know how."
WHAT AM I DOING? "How I'd have managed, coped
today without him. He's so, well so reassuring isn't he, so
giving." Get out, I must....

He rubbed, sucked those breasts. For nothing.

"Just by being here, just having him near was
enough...." Crackell's failed you, didn't you know? "He's
going to be head of that new department, he has" what?
"an excellent chance. Did you know that?" Whatwhat.

"The head, he's going...."

"Yes. Isn't that nice. He told me, he said...." It doesn't
matter. Feet. Legs from standing. Voice. Other words.
Thunder beyond the trees, I can't.... I don't want, I don't
want to play!

"...that trouble at home...."

I'll never, that's all...hear me hear on the tracks at
night! HE WILL NEVER GET OUT....

What if somebody really was and letting them out? Hah
for chrissakes, that'd be great! But where, a bunch of cows
at night, where'd they go, what would they do?

"I mean it must be terrible not to be able to give a man a
baby, not to be able...you know, and that's their problem,
that must be their problem Felix, don't you think?" Dull.
"Felix." What's she....

"What, I'm sorry. Who?" People.

"Oh you...." Thin lips. "Weren't you.... Felix Oswald
you weren't even listening to me...."

"Those people, what are they...." Pointing to the kitchen door, they gather to see. "I wonder what?" Staring at
Frieda.

"Felix, is that somebody singing?" Some yes.

"It certainly sounds...."

Goddamn Frieda! "What is it," I told her Val. I. What
does she know? "Who's singing aunty, is that someone
singing?"

"Yes its...what's his name...." Who? "Crackell...."

"Lucan?"

"Yes."

"You mean he's *singing*?" Wildly, what in Christ?

"And he has a very pretty voice."

"Oh," Susan crumbling: prunes. "What's he...."

"Singing? I don't know, I've never heard...."

"But he must." Off she, "he just has to stop! poor man, he...." Door; "Let me through, excuse," me door, I pause:

> A very strange enchanted boy
> They say he travelled very far, very far
> Over land...

His voice. Unwilling, whose voice?

> ...one day,
> one magic day he comes her way

he's there again, there! don't you see? Felix eager because of the shadow, again, a silhouette for me in the narrowing passage, it sees yes it does! it stares and who is it. "Who are you...." who's that? But it turns from my reaching arm. "Please stay!" and at that corner is gone. Christ its urgent, crucial yes, and maybe they'll know; "Who's that, did you see? who's that person just ahead?"

"Which," and slowing to stop, they turn: "which one?"

"What person, I didn't see...." Dark and somehow nervous they pause. "We can't...."

"There are all kinds of people down here."

"I didn't see anyone."

"And even if we had." Voice insists: "Even if we had we can't, it'd be silly to think we knew them all."

"But he was with you!" waving, pointing my arm, "back there." He was, they. "You must know him...."

"No, no" dismissing. "There are too many."

"In the pipes, remember? With the crowd, that terrible crowd and he was with you up in the...." Blank faces waiting, bodies deformed, but they have to! "You must remember, in the pipes? then he came on ahead and just now, right there," pointing to the corner. "He motioned to me from the corner."

"I certainly didn't see...."

"At any rate its not important." Abruptly: "We've lost too much time already, let's go." They follow with Felix defensive, sure they're acting, that's it! they know alright but they won't tell.... "Come along you, come along. We have to keep going." Legs scuttling and there's no need, he doesn't have to get impatient, not like that....

He's still ahead, he can't have turned, I'll find him there's no way out, there's nowhere to go: sound of their feet. And well, since they decided to lie, to hide...what's that? Up ahead, its him! "Look there he is!" a stumbling run, my phantom out of sight. Desperate I must...pushing past them: "There, he's gone I told you, there! you can see...." Roughly through, I have to, find him, barging frantic from their hands and bodies resisting. "LET ME GO!" And fighting now, I swing and twist to free....

"Just a moment, just." But I won't, I spin in their hands and cry.

"I have to go, I have to find him!" Panting, held, pressed harsh on the wall with his face, cold-voiced he leans:

"You can't go rushing off on impulse."

"But I know him."

"No you don't!"

"But I do, I've seen...."

"You can't know him...it happens often." He speaks softer as they hang on. "They think they recognize something, then they forget everything here and rush away...." Its happened, they've seen it before: from above there's a draught. "They never find it. Usually they come back ...sadder, of course, and with nothing to show...they're worse off really." Squeezing hand as they nod. "We can't wait you know, we never wait for long...so they drift back here...." Warning, or threats? "Well they almost never catch up. They just roam around in the shadows...."

"You've seen them!"

"Hopeless lonely men."

"They're deadbeats...." Reasonable, be.... twisted about me.... be reasonable voice and I was, I'm sure and the bastards stopped me, grabbed me! He paused and then he turned away; a beckoning shape at the corner just for....

Bursting Felix! "Come back, hey you...." Leaping they clutch at his clothing they seize his coat as he twists and he turns. "Hold him!"

"For chrissakes, don't let him...." Desperate he slips like an eel from the coat and he's free! To the corner without a thought, he leaps from their voices behind: "Don't, don't be an idiot!" Beyond them, solitary Felix gone too far

she's what's she? Black dress: "Please! just a moment.

Just a moment please." Voices fall, they. "I would like....
Upstairs...." the museum! "In Martin's poor Martin's...."
Words, "his room," GODDAMNIT! museum. "I'd like
you to know. We're making his room into a memorial."

"What a good...."

"Poor woman."

"A good idea...."

"We're collecting all of his.... all of the things he lived
with, loved so well...." The earth. Plop. "And I'd like,
Mister Baillie and I would like...." Slow motion. "...come
on, all of you.... we'd like you to see...." It doesn't matter....

Ann briefly in the other room; resigned...grey eyes, I
need it doesn't.... What's happening?

"Felix. I told you something, eh? I said I'd...." Teeth, his
face. Eyes. "I've done it, old Max has hee! I've done it
alright." Bodies.

"What?"

"In the punch."

"You what?"

"Alcohol." Whisper-whisper what did he say? "Absolute alcohol in the punch." He's put, laughter, shit, this, oh
no, too much!

"You son-of-a-bitch."

"I did, I told you...."

"Didn't!" his shoulder.

"...indubitously, I...." did the bastard hah did he...shit!
if they knew, they'd.... "I had a flask, you know how I...."
Harsh "wait till we tell them, eh Felix? Wait till Jerry
hears, he'll...and Pat" too much too much "Oh no!"
Laughter, our arms, baby-baby, his shoulder, yes, what
can an old man? "You can't cross old Max" pleading,
"they'll learn...." It doesn't matter

in gathering light on this narrow hill: Felix running
from their voices, but they don't follow. A long rectangle of
colder light with doorways firmly closed, small wooden
doors on either side: too small, I'm sure, and old, cob-
webbed, they haven't been touched. Silence all around,
that's good! he must be still ahead, I can't have lost him;
listening for signs in the bright air to my face and climbing
higher. Careful on like this and on to hear, to see some
figure at this corner, the next and after that another

what voices? elbows, shoulders, where is he? Shrieks.

"Get out of the way!" The room, Martin's. Where is he? never get....

"How could you, how?" Martin's room, we're making a kind of. "That's what I want to know...how could you...I don't...." Susan. Crackell together, he's certainly. "..hardly into the ground, he's...." Excitement, what in Christ? Together. Terrible laughter in my head, her tear-stained. What have they, what's going?

"What's going...."

"Oh Felix!" Oh.

Boom.

"What?" Museum for chrissakes!

"Felix!" Careful, I've got laughter.... "They were... oh...." Hand, her eyes; tears. "I came in and found them, they were," savage, "they were smooching." WHAT?

"We weren't! How can you say...."

SMOOCHING!

"You were, they were weren't they, you all saw them didn't you, you saw them!"

"MADAM! Mrs.!" empty, reaching his: "Mrs. Baillie, you don't.... NO!" Panic searching, crowded door. Run. "You can't believe...."

"And on my Martin's bed, the...." Too much, they ha! ha-hee I can't, too much, oh HAWH-HAWH! hands spotted, "I think I'm going mad" HAH-HAH....

"We were only talking!" tears plop, shouting GOT YOU trembling at each other gawd, oh hee-hee-hee-heee-haaaawh!

"Surely you can't...." gasping breath he'll never. "Believe me please, believe...." Flushed and turning this way, that. "I'm here officially, you see...." And this, boom-boom.

"I'm so ashamed, how could you?"

"Oswald! Felix...you believe me...."

Crazy my OH HAWHAWHAWH! my face to bastards, lurching: the blurring door, his breathing call, bodies as I come, voices:

"Come back!"

Come back

"...disgusting...."

"FELIX!"

"...is he crazy or something?"

What

cold and bright, squinting Felix in opening sunlight, I'm out: pausing to stare at a rising hill at evergreens with new snow and silence. Cautious as in a dream, for where am I, what place is this? moving to where the snow begins and there's not a mark! not a scar, just crystals of fragmented sun.

Its really beautiful. The snow is clean and its drier than I thought....

Irresolute at the edge. Staring to the left, its a ravine alright, and then to the right. Irresolute. Which way. A ravine, with fine trees and a frozen stream. What's that! from the bushes there? Stepping carefully in his street shoes, picking his way on the powdered surface with ice beneath...its treacherous! Shit, be careful. Its beautiful alright, so cold and I'm not dressed for it. Left my goddamn coat behind. A sudden slide, wild jump! then fall dear! God, I crash like a. Bounding to my feet hah, and brushing whisk-whisk hand to my thigh, I must be...careful. Hah. Very cold hands, into my pocket and my feet are soaked. Got to be pretty careful, bruised like I am...could break a leg and freeze to death alone out here, completely. Across the clearing with breaking crust beneath and I'm in it up to my fucking knees! savage oh my shins.... I'll slide the old feet, skate on the surface like this where its new.

I wonder what it was, a raccoon? maybe an otter or something, a big cat? Skirting the hillock, peering among the bushes full of snow, then up to branches against the sky.

A cigarette: cold smoke, tasteless. What's that? Somewhere traffic above me. I wonder where this is? Smoke from its tip in my hand; brightening. Did I imagine him, were they right after all? He didn't come out here and that's for sure...perhaps I passed him, maybe...it doesn't matter I guess, it doesn't matter.... Shivering cold without a coat for chrissakes, stamping feet.... I have to keep going....

Movement there, a bird, another! and a squirrel...the woods have life, he runs on flatter ground beside the hill and around this brush to.... Fifty yards ahead, no more, this huge, a fire of glowing logs and swirling heat untended; whole trees for chrissakes, dead trees burning in a pile and there's nobody...Jesus, that's great! A hut for storage, for lawnmowers in summer and drums of gasoline. Door ajar as he circles wide, he must pass by: careful, two of them sitting in there, smoking and drinking from coffee mugs in the gloom. Good Christ he's a big one and strong from the world, look away! he's seen you.... But you MUST go on! Stiffly Felix, hands deep-thrust, do I turn and nod? I can't, don't want.... He turns to a breaking grin and offered cup, a motioning arm from bright green, nice the green work-man's hut behind him now; Jesus Christ, I got you can't, I can't! he shakes his head, forgive, I can't...then running ahead impulsive to the heat, he's running, skipping, free-sliding....

Communion

For
Selena,
Jake L. and Peter C.

Communion was first published in November 1971 by the House of Anansi Press.

Space is always between us
and time is inserted in us like a disease.

Barbusse

Why does she come each morning like this? A ritual perhaps, but not for him: he's happy enough beneath the covers, arms against his body, hands together at his throat.

Christ knows he doesn't need it! with knees pulled up under his chin for protection, the body curled around its own belly like this, anyone can see he doesn't need it. Yet here she comes with cigarettes, matches and the white plastic holder...

Why?

Deliberately from the door to the chair beside his face and sitting, staring impassive as he sleeps. She hears her spring morning at the open window. She hears birds in the eaves and she hears the trees, a car door slam. She hears the starter before the engine catches, then she listens to hear acceleration to the corner; tipping her ear slightly, she squints her eyes after the diminishing sound. It doesn't take long. And then there's only the city and the imperceptible sound of his body's sleep.

She rises, she puts the cigarettes, the matches and the holder beside his pillow and, bracing her feet on the floor, her knees against the bed, she takes a deep breath and tries to wrestle him onto his back. He resists. She tries harder. He curls in upon himself like an armadillo, but grunting and clutching, sweating now and heaving, she begins to gain the advantage: he's weakening, one of his arms comes loose: vainly he struggles to re-enclose himself but the circle's broken...it's just a matter of time. She hears a high-pitched whimpering in his throat, and knowing the muscles that strain in his chest, the burrowing face, she pauses. Clever. With left hand on his right wrist, elbow against his belly and into his hip, and her right arm under his shoulders, she seems to give in to him. Very clever. His body, surprised at this unexpected freedom, relaxes (will it never learn?), the whimpering dies . . . and at this instant, so beautifully timed, she surges to her feet and grunting flips him onto his back.

Things proceed as usual.

Felix open on his back, he breathes the end of sleep . . .

Cigarette in her mouth, she rests. It's getting harder all the time, she isn't getting one bit younger: once it was strength alone that did it, she walked in at seven and simply rolled him over. But those days are gone now: more and more she has to rely on the advantage that comes with experience. But then he's more stubborn too . . .

She lights a cigarette and slips it into the holder. There are birds outside and trees that press about the house: the sun is shining, rather pale at this hour, but shining nevertheless as she leans forward to brush her finger lightly at the corner of his mouth. He shivers, he searches blindly with a sucking noise, his face is pained, is drawn in lines as his mouth searches suck suck. Such an anxious face!

By resting her elbow at his side she keeps the holder steady; her arm along his chest, she bends and reaches, pinching the nostrils to stop him breathing through his nose. It's the only way. Otherwise he simply puffs, breathing sleepily all the while, and the smoke scarcely passes his lips, hardly gets into his mouth, let alone into his lungs where it's needed, where it does the most good. The effect is immediate. The tip glows more brightly, it fades to greyness, then it glows again, it fairly crackles! Miniature forms collapse upon themselves as he exhales. But the rhythm's still uneven, it's not bad, a beginning, but uneven . . .

Sometimes the smoke goes down the wrong way, gets into the gullet or whatever and he's overcome, he's doubled up and blue with the lack of air. It was frightening at first, she used to think he was actually going to die, but since he never did she's learned to put up with unexpected things from time to time. One morning last winter he wouldn't open his mouth to take the cigarette. Even when she held his nose shut tight he wouldn't open up . . . his body heaved, convulsed as if to make sure there was no way, and then he just lay there turning greyer and greyer until a purple ring appeared about his mouth. Terrible, as if he didn't care, he was so calm, he didn't move and she panicked. It was the spreading private bruise, that blackening beneath the skin, she couldn't look away, she could only stare...and growing certain that he'd finally win, she lost her head completely. She savagely pinched at his nose, twisting the holder she tried to pry his body open at the mouth, she pleaded and coaxed, she cursed him, she promised intolerable things but he wouldn't hear, he'd simply stopped breathing. And he wouldn't have started again, she's sure of that, if she hadn't reached between his legs and gathered his genitals in her hand. She gave a tentative pull...unconvincing...so she squeezed, violently she twisted until he bellowed, he gasped, he started to breathe...and before he could close again she'd pushed the mouthpiece in and won!

That was an unusual morning; but the question of tempo is automatic. The problem is to press firmly and rhythmically on his chest while keeping the nostrils closed and holding the cigarette in his mouth at the same time. None of these things can be neglected for a moment. For example, if she doesn't maintain a constant pattern of pressure on his chest, then she'll never regulate his breathing...however, if in concentrating on this she forgets the nostrils, if air seeps into his head in any way except through the mouth, then he'll simply breath without smoking at all. Finally, even if she manages both, but doesn't keep the cigarette holder firmly in his mouth, if she lets go even for an instant, then his jaws part, his lips slacken, open like an old man's, and the cigarette falls onto the pillow and rolls down to where the throat meets his shoulder.

Perhaps it sounds more difficult than it is and it's true that at first she'd longed for another hand, two extra fingers even, just to snip the nostrils shut. She'd begun to wonder, to plan even, to see if perhaps there was some sort of equipment, a machine...A clothespin, for example, placed carefully on the nose, it seemed an excellent idea, almost like two extra fingers, perhaps the clothespin would do. But he was offended, he'd groaned and thrashed about, his arm had swept up and thrown the clothespin against the wall.

That had been a disappointment. Leaning to enclose his nose securely in the crotch of her thumb and index finger, her hand extending down so the tip of that same thumb and finger can steady the holder in his mouth, she remembers the sense of failure. Yet at the same time she'd never fully despaired, never seriously, and that's something after all; not once has she really considered giving up... What's more, her perseverance ultimately produced the technique she's using now and it works well too: her right hand, placed as it is, successfully looks after the nose and the mouth (both of them) and leaves her left hand free to lean upon his chest, impose this healthy rhythm on his breath.

Leaning her weight, pressing and counting, "a thousand and one" with grey smoke issuing from his mouth ...briefly she holds...then "a thousand and two", withdrawing she sees the fire as his lungs are filled. And so it goes. She fights him resolutely, pressing again ("a thousand and one"), she feels the slobber from his mouth, she pauses...and withdraws.

The next cigarette is ready in her mouth as, poised, she forces his lungs empty, and then with amazing speed her left hand grabs the holder and brings the glowing butt to light the new one; at the same time, her thumb and index finger have pinched his mouth shut and that's important, so he can't breathe and break the cycle. Ashes fly as she ejects the butt into the ashtray, exchanges the empty holder for the cigarette in her mouth, firmly inserts the latter into the former and, letting go of his lips, jams the holder back into his mouth. He gasps, she lurches to maintain the interrupted tempo, "a thousand and one" and they've hardly missed a stroke...

It's going very smoothly this morning.

Soon she stops the regulating pressure, stops the counting and relaxes somewhat back on the chair: she smiles, an imperceptible smile on her large face and hears again the birds, a car in the street, the day outside and sees the lines about his eyes, his mouth in rhythm now and knows the worst is over, that soon he'll be awake.

Keys, in hand and ready, cautious he leans his face to the glass and peers inside: it looks clear enough but he can't be sure, it's nowhere to be seen and that's ominous; it's not on the counter by the cash register, nor crouched as it is some mornings on the door leading to the back rooms. Where is it then? Methodically he searches as best he can; because of the relative darkness inside, the street's reflection on the glass and so forth, it isn't easy... he concentrates though, shading the glass he stares into gloomy corners, he even crouches to improve the angle; kneeling on the sidewalk, he tries to see if it's above the door. It doesn't seem to be but he can't be sure so turning the key, carefully bracing his shoulder he inches the door open... pausing to listen... but he can't hear it. All the usual sounds, the morning sounds: snuffling and groaning, breathing and sighing, all this and more; the brush of bodies, and madness of the talking birds, the chains and the scampering claws in metal wheels. But no Sammy, where is he? Door open a bit more until there's almost enough room to sneak through, it's looking good. Pausing to listen, then whipping it open and lunging inside, slamming the door just as he drops with a shriek from the transom, a chattering howl, the cunning bugger was there all the time! Pounding his fist on the door too late, face of a woodcut devil, then leaping to the counter he turns to stare; his angry shrunken face for a moment, and then he's gone.

Felix trembling inside because of the shock. Even though he was expecting some such assault, even though he's been through it, or something like it, morning after morning now, ever since taking the job, he still finds the shrieking accusation, the wizened face, the snarl profoundly disturbing, far too personal in fact. As if it's his fault, when he's only the employee, nothing more than an employee and yet every morning the stupid bugger comes at him like this, pinches up its nasty face in rage, charges about like a madman and rushes off into the other room.

Glancing to see that the cage is open, that the monkey will be able to get in alright, he picks up several super-market bags and strides into the back room. Along the length of the room there are three aisles between the cages, and in these cages (depending on their size, whether they're on the first or second level) there are dogs and cats, a raccoon or two, a skunk, sometimes tangled creatures that he doesn't quite recognize, and in the corner of the room, in the highest cage, there's an owl.

Now, with Felix pausing inside the door, with Sammy's violent anger, all the animals that can stand are on their feet, they press against the wire or cower back, they snarl or howl, they chatter and moan amongst themselves as he starts down the aisle. The monkey's hiding somewhere, but that's alright, he knows! Felix blows into the bag, squeezing the mouth shut as he draws another breath, blowing again with the paper stretching, the wrinkles vanishing as it fills with air. Down one aisle like this and up the next with still no sign of Sammy, he must be somewhere poised, but he hears alright and soon he'll make his move. Relentless pursuit in the growing excitement of caged animals and blowing out he turns the third corner, at the end of the second aisle, and then the fourth, the last and sees him, yes! he shouts, Ho-Hoh! And rubs the bag against his chest in warning, the monkey screams up onto the cages out of sight and scrabbles away as Felix smashes his hand against the bag. Mercifully it works, on the first try too, it explodes and more than fifty animals panic.

Blowing mightily on the second bag, Felix moves to cut Sammy off at the door because it won't do to let him out there yet, he's not ready, he's not desperate enough for his cage, he might think so, he might even get into it but he won't appreciate it. Not yet. He'll complain all morning.

Dogs cringe away from his legs and howl as he passes. He rustles the paper while gathering air for another blow, preparing himself; not a motion wasted or a moment lost, momentum is the watchword here, for Sammy thinks he's hiding but Felix sees him, yes he does, he sees him over there beside the owl and creeping up behind him bursts the bag! It retreats in growing confusion and fear, he follows with the third bag in his hand, the monkey bounds for the door and still he follows, he's gasping now, he's dizzy with Sammy retreating as the bag begins to stretch, retreating from the room and into his cage. Very good. But Felix won't relent, not yet; he stalks to the door to make sure, he pauses, he rubs the bag against his chest and Sammy whimpers; very good, there's no need to break it now, no need at all. He can walk to the cage and say "Hello Sammy", he can reach inside and stroke the skeletal body, he can say "Morning baby". Scratching under the chin, seeing skull beneath the hair and stroking its head: "Do you want some breakfast Sammy? that's what you want, you want some breakfast."

O   O   O

By the ceiling a window, a window with iron bars on the outside. The television is in the corner of the room. Blue light on his hands. No sound. Light on his trouser legs. He has eaten because it is evening, because it is almost night. Soon he'll leave the room, he'll walk to the stairs, he'll mount them to the landing at the side door, and with only the slightest hesitation, he'll slip out into the alley.

Very soon now. He drinks from a bottle, he smokes: blue light on his hands. What will they be doing tonight? What will he see them doing?

He moves with unfamiliar grace, his feet make no sound. Vaguely swaying lights above as he descends to the floor of the ravine. He avoids the white road, he slides through underbrush, a path along the edge, he walks beside the road because sometimes there are others, there are cars without lights, there are figures, shadows in the corner of his eye.

And tonight there is a car, he knows where to look, he sees it, heart's rhythm and muscles tightening, mouth parting, he pauses: leaves shiver about him, a light evening breeze on his face. He stares at the motionless hulk of the car. He can almost smell it.

From halfway up the side of the ravine, above it, he begins by throwing pebbles, a handful of them, and then another, they rattle through leaves and branches on their way. He hears them hit the car, clattering as they rebound into the dark. He can't see, but he can imagine their shock; that pleases him. Will loverboy play the hero? will hotpants jump out on the attack? He hopes so. Grinning excitedly, holding the brick in his left hand he hopes so, he can hardly contain himself, he stoops for another handful of pebbles and at that moment the engine starts. The car backs onto the white road, he transfers the brick to his right hand, he lobs it like a grenade...

Very close now, creeping closer, he pauses: leaves shiver about him, a light evening breeze on his face. He stares at the motionless hulk of the car. He can almost smell it.

The brush of bodies. They groan perhaps, breathing and sighing, the noise of their bodies: even closer to the glinting metal, if he reached out now, they don't know he's here, so close to them, teeth bared, eyes white, he could reach right in the window, he could put his hands on them gently like this... He straightens, he rises from the brush, he sees them, he reaches, fingers extended, staring he reaches in, he sees her long white legs convulse like spastic arms.

O O O

His mind is full of images, rationalizations, half-formed words, with escape routes closing before he knows, all the familiar structures of guilt: instinctively he stops before the dog, the husky, and drops to his knees in front of its cage. Withdrawn as usual against the inner wall, unmoving, it watches him with cloudy eyes as he bends closer.

The sun shines or it doesn't, it's winter sometimes and sometimes it isn't: the body struggles from sleep, dresses itself according to the season, eats and comes unwilling into the world's routine. But then, unexpectedly, there's a moment when he senses he could fall right out of it all, out of the whole thing, and his bony face contracts, it falls in upon itself like blood.

Riding sometimes in trains, in cars; resting against the glass, falling each mile further into himself: dry roads empty, occasional barns with homes in shadow and always the coloured fields, the geometric fences on the land. Mile after mile. He can't remember the first time it happened and can't be sure it ever did. It might have been an early morning on the way to summer camp. It might have been. A field rising to bush, trees crowding from the sky's edge and there, into the trees, an entrance leading away and he sees himself climbing the field in silence, sees a boyish figure alone, pausing, then striding as best he can from sight.

Gaunt white body unmoving, but it's still alive, and that's something: dull eyes, they watch him rising, watch him straightening to stand and there's tension somewhere, an accusing stink and shallow breath. And then he hears the others: snuffling and groaning, breathing and sighing, all this and more; the brush of bodies, and madness of the talking birds, the chains and the scampering claws in metal wheels as he starts his methodical search. Down the first aisle and up the second, peering into cages, poking a ruler at empty bodies and it's easy to tell the dead ones for limbs have stiffened, their eyes are unresponsive. He hits them as hard as he likes and they don't move. Sometimes he's mistaken of course, sometimes they're sleeping or sick, they lurch from the ruler and then he leans to soothe and reassure, he apologizes and when the animal is calm again he goes to the next cage. It's not a hard job. Whenever he's sure, he leaves the cage door open as a sign and by the time he's finished this morning there are five of them, five bodies to collect, wrap and stuff into green garbage bags. Fortunately none of them are very big. Big animals are difficult to handle, a leg or two is always in the way, the bag isn't big enough, and they certainly don't fit into the garbage cans. But that's not a problem today. A couple of lap dogs, a cat and two mongrel puppies; they hardly take any time at all.

Bell ringing in the shop. He's here: jaunty steps and whistling, things clatter as Peter Walters appears in the door. "Oswald. This place stinks." Into the room, glancing here and peering there. "The cages aren't cleaned, look!" Grimacing "Ugh. No wonder." Bright blue eyes. "What have you been doing? Good grief man, it's... It's almost ten o'clock. Why you should...how do you expect...oh no...Oswald, you know better than that! Come here." Over to the cupboard, opening the door and pointing. "Come here and look. Those cages should be clean by now." Pink nail healthy, white where it grows beyond the quick. "Nine forty-five, you see...that's quarter to ten. These animals should be coming in from the yard, the cages should be sparkling and you've hardly started." Staring from Felix to his lousy schedule, then closing the door again. "That's the trouble with you Oswald, that's the trouble alright...And I say this in all seriousness, in kindness, I hope you know that because, well, because I like you. Yes. I do, I like you Oswald. Don't ask me why. But I do." Cigarette into the mouth. Flick goes the lighter. He stands in clean shoes, smoking. He actually admits to liking Felix Oswald.

O   O   O

Sometimes a stream then, a creek that leads from sight among the trees, and other times it's just a suggestion, an opening image as he's carried by. His body's empty with the journey and he cannot speak.

Cool on his forehead and dirty, the window between him and that figure in the field. It happens often. In trains sometimes and cars, resting passive against the glass, falling with each mile further into himself.

O   O   O

"I hope you know that because, well because I like you. Yes. I do, I like you Oswald. Don't ask me why. But I do." Cigarette into the mouth. Flick goes the lighter. "And I think I can help you get more out of life." He stands in clean shoes, smoking. And what's all this pigshit about liking anyway? Likelike means nothing from him! what's he willing to do, will he… "Let's sit down Felix." Will he produce the bottle and this time a second glass? Pouring, and Felix reaching, lifting it to his mouth. "You're doing a fine job here." The world going by in the street. His smile's not so bad now, not so exclusive. And maybe he really does like him, for at some point he leans, he appears to be human, he leans and asks: "What do you really want Felix?"

"I'd like to die."

"These are sick animals, Felix, sick and it shows in the quality of the stool. Have you ever thought of that? Diseased shit Oswald, the cages are, the cages…" With tears in his voice he looks at his watch. "At almost ten in the morning my cages are full of diseased shit! That's the problem alright and there's no excuse. No. Absolutely none." He pauses and Felix perceives the trouble with that face. He might have been bothered by it before but he doesn't remember. Now the problem is obvious: it looks like the topographical map of uninteresting land. Everything is too small for the size of his head, too crowded there in the middle of his face. "I don't know what you do with your time, daydreaming, moping about."

Even if he did say, who are you Felix? what do you really want? it would be a lie, an intimate lie so that Felix might not notice at first.

"That dog for example, the husky. You spend far too much time with that animal, you really do." He fills a certain space here in the room, he talks. "I don't know what you think you're doing because it won't get better you know, there's nothing we can do." Felix shifts uneasily; he isn't needed for this talk, he doesn't want to hear it again. "Not a dietary problem, not nitrogen trichloride, that's fairly clear." Scratching at his ear, finger poking in to wriggle thoughtfully. "There's been a dramatic, as you may or may not know, a dramatic decline in the incidence of hysteria due to dietary factors." Pausing. "And it's certainly not parasites, no, not parasites. Not in this case." The smile has permanently returned and his voice is precise. "So it must be genetic, eh? An hereditary taint, derived from one or other parent." Felix doesn't believe this, not for a moment. "Yes. And that means..." In fact he starts, eyes rolling as if to speak, to contradict, his chest heaves painfully, his hands convulse against his thighs. "That means there's nothing medical science can do." And still the words don't come. "Particularly when the patient experiences epileptiform fits like this one does." It's always the same.

○   ○   ○

That blue light on his hands, on his legs. The stairs, that door, the alley. Why does he do it? He moves with empty grace, his feet make no sound, he slides through underbrush, a path along the edge, he walks beside the road because sometimes there are others...

He stops under the railway bridge. He's almost there, he'll smoke a cigarette. Then he'll cross the stream and climb to the pavement, the lights, their house. What will they be doing? what will he see them doing tonight? He hears water rushing against the concrete support, it stinks of the cemetery half-a-mile ahead: seeping among the graves it gathers in pools, he remembers the pools, it overflows and fed by the city becomes a stream that smells of bodies.

By the garage, excited because nobody knows he's here, pressing himself into its shadow with leaves resting on his shoulders. There are lights in the apartment but nobody appears in the windows. Music from a radio, perhaps a record player, is playing somewhere. He doesn't recognize the song. Noise from the traffic on Yonge Street, soothing, like the sea, although he has never heard the sea, or wind rushing across the land, some land, somewhere... Resting his face against the brick, he's breathing easily because he's in no hurry. In a minute he'll climb onto the garage roof, using the fence and one limb of the tree, he'll wriggle forward and lie unseen to watch them...

○ ○ ○

Walters, hands in his pockets poking at his balls, feeling himself stiffen delightfully as another woman turns from his smile, is confident that Felix is really trying to re-establish himself in his employer's esteem. And that's a nice thought. But perhaps. Sudden excitedly, he cannot breathe, for in a purple sweater, coming across the street are the biggest boobs, oh Christ he's ever seen! His hands are fiendish in his crotch, his smile is a hardware store. He retreats behind the counter as she pauses, will she come in? He can't believe, he won't... The sun shines only on this woman's hair, her enormous breasts. Will she come in? He can barely look at her. Will she? He leans to offer his most urbane smile. She's irresolute. Desperately he smiles, he grins. But even that doesn't do it. True she does acknowl-edge him, and that's hopeful. A nod, a gentle inclination of her head, yes, an imperceptible widening of the eye, he's sure of that. He saw it. But still he won't allow himself to believe she'll actually turn the necessary forty-five degrees and and bring them in... it's all too much to hope, too much. He catches his breath as she shifts, she seems about to... Which way? Small teeth gnaw on his lower lip. Come in, come in, he commands in silence. Come in! She's making a decision. She glances on up the street, her breast swells. His morning begins to fail. And then at her watch. Hot kisses on her wrist and up her arm, his hands on her shoulders, hers in his pockets, she's turning, she's yes! To her right on her plump legs, thighs in his doorway. Opening. What does she want? Her breasts envelop, his stomach's sinking as he smiles and smiles. The door closes behind her...she prepares to speak, to open her mouth. He can't stand it any longer. She's going to speak! He presses himself against the counter, he closes his eyes, he opens his eyes. Her reaching mouth is just for him, her huge and naked breasts for Peter Walters...what does she want?

"I want a dog."

Oh Christ I'm yours!

O O O

Felix crouching before the dog. Surely it's getting better. Now, because all the cages are clean and Walters is out there talking to someone, he has time to smoke a cigarette. Surely it's getting better. Hunkering down, his feet flat on the floor, his thighs tight against his calves, his long arms hugging his legs, he stares and smokes.

Felix smoking and wondering if he should open the cage, reach in and scratch his fingers between the yellow eyes, grab the hair at its powerful neck in such a way that the animal would know it had a friend. Maybe it's too soon for that.

Teetering forward, watching the eyes, appraising: important to see if it's safe. It could take his arm off; he knows that. Still, it is getting better. Every day it's more alive, almost responsive. At first there was nothing in those eyes, not a thing: no shadows, no light, just yellow diminishing without depth. Then one morning, several days ago, Felix saw something shiver inside the pupil, it was like something opening, something flashing deep beneath the surface. It happened very quickly. Most people would have missed it completely. Indeed it might not have happened for anyone else; it may well have happened *because* of him. Felix hardly dares to think about it, hardly dares to hope.

Perhaps this is the right moment. Perhaps some gesture, reaching in and scratching with his fingers between the yellow eyes, or grabbing the coarse hair at its neck, perhaps some trust, some intimacy of this kind is called for now, at this very moment. It's hard to tell.

Certainly the voice alone isn't enough, it never is: Felix can coo incessantly, nurse with words, he can lean lower and lower until his face is on the floor, even with the dog's, his body sprawling in the aisle; but all the loving sounds that Felix has uttered in the past thirty minutes have not, and can never unlock the mesh door, have not and never can give the animal what it needs.

And so he reaches up to unlock the door. Does it tighten as he reaches, touches the bolt? What will it do, it seems calm. It stares at his hand. the metal is cool on his fingers. He pauses a moment. His long body in the aisle, his head resting on the linoleum, he does not move: his arm is raised as in a salute. His fingers are cool on the metal. What will it do, is it smiling at him? It appears that the dog is smiling at him. He slides the upper bolt and the mouth opens imperceptibly, the lips are drawing back in a smile. Still its head rests on the floor of the cage, his head in the aisle. It watches his falling hand to the lower bolt and the eyes seem blank again, from far inside a sound begins, a cry. Perhaps it doesn't understand. It occurs to Felix that he should have raised himself from the floor *before* opening the bolts, *before* the dog, realizing something new, something unexpected was happening, began this terrible noise...

What to do? The stiffening body, that cry, the bristles jagged on its spine, he doesn't know what to do! He lies with his hand on the second bolt and imagines rising to his feet, crouching to slide it open, opening the door. And the dog explodes, hurling its eighty pounds against him, bursting from the cage with snarling froth and pain, the noise! the terrible noise and pain... That's a real possibility. And yet. He's loth to stop now when he'd been so sure: it had seemed exactly the right time, the dog expectant, responsive, waiting his hand, the perfect moment, the gesture, the friendship... It seems too bad. Really too bad. It stares intently at his hand which rests uncertain still on the bolt. The sound in its chest is like an electric motor. Felix doesn't know what to think, he doesn't know what to do and since there's no easy way out, he stops thinking. It nearly always works. His mind is empty, his eyes are closed. Time passes. It becomes clear that he isn't going to undo the second bolt. It always happens. He opens his eyes. The room is the same as he rises to his feet. His voice has begun to soothe, placate again as he reaches for the upper bolt; he's hardly aware of the dog. His mind is empty. There's a vague regret, of course, a sadness, but he's used to that.

He stands with his fingers on the lock and if he thinks at all, he finds it difficult to believe he ever really intended to stick his arm in there. The morning has made him sleepy. Bright sun on the windows and the room is uncomfortably warm. He wonders, for a moment, what he's doing here. Irresolute in the distinct and separate noises all around him, he wonders what he's doing in this airless room with cages in tiers, with shuffling animal bodies and the heat...

O   O   O

"Why yes, of course I can help you." She knows alright, that's clear enough: she sees, she must, his eagerness and imperceptibly she's smiling. "I'd be delighted hah, no trouble at all."

"After work." She stands on both feet, her legs slightly apart, balancing evenly on both feet, she leans toward him.

"Are you sure it's..."
   Jesus "Yes, I'd be..."
"About what time?"
"Five."
"Five-thirty?"

"Certainly." It's already after work, they're returning from the kennels.

"It's very kind of you doctor." She's called him doctor! "It's hard, you know. When you don't know the city." She doesn't know the city, doctor I don't know the city! He stares intently at her face. Steady. Steady. Returning from the kennels, or even better, they decide to have a drink and then another. Is she married? There isn't a ring, but she looks married. Her face watching him, he hopes she's married. A drink in some nice bar then, her breasts heavy on the table as she leans for a light and before long it's too late, the kennels are closed. She wants it as much as he does, that's pretty obvious, he can tell: her breathing's shallow and more rapid...

"I'm sorry," smiling. "What's your name? I don't know your name."

"Anderson." Does she pause, or is it his imagination; is she evasive? He'd like that. "Mary Anderson." And smiling brilliantly, is that sweat on her lip? Married, a bit of danger, he'd like that. "I'm sorry, I should have..." Her eyes, more calculating into his.

"Oh no, that's." It's sweat, he finds it irresistible, she's sweating. "I'm Peter Walters." That's very nice.

"Hello Peter Walters."

"Hello Mary." He eases off the counter, no need for that, and his day expands with sweat on her lip, her breasts, his mouth, hands, his...No dinner, no. He passes quickly over a supper of some kind, candlelight, very nice with wine, but why not drop by my place for a nightcap? Why not? A smoke, he searches in his pocket. They're by the ashtray. "Would you like a cigarette?"

Thanks. Reaching. Reaching "Thanks", she's in his bed. A wildcat. Her fingers touch his hand as she inhales, she agrees to everything, maybe she'd. He's always wanted a...Fantastic! No question of that lingering touch: steadying his hand, on his face more like it, his eyes, now tracing intrigued the line of his mouth and he can try it, yes, she's not like the others.

Poking into his belly button, scraping index fingernail up his thigh and the certainty that she won't be horrified, afraid, it's right up her alley, fills his head with blood, it glints in his eyes...His legs are like rubber, he can hardly get out of the room to put it on.

Peter Walters on his hands and knees, fiercely lustful, a dog, a wolf, he pauses to sniff and growl at the bedroom door. It's cunningly designed. A canine mask covers his head but leaves his mouth, his own fangs free: dog skins have been tailored to fit over his shoulders and along his back to the bushy tail. Surprisingly white underneath, blue-veined at the belly, he's naked from mouth to thighs.

A flesh-coloured strap buckled under his chin, another across his chest, two more between his legs, hold everything in place; sleeves to the wrist for his arms, to the knee for his legs, are secured by elastic. It's beautifully made, it never slips or binds: the straps at his thighs tend to chafe in hot weather, but only because he's plumper now.

There's a piece of wire in the tail (he thought of that himself), stiffly it rises behind him, jerking from side to side as he crawls towards her. He snarls. She understands immediately, she understands! She moans. His small red penis rises like a finger as she moans. He howls, she whimpers. Raising his face in gratitude, his muzzle to the ceiling, he howls and howls! With burning eyes she watches him pad to the bed, she whimpers more excitedly, she rises on all fours, she...

Chaos in the room behind. Good God, turning to the door "Excuse me", what in hell? A madhouse, they've all...

"What's that?" Her eyes, oh doctor...

"Just a." The husky, the fucking... "Excuse me." Smiling professional, grimly smiling. "Just a minute, it's just." And Peter Walters through the door to restore order. "Don't go away." Darting his head back, her breasts, smiling "Don't go away." And then between cages with animals launching themselves against their doors, swelling and spitting, it's a madhouse, a crazy ark because of that goddamn dog and Oswald. What's he done to it? staring, muttering privately. What if she leaves? hardly a glance for Oswald standing and it's another fit of course. A bad one by the look of it. Totally hysteric, and that's enough, it'll have to go: the dog is completely out of control. Horribly contorted it screams, howls, and Walters decides to make the phone call. There's no curing it, and they might even pay extra for a specimen as strong as this. The great white body crashes repeatedly against the cage as he watches: the whole tier shudders, but the bugger should collapse anytime now. Really stupid, a frenzy of stupidity, what brings it on? Growing weaker, it stiffens brutally, the foam at its mouth is red with blood, it falls jerking to the floor, it shakes, and flutters and then lies still...

As its silence spreads Walters hears a sound unlike the others, a rattling mechanical noise and it's coming from right beside him. Curious he turns to Felix Oswald, sees the chattering teeth, the eyes, and is suddenly, Oswald! "Oswald" for chrissakes, "Felix are you alright?" Reaching for the arm, touching, feeling the tension and soothing, "What's the matter Felix?" with his voice and hand, "You'll be alright, you'll be..." Felix stares for a moment at Peter Walters and then begins to cry.

O   O   O

He comes to the street and into the sun. It's two blocks to the subway station, and today there's no sign of a bus. His long legs carry him unthinking. Automatically he adjusts his stride so that his left foot hits the lines on the sidewalk. He's particularly anxious to get there and even with his coat open, flapping about his legs, he begins to sweat, it's because of the effort, the sweater, his winter coat, the sun...

When he bursts onto the platform his body is damp. He can feel the heart alive in his chest: he senses vague pains, he reaches under his sweater, inside his shirt so his fingers are in the armpit, his palm across the nipple, and he presses roughly, he digs his fingers into the moist flesh and leans to stare down the track. There's only an hour for lunch. No sign of the train, not yet. But here are children chasing among themselves: they appear to be spitting at each other; they make exaggerated hawking sounds in their throats, they rush about noisily, bumping into men and women who, in turn, push back at the children, their mouths opening and closing as they reprimand them. Several have left briefcases on the platform now, so they can run about more freely. One little boy, standing by himself, appears to be crying. Felix watches them and sees that they spit like children with the fronts of their mouths, their lips, and their spittle is frothy and inconsequential. There are many travellers waiting, so he hasn't just missed a train. He finds that reassuring. At the same time in their frenzy the children may not see that briefcase by the edge, one of them, looking back over its shoulder as it flees could very easily trip over it and fall onto the tracks. And the train is coming. It could easily happen. He hears it to his left, but the children don't. They continue to chase each other, laughing shrilly: one little girl, perhaps because of her long hair, is being pursued by several boys at once; she darts this way and that in her attempts to elude them. The train hurtles into the station, he can see where the spittle gleams in her hair.

O   O   O

Standing by the window perhaps. Vaguely aware of the garages at the end of the garden, the catalpa, the sound of a commuter train on the bridge. Not really. Pretending...

Everything dirty, seedy from winter. His hands have no strength. His fingers are trembling. He turns from the window and sees himself reflected in the mirror: he crosses the room to his reflection, he can almost count the hairs in his beard.

On the subway, not sitting, standing in the corner so that he touches no one, nobody can accidentally brush against him with their bodies because of a sudden stop, or even, as can happen, because the cars sway as they rush from station to station.

O   O   O

Davisville, past the cemetery, into the tunnel and then St. Clair. Felix on his feet before the train has stopped, even before they've entered the station: he's first to the door and out, he races up the stairs, through the turnstile and into the street. He sprints across St. Clair and heads north on Yonge. Time is passing. He darts among window shoppers in the sun. Although his body seems awkward, his passage uncontrolled, he threads among them expertly, he never contacts, never touches or is touched: it's almost as if he wasn't there at all.

She's there though, that woman again, perhaps still leaning at the corner. Enveloped in a huge scarf, she pulls it about her head and shoulders: she watches from the other side of the street. Nobody has ever spoken to her, no one has followed her home...

Felix walking more freely because the shops are behind him and there are few people near the Church. Some old men, that's all: crouching on benches they examine their hands, their bodies in the sun.

The journey is interminable. He's only now at the gate, it takes him forever to pass the office and he has to follow the drive for thirty yards up the hill before it curves to the left. Felix leaves it here, he continues straight ahead, he walks on the graves, their headstones cut with names, beloved father, strange names lost in memory.

At the crest of the hill he barely pauses, he knows his route; this is where the ravine begins. There are no graves here, no trees: a shallow valley from the north to the south, it tumbles to dead elms, underbrush at the cemetery's southern edge; and there the stream, foul smelling, issues from the ground. He reaches the bottom, running to maintain balance, and crosses quickly.

Often he has walked here almost for pleasure. One summer afternoon he watched a ground hog there, yes there, he could see the mound if he'd only look. But he does not look. And to his left a pile of broken monuments. Fragments of a wing, a face: the scattered headstones, chunks of marble as he passes. Earth sticks to his boots as he climbs to rejoin the road: ice clings in the roots of trees. He's out of breath, he slides, his heart is pounding, but he's almost there.

Mausoleums through the trees above him, he knows them: he's stared through barred windows in metal doors at luminous angels and virgins, at wreaths, at ivy frozen in the glass. He's tasted chemical smells that once were Eatons, Wycliffes, men and women, their children: he's seen them stacked in the light of memorial windows.

The gross man in the hockey sweater is leaning on a shovel and smoking. He's incredibly fat and standing very still. Yellow mud from the hole adheres to his feet, they appear enormous, as if wrapped in dirty blankets. He's looking the other way and doesn't see Felix: or if he has seen him, he makes no sign. Perhaps he pointedly turned away, perhaps he doesn't want to acknowledge Felix Oswald for some reason known only to himself. People can be like that. For example, even though Felix has seen the man before, it's impossible to mistake him because of his immense size, he must weigh three hundred pounds, even though he has seen him with his shovel, his blue construction helmet, in all seasons and at all times of the day, and even though the man has seen Felix, neither of them has given any indication that the other exists. Despite this and for some time now, Felix has wanted to speak to him, to walk up to him and say "Excuse me" or "Good day sir". It would be pleasant to smoke a cigarette with him, perhaps he has a bottle of wine in his suitcase and they would sit on the steps of a mausoleum, talking or perhaps not talking, perhaps just eating their sandwiches, smiling occasionally, passing the wine back and forth and if everything worked out, Felix might introduce him to the stone ladies.

And there they are. He begins to run. Twin sisters, he's sure they're twins and they're waiting for him. Sitting at either end of the stone bench, each resting a cheek against the back, staring at each other, they wait: their outside arms are raised, identically, with the inside wrist against the forehead, the elbows up and back, lifting their breasts. They watch each other. They reach with their other arms, their opening hands along the stone and will never touch. They're so beautiful. He pauses before them, he glances from one to the other as if for a sign, from profile to profile. They're bigger than he is, probably six and a half feet if they stood up: they've got good tough bodies naked to the waist. He knows their breasts, the muscles of their bellies, the strong thighs under the stone draperies gathered about them as they sit.

Very close to them now, he pauses: still looking from one to the other he comes to sit between them on the bench, right in the middle. That's important. One day at the beginning he measured the full length of the bench. It's fourteen feet long. Then he found the exact centre by walking seven feet from the end: with a white-washed rock from the flower bed, making certain he was unobserved, he scratched his mark into the stone. It's still there. And he's come to sit precisely on it, every lunch hour for months.

Felix sitting with a buttock on either side of the exact centre of the bench; reaching into the bag for his lunch. Perhaps they don't care: he can't believe that. Biting into a meat sandwich, he knows it's important that when he first arrives, he sits in the dead centre like this. He mustn't show any preference until he's finished eating. In the same way, they continue staring through him, at each other, as if he wasn't there. Methodically he eats. He chews his food well and washes down the wads of bread and meat with orange juice. Afterwards, when he's finished, when they've got this stasis to support them, he can, and usually does nestle up close to either one or the other: he can spend all his time talking to one of them, with nothing more than mere courtesy for the other, and sometimes not even that; sometimes he becomes so preoccupied with one, with the intimacy they have, the excitement, that he ignores her sister completely, and still there's no awkwardness. Even when he leans to circle a nipple with his mouth, or when he fondles the breasts, the belly, rubs his hands longingly over her thighs, even when he kneels on the bench beside her and takes the stone face in both his hands and covers it with kisses, poking his tongue in at the mouth, her eyes, licking her jaw greedily to the ear, even with all this, there's never a hint of jealousy. It's worked out very well.

The limousine, black and official, the sun glinting from its polished surface, slips through the trees before he sees it: next, and close behind, comes the hearse. They make no sound and Felix, eating his apple, is at first unaware of them. When he does look down, when he sees them, more cars have come over the hill, big rented cars with important mourners, and the procession, in slow motion, glides among the headstones. For a moment he believes they'll go to their left, follow the road that swings away to his right and into the cemetery's heart. But they don't, they take the other fork. One after the other. In complete silence: they pass from right to left in front of him. He can hear them now, can see faces looking at that young man sitting between two stone figures on a memorial bench eating an apple.

The first car stops at the public mausoleum, then the others, the line contracts: figures clamber from the black limousines at the front and he suddenly remembers the chapel, sort of the chapel inside, a vacant-smelling room, like a courtroom, with pews and an altar for the body. He understands. Behind the screens on either side run halls, four to the north and four to the south, high-ceilinged halls, their only light from frosted windows at the end; he's walked them often, he's read the names, peered into cells at plastic wreaths, at mouldering flowers, he's breathed the dead air and stared at corpses filed in drawers to the roof.

Voices suddenly, doors slamming and Felix averts his eyes as people, singly and in groups, march from their cars: soberly dressed, they straggle to the steps, to the hearse brilliant in the sun ahead of them. There are children too;

in little hats and ties, with tiny purses and polished shoes, they trot beside the adults, their pinched faces acknowledge him as they go.

A terrible commotion from ahead! Violent cries indistinct with distance... there's shouting near the coffin, it's at the door now: scuffling feet of mourners at the rear, sensing drama they quicken their pace, literally dragging their children to the bottom steps, the edge of the crowd; impatient they struggle and crane to discover the source of all this shouting, these accusations. Felix is drawn unwillingly. Leaving his friends, they understand, he approaches the crowd: it surges on the mausoleum's steps, something violent is happening at the door, the crowd convulses. Everyone strains to see. Felix can't be sure but apparently two people, at least two people, although others are taking sides, two women, he thinks, are at the centre, they're shouting hysterically, he can't make out what they're saying, he can't even be sure that the two of them are opponents, perhaps they're taking on everyone else, perhaps there's more than one centre to this. Apart from it all, hands down by his side, he watches. A child, a little girl in blue velvet and patent leather shoes, a tiny child with brass buttons and long hair, growing tired of the crowd because she can't see anything, or maybe she's not bored at all, maybe she's afraid for even Felix is uncertain, yes, something violent is building, she's probably afraid, she wanders away from her mother in the direction of Felix. He can't know if she sees him or whether it's only chance. The sun shines in her hair, the wet earth sticks to her shoes as she comes. Her mother, greedy to see, clawing into the crowd, hasn't missed her yet. Felix is transfixed. Turning he sees his friends, the one staring past her sister into his face, and behind them, the gravedigger in his hockey sweater standing by a blue tree. He's left his shovel somewhere and watches the scene intently. The crowd still boils about the coffin, the voices still shout with more and more of them protesting. The child is crying piteously. She totters aimlessly among the ornamental bushes, the naked hedges by the road. Felix doesn't know what to do. He should do something. Should he try to find the mother? It would be better if he tried to console the child; but how do you do that? Stories and songs, you tell them stories, dandle them on your knee... Felix remembers stories, a long time ago, there was someone, a man, a woman, it doesn't matter now, perhaps it was a maid, a housekeeper, someone told him stories and that's the important thing. He remembers liking them; now, because her cheeks are smeared with tears, with dirt from her little hands, he remembers a lap, a heart beating inside someone else's body; he remembers a voice, or is this all imagination, has he made it all up? a voice telling him of wolves with glittering eyes, they encircle the campfire of a traveller far from home, in winter, an especially deep winter so that food is scarce everywhere and the wolves, desperate with hunger, shift closer as the fire dies: shuddering awake he sees their shadows nearly on him, he can smell their bodies! frantically he throws wood on the coals, sparks fly in the towering night, he shouts but they've grown accustomed to his noise and fear him no longer. He has only the fire.

It's a good story, but it would only work if he knew the child, if they had time, only if she trusted him. Watching the blue velvet jacket, seeing her uncertain body, Felix realizes you can't force the kind of intimacy necessary for a good story, certainly not with this sad long-haired little girl. He'll have to think of something else.

Perhaps a trick of some kind would divert her. Years ago there was a person who could eat light bulbs. Felix thinks he's in New York now. And once he'd seen a man sterilize the point of a safety pin in the flame of his lighter, grasp some of the loose flesh at his throat, just above the Adam's apple, and push it through. Kids would love that, he's sure they would, he'd cheer her up alright, if only he could do something like that...

It's definitely too late to turn away now. She's so close, the dejection in the fall of her shoulders, the despair, yes it's almost despair he sees in her face, she's so obviously in pain that he can't ignore her. The gravedigger, still standing by the evergreen, must see, must know: so there's no turning away. She's less than twenty feet from him when her mother calls, she's finally noticed, the shrill voice carries clearly, and if she continues in the same way she'll pass within a couple of yards of him. She doesn't hear her mother and she doesn't appear to have noticed Felix, or if at some point she did see him, perhaps for some reason she actually set off in his direction at the beginning, it's fairly clear she doesn't see him now. He understands that. Partially concealed by her hair, her eyes are empty. She doesn't respond to her mother, although the woman is rapidly gaining ground on her. It's a big woman and obviously very upset, worried about her baby, she runs awkwardly, and although the voice is clear and strong, he can't make out the words. Felix takes a half step, he says: "Your mother. Little girl your mother." How best to continue? "Your mommy's calling you." The only response, and he's not sure of this either, is an imperceptible quickening of her pace. Surely she must hear the familiar voice calling her name, surely that's what she wants? But weeping she continues toward him, so Felix takes another step. "Little girl" he says again. He's getting involved despite himself: he raises an arm, his right arm, he points at the woman who's stopped shouting now, is slowing down, has stopped calling the child's name because she's out of breath, her face is swollen, red, her eyes harsh with unaccustomed effort. But the child will not be warned. Felix has tried, he's pointed, he didn't turn away, he's even spoken to her. It's not his fault the woman is closing in, is reaching, it's not his fault the child reacts too late: she dodges, tries to slip away, to free herself from the hand on her blue velvet shoulder, accusing voice, voice and the sudden blow, in the face, she hits the child with her open hand, she hits again, he hears the dead sound of flesh on flesh.

○　○　○

It's always the same, out the side door into the alley, it must be dark, or almost dark, he's wearing running shoes and goes directly to the park, into the ravine, he walks in the bushes beside the road until he comes to stand under the railway bridge...

He's done this before. Listening at the back door. Nobody's home, there are lights but nobody's home, he's sure of that: listening to the empty house, entering, he's done it many times. Trembling violently he closes the door, he walks through the kitchen and along the hall to their bedroom, his sneakers make tiny kissing noises on the hardwood. Everything is clean, the rooms are clean, they smell of furniture polish, soap, perfumes and powders, wax, there are fresh-cut flowers by the piano and a bowl of fruit on a stand near the bedroom window.

She's taller than the average woman and full-bodied, nevertheless he looks absurd; even after choosing the fullest, most shapeless clothes from her cupboard he still looks absurd. Usually he settles for skirts and sweaters, but this evening he tries on the purple and black terrycloth muu-muu. He undresses quickly, exchanges his underwear for hers, padding the brassiere with his socks, one in each cup...

Exciting as it is, it frightens him: standing in her brassiere, her pale blue nylon panties, seeing himself grotesquely reflected in her full-length mirror, he knows how vulnerable he is. What if they should come back, how could he possibly escape if they came back? He darts to the window, his body deep into the mirror, then back to the hall, in order to make sure they're not returning because he knows they'd laugh at him, regardless of their initial shock, maybe even fear, they'd pity him soon, they'd laugh and laugh, they'd tell their friends...

O   O   O

Past the fat man, among the monuments, the line of mausoleums, the brow of the hill, scattering earth as he charges into the ravine, Felix struggles up the other side to the road, gasping for breath, sweating but he can't slow down, there isn't time; through the gate, blindly on to Yonge Street. Fighting his body, straining for his second wind because it's come to him, Jesus Christ! he can't believe he didn't see it immediately, hasn't known it all along, he prays he's not too late. It's obvious Walters will call the bastard, maybe he already has, perhaps the vivisectionist...

Exhausted, his body's hurting him now, resisting him, but he won't give in. The dog has been taken, it's too late but he can't stop. Too much is happening. He runs through lunchtime crowds and he has no idea of how he'll save it, what he'll do tomorrow, whether there's anything he can do. Even if he put his mind to it, even if he did concentrate fully, examine the problem realistically from all its various points of view, he'd find no answer.

Seized in a red fist, struggling she looked into his eyes.

He trots into the subway station, back through the turnstile, and on to the platform. It's best not to think at all. The train arrives at the same time as Felix: that's a sign, an omen, it means he's being given a chance. Now if there's a good bus connection at Eglinton, if the same thing happens there, he'll come to Walters with, not with assurance exactly, not with confidence; with something like grace. Harmony. He hopes so.

Occasionally, not often because he isn't a stubborn man, not a man of principle, he'll remain standing on some spot, a particular square, until the doors open directly in front of him, so he can walk right in. Once it took seven trains, but he wasn't going anywhere, just out to the end of the line, so the time didn't matter.

It isn't that he hadn't wanted to act, certainly he wasn't indifferent: he'd tried to warn her, he's sure of that; he'd stepped towards her, he'd spoken, he'd pointed with his arm, what else could he have done? but she hadn't noticed him, why don't people notice him? Perhaps the tears blurred her vision, perhaps she was blind! It makes a difference. That's why she couldn't be warned, she was blind. It's not his fault.

Why didn't she hear him? He spoke, he said "Little girl", he's certain he did. She could have heard him even if she was blind. And she looked at him. There's no denying that she looked at him. He can't forget that look.

How could he have known the crazy woman was going to beat her? You don't expect that kind of thing: Christ no, not a physical attack, who's prepared for that?

Out of breath from running in the earth, her face admittedly ugly, coarse from exertion, but not brutal, not even angry: distracted, almost automatic, her voice muttering something or other without emphasis, without anger, as she struck the child back and forth across the head.

Stop it! he'd tried, it frightens him to remember stop it! for chrissakes she's crazy, what if she kills her? But the words wouldn't come. Trapped inside his body, he stared out through his eyes, he couldn't move, he couldn't speak...

O   O   O

...Fiercely lustful, a dog, a wolf, he pauses to sniff and growl at the bedroom door...he crawls towards her. He snarls. She understands immediately, she understands! She moans. His small red penis rises like a finger as she moans. He howls, she whimpers. Raising his face in gratitude, his muzzle to the ceiling, he howls; revealing his opening mouth, his soft underbelly, he howls and howls! With burning eyes she watches him pad to the bed, she whimpers more excitedly, she rises on all fours, she...

But first he must undress her, that's essential: she has to be naked for everything to work. A few drinks somewhere and then back to his place, he's got it all clear in his mind. Lots of laughs, but they both know he's just priming the pump. Because she wants it alright, he can see that, Christ the way she looks! she's horny as a toad, he pours the drinks and joins her on the sofa.

It doesn't have to be in the bedroom.

The sun is hot on the shop window; women pass by in both directions, some of them cross the street, but Walters doesn't need them today.

With burning eyes she watches him pad to the bed, she whimpers more excitedly, she rises on all fours, she shudders as he snarls, those full breasts quiver as she lifts her head, her face, exposing her throat, the stretching tendons...impatient she strains, rolling her eyes, baring her teeth she waits his approach...

Right away, even before tasting the drink, she buries her face where his neck joins the shoulder. Her hair smells of sweat. He puts his right hand on her left breast. They're bigger than he thought! his hand can't contain it all, it bulges away like a balloon full of milk, he's overwhelmed.

Automatically he kisses her eyes, his sucking lips down the length of her nose: her mouth is small, it opens for his tongue, her teeth are pointed. He undoes her dress, slips his hand inside her brassiere and pinches the nipple. Her brown eyes watch him. He kisses them shut.

He'd swear the breast is growing in his hand. It lolls

uncontrollably on her chest and the nipple's like a walnut. Kissing her chin, then her throat, he undoes the remaining buttons down the front of her dress. There are seven in all: they're not too small and she moves helpfully under his hands and mouth, he doesn't have too much trouble.

She smells like roast beef.

She lifts her hips so he can remove the dress. She lowers them. Receptive she manipulates him, she's not impatient like some, not embarrassed, she grabs her tits, he bites her belly. Fantastic!

But his heart isn't in it it's true, he doesn't know why at first, he tries to concentrate…the costume is cunningly designed. A canine mask covers his head…dog skins well tailored to fit, his back, the jerking tail, blue-veined at the belly, he's naked from mouth to thighs.

She does everything he wants.

…fiercely lustful, a dog, a wolf, he pauses to sniff and growl…

But she has to be naked, they both have to be naked. It won't work if he skips the preliminaries, Walters knows that better than anyone else he knows just how tenuous the scene is. So he re-devotes himself. He tries to slow everything down.

There's the question of her underwear. A half-slip, what colour? babyblue, the same as her brassiere and a garter belt, that's inescapable, a bit old-fashioned perhaps, but very nice with rosettes, tiny pink and white rosettes: he sticks his tongue in her belly-button and the slip comes off easily. Intently he nibbles, licks the white flesh of her thighs, down her legs as he slowly removes the left stocking. He does the same for the right one. She seems to like it. She rolls her head from side to side with little sounds and her arms flop about. After the garter belt, he tries to remove her pants with his teeth, but she starts to giggle, that's fatal, so he stops, pretends it was a joke…

It's almost time!

Naked she reaches. All he has to do is get out of his own clothes as provocatively as possible, she's watching him, do what's necessary to maintain, intensify the mood, perhaps take her into the bedroom yes, or should he do that before he undresses? yes.

And then he can…

How many times is this? It's never been so good, the expectation, Christ the longing as if it's never been done before, this is the first time! he kisses her here and there, squeezes a little, chews on her breasts, her mouth, takes a big swallow of his drink, he lifts her from the couch, it's never been so good, he carries, he can hardly stand it, he's light on his feet, her mouth is alive in his flesh...

Peter Walters on his hands and knees, fiercely lustful, a dog, a wolf, he pauses to sniff and growl at the bedroom door. She stares incredulous. Small hand to her mouth, what's that! she's starting to laugh, a spluttering giggle, the laughter exploding, her nude body convulsive on his bed. He growls. She isn't supposed to do that! Her breasts jiggling with uncontrollable laughter. He raises his mournful face, baring his fangs he rolls his eyes...She's supposed to...

Perhaps if he frightened her.

Baring his fangs, his cruel mouth in a snarl, he strains towards her, he desperately snarls from deep in his chest, but it doesn't work. On the contrary. She collapses again, writhes helplessly, her laughter bounces off the walls. she's not supposed to do this at all. He howls piteously, cringes and tries to meet her eyes, he rubs himself against the door, he whimpers while she watches him intently. She manages to speak: "A puppy dog" she says, her face suffused, "How sweet, an itsy-bitsy puppy dog." She stares. "Oh Christ!" she cries and unable to continue throws herself back on the bed.

He pants and snuffles uncertainly. He's afraid, he doesn't understand: perhaps she doesn't like him after all; he pads towards her, pausing often to watch and listen. Because of the mask, but more because of the terrible shock he can't see that Mary Anderson is almost hysterical. He's aware only of her hip, the powerful buttocks as he crawls closer, sniffing, cautiously closer because the laughter's stopped, she doesn't seem to be, her body quiet, he hopes she doesn't start again, she isn't laughing anymore: she's not supposed to respond like that, his head is boiling, she shouldn't have done that. He's at the edge of the bed and she still doesn't move. Her white ass looms invitingly large. He feels more secure because her breathing is agitated, she's clearly excited, she wants it alright, there's no doubt about that, she wants it! He puts his front paws on the bed and whimpers seductively. The laughter was a mistake, these things happen: he should have prepared her better, given more warning. He's willing to forgive her.

Fiercely lustful, a dog, a wolf, he pauses to sniff and growl at the bedroom door...he crawls towards her. He snarls. She understands immediately, she understands! She moans. His small red penis rises like a finger as she moans. He howls, she whimpers. Raising his face in gratitude, his muzzle to the ceiling, he howls; revealing his opening mouth, his soft underbelly, he howls and howls! With burning eyes she watches him pad to the bed, she whimpers excitedly, she rises on all fours, she shudders as he snarls, those full breasts quiver as she lifts her head, her face, exposing her throat, the stretching tendons...impatient she strains, rolling her eyes, baring her teeth, he leaps to the bed, she bounds away. He follows. She snaps playfully at his flank. He growls in his chest: she's trembling as he circles close, sniffs the gentle flesh of her buttocks, smells the ripe earth, tastes...

"FUCK OFF YOU PERVERT!"

Frightened and turning, grabbing the coverlet about her, she's staring at Peter Walters in his dog suit. His chest and front paws are along the bed; the rest of him still crouches on the floor.

He doesn't understand. She isn't supposed to react like this, she mustn't! she's supposed to, he was so sure with burning eyes she watched him pad...And she laughed! Surging blood inside, this snarl, it twists his mouth and viciously...

She screams as he leaps, she tries to escape, he drives for the throat, she twists, she fights, and is helpless.

Soft white victim, her fat legs kick the air: too terrified to cry out now, she groans, she begs forgiveness, mercy from the beast, she promises much...

But it's too late. His paws on her face, he hears nothing but her heart; he forces past her arms and bites deep into her throat, tears flesh, tastes dark blood pumping between his jaws.

O   O   O

Just because the dog, clearly exhausted, drained, just because it's sleeping in its cage, relaxed now, secure, it doesn't mean that Walters hasn't phoned, Felix knows this: it doesn't mean that everything hasn't been arranged. He isn't fooled for a minute.

Standing in the aisle, the dog completely unaware of him, Felix realizes that he must act. That's obvious. He can't ignore it. He doesn't know what to do.

He can't just open the cage, the back door, the gate to the lane and shoo it out into the city. He can't do that because there's no guarantee the dog would go, and even if it did, even if he chased it out with a broom, a shovel, nothing good would happen to it. It would be hit by a car; or the police would be alerted, somebody would report seeing a great white husky, perhaps mistake him for a wolf and the hunt would be on. They'd recapture him immediately, certainly before he got to the ravine. The dog would have one of its seizures, the police mistaking it for a rabid animal would shoot it to death.

And even if it does, by some unlikely chance, survive the traffic, even if it manages to elude the police, the Humane Society, even if it finds its way to the ravines, what will happen to it then?

Nothing good.

Early in the winter, before Christmas he remembers, a timber wolf came down the Don Valley Parkway right into the city, almost to the Lakeshore before it was recognized and killed. How did it get so far? Did nobody see it, or did they just glance from their cars and mistake it for somebody's dog? There's no way of knowing. The newspapers said it was very young, a pup really, that might help to explain it, they said it was starving, you could count the ribs on its skinny carcass. A policeman shot it with his service revolver.

So what can he do?

He can't hide it in the cemetery, the fat man would know immediately, and even if he didn't want to, even if his sympathies were with the two of them, the young man and his dog, and that's improbable, he'd still have to report the presence of a white husky among the graves. And that would be the end of it; people don't like that sort of thing.

Felix hears a kind of cry, the animal shudders but it

doesn't waken: one of its paws trembles and then is still. The belly rises and falls agitatedly as the cry, a thin vulnerable sound, continues...

What does it dream?

He'd like to take it back to the woods. That appears to be the natural course of action: it would be the best thing. Driving north as far as the roads go, if he had a car, past towns and villages, back into winter until somewhere, in a clearing perhaps, by the edge of the bush he releases it. That's the best thing, the natural thing: it pleases him, seeing it slip from the car, pausing to smell the air curiously, defensively, then breaking into the tireless searching run of wild dogs, the wolf...

That's all very well, but whatever he's going to do he has to hurry. Walters has surely phoned, he probably phoned as soon as the woman left. If he did, and if the dog's going to be saved, then it has to be done right now.

$$\bigcirc \quad \bigcirc \quad \bigcirc$$

Through some opening, a stream perhaps, where does it lead? running shadowy among evergreens, beneath the sky: running some hidden path, instinctive...

It's winter. The stream bed is frozen, the sky is empty: Felix stands by the road, his body's breath billowing into the air. The dog is gone. He watched it trot easily to the forest's edge, he saw it pause at the entrance, it turned to stare briefly back to where he watched from beside the car, and then it was gone.

Shadowy running among evergreens heaped with snow, instinctive running with Felix trembling on the road. It's cold but he doesn't feel it, he isn't aware of the wind: he hears only the brittle earth resisting spring.

Without noise, meanwhile, unravelling above them is the vapour trail of a jet, Felix doesn't see it for a long time. He's staring at the darkening forest as if expecting the dog again: it doesn't come and it won't, he knows that. But still he stares, he hears the uncertain silence of dying winter, the hollow pressure of the land and is suddenly cold. Returning quickly to the car he sees, pink on the evening sky, the tattered remnants of an aircraft's flight.

Driving south, his headlights dashing from heavy trees

on either side, perhaps the radio's playing, he concludes it
was American. They're everywhere. Loaded with hydro-
gen bombs they fly hour by hour, year after year; they
don't go anywhere, they don't do anything.

O O O

Peter Walters smiling, leaning in the doorway. "You can't
deny it's the first time you've taken a short lunch hour."
His smile as he rubs his right palm on the outside of his
thigh. "If you don't mind me saying so, it's the first time
you haven't taken a long lunch hour. Ha!" Felix aware,
there's nothing novel about this: he's surprised however
that Walters closes his eyes, what's the matter with him?
he's never done that before. He sees the plump hand up
and down the pant leg, up and down intently: the eyes
remain closed.

"It's the dog" he tries. "I wanted…"

"I know!" Walters alert suddenly, watching. "You don't
have to tell me anything Oswald. I know your concern for
that dog. I think you're crazy, but there you are." Coming
into the room. "That's not what we're talking about
though. We're talking about you rushing out of here every
noon hour. Right on the button. That's what we're talking
about." Walking towards Felix, arm outstretched, pointing. What does he want? one foot and then the other, his
body swaying heavily as he comes. "Rushing off to wherever it is you go. Ha! don't think I haven't noticed, it's as
plain as the nose on your face." Intimate, his white teeth,
what does he want from Felix, why is he reaching? "Anybody with any sense can see it Oswald." Taking the left
bicep of Felix Oswald in his right hand, squeezing signifi-
cantly, leaning to say: "And I think it's great!" breathing
his sweet breath and squeezing. "A man needs his nookey."
Guiding Felix into the office, turning, presenting this grin.
"Isn't that right Oswald? every man needs a bit of nookey
now and then." Felix standing in the office, his employer
pinching the inside of his arm, what's going on? he has to
know about the dog, and besides this hand on his arm, the
voice. He hasn't any choice. "It's only natural."

"Oh yes" what? "I think so."

"Tell me about her." Going behind his desk.

"What?"

"Is she good?"

"What do you mean?"

"GODDAMMIT OSWALD!" his arm crashing on the desk. Terrible sound. It frightens Felix because it, crashing sound like that, it's unexpected. "Tell me the truth." He stares at his employer. Something struggles in his cheek, he can feel it bumping on the edge of his cheekbone. He wonders if Walters can see it. "I can read you like a book, you know that Oswald, you don't fool me one little bit, so don't think you do." His sleeve is dangerously close to the little glass. Felix sees the sleeve moving near the glass and considers, briefly, should he tell the prick he might spill the drink, he's going to spill the drink, the way he's moving his arm, the way the arm is moving, it's quite possible it will hit the glass, it will probably knock it over, it's surprising he hasn't knocked it over already. Liquid in the glass vibrates. The desk top is white. Felix sees an amber shadow with its core of light on the white surface. The muscle continues to jump in his face. Walters continues to talk, his voice concluding things, there's nothing new in all of this, he's not asking questions or anything, Felix can tell that, there's no need to answer, he's not soliciting advice, he's not revealing anything either. All Felix has to do is acquiesce.

O   O   O

Sleeping breath against her shoulder, the perfume of her body: silent first light, perhaps curtains swaying, he slides from her bed, he stands naked in the morning air; seeing familiar objects about the house in the gathering light, he smokes a cigarette. Houses in silhouette, the trees; fences, squat bushes at the edge of the ravine, and air from the window drifting against his belly, encircling his thighs. He licks the palm of his hand, absently he smoothes at his belly, he rubs wetly among the gathering hair, his body's still, he licks again, tasting the earth smell of sex, he smoothes his thighs, the air is cool where his hands have traced, the morning at his body, he smokes in silence. Only the rustle of fingers on his own flesh, the sound of her body as she moves; he throws his cigarette out the window and at that moment sees two men dismantling a car, he hears the dull clang of metal on concrete. They work methodically, but very quickly, they're obviously experts, perhaps they're pit mechanics from Mosport. Not long ago he would have been appalled, frightened too, he would have shouted, phoned somebody, maybe even scrambled into his trousers and run barefoot into the lane to confront them; but this morning it doesn't matter.

He turns to her. She's pulled the covers over her head. Suddenly the distance between them, his body and hers, the space is intolerable; he knows he must leave before the child wakes, but he gets back into bed and holds her, half-waking she receives him, he says her name, her breath is in his mouth, their bodies wrestle in slow motion, they slide through the air like fish.

O   O   O

A band of sunshine bright on the window sill. Felix realizes there are people in cars who pass each other in the street and he remembers the afternoon last summer when he watched the groundhog. It hadn't done very much. On the contrary it seemed merely to be looking for something, its blunt body crossing and re-crossing the area around its home; it had stopped now and then to rise on its hind quarters and watch him nervously. He hadn't moved. Eventually it scuttled into its hole, without finding whatever it had been looking for, or at least not obviously, then it must have turned around for the head re-emerged, just the head, it was almost indistinguishable from the earth, and it lay like that for a long time blinking against the sun. After a while Felix continued his walk. He sees the sky, a washed-out blue, the sky still looks cold although the sun is shining. He had been close enough to see the colour of its eyes. It amused him to think of it burrowing among the graves.

"Felix" he says hollowly. Waiting.

"Yes?" politely.

"Her old man's away during the day, is that it?"

"No, no it's not that."

"And you sneak around there for a bit of nookey, eh? every day you..."

"No, it's, no...I..."

"C'mon Oswald." His face demanding. "Don't lie to me Felix."

"She's pretty good."

"Aah!" sighs Peter Walters. "That's better." Smiling he leans with his elbows on the desk again. Felix finds it something of a relief. The sleeve moving near the glass, the amber shadow with its core of light, the white surface. "And I'm right aren't I? she's married." Felix nods. Walters shifts his chair closer to the desk, he pours two more drinks, he wiggles his buttocks, settling into the chair, he smiles. "Good for you Oswald." Sipping his drink this time, he says "Good for you." He raises his face, he's ready for the next admission.

Now, and this is more difficult, going to her again, knowing the hair shrouding her face, knowing she waits for him: almost unrecognizable towards the afternoon sun, his feet ring on the frozen road, trees are scattered up both sides of the ravine, their long shadows blue on the snow: this morning he saw a hawk, he's almost certain it was a hawk, it floated from sight behind him as he left her.

It's so easy.

Her long body in his arms, strands of her hair in his mouth as he climbs on to the breast of the hill. Paved roads. Children playing in the alley. The house and she's waiting for him, reading the paper at her kitchen table, she'll turn as he comes in the door, light from the window in her hair, on her cheek...

Behind him, under the railway bridge, the lean woman with two greyhounds: pausing at the edge to catch his breath, looking down through tangled branches he sees the searching dogs, he stares into her face, she's stopped walking, she seems to return his look, he raises his arm as a sign but she doesn't respond.

O O O

"C'mon Oswald, please! c'mon..." nodding pointedly towards the other room, but Felix doesn't understand, what's he doing that for? Then he remembers the dog. "Just between men eh? just between ourselves." That's what it's all about. "C'mon, don't be bashful, Christ I can tell you things! like that broad who was here this morning, you saw her. Have you ever seen tits like that before? Fantastic! Right? Well I'm..." Inadvertently they stare at each other. "You know..." Studiously examining the plump hand in sunlight, Felix nods, suggesting that he does. "I'll bet she screws like a mink." Felix nods again. Cars fill the street, he can hear them. The sun is brilliant on the desk. "Well? For chrissakes Oswald, go on!"

O   O   O

It was unwilling to leave. They stood facing the forest's edge, Felix and the husky: trees black between snow and the sky, their breath like smoke as he crouches, he leans his face against its skull, he talks. Contracting with the cold, the car cracks mechanically but he doesn't hear, he hears his voice, he feels the road beneath his knees, a muscular throat and shoulders under coarse hair, he hears the animal's heart, the thawing earth.

Felix stands by the road as it trots uncertainly to the entrance, seeing it pause, it stares over its shoulder but he can't see the eyes. Then it's gone, a white body against the trees before it vanishes. The snow's surface is broken in an arc between him and the trees, it fills with shadow as he watches: the night is immense, he's cold as he returns to the car. Running among evergreens a dog, a wolf at the other end of that track, the searching run of wild dogs...

He's opening the car door when she speaks: a woman at the edge of a field near the shell of a building, an abandoned school house that he hadn't noticed, perhaps it's a deconsecrated church. The wall behind her has crumbled away, the roof has gone, the windows are empty and snow drifts high on the inner walls. Where has she come from? Her silhouette is completely without detail, although it appears she's wearing a parka with the hood up. She speaks again. She turns and starts back along the side road, she doesn't acknowledge his voice but he follows her anyway. The wind is gusting stronger, the footing treacherous. He can barely see the tip of the ruin now, to his left, above a snow bank, he leans into the wind, trying to catch up he begins to run, almost in slow motion, it's difficult, there are ruts, tracks of cars beneath drifted snow, he slides grotesquely, she turns and smiles, he's close enough to see her smile, to hear her laugh, she veers from the road, scrambles over the fence, he follows her into the field, the moon is bright, they struggle thigh deep and fall, and rise, they're laughing like children as he grabs her, she reaches, pulls him down, her mouth is cool, there's snow melting on her cheek.

The sound of their boots on the road: his arm over her shoulders, her body walks at his side. Wild clouds blow around the moon. They walk into the shadow of the building and a distant farm dog begins to bark; they can't help hearing its thin, insistent voice as they descend to the car, they pause to listen on the road, holding each other they stand in the towering night.

$$\text{O} \quad \text{O} \quad \text{O}$$

"You're some kind of fucking pervert, that's what you are." Methodically emptying his glass with Felix staring at him. "I know where you go, I've followed you…" This can't be happening, it mustn't happen. Walters pouring whiskey into the shot glasses. Felix feels the muscle jumping in his face; amber shadows on the desk, cars pass each other in the street. All he can do is wait. "There isn't any woman is there!"

"She's pretty good…"

"C'mon Oswald, don't give me any more of that bull. I've followed you, I know where you go." Felix continues to stare at Peter Walters who is shaking his head now, puffing his cheeks and forcing air from his mouth. "I mean Jesus! trying to stick it in a statue's ear, I never came across that before…you're one of your actual Kraft-Ebbing maniacs…"

"I *said* she's pretty *good*!" Both of them startled. They stare at each other across the white desk. Eventually Walters, is it insensitivity or bravado? tries to ignore what has happened. He clears his throat, but it's too late.

"I've followed you," his voice lacks conviction. "I know where you go, you go to the graveyard."

"*Listen* you sonofabitch! you *believe* me, alright?" Felix standing. Walters collapsing. It's superb. The mouth open, the eyes have lost their focus as he struggles to reassert himself:

"Trying to stick it in a statue's ear, I never came across that before. Sucking on a stone boob for chrissakes, Oswald you're a..."

"Woofwoof."

"Oh." An expiration scarcely heard, a mouthful of air from his lungs as his body opens, that's all: sweat bursting from his forehead as he turns away.

"Woofwoof WOOF!"

"C'mon Oswald, please! c'mon..." It delights Felix to see the fat hands trembling. "Christ I can tell you things! There's no need to bring that up, no need..." He tries to straighten himself in his chair. "Like that broad who was here this morning, you saw her. Have you ever seen tits like that before? Fantastic! Right? Well I'm..." Felix pours himself another shot: fat hands opaque in sunlight, the voice appealing now, almost begging, it was so easy! why couldn't he have done it earlier? "You know," hopefully. Felix nods, suggesting that he does. "I'll bet she screws like a mink..." Sipping his whiskey, grinning uncontrollably, Felix nods again. Woofwoof. He puts his glass on the desk and lurches to the window to contain his elation: he can do what he wants, it's incredible! he knows what he can do...

"I'm seeing her tonight Peter and I wondered." Staring at himself reflected in a window across the alley. "I'd like to borrow your car."

O   O   O

Because there's so little time to think he walks up to the cage, explains briefly to the dog what he's going to do, why he's going to do it, and then opens the door: it surprises him that the animal doesn't move, it hardly acknowledges him or the open door, it lies with only a sliver of light in its eyes.

He speaks to it but it doesn't respond. He coaxes, even pleads: finally he commands, he shouts harshly and rattles the door; that doesn't work either. He's bewildered. Leaving the cage door ajar Felix goes into the office, sits down in the chair and pours himself a small glass of whiskey. What must he do now? Stupid fucking dog. He tries to compose himself, to relinquish everything not related directly to the problem, to open himself in such a way that the solution, there must be a solution, the solution will become obvious. Certainly he mustn't allow himself to think. His heart beats painfully with unfamiliar excitement because it appears something is going to happen, he can't recall anything to match the possibility of his triumph. Walters' hands rubbing aimlessly between plump thighs.

He drinks from the little glass and notes that the whiskey has lost its bite: he goes to the window, opens it from the top, and methodically breathes cold air in through his nose. He must become blank, an empty organism, but it saw him, he's sure of that, it knows the door is open so why doesn't it respond? It's probably afraid. Staring at empty yards, at fences, dirty windows, feeling the cold air in his nose and throat, he discovers that it's afraid. He isn't surprised. His hands have no strength. As he lights a cigarette he sees that his fingers are trembling. Felix Oswald smoking by a particular open window: he senses vague pains, he reaches under his sweater, inside his shirt so his fingers are in the armpit, his palm across the nipple, and he presses roughly...

Clearly he must acknowledge the animal's fear, he must reassure it with everything at his disposal: he must talk gently, explain that they're going to drive north to a field by an empty road, an opening in the bush, a frozen stream perhaps; he must reach in, scratch with his fingers between the yellow eyes, grab the coarse hair at its neck. Outside in the yard a black and white tomcat stares into a small tree full of sparrows. Felix hears their idiot voices: he remembers, there are wicker travelling cages in the front of the shop and probably a blanket in the cupboard...

$$\bigcirc \quad \bigcirc \quad \bigcirc$$

He doesn't stop under the bridge or even pause at the top of the hill, he hardly notices the foul stream, he walks on the sidewalk to her door and because the light is on, he rings her bell. He's never done it before.

He hardly knows her, this is the first time he's been in her apartment, he's drinking her scotch, smoking her cigarettes: sitting across from her, pale eyes, she doesn't move, he believes she stops him when he tries to leave, listening to her records and telling her incredible things about himself, telling her: "Once upon a time when I was much younger, it was in Ottawa I think, it must have been in Ottawa and everything was so much simpler, I had a parrot, a green and yellow parrot with scarlet on its shoulders. His name was Harold. He could bark like two dogs at the same time but he refused to talk, he screamed and whistled and barked incessantly, they go crazy you know; he was a gross and vicious bird: everything he ate turned to shit immediately so I gave him to the zoo..." Does he tell her of the pain he senses in the raw meat and membranes of his chest? Why is he telling her this, has he actually said it? "I've never encountered a situation in my own life where I could have behaved differently, everything that has happened, or not happened to me, because of me, all of it has been inescapable."

"Don't say that."

"I believe it."

"That isn't good enough." They listen to the music. "I believe all kinds of things but I don't let them make any difference... Why do you make everything so difficult for yourself?"

Getting up from the chair, asking her: "May I touch you? I have to touch you," kneeling in front of her, taking her face in his hands, she watches him: the muscles along her jaw are tense, her light eyes do not give him anything. He kisses her forehead. Her hands, resting along her thighs, do not move. Returning to the chair, that's all he wanted, that's all he wants...

No it isn't.

She says "I was at a party Saturday night, maybe fifteen... all old friends except for a few of us, we were strangers, almost strangers. It's weird. I was really horny, I'd have gone with anybody, I mean it, man or woman, it couldn't have mattered less..." Still she doesn't move. There's a scratch on the record: they hear its predictable tick, and then... tick... and then... The muscles in her body tense under his hands. He wonders if maybe he does make things difficult for himself, he'd like to believe that; it would suggest there was another way... She says: "I was at a party Saturday night, maybe fifteen…all old friends except for a few of us, we were strangers, almost strangers. It's weird." There are fresh cut flowers by the piano. Everything is clean, the room is clean, it smells of wax. "All of us together in this guy's house and the basic emotion was hatred, all of us felt it one way or another. There wasn't any reason, it just happened. Like, it could have been, you know, friendship…nostalgia, but it was hatred." They look at each other and he is uncomfortable.

"But why not? It's just as human." Her hand moves to push back strands of her hair: the white face is strangely delicate. What is it that he wants from her? "Everybody tried to be nice because they knew, we explained and apologized, backed away from scenes…"

"I need to lie down with you," to hold somebody.

"Just a minute…No matter how we tried it had to break out somewhere." He goes to stand by the window. Shadows at the end of her garden, the sound of a train on the bridge. Everything is dirty, seedy from winter. His hands have no strength. Her voice is matter-of-fact: "I don't know why I did it…when he said goodnight I hit him across the mouth with my hand…why would I do that? I didn't know him, I hadn't even spoken to him…" He turns from the window, raises his hand as if he has something to say and discovers that he doesn't. He stops in mid-gesture. Immediately it's clear that she's seen him, she expects him to continue, she waits…"Why would I do that?"

O O O

He left early to beat the traffic but it didn't work, he's never seen so many cars: caked with salt and dirt they creep, wait…As he approaches the expressway traffic thins out, they begin to move faster, Felix cuts from one lane to the other, he curses stupid drivers, air bursts at the windows and the husky shifts in its cage unhappily: he switches on the wipers because transports, speeding cars hurl dirty water on his windshield, his hands are sweating, he holds the wheel lightly and doesn't think.

North on the airport road. The animal's body curling in on itself behind him. It whimpers as if dreaming. Small factories on either side of the road and ugly subdivisions. Indian Line to highway 50. He turns on the radio. Across from the race track a tree full of starlings, thousands of them crowded in its spiky branches, their mottled bodies ragged in the wind. He can hear them as he passes.

Into the Humber River valley at Bolton, rising northwest to Palgrave where the snow begins again, west on 9 to Ballycroy, villages year after year in drifted snow: a woman in Palgrave raped and murdered in her bedroom, within months another, in another town and her eight-year-old daughter heard it. He turns on his lights and smokes another cigarette.

Orangeville, then north through Camilla with the pale headlights of approaching cars, Primrose, Horning's Mills, driving back into winter, the sky grows pale, then dark between metallic clouds and the horizon. Farms are farther apart now, their front doors sealed for winter and trees crowd to the highway's edge; the beams of his headlights thicken with blowing snow. The dog hasn't made a sound for over an hour. He'll turn from the highway, he'll drive on concession roads to a place he knows, past an empty farmhouse with one apple tree, he's been in the house, he's heard her snowboots on the stairs, heard their voices echoing through its rooms...

The highway has been rising imperceptibly from the lakeshore, he doesn't know how far, perhaps a thousand feet, so that after he leaves it the road lurches unpredictably into ravines, hills swell beneath him, he knows the land drops sharply to Georgian Bay just beyond a particular clearing by a heavy stand of evergreens. He turns halfway to the dog, he speaks to it. There's no response, at least he doesn't hear anything and it's too dark to see: he begins to talk, he explains, encourages, rhythmically the wipers thump, he's driving automatically, he knows what he's doing, he's soothing the dog, he's turning left, in a little while he'll turn right again: he passes houses without lights clustered at crossroads. The hills become longer, steeper, until he reaches the plateau: the wind is blowing from west to east across the road, they pass the farm, he can't tell if it's still empty, it hasn't mattered for a long time, he hardly looks at it. He continues past the shell of a building, an abandoned schoolhouse, perhaps it's a deconsecrated church. One wall has crumbled away, the roof has gone, the windows are empty and snow drifts high on the inner walls. He stops the car and turns off the engine. He zips the coat tightly under his chin, he pulls his woollen hat down over his ears, puts on his leather mitts and gets out. The wind abates. Fine particles of snow lift from the edge of drifts above the road, they powder his cheeks as he stands, but even that ceases; an immense stillness engulfs him, pale stars emerge in the evening sky, the field shimmers between them and the trees. Eventually he walks around the car and opens the door.

The husky is unwilling to come out of its cage. Felix understands that, the animal's confused, disoriented by the drive, it needs to be reassured. Dragging the cage, manoeuvering it out the door isn't easy, but he manages: short of breath, almost impatient, he explains everything: when the cage is out he lowers it to the road and undoes the wicker door. The dog doesn't move. Perhaps it's dead, that's unlikely. Maybe it's sick. He gets down on his knees to peer inside but it's too dark, he can't see a thing. He's suddenly afraid to put his hand in and he doesn't have a flashlight; he straightens and leans against the car. If he upended the cage he could shake the son-of-a-bitch out onto the road. That's a possibility: at least it's something he might be able to do. Standing against the car he closes his eyes; the dog should appreciate, at least understand that its freedom is being restored, it should, no matter how cautiously, he recognizes that suspicion is natural and therefore desirable, it should at least poke its fucking head out of the cage, it should see what Felix has done, is doing...

Maybe he's expecting too much too soon: opening his eyes he avoids looking at the cage, perhaps it needs a little time, he stares emptily into the sky. Insubstantial clouds. Time passes. He waits with his face upturned until his neck begins to hurt. Then he slowly tilts his face forward, lowering his gaze, the sky is endless, the tops of trees against the stars, their brute mass without detail and then the field, the snowbank and the cage. But no dog. Trying to contain increasing vertigo, Felix hunches to the ground, his voice is desperate, begging...

Dragging the cage beside the car. The footing is treacherous, there are ruts, tracks of cars beneath drifted snow, he slides grotesquely but he doesn't fall, he's pulling the cage to a spot directly in front of the car, about thirty feet along the road. It's one thing to do. He goes to the car, turns on the headlights and returns in their glare with his shadow huge and broken on the snow. He crouches to open the cage again, he shifts to avoid the shadow, he doesn't know what to expect: the white body curls away from him. The head is buried in a corner. He speaks to it purposefully, he demands obedience, is rewarded by a sound, he's sure there was a sound, he orders it from the cage, it appears the dog is trying to move, there's tension in its limbs, Felix commands more forcefully, he snarls it lurches trying to turn, it falls, he hears the warning rattle in its throat, can see the gathering spasms...

Why does it terrify him?

He scrabbles to his feet, he runs to the car and slams the door. He begins to cough, his chest explodes, his mouth fills with vomit, he opens the door and spits onto the road, he's choked with rolling spasms in his chest and throat, the contents of his stomach burst from his mouth and nose. Perhaps he's dying. It happens like this, explosions, treachery inside his head, everything silent, a spike of ice in his chest, the body's puke dribbling from its nose...

He gets out of the car to wash his face in the snow. Kneeling at the edge of the road he rubs until his skin hurts, then he dries it with his knitted hat: he bends to rinse his mouth, it takes more snow than he thought because it melts to almost nothing; he forces his head back, exposes his throat and gargles ineffectually. Spitting thick saliva beside his knee he reaches along his gums with his tongue for chunks of vomit. He spits again. Fresh snow in his mouth and his teeth begin to ache with the cold, he gargles again and spits. His knees are cold, his face is stinging but he doesn't get up. The snowbank, from where he kneels, rises to meet the sky and since the car is behind him nothing but the stars has any form. They do not move. There are no clouds...for an instant there is no distance between objects, no objects, a consciousness, only an idea...gradually the impression of the icy night on his eyes, a noise in the distance, his knees melting the snow beneath him, the car cracks mechanically, contracting with the cold but that's not it. He stands. He has the uneasy sense that something has happened, an emphasis has shifted in some way, nothing is certain: the trees, the sky remain the same, the field's unchanged. It doesn't make any sense. Supporting himself against the car he returns to its open door. A light breeze on his cheek, the whine of an engine carried from the highway: it sounds like a truck, he hears the farm dog. Shutting the door, he walks to the cage in the middle of the road and as he expected it's empty: running easily among the trees, the tireless run of wild dogs, the wolf. He knows it's too late, but he stares at the shadowy trees, searches the edge of the woods as if for a sign. There isn't one of course; the landscape contains nothing, it might as well not be there...

The dog is in the car. He discovers it when he opens the back door to replace the cage. The interior light goes on and there it is. Cowering on the floor, it stares at him from the corner of its eye. He doesn't understand, why is it in the car? He says "You'll have to get out of there," he speaks formally: "get out now, out!" It stares at him. He crouches by the open door, he smells wet fur, leaning over the seat until he's level with its breath. "If you don't screw off they'll get you, please go, they'll take you to the university, they'll cut you open, they'll put wires and everything into your head." It doesn't understand. "Don't you understand? they're waiting to zap you, they'll fry your goddamn brain." Its breathing is light and rushed, how can he expect it to understand, what is there to understand? He's come this far on his own.

Very calm, without emotion, he walks around to the other side of the car, he opens the door and returns to the cage. There's nothing to be said. He must simply force the animal from the car, close the doors and drive away. He can't use the wicker cage as a prod; the space between the seats is too narrow, he must think of something else. All possibilities exist at the same time, in space like a tapestry: he can dismantle the cage and try to straighten one of the supports, he can find part of a fence, he can roll the spare wheel, there's enough room, he can kick at the dog, push it out with his snowboots, it's too bad he doesn't have a ski-pole, the dog will resist, the fences in this part of the country are ideal, a tire iron or the jack, the spare wheel.

He's unwilling to hit the animal; he could injure it;

unless everything else fails; he leans on the red metal jack, it presses cruelly into the sinews, bone and muscle, the whimpering grows in strength. They are both without anger. Felix bending into the car, forcing methodically, he doesn't think, he has no sensation, the husky resists. It's only a matter of time, it can't win. Felix knows that. The only question is how much, what kind of pain will he have to inflict before the animal capitulates?

Even when it's finally on the road he can't slam the door because, as he pushes its head out with the jack, it sticks a leg back in, he taps the leg carefully until it's withdrawn, only to find another one, or the head again. He's cold, his mouth tastes awful: he'd like to be in the city. It goes on and on. The dog breathing intently, whining in its chest, Felix pulling the door shut; why is he doing this? Eventually he succeeds. The husky is outside, it stands on its hind legs and paws at the window, he can hear it: he closes the other door and climbs into the front seat. He sits with his hands on the steering wheel, he doesn't know how long he sits with his hands on the steering wheel. He's trembling. The dog is at his window now, its paws scrabbling desperately, it barks suddenly, an abrupt explosive sound, it frightens him: it's the first time he has heard it bark. He gathers saliva, trying to cleanse his mouth, he lights a cigarette and starts the car. The dog barks again, it falls away from the window as he accelerates, the rear wheels slide as he gathers speed, it runs beside him, the night is immense, he doesn't know the road in this direction, he doesn't know where it leads.

He's driving faster than he should, he mustn't go off the road, he mustn't get stuck, the husky's loping behind him. This isn't the way it was supposed to be.

○   ○   ○

If, when he reaches the floor of the ravine, he turns right instead of left, if he climbs the small hill to the road and descends across highways to the railway tracks, he's in the Don Valley. It must have been beautiful before the war. The river meanders as a river should. He can see sepia figures with parasols, gentle men with shiny boots, they drift silently beneath great black trees with rough bark, but the trees are dead now and the water is foul. In the guts of the bridge above him a subway train rattles to Bloor Street. It's almost spring, the wind is cool: dirty water swells powerfully to the lake, eddies, whirlpools convulse to the surface and vanish. Felix crouches at the edge, on a sandbank, with a mountain of filthy snow and salt on the other side. Clearly pressed into the wet sand there are the tracks of animals, exquisite icons, he doesn't know what they are, he touches them with his finger. He doesn't know what they mean. He stands. There are trees, obviously different kinds of trees. He stares at them. They have names, he doesn't know their names: they are different from each other and unique, some have rough bark, others are smooth, some are tall and slender, others burst greedily from the earth, and birds, he hears their separate voices; following the edge of the river he startles a flock of hundreds, they spring from dead weeds stuck in the snow. All about him there are signs, strange birds chase each other on an empty sky, he threads through husks of summer plants, their pods open and dry like insects. He does not want them to touch him. The snow is melting, the river grows. Even here, all around him, there are animals, they watch him pass. He doesn't know.

He knows that he has loved her but no longer understands what it means. Standing by the window. Laughter and applause from the front room. He stares at the garage: it's dusk, he will go for a walk. There is music now from the television, it makes him angry: in front of the set, her legs tucked beneath her on the sofa, the delicate perfume of her body, he needs her, needs to lie down with her, they cannot do that. Why can't they? Heavy shadows at the end of the garden, the catalpa black against the sky. He goes for another drink, she turns her face to him, he's aware of her face, he doesn't respond, he goes into the kitchen. He should have looked at her, he should have touched her. "Do you want a drink?"

"I . . . I don't think so."

Sitting in an office on the seventh floor, at some point in his life, staring where his reflection should be in the win-

dow, he becomes aware, imperceptibly, of a large bird
flying towards him, he can't believe it, he waits for it to
slow down, to wheel away from him, but it doesn't, it
intends to imbed itself in his chest, fiercely he sees its eyes,
the yellow beak as it explodes against the glass.

Is that someone on the garage? he's sure it wasn't there
before: a shape of some kind, a form, almost like someone
lying up there observing him, but that's unlikely. He takes
a mouthful of whiskey and tries to determine if someone is
watching as she comes to stand behind him, she puts her
arms around him, a hand inside his shirt against his belly,
she rests her body against him. Is she crying? He turns to
her. It isn't any good, he doesn't know what to feel, it makes
him sad to know he has nothing to say. It's night now. A
train crosses the bridge as she speaks: "I'm sorry." Her
mouth remains parted, she doesn't expect an answer.

"So am I." He touches her face with the tips of his
fingers, lightly brushing her forehead, her cheekbones, he
is particularly uncertain because the watcher is waiting to
see what they will do next. With his hand at the back of her
neck he pulls her against him. It is merely awkward, at
first, but it quickly becomes embarrassing: she steps away
and returns to the other room. He returns to the window.
Perhaps if he turned off the light and crouched by the
window he could see a wiry silhouette rise to stand beside
the tree.

○　　○　　○

In front of him a car bursts over the hill, driving fast it
appears instantaneously, it blinds him, he swerves to the
roadside: its horn blares once and then it's gone. Felix
struggles to keep the car moving through drifted snow, he's
sliding in deeper, he stops the car and puts it into reverse,
he accelerates, it begins to move, the wheels are spinning,
his hands are clenched, he throws it into drive, then reverse,
rocking his body with the car he makes it back onto the
crown of the road. He lights a cigarette and smokes without
moving. There's a gentle wind now; the sky is full of stars. If
he doesn't come to a concession road soon he's going to
have to turn around and drive out the way he came in.
Where is the husky? possibly it has left the road, it had been

right behind him. He searches carefully but there's no sign of it. He gets out of the car to pee, his body doesn't work very well, it's as if it doesn't understand, all his muscles are contracted so that he has difficulty in straightening himself, it occurs to him that very old men must feel like this. Fumbling beneath his coat to find his fly he hears it, he knows it's the dog, he knows it's been hurt, it's gone mad, it's been injured: his feet on the frozen road, he's supporting himself with both hands along the car so he doesn't fall, it's having a fit, a noise, a strangling, the sound of his feet, the wind, peering ahead he sees it crushed beside the road, it struggles in small circles, it flops from side to side like a fish. Standing over it he tries to understand. Bone protrudes from its side and the snow is black with its blood. He doesn't understand, he can't stand the noise! kill it to stop the noise, he doesn't know how to kill it, he falls as he tries to turn away, his knees bang stupidly against his chest, he's bleeding from the mouth, he doesn't feel the snow against his face. He doesn't see the husky die.

○　○　○

Ritson awakens. It's predictable enough. This afternoon, like every afternoon at the same time, the need to urinate wakens him. Since he's not yet prepared to wet himself, he can resist the pressure but he can't ignore it. So he wakes up. Manoeuvring onto his back, he opens his eyes. There is no light, not a glimmer, he'd be astounded if there were. Lying on a mattress, in a windowless cubicle, not a cell, in the deepest corner of his basement, he acknowledges there is light in the city, but it never penetrates this far beneath the street.

On his back in the dark, it's like sleep but his eyes are open, the empty house above him, so many rooms, the furniture covered with sheets to protect it, he remembers a woman, she must have done that before she left. Or has he always been alone? He remembers many women, and children, some of them had children in their arms, they prepared meals of soup and sandwiches for children coming home from school. It doesn't matter. He must get up, the pressure on his bladder insists, he closes his eyes, he opens them again. Children skating on a river, their red toques brilliant in the sun. Their voices come to him in the wind. It's possible he played a musical instrument of some kind, a violin perhaps, some instrument that he could carry with him.

He's convinced, not without reason, that he's appreciably weaker, his body less effective. The pain is no more intense, indeed it may have diminished, but that's neither here nor there; pain has come and gone with the brute regularity of the tides for as long as he can remember. Inevitable; but it has no more bearing on his true state than the beating of his heart, for example, or the alternate expansion and contraction of the lungs inside his chest. But when he attempts to stand he can see that the process of disintegration in his body has continued while he slept, it may even have accelerated. His spine doesn't bend easily, it's as though the individual vertebrae cling to each other and even with help from his arms, the muscles in his belly are incapable of pulling him into a sitting position. He rolls onto his side, drawing his knees up to his chest, levering with his arms, he flops onto his belly, he struggles to raise his trunk from the mattress, to rise onto all fours, his arms are too weak, he collapses, his face bangs rudely against the cellar floor. It's probably like this every day, soon the strength will return, he lies motionless with one arm beneath him, his face is pressed against the cement.

If he doesn't manage to get up soon he'll have to pee here in his bed and he's never done that before, at least he can't believe he has. He has vomited, that's fairly certain, he's clawed himself from sleep, his throat and lungs choked with half-digested food, and in the past, dreaming of boys and girls, a hayride perhaps, young limbs entwining him, their voices, hands, the smell of the hay, their bodies, he's woken with hands between his legs, the unfamiliar noise of ecstasy. If it happened, it was a long time ago.

Manoeuvring onto his back, he opens his eyes. On his back in the dark, it's like sleep, the empty house above him, so many rooms, the furniture covered with sheets to protect it, he remembers a woman, she must have done that before she left. Or has he always been alone? He remembers many women, and children, some of them had children in their arms, they prepared meals of soup and sandwiches for children coming home from school. It doesn't matter. He must get up, the pressure on his bladder insists, he closes his eyes, he opens them again. Children skating on a river, their red toques brilliant in the sun. their voices come to him in the wind.

○   ○   ○

Felix stops by the car, he's afraid, he turns to look at the corpse. Even if he did kill it, it doesn't matter: beneath stars, the dead of winter, no harmonies, there's nothing known, nothing not known; he's trembling against the car, the occasional naked tree, the brittle earth, he doesn't tremble because of the fear, not even because of the cold.

What does he have to do?

Deathly cold, shaken by uncontrollable tremors, he drives back down along the road they entered. Snowbanks on either side, he accelerates beneath the sky. It was dead when he revived, beside him, nestled against him, its great body against him: he had stumbled away from the black snow, he had paused... Descending to the lake he turns to the right, the heater is beginning to thrust warm air into the car, it isn't enough. He failed. He doesn't understand. The road rises and falls with the land, he passes houses without lights clustered at crossroads.

○   ○   ○

Leaving by the side door, into the alley, it's dark, he's wearing running shoes and goes directly to the park, then into the ravine, he moves with empty grace, through underbrush, a path beside the road because sometimes there are others...

Under the railway bridge, he smokes a cigarette: cupping it secretively in his hand, he hunches down with his back against the concrete column. He listens to the stream rushing over rocks and garbage. It stinks of the graveyard. There was a boy who lived under a bridge, maybe even this bridge, there are lots of places to hide, he grew up under it in the middle of the city and nobody knew he was there. He'd come out at night to forage for food like the raccoons. He would have gone to the country, it might have been different in the country, but he didn't know it was there. During the day he'd cling unmoving among the supports high above the ravine and watch strangers walking dogs, he was afraid of the dogs, he saw boys and girls playing together, riding their bicycles; occasionally there would be lovers lying together in the long grass, he'd see them, their private urgency and after they'd gone he'd descend to where their bodies had crushed the grass and lying on his belly, with a long freight rattling over the bridge above him, he'd weep. He knows how the rabbits move nervously at dawn and where the groundhogs live, he's seen them killed by dogs.

At night, when there's no longer the noise of traffic on Yonge Street, with winos sleeping heavily in the bushes, he emerges from the ravine, he must eat and knows which houses are likely to be open and where there are no dogs. He's motionless by the catalpa, he's watching, listening, then he vaults the fence and moves quickly to the back door and slips inside. He's selective by instinct and rather than have them miss anything, begin to watch for him, he'll visit three or four houses, taking a little from each. He drinks from the milk bottle, there's cold meat in a drawer beneath the freezer, he takes some fruit, several slices of bread, he puts it all in his pockets, picks up a tomato, takes another mouthful of milk and starts for the back door...

Excited because nobody knows he's here, there are lights in the apartment window, but he can't see anybody inside. Music is playing somewhere, he doesn't recognize the song: noise from the traffic on Yonge Street is curiously soothing, like the sea. Using the fence and the tree, Fripp climbs onto the garage roof, he wriggles forward on his belly, excited because nobody knows he's here, he presses himself flat on the gravelled surface. A bearded man appears in the window, it's the husband, he stands looking out with a drink in his hand. There is a bed behind him, a doorway with light in it; the music has stopped. Night air is moving imperceptibly against his face as she appears in the doorway, the woman walking up behind him, she puts her arms around him, he doesn't move, her hand is inside his shirt. If they speak he cannot hear them, if there are sounds in the apartment, he doesn't know: they remain motionless, he imagines their breath, the rustle of clothing as he eventually turns to her. He takes her in his arms. She turns from him, he reaches after her, she stops to look at him from the doorway, his arm is still extended, she steps forward and sits on the bed, she's reflected in a mirror on the wall, she lies with her face in her hands, the man walks to stand over her, he touches her as if he'd never seen her before. She doesn't move. He touches her shoulder and still she doesn't move, he's saying something to her; she presses her face even more tightly into her hands. The man comes to the window. He empties his glass and lights a cigarette, he stands smoking, staring out at the end of the garden. Without turning his head he says something, the woman raises her face to stare at him, her long hair over her face like a mask: it isn't any good, the man turns, the woman stands, pulls her dress up her body over her head, she is naked except for bikini pants and her back is crisscrossed with lacerations as if she has frequently been whipped. He sees her reflected in the mirror, she is standing very still, her body is white and soft even from this distance, her breasts are heavy. He does not know what is happening, the expectation is like panic. She bends to the bed, she kneels on it, she stretches herself face down along it, the man comes to crouch over her, he leans to put his mouth on her wounds, they look like decorations in her flesh, his tongue traces them dutifully, there's no passion, they don't appear to be moving at all. Her eyes are closed.

O   O   O

Now, and this is more difficult, going to her again, knowing the hair shrouding her face, knowing she waits for him: there are trees scattered up each side of the ravine, this morning he saw a hawk, he's almost certain it was a hawk, it soared on ragged wings.

Her long body in his arms, strands of her hair in his mouth as he climbs out of the ravine, he vaults the fence by the garage, she's waiting for him, she'll turn as he comes in the door, light from the window in her hair, on her cheek.

A bottle of chilled white wine, it's a ritual, either of them might have bought it: they're listening to her records. Bright on the wicker place-mats, the afternoon sun is still warm; the wine glass focuses a shimmering patch of light on the table by his hand. She reaches across the light to touch him. He goes around the table, he kneels before her, he burrows his face into her lap, his hands under her skirt grope for her thighs, her buttocks spreading as she sits: her hands are in his hair, she traces the muscles from his neck into his shoulders. They do not speak. She's watching him. He loves her, he raises his face, she kisses him, her mouth is full of wine, he drinks: she reaches for her glass, her eyes are moist, pressing her mouth to his she dribbles wine, warmed by her body, into him; he loves her, his tongue is swollen against her teeth, she resists, she rejects and receives him; with mouths bruising together they re-explore familiar innocence. The floor is beginning to hurt his knees. His hands are at her hips, his thumbs pressing into her belly, his fingers stretching towards her buttocks, he levers himself from the floor, it's only briefly awkward, she stands with him, they embrace, her long body in his arms; then taking the bottle of wine, what's left of it, they go into the bedroom.

It's so easy.

Her long body in his arms, strands of her hair in his mouth, still gentle they undress each other, a shaft of fading sunlight across his body and hers, he spills wine on her breasts, her belly, and drinks; laughing she presses him onto his back, her fingers, mouth and teeth at random on his body. With her again, for the first time again, he understands.

"You make me beautiful."

Her long body in his arms, strands of her hair in his mouth, the urgent sounds of their bodies, passion growing like fear or anger, they clutch and bite in desperation, it breaks, they're tumbling together into loneliness and awe.

○　○　○

On her street for the first time in daylight, he walks past her house, there's no sign of her: a stark tree on the lawn, the windows are clean, there are bright curtains; he stops as if to light a cigarette. He doesn't know her name.

He will tell her, he'll say: "I've never encountered a situation in my own life where I could have behaved differently, everything that has happened, or not happened to me, because of me, all of it has been inescapable." She watches him. Does she understand? her hands are curled in her lap, he's drinking her scotch, smoking her cigarettes: sitting across from her, pale eyes, she doesn't move, he believes she stopped him when he tried to leave, listening to her records.

He will say: "I've never encountered a situation, in the lives of my friends, when they made any kind of choice, when they could have done anything other than what they did do. Choice" he will say, "describes what might have been."

"That's a useless idea."

"I believe it."

"That isn't good enough." They listen to the music, she doesn't understand. "I believe all kinds of things but I don't let them make any difference...I hardly know you...Why do you make everything so difficult for yourself?"

Her street in daylight, he walks to her door: a stark tree on the lawn, the windows are clean, there are bright curtains, everything is clean; it's the kind of apartment that will have fresh cut flowers, it will smell of wax, of furniture polish. He steps into the vestibule, her name is printed beneath her doorbell. Urquhart. Mr. and Mrs. D. Urquhart, he rings the bell. He's forgotten his role, what he was going to say, she'll know, she'll cry out protesting...

She's taller than he thought, her hair is almost black, she looks at him impersonally, her black hair over her shoulders. "Yes?" Her voice is clear and open, he cannot meet her eyes, surely she suspects... "May I help you?" He must answer, he hears his voice:

"Are there any, do you have any odd jobs, you know ...work around the house?" He manages to glance into her face, he doesn't know where that idea came from, certainly she'll refuse him. "Please...I'll do anything..." Calculating, she stares at him easily, there is sunlight in the room behind her, the flesh in the opening of her shirt is white, his mouth and throat, even his teeth are dry, he's seen her breasts, they're even bigger than he thought, she must know, surely she suspects, she's opening the door! it never happens this easily, is she alone? he listens intently, but there's no sound from the apartment behind her. She's alone and she's opening the door, she's stepping backwards...

"Come in. I'm sure there's something." Trembling violently he closes the door, he follows her in the hall, her hair comes right down to her ass, his sneakers make tiny kissing noises on the hardwood. Everything is clean, the rooms are clean, they smell of furniture polish, soap, perfumes and powders, wax, there are fresh cut flowers by the piano and a bowl of fruit on an ornate stand by the window. There is an enormous black brassiere drying on a radiator in the bathroom.

Several women at a table by the window, they're laughing richly. They appraise him in the doorway, it's disconcerting. The table is covered with open beer bottles: she leaves him to drink from her glass, he watches the life in her throat as she swallows. "He wonders if there's anything he can do around the house." Dragging deeply on her cigarette, their buoyant voices overlap; it's as if she's devouring the smoke.

"Well he should begin with a beer."

"For strength."

"He says he'll do anything." Languorous, they're superbly flushed with drink, their bare arms and throats in sunlight; they confidently reach and drink, they cross their thighs and stretch. He can only grin foolishly and take a beer. The watch him drinking.

"What do you do best?" She speaks to him from a chair beside the stove, he doesn't know what to say. Her hair is short, curled about her ears and her smile is gently mocking. There are pearls around her neck, they rest on her small bosom and for some incredible reason he is able to say:

"I don't know."

"There must be something." Although they're observing him in such a way that he knows they must have some understanding amongst themselves, it's almost a plot, certainly some pre-arranged agreement, and although the nature of his response is obviously very important, it will certainly determine how they are going to deal with him, despite all this they aren't hostile, they aren't baiting him, on the contrary, encouragement emanates from them like perspiration, like the odour of their bodies. It makes it possible for him to continue.

"Well. There is one thing, I guess…"

"What is it?"

"Well." They wait patiently, he really must try, he doesn't want to disappoint them. Sun shining on the brown bottles, the women, small green plants, the whole scene in sunlight, there is dust and smoke in the air; Urquhart reaches to the ashtray, her black hair covers her face, she isn't wearing a brassiere, she taps her cigarette and straightens, she flounces her hair back from her face, he hears a bird outside, he knows what he will say: "When the time comes, when it's absolutely essential, I can walk from here to there." He raises his arm and points, he sees his hand in the room. "To the back door there."

It is Urquhart who says: "Not everybody knows that." They prepare a chair for him between her and the woman with the pearls. He sits in it. His bottle is empty so they give him another. He notices that the blond girl, obviously the youngest of them, she isn't much more than twenty, she only has one arm; the sleeve of her black sweater has been removed and the arm hole cleverly mended. She's very pretty by the window, she smiles at him and the smile remains: she watches him drinking and talking.

Later, when she is naked, her breasts marbled with miniature blue veins, he sees that the shoulder curves smoothly, uninterrupted into her side, there's no sign she ever had an arm. He stands in front of her, he cups his hand where her arm should begin, her body is cool, her eyes are closed, she puts her hand on his and speaks his name.

Urquhart has taken the necklace, they're not pearls at all, they're tropical seeds of some kind strung on elastic, she puts it over his head and bending her face close to his, her arms are around him, her hair, she grins wickedly… No she doesn't, she rests her face wearily against his throat. He is standing by the sink. She returns to her chair. There is a silence and then she says: "I don't know. I'm overwhelmed with a sense of exhaustion. It happens every time, I'm sitting with a man and I suddenly realize, there's nothing here for me, he doesn't know who he is, the poor bastard's hardly alive…" He goes to stand by the window. Shadows at the end of her garden, the sound of a train on the bridge. Everything is dirty, seedy from winter. His hands have no strength. Her voice is matter-of-fact: "Why am I always

attracted to empty men?" They sway with her words like
branches. "Impotent men, not necessarily sexually, it's a
question of manhood." He turns from the window, raises
his hand as if he has something to say and discovers that he
doesn't. He stops in mid-gesture. Immediately it's clear
that she's seen him, she expects him to continue, she almost
shouts: "It's not me you know, it's not us!" Her dark
mouth remains slightly parted as she waits, he can see her
teeth. It's not that she's angry, on the contrary; the
one-armed girl is weeping without noise as she lights a
cigarette. He understands, he wishes there was something
he could say. He can't think of anything. "What in hell's
happening to you guys?" A yellow cat appears in the
window behind her; standing on its hind legs it scratches
on the glass to get in.

The icy road against his face, he doesn't know where he is
at first, he can't remember: he feels the coarse hair of its
cold body in his arms, he's deathly cold against the earth.
He finds it almost impossible to move, he doesn't know
why he should try to get up. It isn't painful. He's been
dreaming, there are voices, is he dreaming still? Lying on
his side with the husky in his arms he can see the shell of a
building beside the road, an abandoned schoolhouse,
perhaps it's a deconsecrated church: a wall has crumbled
away, the roof has gone, the windows are empty. The
easiest thing would be to sleep again, he doesn't know why
he struggles to get up, but he does, he wrestles free of its stiff
body and the pain begins, he's on all fours, his body's
possessed with systematic shudders that almost cast him to
the ground. Felix on his knees, sobbing, he can hear his
noise, he gathers himself, he rises to sway above the dog,
the snow is black...

By the ceiling a window, a small window with iron bars on
the outside. The television is in the corner of the room.
Blue light on his hands. No sound. Light on his trouser
legs. He has eaten because it is evening, because it is almost

night. Soon he'll leave the room, he'll walk to the stairs, he'll mount them to the landing at the side door, and with only the slightest hesitation, he'll step out into the alley.

Very soon now. He drinks from a bottle, he smokes: blue light on his hands. What will they be doing tonight? What will he see them doing? He crosses the room because there are dark figures swooping back and forth across the screen, he turns up the sound; the crowd roars with excitement as the players dash from one end of the rink to the other. The Leafs and New York. He takes a mouthful of beer and settles into his chair. He knows each Toronto player by the way they move. At the end of the first period, Leafs leading, he goes to the refrigerator and opens two bottles of beer: returning with them to his chair he's vaguely aware that he isn't going out, it's getting late, he's certainly missing something, what are they doing? He flicks from channel to channel until he finds a baseball game, he doesn't like baseball but it will do. He'll go out later. After the hockey game. He'll move with grace, his feet make no sound: swaying lights as he descends into the ravine, he avoids the road, he slides through underbrush, a path along the edge.

He's sitting by the telephone. He's dialing her number: he doesn't feel anything. He stops dialing her number. He goes to the baseball game and turns off the sound; he returns to the telephone, sometimes her husband answers and that's good too, sometimes nobody answers. His hands are trembling, there is no strength. All sounds are separate and hugely magnified. Cars in the street, the noise of his body: although the clock is on the other wall, it sounds as if it's pressed against his ear. Her phone begins to ring, it rings again, her voice, she answers his call, he starts to talk, she hears him, his tongue is swollen, his mouth is full of meat.

The camera follows the players to their dug-out until the commercial starts. He estimates that ten minutes have passed, he switches back to the hockey game: the players are returning to the ice. He takes a mouthful of cold beer and watches them skate gracefully about the rink, the referee blows his whistle and the second period begins. He settles expectantly into his chair. The room is dark except for shifting light from the game, blue light on his hands, on his legs as he drinks. Sometimes there are a lot of small figures scooting up the ice, then from another angle there are two or three, they fill the screen, they crash together against the boards, they either slide apart as if it didn't happen, or they strike out automatically, they drop their sticks and gloves, they grapple together and fall again, the crowd roars and there's a commercial. He drinks the last of his second beer as the period ends without a score. Several women appear on the screen, they're rubbing themselves against a bum-faced man who's extolling a car; his voice is American: the women are rubbing themselves against the car now, they lie along the hood or lean against a fender with their mouths open greedily, they stare into the camera. He goes into the bathroom and masturbates. On the way back he gets two more beers from the refrigerator, he's just in time for the final period.

Soon he'll leave the room, he'll walk to the stairs, he'll mount them to the landing at the side door, and with only the slightest hesitation, he'll step out into the alley; it's always the same, sneaking out the side door into the alley, it must be dark, he's wearing running shoes and goes directly to the park, into the ravine, he walks in the bushes beside the road because sometimes there are others, a car perhaps, but not tonight. He doesn't stop under the railway bridge or even pause at the top of the hill, he hardly notices the foul stream, he goes directly to the catalpa and climbs the fence. He's done this before. Listening at the back door, there's a light in the hall, but they are sleeping, he's sure of that: listening carefully, entering, he's done it many times. Trembling violently he closes the door, he walks through the kitchen and along the hall to their bedroom, his sneakers making tiny kissing noises on the hardwood. Everything is clean, the rooms are clean, they smell of furniture polish, soap, perfumes and powders, wax, it is dark, but there are flowers by the piano. The bedroom door is open. He waits with his shadow on the wall; he must be certain they're asleep. He can hear them. The house creaks meaninglessly. He doesn't know how long he stands listening to them through the open door, it doesn't matter. One of them, it's her, she's lying naked in her bed, she rolls over, she sighs, he recognizes the sound, he leans against the doorframe. The smell of her body, her breath faintly stale with cigarettes. His gigantic shadow precedes him into the room, he makes no sound, it's as if he isn't there: ecstatic because they don't know he's standing at the foot of their bed, he stares at them, they don't know he's staring down at them like this. From the corner of his eye he sees himself in the mirror on the open cupboard door. Curtains sway in the moving air. She's lying on her side, her face pressed against his shoulder. The noise of a machine cleaning the street; the sound of its revolving brushes as he comes to stand by her head. Then just the sound of an engine as it turns the corner. Bending he places his lips gently at the corner of her mouth. He feels her sleeping breath, her mouth is dry. He draws back from her as she stirs, he mustn't move, he hardly breathes as she shifts onto her back: sighing again, she moistens her lips with her tongue, he wonders if she's dreaming. Muscles contract in her face, he'd like to know what she's dreaming, does she dream of the bearded man sleeping on his belly beside her? Does she dream of her lover? She's smiling in her sleep, her eyes are in shadow, perhaps they're open! perhaps she's looking at him, she's smiling at him, her arms emerge from beneath the covers to enfold him, she draws him to her, her mouth opens against his, she arches her long body, his hands are in her black hair, he holds her delicate skull in his hands. No, it doesn't happen like that. She'd be afraid, if she opened her eyes and saw Fripp leaning over her like this she'd cry out, she'd be terrified. It's not possible that she'd reach with her white arms and draw him to her body. Anyway the man would hear them, he'd waken without them realizing it and although there's a chance that their lust would excite him, that he'd encourage them with sly caresses, obscene exhortations, perhaps he'd even join them, but that's unlikely, there'd undoubtedly be a scene, maybe a violent one. He watches her sleeping face, her body beneath the sheet. Her black hair is on the pillow and on her shoulder. He's seen her breasts, the black brassiere, they're bigger than he thought, he reaches to touch her, he doesn't touch her. He's crouching beside their bed, he doesn't know what to do.

O O O

"Memories are like bad dreams." Ritson's voice, it doesn't sound like a voice, he hears it in the dark. "They torment me so. That's why I live in a cellar, it must be: I am lonely, but I am away from it all. That must be the reason. I have had to get used to it, it has not come easily. How could it? It is not man's nature to live like an animal." Perhaps he has said this before. If only he could get up, he doesn't want to wet himself. Did he get up yesterday? it seems to him that he did, but it's possible that he has deteriorated to such an extent, and in such a way, that he hasn't noticed; and it's the not noticing, after all that's the measure of real and significant deterioration, perhaps it has gone so far that he didn't get up yesterday, that he won't be able to get up today. "A basement is not an ideal place to die." That voice again, his voice. At the same time he doesn't appear to smell of stale urine, that would suggest he'd been on his feet yesterday. But not necessarily. It could just as easily mean that he's subsided to the point where he doesn't have to pee every day, that the pressure he now experiences is a reservoir of urine that's been collecting for several days. The body's organs do decay in this way, its processes do break down, there's no question of that. It isn't surprising. There was a time when he was able to pee as many as fifteen times in a single day, the urine rushed from him in torrents. but that's history too, and there's no reason to hope that it will be possible every day, any more than it was possible, say eighteen months ago, to believe he could then continue to pee more than seven times a week.

If he allows himself, he'll pursue this sort of speculation forever, he'll exhaust every combination of possibilities, and even though it's challenging for the mind, even though it could prove to be more or less diverting, it has nothing to do with him lying here, on his back, his body undeniably weaker than he has ever known it to be. A cellar is not an ideal place to die. He rolls onto his side, drawing his knees up to his chest, levering with his arms, he flops onto his belly, he struggles to raise his trunk from the mattress, to rise onto all fours, his arms are too weak, he collapses, his face bangs rudely against the cellar floor. It's probably like this every day, soon the strength will return, he lies motionless with one arm beneath him, his face is pressed against the cement.

"Memories are like bad dreams." Ritson's voice, it doesn't sound like a voice, he hears it in the dark. "They torment me so. That's why I live in a cellar, it must be: I am lonely." There's a woman, a fine-looking woman, wide-hipped and full-breasted: she's shrouding the furniture, her arms are naked, she shakes white sheets, they billow over the stuffed chairs, they settle noiselessly on the sofa. A purposeful young woman, she doesn't look more than thirty-five; he isn't confident that he knows who she is. Who is she? Bending she adjusts the sheets, she tucks them under the legs of the furniture. She brushes hair from her brow and sighs. He doesn't understand why she's doing this, why doesn't she acknowledge him? it's as if he isn't in the room. She pulls the blinds down, one by one, she draws the curtains and then, still without looking in his direction, she goes into the other room, he can hear her, he finds himself in the doorway. Because in this room, too, the blinds are down, because the curtains are drawn, he cannot see her. Where is she? alone into the room he knows she will not see him. He hears an unrecognizable sound from the corner of the room, a slight repetitive sound, he opens the cupboard, she's in the cupboard, her feet no longer touch the floor; her face, although contorted, is brutally serene; her tongue is swollen, it lolls from between her teeth, he sees that she's bitten it, there's blood in her mouth, it's boiling onto her chin: bulging from their sockets, her eyes stare hugely over his shoulder into the room. The noise is caused by her fist; compulsively, as if counting time, she's tapping the cupboard wall with her fist. He's appalled by the calm in that body beneath her blackening face; all the energy of death is in her face as her body rotates imperceptibly.

Manoeuvering onto his back, he opens his eyes. On his back in the dark, it's like sleep, the empty house above him, so many rooms, he remembers the woman, she must have done that before she left. Or has he always been alone? He remembers many women, and children, some of them had children in their arms, they prepared meals of soup and sandwiches for children coming home from school. It doesn't matter. He must get up, the pressure on his bladder insists, he closes his eyes, he opens them again.

Children skating on a river, their red toques brilliant in the sun. Their voices come to him in the wind.

○   ○   ○

Leaving by the side door, into the alley, it's dark, he's wearing running shoes and goes directly to the park, then left into the ravine, he moves with empty grace, through the underbrush, a path beside the road because sometimes there are others, there are cars without lights, there are figures, shadows in the corner of his eye.

And tonight there is a car, he knows where to look, he sees it, heart's rhythm and muscles tightening, his mouth parting, he pauses: leaves shiver about him, a light evening breeze on his face. He stares at the motionless hulk of the car. He can almost smell it. Circling up the side of the ravine so they won't see him; he wonders if they're screwing. He hopes so. Pausing to stare down at them he thinks of hurling a brick or something, bouncing it off the roof. He stands grinning in the dark. There's no sound from the car. The wind has gone, he hears traffic somewhere above him; he'd never do a thing like that, he knows it'd scare the shit out of them, they'd probably never make it again. He stands without moving: there are animals, he hears them in the dead leaves, the night sky is full of bats and owls. He no longer cares why they have no place to go, why they have to come here, inviting almost certain detection by the police who patrol the ravine with searchlights on their yellow cars. It doesn't matter, it's true the car is there, it might as well be empty. He doesn't understand how he could have been tempted to crawl closer to the glinting metal body, the brush of bodies perhaps? He knows how pathetic that is. They groan, breathing and sighing, the noise of their bodies, he sees them, they don't know he's here, so close to them, teeth bared, eyes white, he reaches, fingers extended, staring he reaches into the car, he sees her legs convulse like arms. What does he want from them, any of them? He doesn't know who they are. He doesn't feel anything. They're there, he's seen the glow from at least two cigarettes and smoke drifting from the driver's open window. He can't make any sense of it, he can't even remember why he's standing above them in the dark, deathly still, as if remembering something he's never experienced.

He's almost there, he'll cross the stream, it's always the same. He smokes a cigarette under the railway bridge: cupping it secretively in his hand, he leans against a concrete column. Water rushes over rocks and garbage, it stinks of the cemetery. Crushing the butt beneath his shoe, he listens intently for any noise that will betray the other, the watcher; he hears only cascading water, the predictable sounds of night and the city above him. Secure that he's not observed, he crosses the stream, he scrambles directly to the entrance and with some difficulty slides the metal cover until there's an opening big enough for him to slip through. Because it's cramped inside, in fact there's scarcely enough room for his crouching body, it's hard to push the cover back into place. He has to brace himself against one wall, it's not so much the weight, it's the angle, he has to rediscover it every time. Tonight, for some reason, he falls into it very quickly, it hardly takes him any time at all and although he's not a superstitious man, he accepts it as an omen.

He twists to enter the conduit at his feet: it's an almost perfect circle; at the beginning he'd thought it was a pipe, but it isn't, it's made of brick. Because it's narrow, he's perfected a slithering crawl that transports him, efficiently enough, up the incline to where it widens at the foot of their garden. But it fatigues him. He lies on his belly listening to his heart. It's remarkably dry and there are dead leaves on the floor of the tunnel. Catching his breath, he discovers that he's grinning in the pitch black; the sound of his heart does not frighten him. The garage, the catalpa are above him somewhere and the house is straight ahead: from here it's wide enough for him to scrabble on his hands and knees to the foundation, it's easy.

Once inside the walls, however, he must be careful. He inches from the basement to the ground floor and peers through tiny holes into the kitchen. The light on the table, reflected in the window, glows in an empty room heavy with shadow: the counters have been wiped clean, a dish cloth hangs from the faucet, and although it's clear they've finished with this room for the night, he waits briefly to be sure. He's seen too much in here, he's seen them together, and alone, he's watched them, Urquhart and her man, their child, as they eat: some nights he's watched the two of them drinking with friends until the kitchen table's covered with bottles and the room is stale with smoke. Infrequently they sing. More often they listen to sentimental music and talk defensively of friends, of ugly marriages and failures: Urquhart usually retires first, but there was an evening when her husband went first and Urquhart was left with a man he hadn't seen before, an intense and animated man who'd apparently returned from some distant place, it had been difficult to hear because of the music. Can he be sure it actually happened? it's impossible to know. Urquhart and her lover leaning together from opposite sides of the table, she talking uncontrollably, he can't hear what she's saying, the man holding both her hands in his, occasionally he reaches, he brushes the hair from her face, and once, she imprisons his hand against her shoulder with her mouth.

He moves easily, without noise, between their walls, he's accustomed to it now: he's observed them night after night and sometimes, usually on weekends, he's remained all day in the structure of the house, moving from room to room collecting minutiae of their lives. They don't know he exists, containing their bodies' history like a mirror. He tries to understand, it's as if he doesn't exist.

The child is asleep in its room, he can barely discern its body stretched out beneath a blow-up of the Beatles. One night he saw Urquhart and her man give the child a toy, it looked like a model gas station, perhaps it was an ocean liner. The child was asleep and after the baby sitter left they woke it up because they couldn't wait until morning. Whatever it was had batteries because miniature lights glowed magically in the dark room and the child threw its arms about their necks, he could hear the excited voice, he watched them standing intimately above the child as it stared in wonderment.

○　○　○

Fumbling beneath his coat to find his fly he hears it, he knows it's the dog, he knows it's been hurt, it's gone mad, it's been injured: his feet on the frozen road, he's supporting himself with both hands, the sound of his feet, the wind, its body crushed and struggling, white bone in its side, kill it to stop the noise! he can hear it, broken, the snow is black, he doesn't understand, the noise, he tries to turn away, he falls...

He's driving back down along the road they entered. Snowbanks on either side, he accelerates beneath the sky. It was dead when he revived, beside him, nestled against him, he'd been dreaming, he remembers a valley full of lilacs in summer rain, mauve and purple at the bottom of an eroded hill, he descends with difficulty because it's steep, yellow mud sticks to his boots: there's a stream at the bottom, he arrives at the bottom, the smell of lilacs bursting on him, the long grasses bend down behind him in a path.

○   ○   ○

In front of the set, her legs tucked beneath her on the sofa, Urquhart's sitting in the noise of laughter and applause. Her husband comes in from the bedroom with an empty glass in his hand. There's music now from the television. She looks at him, he doesn't respond, he goes into the kitchen. She buries her face in her hands. His voice when he calls from the other room, is matter-of-fact: "Do you want a drink?"

"I...I don't think so." She hesitates, she springs to her feet and shuts the television off. When the husband, ice ringing in his glass, passes through again, she's standing with her back against the white wall, splay-fingered hands pressed against it at her sides. In order to get where he'll be able to see into the livingroom, bedroom and bathroom with a minimum of movement, he'll have to creep within two inches of her, he's never been this close; she's still there, he's hardly moving now, does he imagine it, or can he smell the delicate perfume of her body? there's a sudden movement, it's happening! her hands bang against the wall, he hears her speak, he stares in time to see her march into the bedroom. Afraid that he'll miss something, he scuttles to the corner, along to the bathroom and around it, and then, with practised agility, into the bedroom wall.

They're standing together at the window; on the other side of the window it is night. They're reflected in the glass. Urquhart is behind her man, her arms are around him, her body rests against his body. Is she crying? The man turns to her uncertainly. A train is crossing the bridge as she speaks: "I'm sorry."

"So am I." He touches her face with the tips of his fingers, he brushes her forehead, her cheekbones, he slides his hand to the back of her neck and pulls her close to him, she rests her face wearily in this throat. She disengages herself and sits on the bed, he returns to the window. He leans against a supporting beam and waits. The room is almost dark and they are unwilling to move.

She speaks his name, she says "I don't know anymore. I'm overwhelmed with a sense of exhaustion." She talks in the shadows. The words are unrelated to her voice. "It happens every time. Like at the party...I was really horny. I'd have gone with anybody, I mean it, man or woman, it couldn't have mattered less..." Still she doesn't move; the man, does he hear her? he's standing with his reflection. "Maybe fifteen people...all old friends except for a few of us, we were strangers, almost strangers. It's weird." Her hand moves to push back strands of her hair: the white face is strangely delicate. "All of us in this guy's house and the basic emotion was hatred, you must have felt it, you knew too...There wasn't any reason, it just happened. Like, it could have been, you know, friendship...nostalgia, but it was hatred."

"I've never encountered a situation in my own life where I could have behaved differently, everything that has happened, or not happened to me, because of me, all of it has been inescapable."

"Just a minute...No matter how we tried, it had to break out somewhere." The man comes to stand beside the bed. He speaks inaudibly and still she's unresponsive, he speaks again. Her voice is matter-of-fact: "I don't know why I did it...when he said goodnight I hit him across the mouth with my hand...why would I do that? I didn't know him, I hadn't even spoken to him..." The man crouches before her: their shadows blend without detail, their two bodies separate, automatically their voices overlap, he's seen this before, he strains to hear what the man is saying but he cannot hear. Urquhart stretches to the lamp on the bedside table, she turns it on: she stares intently into his upturned face and her voice silences him. "Why am I always attracted to empty men?" He lowers his bearded face to her lap, his hands are moving beneath her skirt. A train is crossing the bridge. How long do they remain like this? his hands groping at her thighs, his voice muffled by her body and she watching them in the mirror, she almost shouts: "It's not me you know, it's not us!" Her dark mouth remains slightly parted as she waits, he can see her teeth. A yellow cat appears in the doorway to his left, it leaps onto the bed and as it curls about itself on the pillow it reveals swollen dugs. Urquhart stretches her head back, staring emptily at her reflection, she runs her fingers through her hair. "What in hell's happening to you guys?" On his knees the man rocks back so that his buttocks rest on his heels, he stares into her face and takes his hands from her body. Peering through rough plaster, he watches Urquhart light a cigarette; she's impatient, even angry: "Will you get up for Chrissakes!" She lurches to her feet and goes into the bathroom.

In order to see into the bathroom he has to edge back, about six feet, to the corner and then to the mirror, he makes no noise. She's brushing her hair. He sees black stubble in her armpit, he watches her tricep flexing beneath painfully white skin; she tilts her head, the hair falls free of her shoulder, her dark mouth is parted, he stares into her empty eyes. She leans her head to the left, she reaches to brush the other side, her breasts shift heavily, they're marbled with miniature blue veins, she's holding her lower lip between her teeth and now her eyes are closed. Abruptly she throws her trunk forward, her tumbling hair, a curtain between him and her body, she brushes and brushes. He hears the brush in her hair; he's close enough to see, just before she straightens, the white scalp at her crown. There's a tap on the door. Turning she shakes her hair into place, she unlocks the door and takes the drink. The man is just visible beyond her, he seems to be pressing against the door, his face is very close to hers: his mouth opens and closes as he speaks, her body prevents him from entering and still he's talking while she resists, she manages to close the door, she latches it, her voice is

very calm: "I'll be out in a minute." She returns to the
mirror as if nothing has happened; as she drinks, her left
hand absently fondles a breast. In a minute she'll leave and
the man will enter, it's always the same: standing at the
bedroom window, smoking and staring into the garden,
he's waiting until she opens the door. He'll come into the
bathroom and after putting his underpants in the laundry
basket, he'll pee noisily and with obvious satisfaction: then
he fills the basin with hot water. He washes himself
meticulously and always in the same order. First his hands,
his arms to the elbow and then, standing on a towel, he
soaps his armpits and leaning over the basin, rinses them
thoroughly: next, his crotch and between his buttocks with
water dribbling down his thighs; when he's finished that,
he empties the basin and dries himself. It never varies.
Bending close to the watcher in the mirror, their eyes are
less than a foot apart, squeezing blackheads from his nose
and forehead, brushing dandruff from his beard, he refills
the basin, he scrubs his face and neck until the skin is red.
Urquhart puts her glass beside the basin, she removes her
brassiere and examines each breast as if searching for
something, then she vigorously brushes her teeth. She spits
into the basin and he's startled to see the blood in her
saliva. He concludes it's from her gums.

○   ○   ○

That blue light on his hands, on his legs. The stairs, that
door, the alley. Why does he do it? He moves with empty
grace, his feet make no sound, he slides through
underbrush, a path along the edge, he walks beside the
road because sometimes there are others...

He stops under the railway bridge. He's almost there,
he'll smoke a cigarette. Then he'll cross the stream and
climb to the pavement, the lights, their house. What will
they be doing? what will he see them doing tonight? He
hears water rushing against the concrete support, it stinks
of the cemetery half-a-mile ahead: seeping among the
graves it gathers in pools, he remembers the pools, it
overflows and fed by the city becomes a stream that smells
of bodies.

By the garage, excited because nobody knows he's here,

pressing himself into its shadow with catalpa leaves resting on his shoulders. There are lights in the apartment but nobody appears in the windows. Music from a radio, perhaps a record player, is playing somewhere. He doesn't recognize the song. Noise from the traffic on Yonge Street is curiously soothing, like the sea, although he's never heard the sea, or wind rushing across the land, some land, somewhere...Resting his face against the brick, he's breathing easily because he's in no hurry. In a minute he'll climb onto the garage roof, using the fence and one limb of the catalpa tree, he'll wriggle forward and lie unseen to watch them...

O   O   O

Fumbling beneath his coat to find his fly he hears it, he knows it's the dog, he knows it's been hurt, it's gone mad, it's been injured: his feet on the frozen road, he's supporting himself with both hands, the sound of his feet, the wind, its body crushed and struggling, white bone in its side, kill it to stop the noise! he can hear it, broken, the snow is black, he doesn't understand, the noise, he tries to turn away, he falls...

He's driving back down along the road they entered. Snowbanks on either side, he accelerates beneath the sky. It was dead when he revived, beside him, nestled against him, he'd been dreaming, he remembers a valley full of lilacs in the summer rain, mauve and purple at the bottom of an eroded hill, he descends with difficulty because it's steep, yellow mud sticks to his boots: there's a stream at the bottom, he arrives at the bottom, the smell of lilacs bursting on him, the long grasses bend down behind him in a path.

He's driving back down the road they entered, descending to the lake; he turns to the right, the heater is beginning to thrust warm air into the car, it isn't enough. He's icy to the core, his fingers are swollen and painful, his mouth is bruised: he almost welcomes the pain. He drives with one hand gingerly on the wheel, the other is pressed into his armpit beneath his clothing. He's failed. He doesn't understand. Why didn't he do something, why didn't? strangling there, the sound of his feet, why didn't he kill it? with the jack handle, he could have, that's something he could have done, he could have killed it in Toronto. The road rises and falls with the land, there are no cars, he passes houses without lights clustered at crossroads.

Driving south from winter, through Primrose, south to Camilla and still the highway's empty, his hands still hurt, driving into Orangeville, turning left at the lights: stopping at the outskirts he turns on his wipers, with difficulty he climbs out of the car, he throws snow on the windshield to clean it, another handful, his body is bruised and stiff, he gets back in. He lights a cigarette. His hands are throbbing. He turns on the radio and sits smoking without hearing the voice. Then, forcing the butt out the no-draft, he accelerates onto the crown of the road.

Through Ballycroy on 9 with music on the radio, driving at night with fields of snow on either side. He believes he did this often as a boy. Driving in a sealed car, a winter night, smoking alone and listening to the radio, climbing into the Laurentian shield, driving for hours and sometimes with others, in the back seat perhaps, with a girl, taut bodied and sighing, their mouths dry, surely it happened to him as well, it must have: sharing Molson's from a quart bottle, the taste of it in their mouths, young bodies, hands at his face, his belly inside his shirt, how can he know for sure? protesting mile after mile, I must get home, it's late, oh please! reluctant thighs and hungry faces in the light of passing cars. And then, one night for the first time, it must have happened, a damp hand between his legs, such a long time ago, the noise of their breathing in the swaying car, the radio, he remembers a small hard nipple between his teeth.

The signal's stronger as he turns south again: radio voices sing of peace, of love and snowbanks collapse upon themselves as he drives into Palgrave, its houses isolated along the road. A woman raped and murdered in her bedroom. He's driving out of winter, away from the snow: black fields and the highway glistens in his lights. He's very tired. He doesn't think about the dog, not now, perhaps never. He'll leave the car for Walters, that's all. Music in a closed car driving very fast, he discovers it's over: he'll never work for that man again, the prick, Felix would have done something, he'd have helped the dog in some way. If he hadn't fallen, if his body hadn't betrayed him, it's like a seizure, he doesn't understand, like a fit of some kind, he doesn't want to think about it. The inside of his mouth is dark and bruised, his fingers are like sausages. Radio voices sing of peace, of love. There was a girl with brown legs, he remembers her name: a young girl with blue underwear, they lay on the livingroom floor. She went away, he doesn't know why she went away. Blond hair and gentle mouth, she lived with him for a week one summer and then returned to California. Music from the hi-fi, she danced in her bare feet, her lithe body and her laughter; she never answered his letters, she wouldn't say anything on the telephone. He knows where she lives. Finally she sent him her picture. She must have had her reasons. Is it because they talked about love? he's convinced they talked about love, they lay together on the livingroom floor: did she talk about her love for him then? It's the usual thing to do. Her name, he recalls, is Morag.

○   ○   ○

Ritson's convinced, not without reason, that he's appreciably weaker, his body less effective: when he attempts to stand he can see that the process of disintegration has continued while he slept, there's even reason to believe that it has accelerated. His spine doesn't bend easily and even with help from his arms, the muscles in his belly are incapable of pulling him into a sitting position. He rolls onto his side, drawing his knees up to his chest, levering with his arms, he flops onto his belly, he struggles to raise his trunk from the mattress, the problem is to get to his hands and knees, it's here that he's most likely to fail: it hasn't always been like this, he persists, he refuses to falter, there was an instant when he doubted himself, at the start, it appeared certain he'd collapse but he held on, he braced himself and won. The rest is comparatively easy. He'll crawl to the chair and pull himself erect.

It's a tiny room, a windowless cubicle, not a cell, in the deepest corner of his basement, he acknowledges there is light in the city, waning afternoon light, but it never penetrates this far beneath the street: the basement, honey-combed with cells and passages, has been in darkness as long as he can remember. As confident as a blind man, he crawls to the wooden chair by the door, he puts both hands on the seat and climbs to his feet. After asserting his balance he leans against the wall for support, he reaches with his arms, he stretches his body towards the ceiling with muscles and sinews protesting, he gulps air vigorously into his lungs, he holds it as long as he can and then exhales. He repeats the process until he's trembling and dizzy. When his head clears he sits on the chair, he slips his feet into his boots, laces them to the top and ties them with a double bow.

It's always the same, the need to urinate wakes him: he's lying on his back in the dark, it's like sleep but his eyes are open, the empty house above him: inescapably the prospect of rolling onto his belly, of forcing his body to its feet, fills him with uncertainty and dread. He has tried to understand. Perhaps he's afraid of failure. There was a time, Ritson believes there was a time when this explanation convinced him, it's all-encompassing, that's attractive, and even more important, it's simple: unfortunately he's concluded that if he was afraid of failure, then he wouldn't involve himself, he wouldn't even try, there must be another explanation. It has occurred to him he's afraid of what he'll find outside the house. Without any doubt, he's convinced there's sound reasoning here: the shattered windows, bodies in the street he's seen it all, men prowling like animals; he remembers tanks, whole blocks united in flame, the sky insanely red and soldiers with guns and clubs. But what has it got to do with Ritson? if the cause for dread lies outside, then it's unlikely he'd go out as eagerly as he does. There's very little need, his requirements are modest and virtually everything necessary for life has been stored here in the basement; despite this, as soon as it's dark he slips out of the house without fear, at least without specific fears, he's expectant certainly, even defensive, but that's endemic. Life demands caution. Clearly then, or at least it seems so to him, there's no obvious cause for his uncertainty and dread. And that raises the possibility he's been approaching the problem from the wrong angle; perhaps he doesn't understand the nature of his experience here in the dark each afternoon, on his mattress, struggling from sleep, the empty house above him. Perhaps he's mistaken, and it isn't uncertainty or dread that he feels, perhaps it's frustration in response to inertia. It's possible. If that's the case, however, what is it that drives him to overcome the inertia? there has to be something.

If he allows himself he'll pursue this sort of speculation forever, he'll exhaust every combination of possibilities, and even though it's challenging for the mind, even though it could prove to be more or less diverting, it has nothing to do with lying here, on his back, his body undeniably weaker than he has ever known it to be. A cellar is not an ideal place to die. He rolls onto his side, drawing his knees up to his chest, levering with his arms, he flops onto his belly, he struggles to raise his trunk from the mattress, to rise onto all fours, his arms are too weak, he collapses, his face bangs rudely against the cellar floor. It's probably like this every day, soon the strength will return, he lies motionless with arm beneath him, his face is pressed against the cement.

○ ○ ○

Why does she come each morning like this? A ritual perhaps, but not for him: Christ knows he doesn't need it! with knees pulled up under his chin for protection, the body curled around its own belly, it's obvious he doesn't need it. Yet here she comes with cigarettes, matches and the white plastic holder...

Deliberately from the door to the chair beside his face and sitting, staring impassive as he sleeps. She hears her morning at the open window. She hears birds in the eaves and she hears the trees.

She rises, she puts the cigarettes, the matches and the holder beside the pillow and, bracing her feet on the floor, her knees against the bed, she takes a deep breath and tries to wrestle him onto his back. He resists. She tries harder. He curls in upon himself like an armadillo, but grunting and clutching, sweating now and heaving, she begins to gain the advantage: he's weakening, one of his arms comes loose! vainly he struggles to re-enclose himself but the circle's broken…it's just a matter of time. She hears a whimpering in his throat and pauses. Clever. With left hand on his right wrist, elbow against his belly and into his hip, and her right arm under his shoulders, she seems to give in to him. Very clever. His body, surprised at this unexpected freedom, relaxes, the whimpering dies…and at this instant, so beautifully timed, she surges to her feet and flips him onto his back.

Things proceed as usual.

Felix open on his back, he breathes the end of sleep.

Cigarette in her mouth, she rests. It's getting harder all the time. Once it was strength alone that did it, she walked in at seven and simply rolled him over. But those days are gone now: more and more she had to rely on the advantage that comes with experience.

She lights a cigarette and slips it into the holder. There are birds outside and trees that press about the house: the sun is shining, rather pale at this hour, but shining nevertheless as she leans forward to brush her finger lightly at the corner of his mouth. He shivers, he searches blindly with a sucking noise, his face is pained, is drawn in lines as his mouth searches suck suck. Such an anxious face!

By resting her elbow at his side she keeps the holder steady; her arm along his chest, she bends and reaches, pinching the nostrils to stop him breathing through his nose. The effect is immediate, obvious. The cigarette glows more brightly, it fades to greyness, then it glows again, it fairly crackles! Miniature forms collapse upon themselves as he exhales. She leans her weight, pressing and counting, "a thousand and one" with smoke issuing from his mouth…briefly she holds…then "a thousand and two", withdrawing she sees the fire as his lungs are filled. And so it goes. She fights him resolutely, pressing again ("a thousand and one"), she feels the slobber from his mouth, she pauses…and withdraws.

The next cigarette is ready in her mouth as, poised, she forces his lungs empty, and then with amazing speed her left hand grabs the holder and brings the glowing butt to light the new one; at the same time, her thumb and index finger have pinched his mouth shut so he can't breathe and break the cycle. Ashes fly as she ejects the butt into the ashtray, exchanges the empty holder for the cigarette in her mouth, firmly inserts the latter into the former and, letting go of his lips, jams the holder back into his mouth. He gasps, she lurches to maintain the interrupted tempo, "a thousand and one" and they've hardly missed a stroke...

It's going very smoothly this morning.

Soon she stops the regulating pressure, stops the counting and relaxes somewhat back on the chair: she smiles, an imperceptible smile on her large face and hears again the birds, a car in the street, the day outside and sees the lines about his eyes, his mouth in rhythm now and knows the worst is over, that soon he'll be awake.

O   O   O

When he reaches the floor of the ravine he turns right and climbs the small hill to the road, he crosses and descends to the railway tracks: Felix on the tracks in the Don Valley. A hundred yards from him, across a field, the river meanders beneath trees with rough bark, he knows somehow they're trees from dream: he crouches smoking, vacantly he stares across the river to the parkway choked with cars, to the apartments above them bleak against the sky. Raucous birds wheel about his head. He can hear their wings. Although it's early, the sun is hot: cars labour to work on raised arterial roads and high in the guts of the bridge a subway rattles to Bloor Street. He waits to see if he'll cross the field to the river, or turn to his left along the tracks. The birds swoop angrily closer. He inhales, feeling the smoke sharp in his chest; without noise, unravelling above him is the vapour trail of a jet.

It's not that he misses the job, he's sure of that, time passes painlessly enough without it: for days now, it must be, perhaps weeks, he's emerged from the house at his usual time, but instead of walking to the subway he's come into the park, down into the ravine, he's turned right, climbed the small hill to the road and descended into the Don Valley. What is it? Wandering in spring's incredible violence, fearful with birds tumbling wildly to the ground, the headlong pursuit of squirrels among branches and out of sight, Felix, he doesn't recall when he first became aware of it, how it was brought to his attention, perhaps it's only just now become clear to him, Felix is impotent with dread.

O   O   O

Felix smoking a cigarette, leaning against a concrete pillar, staring out into torrential rain, it's almost vertical now, it covers the highway with miniature explosions as cars with pale headlights crawl past him, drivers hunched and intense, they don't appear to see him or his sign saying CALIFORNIA, and if some do, they don't acknowledge him. The thunder has drifted overhead in its journey from the west. Lightning flashes sporadically, and the air is full of water. He's beginning to feel uncertain. He crouches to rest his legs, bracing his back against the pillar he listens to the wheels of a transport braking on the overpass above him. He watches it descending into view, he gets automatically to his feet, he holds up his sign, he smiles hopefully, he sticks out his thumb, perhaps if the driver sees him smiling, perhaps he'll stop, he sees the shuddering, hears air brakes as it drifts by him, huge wheels protesting as the driver steers onto the shoulder of the highway. Felix running with his knapsack in the pouring rain, into the exhaust, beside the gleaming trailer to its cab, the door is opening for him, he hoists himself up the step and scrambles, dragging his bag with him, he slams the door. The truck does not move. Brushing wet hair from his eyes, clearing rain from his face so he can see, Felix is startled by the voice: "That's a bitch of a day baby." An echoing bass voice, it fills the cab.

"Yeah, I'm...thanks..." Brown eyes appraise him from a ferret face, what's he waiting for? the mouth opens in a thin smile, Felix is disconcerted, he averts his gaze: the man's white eyes staring at him, his face resting on the steering wheel. Rain hammers on the cab, the wipers thump back and forth. "I'm going all the way to California." He wonders why the man doesn't drive on, but he doesn't, he just sits there with his delicate hands like paws on the wheel, he's gazing at Felix, it's as if he's expecting something, Felix doesn't know what to do. "I know a girl there, she lives in San Mateo county." Cars and trucks pass them in the rain. The floor is littered with sandwich crusts and paper. "Her name is Morag." There's a movement to his left, he looks, the driver is nodding his head. "I met her one summer and then she went away."

"I could tell right away you weren't a chick, you know that baby?" Felix hears the voice, a resonant, engulfing voice. "Chicks wouldn't be out here alone." He leans finally to stare back along the 401 in his mirror, he shifts into low and begins to accelerate. "Once I picked up a coupla, hippie chicks, you know. Most times there're guys with them but not these two. Shit." Wipers thump as the engine strains to gain momentum. "Real jailbait, the two of them, little tits and long hair... but nothen, fuck-all happened." Reaching down beside the seat, his hand re-appears: "I even showed them this BANGBANG! I said." He presses a pistol against Felix's cheek, he's chuckling, the metal's cold, he holds the accelerator to the floor with rain beating on the windows, the floor is littered with sandwich crusts and papers. "I told em about all the guys I killed, I thought maybe it'd make em hot, you know what I mean?" Felix nods, the muzzle bumps against his cheekbone. "All I did was scare the shit out of em." He laughs and Felix tries to smile, he wonders if he can grab the gun in time.

"Is that..." Blurred by rain on the windshield, headlights from oncoming cars; he tries to speak.

"You mean is it loaded?" Felix nods. "Fucken right baby." Laughing explosively, the muzzle bumps against his cheekbone; blurred by rain on the windshield, headlights from oncoming cars hurtle out of sight. The pistol is removed. Felix looks, he doesn't know how to refuse its compact weight, he discovers his hands are sweating. "Women are funny chicks." He's driving with both hands on the wheel again, he turns to Felix, his voice like stereo, he grins: "Were you scared sweetheart?" Felix doesn't respond, he doesn't know what to say, the stench in the cab is beginning to nauseate him. He opens the window. The rain abates, they're driving fast in light traffic, they're approaching the airport road, Indian Line north to highway 50, for an instant he believes they're going to turn, he struggles to protest, he opens his mouth but the words won't come, his body's drenched with sweat, they do not turn, they continue accelerating westwards. "My name's Fripp." Felix can't reconcile the strength of the voice with this wiry man, the laughter. "What's yours?" He can't be sure, but he believes there are insects crawling up his legs, he swats at his calf. The floor is littered with garbage.

"Felix Oswald." He sits with the automatic pistol, it's got a wooden handle: he raises his arm, extends it from the shoulder, he's aiming at a car in front of them, his index finger along the trigger guard.

"A buddy of mine beat me to one outside Kingston. Shit." It seems so small, a toy car scooting along the highway, he finds it hard to keep his arm still in the swaying truck, he curls his finger around the trigger. "Shit. I saw her as I was coming into the restaurant there, a big blond cunt with her thumb stuck out, just like that! before I had a chance this buddy of mine stopped for her, he was just pulling out, the lucky bastard." Felix, his arm extended from the shoulder, he braced himself, squinting he aims at the toy car with his finger on the trigger. "I saw him later, I said ah, How far'd that blond cunt go? all the way, he said, all the fucken way." He's driving with both hands on the wheel, he turns to Felix, his voice is like stereo. "Maybe she wouldn't of done it for me. Some women are funny that way, you know what I mean? they'll do it for some guys but not for others…"

Felix sits with the automatic pistol, it's got a wooden handle: he raises his arm, extends it from the shoulder, he's aiming at a car in front of them, his index finger along the trigger guard, it seems so small, a toy scooting along the highway, he finds it hard to keep his arm still in the swaying truck, he curls his finger around the trigger, this is the way it's done, you squeeze the whole hand like this, very gently…Fripp is watching him, Felix returns his gaze and smiles, he lowers his arm until the gun is resting on his thigh and the man begins to laugh. His hands are delicate on the steering wheel, he's watching Felix with sharp white eyes and laughing richly. "Baby you should of seen your face." He reaches to take the gun, his hand is cool, Felix sees it on his own. "You should try it some time, you know what I mean?" They're driving fast in light traffic; the fields on either side are flat and green. He's sure there are insects, bugs, he feels them scuttling inside his clothes. "You should try it."

"No, I...couldn't."

"Baby you should of seen your face."

O   O   O

As confident as a blind man, he crawls to the wooden chair by the door, he puts both hands on the seat and climbs to his feet. After asserting his balance he leans against the wall for support, he reaches with his arms, he stretches his body towards the ceiling with muscles and sinews protesting, he gulps air vigorously into his lungs, he holds it as long as he can and then exhales; he repeats the process until he's trembling and dizzy. When his head clears he sits on the chair, he slips his feet into his boots, laces them to the top and ties them with a double bow.

As confident as a blind man, Ritson steps into the narrow hall, it's only a passageway, his shoulders brush each side as he shuffles past the stairs, he turns right and then left, into the toilet. He's surrounded by rooms, cubicles in the dark. Standing in the noise of his piss, feeling it flow through the flesh in his hand, he responds predictably and for the first time today, he accepts that it has begun again: he'll climb from his basement to the ground floor, he'll eat a certain amount of food and when it's undeniably night, he'll go out into the streets. He'll keep to the alleys and sidestreets, he prefers back alleys, laneways tortuous among foundation walls of factories, warehouses, he walks slowly and with difficulty and despite the pain, he's learned to make no noise, he misses nothing even though his face, whenever possible, is turned inward to the wall, his fingers trail reassuringly along their uneven surfaces, he listens defensively, he hears others, the feral strangers, he crouches motionless in the dark, it's as if he's invisible, he can see the struggling shapes, he hears the scuffling feet, the brutal gasping breath, the sudden blows and kicks, then moans in the dark and sometimes cries: Ritson crouching with the gun in one hand, the other lightly on the wall behind him, he waits until it's over, until they've risen from the body and, brushing at their clothes, return into the shadows.

It's not clear in what way he knows this, but Ritson believes there was a time when he could venture out of his house during the daylight hours, there must have been. Memories are like bad dreams. Leaning into the stink of his urine, he flushes the toilet and leaves the room. He can't imagine that he came to this city at night, he hasn't always lived in the basement, there was a time, there must have been. "Memories are like bad dreams." Ritson's voice, it doesn't sound like a voice, he hears it in the dark. "They torment me so. That's why I live in a cellar, it must be: I am lonely, but I am away from it all. That must be the reason. I have had to get used to it, it has not come easily. How could it? It is not man's nature to live like an animal." Perhaps he has said this before. Does he remember or does he dream? Cedar boughs, he knows what they smell like; a child, children of different ages. It doesn't mean anything. Nothing happens for the first time. He urinates, flushes the toilet, comes to the stairs and climbs out of the basement; it's like the beating of his heart, for example, or the alternate expansion and contraction of the lungs inside his chest.

Ritson with the gun in one hand, the other lightly on the wall behind him, he sees others, the feral strangers, he crouches unmoving in the dark, his hands are sweating, he raises his arm, extends it from the shoulder, his index finger along the trigger guard, it's as if he's invisible, he can see the struggling shapes, he can hear them, they don't know he's here, so close to them, teeth white, eyes staring, he could almost reach out and touch them, he curls his finger around the trigger, he squeezes, the first one doesn't hear the explosions, he fires methodically, he never misses, they're dead before the impact throws their bodies to the ground.

As confident as a blind man, Ritson steps into the narrow hall, it's only a passageway, his shoulders brush each side as he shuffles past the stairs. He's surrounded by rooms, cubicles in the dark. Standing in the noise of his piss, feeling it flow through the flesh in his hand, he accepts that it has begun again: he'll climb from his basement to the ground floor, he'll eat a certain amount of food and when it's undeniably night, he'll go out into the streets. He'll keep to the alleys and sidestreets, he prefers back alleys, laneways tortuous among foundation walls. He's able to cross narrow streets, resting his hands lightly on the wall behind him, making certain he's unobserved he closes his eyes, he launches himself into a desperate run, he knows how vulnerable he is, what if they see him? reaching for the wall on the other side, he makes it if it's not too far, he clutches at the buildings, the substance of the city, he's terrified of open spaces, the sky: occasionally he loses his nerve, perhaps he's confused and changes direction, it can happen, the wall isn't there, he panics, lurching with closed eyes, stretching his arms, searching, he hears his voice, he falls to his knees, he presses his hands, his face against the earth, he doesn't know how it happens, he doesn't know what to do, he crawls blindly...

O   O   O

Felix returns his gaze and smiles, he lowers his arm until the gun is resting on his thigh and the man begins to laugh. His hands are delicate on the steering wheel, he's watching Felix with sharp brown eyes and laughing richly. "Baby you should of seen your face." He reaches to take the gun, his hand is cool, Felix sees it on his own. "You should try it some time, you know what I mean?" They're driving fast in light traffic; the fields on either side are flat and green. He's sure there are insects, bugs, he feels them scuttling inside his clothes. "You should try it."

"No, I...couldn't."

"Sweetheart, you gotta wait and see." The hand is cool, Felix sees it resting on his own, the delicate fingers, he knows the ferret face watching him, he relinquishes the gun. Fripp replaces it beside the seat: lighting two cigarettes, Felix gives one to him, he can't look at him, they're driving very fast, grey smoke is sucked out the window. "I thought it'd make them hot, sometimes it makes em hot, you know that baby?" Felix scratches inside his shirt, whatever they are they don't seem to bite; inhaling he feels the sharp smoke in his chest, he senses vague pains, his fingers are in the armpit, his palm across the nipple, he presses roughly, he digs his fingers into the moist flesh and stares out the window to his right. What's he saying? they're driving very fast, his voice fills the cab but Felix doesn't understand; past exit roads for Kitchener, then Preston, bland fields in tentative sunlight, Woodstock and London with Felix slouching, staring through the glass, falling each mile farther into himself: sideroads empty, occasional barns with homes in shadow and always the fields geometric on the land. Mile after mile. He can't remember the first time it happened and can't be sure it ever did. It might have been an early morning on the way to summer camp. It might have been. A field rising to bush, trees crowding from the sky's edge and there, into the trees, an entrance leading away and he sees himself climbing the field in silence, sees a figure alone, only briefly pausing, then striding as best he can from sight. "Got my first one in Buffalo, he went down like a bag of shit, you know what I mean? Baby, you listening to me at all?" Felix turns, white eyes in a narow face, he nods. "You never aim for the head, shit: the head's too fucken small, you go for the gut, it's full of stuff they need." Both hands on the wheel, driving in the late afternoon, his voice is immense. "There's just a little hole where it goes in, but it comes out the back like a fucken cannon." They stare at each other, Felix has to look away: he sees a bird with ragged wings, poised above the fields, it drifts easily ahead of them, it's rising as they pass: turning he watches it from the side window until it's just a speck, until he can't see it anymore.

Sometimes a stream then, a creek that leads from sight among the trees, and other times it's just a suggestion, an opening image as he's carried by. His body's empty with the journey and he cannot speak. Would it have been different if he'd prepared the dog in some way? it might have been, if he'd taken it for walks maybe, gone north with it, given it a chance: he was precipitous, panic, it must have been panic, he didn't think, he should have, he should have what? He could have killed it in the cage. Nothing is certain. How can he know? Cool on his forehead and dirty, the window between him and that figure in the field. In trains sometimes and cars. One day he will wake and discover that he isn't sure whether it happened or not, it won't matter; he'll feel guilt, the familiar patterns, but the husky, what will it mean to him then? Driving past Chatham with night overtaking them:

her eyes, luminous, did it happen in Ottawa? crying in somebody's hall, is this true? in some obscure way he too is guilty, he wasn't there. Past Chatham, on towards Windsor with the sky rising mountainous behind them, they're driving against the earth. Mile after mile. His mind is full of images, rationalizations, with escape routes closing before he knows, all the familiar structures of guilt.

At some point they stop for coffee, they climb down from the cab, he remembers the body walking beside him, they don't pause by the cash desk inside the door but go directly to a booth in the corner with Fripp waving, shouting recognition as they pass: there are introductions, a woman with purple nails, a man with a cigar, there are others, Felix doesn't recall anything happening. He has the impression, he doesn't know why, that they talk about him as if he's somewhere else. Drinking coffee, eating and smoking.

Towards Windsor with the sky rising mountainous behind them, they're driving against the earth. Mile after mile. It wasn't his fault, he'd have done something, he'd have helped in some way. If he hadn't fallen, if his body hadn't betrayed him, it's like a seizure, he doesn't understand, like a fit of some kind, he doesn't want to think about it. "Her name was Morag." Fripp grins, he touches Felix on the knee. He could have killed it in the cage.

"You light me a smoke baby?" Startled by darkness in the cab, it's almost night, the white teeth, his white eyes in shadow now, Felix looks away: with two cigarettes in his mouth he bends to the shifting flame, he inhales, he knows that Fripp is watching him. What is it? He gives him the cigarette and lights his own. "I really like you Felix Oswald, you know that?" Felix doesn't understand. On both sides of the highway, bare branches rise from the darkening land, there are houses without lights, in the distance he can see towns, they're coming to a city, to the river, soon they'll be in Detroit.

The headlights from approaching traffic hurt his eyes: there are restaurants and motels by the road, he sees service stations with multi-coloured pennants reaching above the lights, low buildings in darkness; he's never been here before, he stares through the glass and nothing is new; people stand by the road, there are traffic lights, everywhere there are cars, and then he sees the bridge, its mechanical shape crouching over the river.

They scarcely pause on the Canadian side, it's unnerving, Felix doesn't know if he should look back at Windsor, what would that accomplish? Conceivably he shouldn't be doing this, he recognizes it might be a mistake, but he can't be sure: the metallic river glistens beneath them, Fripp accelerates slowly to the hump of the bridge, talking all the time, and Felix discovers that he's actually thinking of opening the door, of jumping onto the bridge and returning to the other side, it's not too late. A yellow sky hangs over the city as they descend. Up river and close to the shore he notices fire, but there are gates, lights flashing ahead. Men in uniforms, they pull open the doors and motion him out, they do not speak to him, they're joking with Fripp but Felix can't hear what they're saying, he wonders what would happen if he walked back up the bridge and went home, would they hurt him? Fripp comes around the truck, he's laughing easily. There are flashing lights, the noise of engines. "They want to talk to you baby, it won't take long." Felix looks back up at the bridge against the night sky, they cross the pavement, they usher him through the waiting room with an American flag on the wall, there are five of them, including Fripp who carries the knapsack: they follow a narrow hall, there are closed doors on either side and heating pipes on the ceiling. They come to an alcove at the end. One of the men empties his knapsack on the floor and methodically begins to examine the contents. Felix doesn't know what they're looking for. It's true he's impressed by their thoroughness, but he doesn't know how to react, he doesn't know what to feel. Standing naked against a pile of cardboard cartons he watches them tapping the heels of his shoes, they run their fingers along the seams of his clothing, everything is meticulously searched, he stares in horror as his tube of toothpaste is squeezed into the wastebasket; he knows that Fripp is leaning against the door jamb with his arms crossed as one man examines the inside of his mouth, the fingers are like sausages and taste of soap; they turn him around and push him forward into a crouch, he's held by the scruff of the neck, one of them stabs an investigating finger up his ass, he's afraid he's going to shit. He almost falls when they release him. Because they haven't spoken to him, nobody has addressed a word to him, they're laughing and talking among themselves, it's unclear whether or not he can ask them what they were looking for, what they were doing to him. He gets back into his clothes without looking at them. Crouching he gathers his belongings together and stuffs them back into his knapsack.

Felix climbs back into the truck. He lights a cigarette, his mouth is bruised. Inhaling he stares through the windshield, the cigarette glows, it fades to greyness, then it glows again, miniature forms collapse upon themselves as he exhales. He'd like to hammer on the window with his fists, but he's afraid: he stares into the dark. When he inhales, the light illuminates his face, he sees himself reflected in the glass. He looks away.

Fripp scrambles noisily into the truck, shouting farewells he slams the door, the great engine catches and they begin to move. Briefly Felix sees figures motionless in the headlights and then the streets are deserted. Something struggles in his cheek, he can feel it bumping on the edge of his cheekbone as they drive, his hands have no strength, he throws his cigarette out the window as Fripp brakes the truck at a red light. They sit in silence. The muscle continues to jump in his cheek. "Hey baby." The sudden voice, he sniffs his middle finger, he thrusts it under Felix's nose. "You wanna smell something, you recognize that?" The cab is full of laughter, it's like stereo. The light has turned green, they don't move. Fripp's white teeth in a ferret face, he's staring at Felix, his face is resting on the steering wheel. "Jesus Christ I'd like to fuck you!" Fripp reaches beside the seat, Felix is sure he did, he throws open the door and leaps to the road, that voice, what is it saying? running beside the gleaming trailer, through the exhaust, he hears noises behind him, he throws himself into an alleyway...

He doesn't know how long he's been walking, it doesn't matter, eventually he'll find the bridge, in the morning he'll find the bridge. He keeps to the alleys and sidestreets, back alleys, laneways tortuous among foundation walls of factories, warehouses, he moves with unfamiliar grace, his feet make no sound because sometimes there are others, he can hear them, in the rubble of a vacant lot, crumbling houses on the other side, he can see them, beneath a yellow sky, they look like children, they're running excitedly about some object on the ground, he strains to see, it's a man, he's crawling blindly, they're taunting him, Felix doesn't know what to do, they're lighting matches, "Stop it!" He shouts and rushes into the open, they scatter with cries of alarm, one of them falls, a twelve-year-old, Felix grabs it by the shoulder, what are they doing? Felix with both hands at the throat of a struggling child, he stares blankly into its face. He doesn't understand. The old man crawls whimpering towards a wall, Felix smells the gasoline as he passes, the child is jumping wildly, kicking in his hands: Felix Oswald, the muscle convulsing in his cheek, they were going to burn him, he can smell the gasoline, where are the others? Felix staring violently into the darkness, the old man's almost to the wall, he can hear the gasping breath, the child has stopped fighting, Felix is hardly aware of him: a yellow sky presses down on the shells of buildings, their boarded windows, it settles on the vacant lot, the small body is limp in his hands, he has to support it, he stares into bulging eyes, the black contorted face, it's dead! a small body collapsing at his feet, the yellow sky. Standing over it he tries to understand. The swollen tongue, it lolls from between its teeth with blood boiling onto the chin, he doesn't understand, he falls as he tries to turn away, his knees bang stupidly against his chest, he's bleeding from the mouth he doesn't feel the garbage against his face. He doesn't see the tentative figures emerging from shadows, they circle closer, cautious, like dogs, they douse his shuddering body from pop bottles, with gasoline, one of them lights a match and Felix Oswald bursts into flame.

○　○　○

itson with the gun in one hand, the other lightly on the wall behind him, they almost got him, he crouches in the dark, his hands are sweating, the stink of gasoline has cleared his head, he raises his arm, extends it from the shoulder, his index finger along the trigger guard, it's as if he's invisible, he can see them clearly in the light of flames leaping from the body of a man, he can hear terrible cries, they don't know he's here, so close to them, teeth bared eyes white, he curls his finger around the trigger, he squeezes, the first one doesn't hear the explosions, he fires methodically as they scatter, he never misses, they're dead before the impact throws their bodies to the ground.